Praise for the David Slaton Novels

"Highly reminiscent of Robert Ludlum's Jason Bourne series!"   —David Hagberg,
New York Times bestselling author

"A must-read for anyone looking for the next great assassin saga."   —*Kirkus Reviews*
on *Assassin's Game*

"The action-filled, high-octane thriller that you have been waiting for. Ward Larsen delivers enough page-turning suspense and globe-spanning action for ten novels."
—William Martin,
New York Times bestselling author,
on *Assassin's Silence*

"A superbly written story."   —Larry Bond,
New York Times bestselling author,
on *Assassin's Game*

"Slaton is the perfect assassin, and this is the perfect action-adventure thriller."   —*Booklist* (starred review)
on *Assassin's Silence*

"A stunning thriller, one that ranks right up there with *The Day of the Jackal*. Frankly, this is the best nail-biting suspense novel I've read in years."   —Stephen Coonts,
New York Times bestselling author,
on *Assassin's Game*

"Sharp as a dagger and swift as a sudden blow, *Assassin's Game* is a first-rate thriller with a plot that grabs you hard and won't let go."   —Ralph Peters,
New York Times bestselling author,
on *Assassin's Game*

BOOKS BY WARD LARSEN

The Perfect Assassin
*Assassin's Game**
*Assassin's Silence**
*Assassin's Code**
*Assassin's Run**
*Assassin's Revenge**
*Cutting Edge**

* Published by Forge Books

ASSASSIN'S RUN

WARD LARSEN

FORGE®

A TOM DOHERTY ASSOCIATES BOOK
NEW YORK

ASSASSIN'S RUN

A Forge Book
Published by Tom Doherty Associates
120 Broadway
New York, NY 10271

www.tor-forge.com

Forge® is a registered trademark of Macmillan Publishing Group, LLC.

ISBN 978-0-7653-9152-0

Our books may be purchased in bulk for promotional, educational, or business use. Please contact your local bookseller or the Macmillan Corporate and Premium Sales Department at 1-800-221-7945, extension 5442, or by email at MacmillanSpecialMarkets@macmillan.com.

First Edition: August 2018
First Mass Market Edition: October 2019

Printed in the United States of America

0 9 8 7 6 5 4 3 2 1

To the men and women of the 23rd Fighter Group
The Flying Tigers

ASSASSIN'S RUN

ONE

It was just as well Pyotr Ivanovic didn't realize he was about to die. As a man who comprehensively enjoyed a good meal, his last on this earth would be free of any misgivings regarding his soon-to-be-issued digestif.

He glanced out the starboard window at a night-shrouded sea, the occasional breaker highlighted in dim moonlight. Lovely as the panorama was, it was far less compelling than what rested before him on the white-linened table. His new chef had outdone himself tonight. The steak before Ivanovic was a choice cut, thirty ounces of grain-fed beef flown in from Australia and seared to perfection. Against that, the potatoes Lyonnais were but an afterthought, the haricots verts no more than garnish. The bottle of Bordeaux, he allowed, did the steak justice, one of the best from his extensive shipboard collection. Thankfully, the new man had learned quickly. Ivanovic did not count calories. He courted them openly, throwing himself upon the culinary altar of any chef who could do them well. Tonight's meal, as it turned out, was more special than most. It was a celebration of sorts, marking the beginning of the most ambitious undertaking of his career.

Which made it very ambitious indeed.

The head of his security detail came through the salon door, bringing a gust of wind with him. October had arrived full force on the Tyrrhenian Sea, the opening volley of winter's campaign. Ivanovic looked up in annoyance, but he knew there was no use in berating the man—that was life at sea.

The ship was called *Cassandra*—ship because no vessel 190 feet long could be referred to as a boat, and *Cassandra* as a prod at his late mother. He still laughed inwardly at that: the ship had already been around the world once, while her namesake, as far as he knew, had never in her life traveled more than ten miles from the miserable Ukrainian village in which she'd been born.

The yacht had been built to his demanding specifications by a man who, if not the finest marine architect in Greece, was certainly the most expensive. The mahogany planking beneath his feet was inlaid with gold trim, and every fitting and furnishing was of the highest quality. Marble floors and columns predominated, so much weight that the poor architect had warned the boat might capsize. Another three million had allayed the man's worries, something to do with stabilizers and ballast to keep the ship upright, and causing Ivanovic to jest that her keel had been laid not in lead but gold. Ultimately, however, he had what he wanted—not a refuge for the odd vacation, but rather a stage, a platform from which all manner of business and pleasure might be consummated.

His thickset security chief padded across the salon. He was dressed in his usual ill-fitting suit, and his only visible accessory—sourced not from Gucci or Hermès, but rather Beretta—bulged obviously beneath a wrinkled lapel. The man handed over a communications printout. "This just arrived," he said in Russian.

Ivanovic took a ten-page printout in hand and removed his reading glasses from a pocket. "Is the loading complete?" he asked.

"Yes. The ship will sail shortly after midnight from Sebastopol."

Ivanovic skimmed the report, which contained an official manifest purporting what was being carried and where it was being taken. He chuckled at the creativity involved, and with some effort extracted the few truths. The destination was listed as Mumbai, which covered things nicely. *Argos*, a ship his new subsidiary had acquired only last month, was to leave Crimea for the Black Sea, then run a gentle slalom through the Bosporus Straits, followed by a left turn into open water. There she would disappear into the Mediterranean's river of commerce.

"Bring me any new updates," Ivanovic said dismissively.

His security man disappeared and he readdressed his steak, his eyes still scanning the paperwork page by page. He was remorseless in his attack, his hands sawing hunks of flesh and plugging them into his mouth. At the other end of the twelve-foot table a young woman sat ignored, but that was nothing new. It had long been Ivanovic's custom to work through dinner—he'd always felt he was at his best behind a good meal, his senses at their most heightened.

"You are not eating," he said distractedly, his eyes pinned on a cargo manifest.

Ursula, the new blonde from a tiny village in Siberia, twirled her fork through a salad.

"It is too much for me," she replied.

He measured a lewd reply, but the sport of it escaped

him. He was already growing tired of this one. She was young and rail thin, eyes as blue and empty as a cloudless midday sky. She'd spent the day shopping on the island of Capri, now three miles off the starboard beam. Ivanovic had no doubt she'd spent every dollar of the ten thousand he'd allotted. What had to be a new dress clung like shrink wrap, and the bracelet flopping on one of her wrists looked like a diamond-studded handcuff.

"When will we leave for Saint-Tropez?" she asked.

Ivanovic ignored the question, sensing a bit of negotiating capital for later use in his suite.

He finished his steak, and with barely a pause the cook appeared with a massive crème brûlée in one hand and a torch in the other. In a flourish of culinary stagecraft, the cook lit his flame and soon had the topping caramelized into a crust that looked positively volcanic.

Ten minutes later, his great belly full, Ivanovic stepped out onto the wide aft deck, which doubled as a helipad, and prepared his customary cigar. Fighting a brisk wind, he managed to light it, and stood in survey of his surroundings. In the distance Capri rose from the sea, and a string of amber to the east outlined the Amalfi Coast.

Earlier today, viewing the harbor of Capri, he'd seen one other ship in *Cassandra*'s league. Ivanovic had checked the ship's registry, and was surprised to find that it wasn't owned by a Russian, but rather a Greek. *Probably that bastard marine architect,* he mused. Twenty years ago it would have been a Saudi, before that a Brit. Today, however, across the Med, the competition was largely between the oligarchs. Men who wore their wealth as a badge in the face of invariably humble beginnings.

Ivanovic himself was a case in point. The son of a Ukrainian pig farmer, he had always known he was destined for more than his muck-booted elder. How *much* more had surprised even him. He'd walked out of the foothills of the Carpathians at fifteen, and within two years found himself in Moscow doing small favors for third-tier mobsters. In time, the grade of both his dealings and the crooks he associated with rose in parallel. And now the bar had risen one last time. To a point that could go no higher.

He heard footsteps behind him, and turned to see his security man again.

"Is there something new?" Ivanovic asked.

"No sir. I just wanted to mention . . . I think it might be safer inside."

"You worry too much."

The security man, whose name was Pavel, and who was the closest thing Ivanovic had to a friend, nearly said something. Instead he stood down.

Ivanovic said, "They tell me Abramovich's new ship will be nearly a hundred meters."

Pavel shrugged. "I wouldn't know."

"A hundred meters. That's a very round number— someone should do it."

Pavel eyed Ivanovic's cigar, clearly calculating how much longer it had to burn. Ivanovic went to the starboard rail as a wayward cloud blotted out the moon. He pulled a long draw on his Cohiba, then flicked a bit of ash into the wind-driven water below.

From a distance, the sinewy young man looking through his scope saw a fragment of white-hot ash flutter down to the sea. The burning cigar itself was bright, like a beacon atop the rotund lighthouse that was Pyotr Ivanovic. He saw another man on deck, yet had no trouble distinguishing which of the two to target. The Ukrainian stood out in any crowd, his height and girth at the limits of human potential.

The shooter was still getting used to the new scope, a synthetic hybrid of optical and infrared imagery, and he was pleasantly surprised. Technology in armaments had never been a Russian strength—manufacturers there had long leaned toward simplicity and robustness. The picture before him was unusually sharp, if a bit undermagnified.

The story behind his equipment had been explained to him by a pair of engineers, this in itself a departure from long-held practices. They told him the scope was not a Russian design, but had in fact been "acquired" from America's leading edge research facility, the Sandia National Laboratories. This was nothing new. Russia had long ago stopped trying to keep pace with the West, realizing it was far more economical to let them do the expensive research, development, and testing, then simply steal the results. It had been going on for decades, going back to the Cold War. In those heady days, virtually every new American airplane was followed within a few years by a curiously similar Soviet twin. A time lag had been unavoidable then, Soviet developers forced to work largely from photographs, which necessitated considerable guesswork and reverse engineering. Now the internet age had simplified things greatly—today Russia simply hacked into computers and filched proven blueprints, shortening the "time to shelf" considerably.

The assassin checked the scope's calibration one last time, then verified the synchronization. It was the first time he'd used this system in the field—even his practice had been limited to tightly controlled simulations. The rifle was at least familiar, which gave a degree of confidence. Best of all, his level of personal risk on this mission was less than on any he'd ever undertaken.

A gust of wind brushed the shooter's cheek. On any other day it would have got his attention, but tonight he ignored it entirely. His finger began to press the trigger and his breathing slowed, the habits of eight years taking hold. It couldn't hurt. Finally, in what could only be termed a playful impulse, he jerked his finger through the final half inch of travel.

The big gun answered, bucking once and belching a tongue of flame. All as expected. The bulky suppressor helped, but there was no dampening the supersonic round. The killer resettled the scope for what seemed an interminable amount of time. He was almost ready to admit a miss when Ivanovic jerked violently.

He saw the Russian's head slam forward on a neck carrying its last neural transmissions to the limbs below. His massive body seemed to hesitate for a moment, like a felled tree deciding which way to drop. Then he cartwheeled over the ship's rail and into the sea.

The splash was momentous.

It was all the confirmation the killer needed. Job done, he tidied up his gear, surveyed carefully his course of egress, and blended into the night.

TWO

Compared to the launch of her dead owner a thousand miles away, the departure of *Argos* from the docks of Sebastopol caused barely a ripple. She was a Russian-flagged vessel, a 312-foot carrier of general cargo. The ship's hull was weathered and her fixtures dated, but there was not a hint of slackness in her rigging, nor any chatter in the hum of her engine. Nearing the end of an unremarkable service life, she'd spent years hauling fertilizer to Syria, a surprisingly profitable niche until civil war brought agricultural production there to a grinding halt. Shifting to more reliable trade, *Argos* had found steady if marginally profitable work running dry goods and machinery between Black Sea ports and the more sedate corners of the Middle East.

The ship's recent transfer of ownership had little apparent effect on her operation. Most of the crew had stayed on in a tight job market, including her skipper, a thickset Armenian named Amad Zakaryan. As sea captains went, Zakaryan was a decent sort, with a reputation as a competent if conservative master who held deep familiarity with the routes he plied. *Argos* was his second command, this for a man who'd been running the Black Sea since he was a teen. He'd started out pulling dock lines and scraping rust, working his way up to master over the course of three decades. In that time he'd seen great change in the merchant marine industry, much of it for the better.

The changes he saw tonight, however, were not to his liking.

Argos maneuvered up the deepest channel in the Port of Sebastopol, a weaving passage through ebony water that did justice to the adjacent sea's name. On display to starboard, as if lined up for inspection, were bits and pieces of Russia's Black Sea Fleet. It was the smallest of that nation's naval commands, comprised largely of ships that were castoffs from the frontline cold water fleets. The docks had grown marginally busier since the annexation of Crimea, and from the wing of the bridge Zakaryan watched the hulking shadow of a destroyer slide past in the pier's yellow-sulfur lights. Being intimately familiar with the harbor, he knew this particular warship hadn't seen open water in five years. Of course he knew why. For an economically struggling Russia, unable to fund major repairs, more of her navy was falling each day to little more than placeholder status. Like mortgaged hotels on a Monopoly board, eye-catching but valueless.

Soon the last wharves slid past, and the channel opened up to greet the black void ahead. Zakaryan issued an order to raise the speed, but he remained on the catwalk. He half turned his head to address the man standing behind him.

"I should know what we are carrying," the captain said. It was the third time he'd posed the question, and while he didn't expect an answer, he thought the business of getting under way might be his last rightful chance to ask.

The man standing by the rail, who wore heavy cargo pants and a thick sweater, gave a classically Slavic shrug. His name was Ivan, or so he said, and his accent was unmistakably Russian. *A Russian named Ivan.* That had been the captain's first thought when they'd met yesterday afternoon. *God help us* had been his second.

There had been little interface when he'd first come aboard. Zakaryan had shown the man to his quarters on the upper deck, followed by a cautious exchange as they stood watching the deck crane lift a series of pallets aboard—none of them was particularly large, but they were obviously heavy based on the creaking of the cables and the efforts of the men on the guidelines. That was when the captain had first asked what they were carrying. The second query came around midnight, after Zakaryan had signed what was clearly a dubious cargo manifest—not unheard-of in these parts. Neither query had gotten a response. Now, with the ship plowing toward open water, it seemed his last chance.

"What if we experience a fire in the hold?" Zakaryan pressed. "My men must know what they are dealing with."

"Don't let your boat catch fire," said Ivan. His hair was close-cropped, his manner blunt, and a pair of squinting eyes gave nothing away.

"What speed should we make?"

"We are in no hurry. We need to breach the Suez six days from now."

Breach, Zakaryan thought, *as if we're blasting through a door.* To Ivan's name and nationality, he added a third descriptor: *army*. It did not bode well.

Indeed, the captain's orders for this voyage were unique in all his years at sea. When it came to matters of storms, mechanical problems, or trouble with the crew, Zakaryan would be in charge. When it came to anything else—where they were going, what they were carrying, and when they would arrive—a Russian soldier named Ivan was in command. Every crewman's cell phone had been secured in a locker under his bunk, and even the two-way radios were off limits, to be used only in Ivan's presence. In Zakaryan's experience, it was an unprecedented surrender of authority, but there had been little choice. The ship's new ownership group, which went by the hazy name of MIR Enterprises, was represented by a man named Romanov who had made clear that if Zakaryan didn't comply, a replacement skipper could easily be found. He'd heard such threats before from owners, yet something told him this new group would go through with it. Whatever cargo they were plying, it wasn't going to be left stacked on a pier for the honor of one journeyman sea captain.

Zakaryan tried a different tack with his new co-commander. "I checked the arrival schedule in Mumbai," he said, referring to their ostensible destination. "The port administration there has no record of our sailing—they won't be expecting us."

"Good."

Zakaryan waited, but nothing else came. Frustrated, he stepped to the forward rail and looked out across a dead-calm sea.

"Do not worry, Captain. All will become clear. In two weeks you will be back in Sebastopol with a very nice bonus."

Knowing defeat when he saw it, Zakaryan bent his head toward the passage to the bridge. "Make speed seven knots," he called out.

"Seven knots?" queried the man at the helm. It was

a decidedly inefficient speed, barely enough to keep steerage.

The captain shot his subordinate a hard look.

"Seven knots it is, sir."

THREE

Notwithstanding its vicious nature, the murder of Pyotr Ivanovic was handled with practiced discretion on the Isle of Capri. Long a jewel of Italy's robust tourism industry, the island was a haven for the well-heeled, and the idea that one of its wealthiest visitors had been shot dead on his mega-yacht was something to be tamped down.

The local carabinieri, who had little enthusiasm for high-profile cases, took a guarded investigative tack. To begin, there was nothing that could be called a press conference—the few details that did escape were more along the lines of whispered insinuations. To his credit, the inspector in charge, a compact and circumspect man named Giordano, checked off squares in his investigatory ledger as best he could.

He began by securing the crime scene, which in this case meant locking down what was nearly an ocean liner. With the captain's assent, the inspector ordered that *Cassandra* remain, for the time being, anchored precisely where the murder had taken place. He then set about determining who was responsible for the vessel, and with no great surprise discovered that *Cassandra*'s chain of title was so impossibly convoluted that its disposition might take months, if not years, to determine. With foul play all but certain, he arranged for a postmortem on the body, and only then shifted to the matter of notification.

Giordano's attempts to locate Ivanovic's next of kin were an exercise in frustration. He began with the ship's safe, which was accessed with the help of the captain, and found it largely empty. There were no relevant legal documents, in particular a will, nor any suggestion of where such papers might be stashed. The crew were equally unhelpful—none of them could remember Ivanovic ever mentioning a blood relative. The inspector's inquiries to the Russian embassy were met with indifference. Ivanovic's lawyer, a man from Kiev whose bluster far exceeded his grasp of Italian law, and whose phone number changed with curious frequency, assured the inspector unreservedly that he kept in his possession papers granting him personal oversight of Ivanovic's estate—and that if Giordano could somehow expedite certain documentations, a ten-thousand-euro "assistance fee" might land in his own account.

The inspector demurred. The phone number changed again.

Because even the most egregious of sinners deserved some manner of last respects, Giordano committed to a chain of phone calls, thirty-one to Russia alone, seeking guidance on what to do with Ivanovic's body after the postmortem. In a hopeful moment, he discovered that the victim hailed from the tiny village of Milove, a tangle of dusty streets set tenuously on the Ukraine-Russia border. He even managed to reach the office of the town church, an Eastern Orthodox house whose deacon lamented that the name was regrettably common in town. No one admitted to remembering Pyotr Ivanovic.

Seeing his murder investigation faltering straight out of the gate, Giordano shifted his focus to the victim's recent history. It took little investigative effort to confirm that Ivanovic was indeed one of the most pretentious, and presumably corrupt, oligarchs to rise from the ashes of the Soviet era—something akin to being the nastiest viper in the pit. This, the inspector realized, was perhaps a solution in itself: Such a notorious character would certainly have made enemies over the years. But how could he track them down?

Giordano decided to begin with the low-hanging fruit. He interviewed each member of the ship's crew, Ivanovic's dumbstruck security detail, and the lone female guest who'd been on board. He dutifully mapped out *Cassandra*'s anchorage that night, and with a diagram in hand, he pressed each of them for any sights, sounds, or intuitions to explain who might have put a very large hole in their former employer. The only result was a wasted day, Giordano getting nothing to pique his interest.

When he was finally out of questions, the inspector gave permission for nonessential crew and staff to depart with their belongings. A young and very pretty Russian girl, who seemed none too distraught—and whose duties on board had been made quite clear by the room steward, who in his interview had mimed certain salacious acts—was also allowed to depart. Giordano bid the woman goodbye in her stateroom, just before going off shift, and as he did so he could not ignore that her manner of dress was hardly that of a grieving lover. She was resplendent in fitted Dior above and Manolo below, and the makeup stand in front of the mirror showed signs of a heavy engagement.

Only after Giordano's departure did she make her

move, presenting to the crew of the launch six wardrobe cases, and keeping to herself a large, and evidently quite heavy, handbag. A young carabinieri lieutenant, one of the small rotating contingent who stood watch over the crime scene, insisted on inspecting the handbag at the foot of the gangway. Inside he discovered nearly one hundred thousand euros, in various denominations, and enough gold coins and diamond jewelry to fill a good-sized safe deposit box. After considerable shouting and gesturing, and in a hopeless mix of languages, *Cassandra*'s captain became involved. The woman claimed that the trove had been gifted to her by her beloved Pyotr. The captain alleged she was pilfering all of it, and that without the cash he would have no means of paying a skeleton crew to maintain the ship. An even more disjointed argument ensued until the lieutenant waved his arms demonstratively to impose his ruling: the woman could keep the jewelry, but the cash and gold were to be returned to the ship's safe. Everyone recognized half a victory, and the deal was struck.

With the flurry settled, and on the second day after Pyotr Ivanovic's death, only the captain and five crewmen remained on board to manage *Cassandra*. All were looking forward to an extended paid holiday on the Isle of Capri.

Refusing to admit defeat, Giordano changed course the next day. Using the ship's log as a reference, he made inquiries along her months-long trail across the Mediterranean. In a call to Cannes he talked to a provisioning agent who claimed not to remember Ivanovic, but who told Giordano that he would be most appreciative if the inspector would forward his company's name and number to *Cassandra*'s new owner whenever the matter was settled. An event planner in

Monaco, who'd arranged a dockside party, angrily claimed to be owed damages for a ruined chocolate waterfall.

Through all his inquiries Giordano sensed not a tear shed nor a voice choked with remorse. It was as if every person who'd ever known the Russian, save for his ersatz attorney, had gone into hiding. For Giordano, it was a departure from his previous experiences involving the death of wealthy individuals. Long-lost brothers and mistresses typically came out of the woodwork, professing to anyone who would listen their closeness to the dearly departed. Bankers and creditors materialized like apparitions, stacks of legal documents in hand. Here, however, it was as if Pyotr Ivanovic, and everything he'd ever touched, was in some way contaminated.

And it was there, somewhere between a village church in Ukraine and a chocolate fountain on the bottom of Monaco's harbor, that Giordano's disjointed inquiries reached their end. Pyotr Ivanovic was known widely across the Mediterranean party circuit, throughout banking and legal circles, and had left a string of bitterly shorn mistresses. When it came to the matter of burying him, however, there was not a single volunteer to the spade.

The inspector was stymied. With his investigation fast grinding to a halt, he was left with a yacht impounded in his harbor, a body no one would bother to claim, and a supporting cast of vermin abandoning a ship that wasn't sinking.

In what was only a fleeting thought, the senior inspector from Capri thought he perhaps should have taken the ten thousand after all.

* * *

Though Inspector Giordano would never realize it, his sputtering inquest into the death of Pyotr Ivanovic did stir one small pocket of interest. It surfaced, of all places, in a conference room in Langley, Virginia. A junior CIA analyst, who specialized in metadata filtering, made an astute correlation between the murder of Ivanovic and a separate inquiry at the agency. The connection was tenuous at best, but enough of a thread that she advanced it to her supervisor at their morning meeting.

To her surprise, the division chief, who had herself been newly promoted, took a keen interest in the discovery. She asked specific questions about how Ivanovic had been killed. The only firm detail was as unusual as it was spectacular—by all appearances, he had been shot by a sniper. If the Italians knew more than that, they were holding their cards close.

In a decision the junior analyst thought speculative at the time—but one that months later would earn them both promotions—the division chief sent instructions to the Rome station to look quietly into Ivanovic's death. They were to begin with AISI, Italy's internal security agency.

Within twenty-four hours, the division chief from Langley, whose name was Anna Sorensen, was in the office of CIA director Thomas Coltrane.

Three hours later she was on the next commercial flight to Rome.

FOUR

If the Italian township of Vieste could be distilled to a single theme, it would be that of light. Even at the height of autumn, sun splashes carelessly across a smooth Adriatic, its reflections capturing a city whose white stone walls seem to lift from the sea. Like most towns on the right-hand shore of Italy, Vieste is a place with a history as hard as its calcified cliffs, where Turkish corsairs plundered and pirates marauded, and where quarreling popes battled for dominance. Altogether, an incongruous heritage for a town whose very name invokes purity itself, drawn from Vesta, the Roman goddess of hearth, home, and family.

David Slaton kept a steady pace as he navigated narrow sun-washed lanes. Were he not preoccupied, he might have paused to appreciate the structures around him. The sidewalks, walls, and arches he saw were cut from local stone, everything square-edged and functional. As a stonemason, his range of expertise had expanded greatly in recent years. Indeed, he was reaching a point where he thought he might be able to distinguish any city in Europe based on a single representative building. On that pastoral Monday morning, however, the stonework of the southern

Adriatic coast was not his priority. The tradecraft Slaton was engaged in was an altogether different variety, one whose success was measured not in what caught the eye, but rather what escaped it.

He drew little notice from the locals, although his sandy hair and Nordic features spoke of a gene pool to the north. He stood over six feet tall and carried a discernibly muscular build—not the inflated thickness developed in a gym, but a more functional, blue collar version. Testament to the stone craftsman he occasionally was.

He'd stepped onto Vieste's main pier twenty minutes ago with an uneven gait, sea legs being an unavoidable consequence of three weeks on a small boat navigating open ocean. The awkwardness wore off quickly, and he moved now with a purpose. He mixed languidly with the crowds in busier sections of town, and more quickly where traffic was sparse. He did nothing to draw attention, and little escaped his eye. A car traveling with deliberate slowness passed uneventfully, and a pair of men loitering near the post office he quickly deemed harmless. So too, the bored guard at the entrance of a bank, and a helmeted delivery driver on a scooter. In each instance, information logged, evaluated, and filed into a mental bin that, were it to have a name, might be labeled: *nonthreatening*. There was of course an alternate bin, but that was thankfully empty. As it had been for months.

The reasons for his caution—there were two—lay a mile behind him in the cabin of an Antares 44 catamaran anchored in the town's blue-aqua harbor: his wife and young son.

They'd slipped into port at first light, *Windsom* riding a following breeze, and set anchor inside the long breakwater. Dawn was Slaton's preferred hour for arrival into any port. It allowed some daylight for navigation, always desirable when approaching an unfamiliar anchorage. It was also invariably a time when senior port captains and customs administrators lingered at their breakfast tables. When *Windsom*'s anchor had struck bottom an hour earlier, it did so with its usual symbolism—in that moment, the two realms in which Slaton and his family existed reached their necessary, and always awkward, intersection. Civilization on one hand, and their commitment to escape it on the other. It had been that way for more than a year, and so far they'd muddled through. A month at sea, then venture ashore to resupply, and perhaps, if things went smoothly, to eat a meal they hadn't cooked themselves and sleep in a bed that wasn't moving.

This morning, in keeping with their private protocol, Christine and Davy had stayed behind on *Windsom* while Slaton set out in the launch toward shore. Customs and immigration procedures required that he present the ship's papers and all three passports. The documents he carried were something less than legitimate, but forgeries of such high quality that they'd never been challenged. At least not in Kuala Lumpur or Mykonos, and certainly not in the Maldives. Every destination, however, had its idiosyncrasies.

Slaton had researched things beforehand, and from a cruising reference manual he'd extracted what should have been an eminently simple process. Vieste, being a minor port of maritime entry, kept no dedicated customs facility, nor was there a standing port office. The only obligation was to report *Windsom*'s arrival in Italy to the local police precinct.

And there his problems began.

He found the precinct building easily, only to discover that it had been abandoned due to damage from a recent earthquake. A notice posted at the entrance stated that, while repairs were being made, a temporary office had been established on the opposite side of town. Vieste being a compact place, Slaton set out on foot and reached the correct district in fifteen minutes. There he encountered another roadblock—quite literally. The street in question was under repair, and barricades denied access to the temporary address. Slaton rounded the block, and soon encountered signs directing him to the new station. Then a third sign contradicted the two he'd previously seen. Slaton drew to a stop on the sidewalk. Apparently the carabinieri's coordination with the ministry of highways, or signage, or whatever directorate was in charge, had gone wildly afield. It reminded him of stories he'd read about World War II, when partisans across Europe altered road signs to confuse the invading forces.

"Welcome back to the real world," he said under his breath.

He spotted a café nearby, walked over, and struck up a conversation with an idle waiter—Italian was one of his better languages, although he spoke it with a Swiss accent, a vestige of his schooling as a young boy. The waiter explained that a water main had cracked, and that most of the businesses on the street had been forced to relocate.

"The carabinieri?" Slaton inquired.

"Yes, they were here for a time, but had to move like everyone else. I heard they are now near the old church."

"Which one?" Slaton asked. Saying that something

was near a church in Italy was like saying it was next to a pub in England.

The waiter gave instructions, each turn demonstrated with carving motions of his hands, that sent Slaton uphill, and some distance away from the harbor.

It went that way for another half hour. A schoolteacher on her way to work told him the police had gone back toward the piers, although she too said something about a church. A shopkeeper had seen a group of police cars near the fish market, while a young mason prepping for a day's work on a tile roof—a man whom Slaton innately trusted—told him the carabinieri had set up shop in a wing of the old Catholic school. The roofer's parting words were perhaps the most telling Slaton had heard all morning: *Welcome to Italy, my friend.*

He would happily have asked a policeman for directions, but he'd yet to encounter one—staffing at this time of day, he knew, would be at its low point. He toyed with the idea of manufacturing a minor crisis, perhaps calling in a domestic disturbance on a certain street corner, and letting the carabinieri come to him. The concept had a certain appeal, but came with complications. Chief among them at the moment—Slaton didn't have a phone. He and Christine kept no standing telecom account, which was a requirement these days for those on the run—the must-not-have accessory. Indeed, one of his regular chores upon coming ashore was to replenish their supply of burner phones.

Slaton was three streets above the wharf where his runabout was moored, staring forlornly at yet another church, when his frustration gave way to alarm. Less than a mile distant, at the far end of the protective breakwater, he saw *Windsom* swinging serenely on her anchor.

Lashed to her stern was a small boat.

A boat he had never seen before.

FIVE

It could have been anything. An overzealous port official or a marine mechanic looking for work. A neighborly welcome from another boat. Perhaps the police were more competent than expected, and had boarded *Windsom* for a customs inspection. Those were the best-case scenarios. Bleaker possibilities governed Slaton's response.

With one look at his distant inflatable runabout, he realized his dilemma. If anything ominous was taking place, he was in a deep tactical hole—as things stood, he was facing an approach to *Windsom* not only unarmed, but with no hope of surprise. It was an unacceptable equation, meaning he had to change a variable.

For an assassin—in essence what Slaton was, despite his attempts to leave that life behind—it is an essential skill to employ a weapon. By extension, the ability to acquire firepower when empty-handed is every bit as fundamental.

He had actually once given a lecture on the subject during a brief stint at Mossad's academy—teaching fledgling field operatives improvisational means of finding weapons. The most obvious choices—military and police arsenals—came with obvious limitations.

Such facilities were generally well guarded, and in most cases, anything stolen was quickly missed. The more immediate problem: As Slaton stood looking down at the docks of Vieste, he'd already spent nearly an hour trying to locate the nearest police station, and he knew of no nearby military base. That being the case, he progressed to the more imaginative chapters of his old lesson plan.

He ran downhill to the pier where his runabout was moored, and on reaching the seawall Slaton skidded to a stop. His gaze settled on two waterside bars. Both were obviously closed, and he ran a quick decision matrix. Gun laws in Italy were strict, but it was reasonable to assume that the owner of a waterside bar might keep a handgun beneath a counter to protect cash drawers or encourage destructive brawls to be taken outside. The problem—liquor was valuable, which meant that the strength of doors and windows on closed saloons, rustic as they might appear, often rivaled those found on banks.

Slaton checked *Windsom* again. Nothing had changed. The small wooden dinghy remained tied off her stern, bobbing harmlessly. He saw no one on deck. No movement in the distant windows. His conviction only solidified—he had to find a weapon *now*.

His eyes swept over a fleet of fishing boats on the far side of the harbor. Many would have handguns or rifles locked in poorly secured compartments. Unfortunately, the docks would also be populated by crewmen prepping for morning launches, locals who would not take kindly to an outsider poking around untended boats.

Increasingly desperate, Slaton was weighing a rash unarmed approach to *Windsom* when he turned a half circle and saw another prospect. Just behind him, in a building abutting a large warehouse, was the local chapter of the *Unione Italiana del Lavoro*. It was the Italian labor union whose oversight ran the spectrum of blue collar professions. In front of him, presumably, was Vieste's longshoreman's chapter.

If there was a commonality on all the world's wharves, it was that they were rough-and-tumble places. Places where hard men worked and smuggling thrived. And consequently . . . places where a union labor boss might want protection.

With a glance up and down the deserted pier, Slaton trotted toward the union office and peered through a grimy window. It was dark inside, no one having yet shown up for work. In the shadows he saw worn office furnishings and bookcases, and a big banner from an old rally was strung across a wall: *PIÙ FORTE INSIEME*. Stronger together.

There was an exterior door just to his right, but it looked solid. Another door farther to his left looked eminently more pliable, and appeared to lead into the adjacent warehouse. Slaton found that door unlocked, and he pushed through on creaking hinges.

The warehouse was cavernous. There were endless rows of shelving, and pallets were stacked high, looking like tiny shrink-wrapped buildings. He heard an engine in the distance, probably a forklift working in some distant aisle. On his right was the union office, and as hoped he saw a door connecting to the warehouse. He spotted a crowbar on top of a wooden crate. Ten seconds and one splintered door jamb later, he was inside.

In the half light he discerned a series of offices along a hallway. He found the *capo*'s desk in the third one. There were three locked drawers, and with the crowbar still in hand, he splintered them open from top to bottom. The first drawer held office supplies. The second, tools, including a blowtorch. This gave pause, but he moved on. Slaton's guesswork paid off in the bottom drawer—a Smith & Wesson Model 19 revolver. It was a relic, a classic six-shooter, but the gun looked clean, and better yet, intimidating. Precisely what a union boss might brandish at a recalcitrant longshoreman. Slaton popped the cylinder open, saw six shiny rounds, then flipped it closed. He slid the long barrel into his back waistband, situated for a right-handed draw. Covering the grip with the tail of his shirt, he hurried back outside.

"Men can be like that," the woman said. "Never around when you need them."

Christine laughed at her guest's attempt at humor, but it belied the fact that her face was etched in worry—she'd turned away from her to pull two coffee cups from a rack.

"Yeah, tell me about it," she replied, trying to keep her tone light.

So far the woman seemed harmless. Christine had seen her coming—that was her assignment when they arrived in a new port. David went ashore to take care of business, while she stood guard. There was no better term for it—standing guard, like a military sentry.

She'd watched the woman row the last hundred yards, willing her to veer away. Instead she'd lasered in on *Windsom* like an arrow to a bull's-eye. When her dinghy was twenty yards off the port beam, the woman had paused. She'd hailed to introduce herself, and politely asked permission to come aboard. It hardly seemed an assault. She explained that her name was Anna Sorensen, and that she'd come to see

David. That had sealed it. The use of her husband's true name—not the one on the passport he was at that moment showing to immigration officials—made any evasion or denials pointless.

It also put Christine on edge.

She filled both cups with coffee. "Cream or sugar?"

"Black is fine."

As she turned toward the dinette where her guest sat, Christine glanced out the starboard window. She'd heard a small engine moments earlier, and was disappointed to see only a fishing dory running past, its faded green hull slicing the smooth water with a teenage boy at the helm. She weighed coming up with an excuse to go above and raise their Jolly Roger amidships. The flag was patently ridiculous, that cocktail-hour joke seen across the world on weekend pleasure boats. For her and David, however, it was something else—the pirate's black-and-white standard was their personal red flag. She decided it wasn't necessary—the dinghy attached to *Windsom*'s stern was all the warning David needed.

She slid into the bench seat across from Sorensen and nestled close to Davy, who was sipping apple juice from a plastic cup. Threat or not, she was going to keep her son close. "Can you tell me what this is about?" she asked.

"I really should discuss it with David first." Sorensen looked at Davy, and said, "So how old are you?"

Davy held up two fingers.

Sorensen smiled, and Christine asked, "Do you have kids?"

"Not yet, but I'm hopeful. I think I found the right guy. Trouble is, work has been getting in the way for both of us."

"Don't let that stop you. You'd be amazed at how adaptable parenting can be."

"I guess you would know."

The comment generated an awkward silence. Both went to their coffee. Sorensen was blond and slender, undeniably attractive. She was also quintessentially American in her accent and mannerisms. Christine placed her as being from the Midwest. They hadn't gotten that far—what part of the country each hailed from—but with her nationality all but certain, Christine saw a short list of possibilities as to who she represented. CIA, FBI—some three-letter agency that lurked on the fringes of D.C.

Not for the first time, she was struck by her unconventional thought processes. A pretty young blonde had come looking for her husband, and Christine's main concern was which spy agency she worked for. Extrapolating further, she wondered if some new reprisal was descending upon them. David was a former Mossad assassin, and his past seemed to haunt them with clockwork regularity. Like a heart condition that never quite normalized.

Sorensen began making funny faces at Davy. He giggled, and apple juice sprayed from his nose. "Sorry," Sorensen said, laughing along with him and pushing a dishcloth across the table.

"So tell me," Christine asked as she wiped Davy's nose, "how did you find us?"

After some deliberation, Sorensen seemed to let a barrier fall. "It took some effort. We asked around a bit, and heard you might have passed through Israel recently. What sealed it was your boat's name. We knew it, and that allowed us to track your movements through a few ports. Connecting those dots in chronological order, we got a general idea of where you were heading. From there a few overheads sealed the deal."

Setting aside the question of who "we" referred to, Christine asked, "Overheads? As in satellites?"

"I know what you're thinking—it's a big sea. But it's not as hard as it sounds. Do you know how many Antares 44s are cruising this part of the Med right now?"

Christine didn't venture a guess.

"Two. The other is docked in Split, Croatia."

"You mean . . . from a satellite photo you can identify a sailboat by manufacturer?"

"I didn't say that—but would you be surprised?"

"I guess not." She blew out a long breath. "It's getting harder and harder to disappear these days."

"Almost impossible, depending on who's looking for you. If it's any consolation, not many countries have the assets we do."

There it was again, Christine thought. *We.*

"So how long have you been cruising?" Sorensen asked.

"A little over a year . . . but you probably know that."

Her guest didn't respond, and Christine had a fleeting thought that perhaps she should have raised the Jolly Roger after all. As a doctor she often dealt with misrepresentations and half-truths. How many times had she seen addicts lie to get prescription painkillers? How many drug reps had she seen exaggerate clinical trials for some new and expensive medication? The difference now—she was on the duplicitous side, while the woman across from her was dealing in truth. At least, as far as she could tell. *That's what I get for marrying an assassin,* she thought.

The awkward interlude went on for a few more minutes. It ended suddenly when David appeared in the companionway. He had a large handgun Christine had never seen. It was leveled squarely at their new guest.

SIX

"Your hands stay on the coffee cup," Slaton said, his eyes alternating between the stranger at the dining table and the rest of the cabin. He saw no one else.

"Not a problem," the blond woman said.

Slaton cocked his head slightly. On hearing those three words, two of his questions were answered. He knew who the woman was. And he knew who she represented.

"Sorensen, CIA," he said.

Christine looked at him, then the woman who was facing her. "You two know one another?"

"We've never met in person," said Sorensen, "but we talked over a satellite link. David did some work for us not long ago in Lebanon. It was—"

"No," he interrupted. "I never worked for you. We had mutual interests in a matter that was settled a long time ago. That doesn't give you the right to show up on my doorstep without warning."

"We need to talk to you about—"

"Stop right there! Before you say anything more, I want a private word with my wife. And before I can do that—" Slaton tipped the barrel of his gun upward twice, indicating that Sorensen should stand. He looked expectantly at Christine.

She protested, "David, is that really necessary?"

Before he could answer, Sorensen said, "No, it's okay." She stood and held her arms away from her body.

Slaton watched as his wife reluctantly patted down the CIA officer for weapons—he'd taught her the basics. She didn't find anything.

"Satisfied?" Christine asked.

"No."

Three minutes later Slaton had reestablished a degree of order in his life. After his wife's halfhearted search, he had frisked Sorensen himself and found her to be clean: no wires, no transmitters, no weapons. He then banished her to *Windsom*'s aft rail.

Christine steered Davy toward the forward stateroom. By the time she returned to the main cabin, Slaton was nibbling crackers and tossing a Nerf basketball at a plastic hoop.

"You let her aboard," he said in a hushed tone, no inflection to imply a question.

"What was I supposed to do? A strange woman rows up and asks for you *by name*."

"You should have sent her away."

"I tried, but she asked to wait. I was trying to be civilized."

"Civilized? What would have happened if she—"

"*Give me some credit, okay?* When she came below I made sure she sat with her back to the companionway. I kept Davy close. I left a section of lifeline disconnected on the port side to signal you how to approach. I didn't raise the damned pirate flag because I knew her boat would be obvious enough." She reached into her rear waistband and showed him their family Heckler & Koch 9mm, the only gun they kept on board. Its grip was marred—not from any firefight, but from accompanying him on various masonry jobs.

"I was ready, David. I did all the things you briefed me to do. But we only arrived here a few hours ago—I can't just point a gun at the first stranger who comes up to our boat. And besides, this woman knew your real name. She didn't appear armed, and I didn't see anyone else nearby. I made a judgment call in an awkward situation. So yes, I let her come aboard."

He heaved a sigh, then motioned for her to put the H&K away. "Okay, I'm sorry. You handled it well. It's just that when I saw the dinghy tied off the stern . . . I was really worried."

"Where did you find that?" she asked, pointing to his new six-shooter. "You looked like Wyatt Earp punching through a saloon door."

"An Uzi would have been better—this was all I could find on short notice." It was another old point of contention between them. At the outset of their cruise, he'd argued that they should keep a comprehensive arsenal on *Windsom. At least a shotgun,* he'd said. *Maybe a semiautomatic with a high-capacity mag.* Christine had countered that they might as well mount an eight-pound cannon in the forward porthole. Of course she was right—having heavy weapons on board would be a customs and immigration nightmare.

"Okay, what has she told you so far?" he asked.

"She said she has a boyfriend and wants to start a family someday."

Slaton stared at his wife skeptically.

"That's it, we made small talk. Do you have any clue why the CIA wants to talk to you?"

"No. But whatever it is, it can't be good."

"So you'll send her packing?"

He hesitated. "Maybe."

"Can you tell me anything about the time you worked with her?"

"It was in Lebanon last February. But that mission is history, and I don't think she came all the way from D.C. to get my signature on an after-action report." He tried to think it through. "On the other hand, I *did* help the CIA out of a tight spot. Maybe she wants to return the favor. Maybe she's here to help us."

This time it was Christine who looked doubtful.

"Okay, strike that." He looked out on deck. So-rensen was standing exactly where she'd been told to, one hand gripping a stanchion as the boat rocked gently. "I'll give her ten minutes," he said, "find out why she's here. After that, I'll send her on her way, and we pull anchor and get the hell out of here."

Christine seemed to let the idea percolate. "All right . . . if you think that's the best way to handle it. I'll keep Davy up front."

They locked eyes for a moment, then exchanged a half smile. A thaw in the making. He reached out and kissed her on the forehead. "You did great."

She gave a wistful sigh. "Are we ever going to go back?"

"Back to what?"

"Our three-two in the burbs with the back deck. Maybe a tree house and a swing set this time."

He didn't answer right away. "Is that what you want?"

"Sometimes."

"And the other times?"

"The other times . . . I realize it doesn't matter where we are." She smiled his favorite smile. The one that could not have been more genuine. The one that still took his breath away. She moved toward the forward stateroom where Davy was chirping away. Halfway there she paused. "I did learn one useful thing from our guest," she said.

"What's that?"

"We need to change the name of our boat."

SEVEN

"You can call me Anna," Sorensen said. "I can't remember if I mentioned my first name when we last spoke."

"You didn't," replied Slaton. "But then, it wasn't exactly a social call."

They'd taken opposite sides of the cockpit on *Windsom*'s aft deck, the ship's big chrome wheel between them. Slaton regarded Sorensen closely, having a face now to go with the voice he'd heard so many months ago. That association had been strictly operational, a mission-oriented comm link. A relationship of mutual necessity. The fact that "Anna" was now sitting serenely on his boat, framed by the shimmering Adriatic and offering first-name rapport, only fanned Slaton's suspicions. He harbored a deep and lasting mistrust of all intelligence agencies, brought on by a series of manipulations imposed upon him by Mossad. Regrettably for Sorensen, his misgivings about those organizations were transferrable to all who represented them.

She began in a reticent tone, telling him his doubts were apparent. "What you did for us last year—the director was very impressed. Everyone was."

"We were lucky in a lot of ways, but it worked out

in the end. I'd suggest you don't dwell on the past. I told my wife I would give you ten minutes. You've got nine and a half left."

Sorensen actually smiled. "Yeah, I remember that about you—no wasted motion." She appeared to organize her thoughts, her blue eyes concentrating intently. "Have you ever heard of a man named Pyotr Ivanovic?"

Slaton thought about it. "Russian, a big-time oligarch. I don't get many intel briefings these days, but at one time he was pretty tight with the Russian president."

"Right until the very end."

"What end?"

"Ivanovic was killed four days ago. He was standing on the deck of his yacht, which was anchored off the Isle of Capri, when someone put a very large hole in his chest." Sorensen paused longer than was necessary.

Slaton actually grinned. "And what . . . the CIA thinks I had something to do with it?"

"It's not a matter of what *we* think. The Russian reaction to his passing has been very acute. Very dynamic. They're making a lot of noise, trying to find out who was responsible. Which implies to us that Ivanovic was either still tight with President Petrov, or involved in something important."

"Or both."

She nodded. "FSB message traffic suggests they're gathering information on assassins-for-hire. To what end we don't know."

Slaton remained impassive. The FSB was the post-Soviet resurrection of the KGB.

She continued, "From what we've heard, attention seems to be focusing on a certain former Mossad *kidon.* A man who supposedly died a few years ago in England, but whose name keeps popping up in places like Paris and Beirut."

Slaton considered it. He *had* been busy, and the reluctance of his entanglements in those places was immaterial. It was one thing to dodge the headlines, but whispers in the intelligence community were harder to evade. Once again, he felt the vortex of his past pulling him in.

Sorensen went on. "When we learned that much, I wanted to get out ahead of the FSB. I tracked you down, and learned that you weren't far away that night."

"You can't be serious! Me a hired gun? I've never taken a dime to shoot anyone."

"Actually, I believe you. But you *were* in the general area that night. You were even on a boat."

Slaton conjured a map in his head. He estimated that *Windsom* had been at least three hundred miles from Capri on the night in question. He wasn't going to bother arguing the point.

"From a neutral point of view," she went on, "you *do* have something of a reputation."

"You're wasting my time, Miss Sorensen."

"Am I? In the gray world that follows people in your line of work, you're something between a ghost and a legend. That could have certain advantages—what better cover for a high-end assassin than being dead?"

He shook his head incredulously. "My 'line of work,' as you put it, has changed. I'm a stonemason now."

Her eyes remained locked to his, but she said nothing.

Slaton tried to read her. "Where are you going with

this? Are you trying to tell me the CIA has done me a favor by not outing me to the Russians? I could almost view that as a threat—and I'm pretty sure you didn't come here with that in mind."

"No. I saw you work in Lebanon. Believe me when I say I wouldn't have volunteered for that assignment."

"What then?"

"It's actually quite the opposite. We want to know why the FSB is so concerned about Ivanovic's death. By virtue of your ... expertise ... you're uniquely capable of helping us do that. In return, we might be able to help you."

"Help me? How?"

"To begin, by deflecting suspicion of your involvement. Maybe we could plant some misinformation, help you take your name out of conversations like this once and for all."

"Clean names are easier to buy than to repair—I can get a solid new identity for twenty grand."

"Can you? I started looking for you two days ago. Now here I am, sitting on your boat six time zones away. You're trying to disappear, David, but clearly there are flaws in your plan."

Slaton canted his gaze toward the harbor as he weighed her argument. Sorensen had a point—she'd found him and his family far too easily.

She said, "The CIA is the best in the world at tracking people down. If I were to give you the latest on how we do it, help you refine your methods—I think you'd be able to keep a much lower profile going forward."

He refocused on her. "What exactly do you want?"

"I want your professional opinion. Come with me to Capri. I'll arrange for us to have a word with the detective looking into Ivanovic's death. I want to see it through your eyes. After that, we go to the embassy in Rome."

"Rome?"

"My team back at Langley is working on this from another angle. You and I will need the secure comm at the embassy to see what they've dredged up." She eyed him pleadingly, and said, "I want to get a bead on what's going on. I want to know who killed Ivanovic, and why."

Slaton's jaw hardened. He knew there was more to it. "I still don't see why you're so interested in this."

She broke into a half smile. "I guess I shouldn't be surprised. You have good instincts—aside from the ones you've already proven. There *is* something else, but I can't get into it yet. I don't even know if you're on board."

Slaton looked back into *Windsom*'s cabin. Through the forward passageway he saw Christine airplaning Davy over the bunk, his son's throaty laughter carrying out over the deck. "How long are we talking about?"

"It depends on what we find. A couple days. I can have you in Capri tonight, and we'll spend tomorrow looking into this."

Slaton viewed that as a nonstarter. "No—I want two days to think about it. If I agree to help, I'll meet you in Rome. The American embassy, two o'clock Wednesday afternoon."

Sorensen frowned. "I'd really like to get going on this . . . although I do understand your caution."

"No. Believe me when I say, you do *not* understand. And there's one other thing. If I choose to get involved, I want you to take my wife and son into the embassy in Rome. They stay there, under lockdown, until my part in this is done. I want the tightest possible security."

"Is that necessary?"

"Probably not. But it's nonnegotiable."

Sorensen heaved a long sigh. "Are you always so paranoid?"

"Old habits. The only thing that's changed over the years is the object of my concerns. I don't worry about Mossad or Israel or a mission anymore. It's all about them now." He nodded toward the cabin. "You'd do well not to forget that."

Sorensen stood, went aft, and began unlashing her tiny boat. Before stepping aboard she handed over a blank business card with a phone number scrawled on the back. "All right. I'll be at the Rome embassy, two o'clock on Wednesday." She climbed down carefully into the rocking dinghy.

"Where did you get this boat?" he asked.

"I bought it fair and square," said Sorensen, "fifty euros. There aren't any water taxis here, and it seemed like the simplest way to get here without drawing attention. I told the seller my inflatable was beyond repair." She settled onto the wooden bench seat. "I think I'm the loser in the deal, though. This thing's got a leak."

Slaton saw a minor puddle along the boat's keel. "Can't be too bad. Anyway, I'm sure you'll expense whatever you paid."

She pushed off with an oar. "I'm sure I will."

"You could almost say it's part of the CIA's navy."

Sorensen laughed as she took a grip on the oars. "I guess it is."

"One more thing, Anna . . ."

"What's that?"

"Don't ever approach my family unannounced

again." Slaton pulled the six-shooter from his waist-band and pointed it at the boat. Sorensen stiffened on the bench seat, then shuddered when the gun went off. A neat hole appeared near her feet, water bur-bling over her shoes.

"Now it has two leaks," he said. "You'd better row fast."

Sorensen did exactly that, pulling hard on the oars as the little boat began to fill with water. The look on her face was something between shock and bewilder-ment.

Slaton turned and saw Christine standing behind him. Davy was below, babbling through a song.

"Was that really necessary?" she asked.

"She wants me to do a favor for the CIA."

"And that was your answer?"

"Not exactly. You and I need to talk about it before I answer. That was a message. Regardless what we decide, I want them to know who's calling the shots."

"You have a peculiar way of expressing your views. But speaking as your wife, I'm actually not that up-set."

"Why is that?" he asked.

"She's very attractive. But at the moment . . . I'm pretty sure you're not hitting on her."

As *Windsom* set sail toward the heel of Italy's boot, the freighter *Argos* was plodding southward four hundred miles east, making slow but steady progress through the Dardanelle Straits.

Captain Zakaryan stood on the bridge as the Gal-lipoli peninsula rose like an apparition in the midday haze. As a casual student of history, particularly regarding the waters he regularly plied, Zakaryan knew well what had happened here a century earlier at the height of World War I. The First Lord of the Admiralty, Winston Churchill, had conceived a daring campaign to wrest control of the waterway, intending to open a second front and break the stalemate in the war to end all wars. Unfortunately, as was too often the case, the execution of a bold military strategy faltered under poor logistics, inaccurate intelligence, and ill-conceived tactics. After a lamentable expenditure of manpower and resources, diverted from the stalled Western Front, the confrontation with the Ottoman Empire in Gallipoli was abandoned after eight months. Only the most charitable historians framed it as a draw.

From high on the bridge, Zakaryan looked down into *Argos'* main hold. As he did, he felt a sense of hopelessness that could not be much different from what those British sea captains had felt a century ago. He had set out from port on a campaign doomed to failure, no choice but to salute smartly while disaster ran its course. For Zakaryan the belligerent parties were far less clear, the objectives more opaque. Yet the sense of impending disaster was unshakable. *Argos* was but a cog in someone's greater battle plan.

If that weren't troubling enough, he wasn't the only one at the mercy of unseen commanders. As captain, he was responsible for his crew, both legally and morally. A part of him—admittedly small—even felt compassion for Ivan, who he suspected was as much cannon fodder as the rest of them. It was akin to a game of chess in which the middling pieces had been removed. A king and perhaps a queen, the rest of the squares filled by common pawns. He looked out over the horizon, and in the distance saw another ship, a thin trail of smoke rising easily from her stack into the misty day. He wondered mournfully where she might be headed.

Though he could not know it, as Zakaryan stood ruminating from his catwalk, two other captains, masters of freighters very much like *Argos* and carrying nearly identical loads, were harboring similarly downcast thoughts. One, a Bulgarian in command of a converted reefer called *Tasman Sea*, had sailed from Cam Ranh Bay in Vietnam three days earlier. The Greek skipper of *Cirrus* had left the Syrian port of Tartus only yesterday. Like *Argos*, both ships made headway on a secretive schedule, and every twelve hours dispatched a message, via secure satellite link, to their new corporate parent. The messages were little more than standard reports of position and mechanical status. What was less routine was where those reports were received: not in some wharfside shipping office in Marseille or Piraeus, but rather in a nine-million-dollar chalet in Davos, Switzerland.

EIGHT

Windsom scythed a fast track south through heavy seas. Bari was in sight ten miles off the starboard beam, Albania somewhere beyond the horizon to port. They'd pulled anchor right away, and set a general course for the open Med. It was a magnetic heading that covered both potential outcomes. If they chose not to get involved, the open waters to the south were where safety lay. Otherwise, a right turn at the bottom of Italy led to the Strait of Messina and the approaches to Rome.

"Davy is out," Slaton said, emerging from the cabin to meet Christine at the helm.

"Heavy seas do it every time," she said. "They rock him right to sleep."

The wind was strong from the east, and the boat moved rhythmically on five-foot swells. With Davy napping, it was their chance for a discussion on how to proceed. Slaton had already covered the essentials of what Sorensen had in mind. Now they'd both had the morning to weigh it.

"So," Christine began, "could the Russians really believe you're responsible for this man's death?"

"It sounds incredible, but they seem convinced Ivanovic was hit by a hired gun—in particular, a distance shooter. There aren't many of those around. If you ask me, the fact that the FSB has any interest in Ivanovic's death raises a red flag. It suggests he was more than just an entrepreneur."

"So . . . what happens if we ignore this?"

"Best case, nothing. We go where the wind blows us."

"Worst case?"

"The Russians come to the erroneous conclusion that I killed Ivanovic. They find out I'm not quite as dead as advertised, and resolve to take some justice."

"Justice?"

"They'd have a few options. They might opt for intelligence sharing between nations. Maybe an Italian detective will show up at an immigration desk in Malta or Sicily, wherever we end up next, and take me into custody."

She blew out a long breath, then adjusted the trim on a sail. Her long auburn hair skimmed across her face in the wind, and she brushed it back with two fingers. Slaton couldn't stop staring at her.

"We've got to make port soon," she said. "Our supplies are running low."

"I know."

"We could head for Greece or Spain. Even if the authorities somewhere take you in for questioning . . . I don't see what we have to worry about. You were nowhere near Capri when this Russian was shot."

"You and I know that. Any investigation governed by rules of law would go nowhere. But it doesn't always work that way. I *have* been involved in some indiscretions in recent years. Stockholm, Geneva, Paris. Truth is, you were mixed up in a few of them. If we don't stay out ahead of this, there are police in a half dozen countries who could make uncomfortable associations. A few intelligence services would also like to have a word with me. And since you asked for the worst case . . . Sorensen made it clear that Ivanovic was tight with the Russian president. If the two of them were tied up in something unseemly, and President Petrov thinks I'm the one who killed Ivanovic— then the SVR itself might come looking for us. And they wouldn't send detectives."

"You really think that could happen?"

"It's doubtful . . . but we can't ignore the possibility."

Christine lapsed into silence.

"There's something else we should consider," Slaton said. "This is the second time in a year that somebody's tracked us down. Our off-the-grid plan isn't working as well as we'd hoped."

"Meaning what? That we dry-dock the boat and try to hide out in Idaho? New names and a log cabin in the mountains?"

"I'm not saying that. But as much as I hate to admit it, there are times when we could use some help."

"Help? From the CIA?"

"At least as a one-off. They could tell us where the holes are in our cover. Maybe even warn us of impending threats."

"You sound like you're leaning towards working with them."

"On its face, what Sorensen is asking for is simple. She wants a little professional advice on how Ivanovic was killed. In return they'll do what they can to remove my name from the conversation."

"But it's not so simple."

"Never is. She's already admitted that there's more to Ivanovic's story than what she's told me so far. There has to be to generate such interest on their part."

Christine made a slight course adjustment, then looked at the navigation display. "Okay, we've got ten hours to our turn point. We don't have to commit until then."

"True. But I don't expect any new revelations between now and then."

She was silent for a time, then looked down into the cabin. "It's been a while since Davy has had a play date. Do they have two-year-olds in Rome?"

"Last time I was there they did—lots of them."

Her voice went quiet as she studied the nav display. "I'm not sure we can make Rome by Wednesday."

"I figured it earlier. It'll be tight, but with these winds I think we're good. We can put in to Amalfi, take the train from there."

She eyed him accusingly.

"I was only covering all the bases."

"Right. Well . . . I guess Rome *is* on our list of places to see."

He moved behind her and put his arms around her waist.

She said, "All the same, if you come up with a good reason to go somewhere else in the next ten hours— I'd like to hear about it."

"Fair enough."

"Now, get up to the bow—that anchor line never got stowed."

"Aye, Cap'n."

Slaton weaved his way up front, his legs bending in concert with the boat. At the bow he coiled the hastily pulled anchor line and dropped it into a stowage compartment. The boat lurched on a big wave, and he grabbed a stanchion to steady himself. He looked out across the sea ahead and wondered if they were doing the right thing. Had he presented the facts evenly, without any bias? Or had he steered Christine to his predetermined course?

Slaton was content with the new life he and Christine had built, no regrets for the practical hurdles or requisite wanderlust. Yet there was a part of him—a very small part—that missed his work with Mossad. The adrenaline, the sense of mission, the camaraderie. Was it some deep-seated character flaw he was only now recognizing? Perhaps getting involved with the CIA was a symptom of his recovery—a kind of delirium tremens for state-sponsored assassins. Whatever the case, he vowed to tread carefully in working with Sorensen.

As the Adriatic fell behind them, Slaton made an internal promise. His decisions in the coming days had to be taken with the greatest care, reflecting his new reality. With Mossad he had put his life on the line, but now he had responsibilities. He had people counting on him in different and very enduring ways.

Most sobering of all, he knew that if his family were ever harmed as a consequence of his actions, he would never forgive himself.

NINE

They arrived in Amalfi on a wet Wednesday morning. Under the cover of a steady drizzle, Slaton located the police station with far more ease than in Vieste, and by ten o'clock *Windsom* was cleared for entry. Slaton made arrangements for their boat to be berthed in a slip for a week, telling the dockmaster that he and his family would be touring Rome—as ever, lies dressed in elements of truth. It was longer than they'd likely need, and would never have been possible at the height of the season. In late October, however, such an unscheduled stay was welcomed with a pleasant smile and an outstretched palm.

Slaton, Christine, and Davy had breakfast ashore. They watched the weather clear from beneath an awning with a spectacular view of the Duomo di Amalfi, the famous cathedral framed by serrated mountains beyond. The end of breakfast brought a return to reality. Slaton purchased a pair of burner phones, got them up and running, and gave one to Christine. Soon after they were on a train to Rome.

Like most young boys, Davy loved everything about trains. His face was pasted to the window as he gawked in youthful wonder at trucks and cows. A distant hot air balloon brought a squeal of delight. It would all be captivating to any toddler, but was especially so for a boy accustomed to palm trees and pods of whales. Davy was reluctant to get off at Rome's Termini Station, as were his parents, albeit for very different reasons. They watched their son's excitement build a second time as their taxi rounded a playground full of children near Villa Borghese. Davy kicked the seat with his heels and gestured wildly to be let out, wanting to join the fun. On any other day they would have indulged him.

The United States embassy in Rome is fronted by Via Veneto, but Slaton called ahead using the number Sorensen had provided, and she met them at a side entrance. As they were escorted toward the building, Slaton gave its exterior security measures a hard look. He had to admit they appeared solid. He saw staggered concrete barriers, metal gates, and multiple layers of guards—professional-grade contractors on the outside, graduating to uniformed Marines on the inner ring. Inside was a screening area that looked thorough, built in the form of a mantrap with sealable entrances on either side. There were cameras everywhere and, most encouragingly of all, a notable alertness among the staff.

He was sure that unseen layers of protection were embedded—motion detectors outside the walls, strategically placed bomb sensors at street level. It was a good setup, but no less than one would expect for a facility that could only be characterized as a high-value target. Comforting as it all was, Slaton knew every security plan had its weaknesses.

"This is the working section of the embassy," Sorensen said as she guided them deep into the building. They bypassed a maze of offices where Davy drew finger waves from men and women in cubicles. A narrow hallway brought transition to what looked more like living quarters. At an ornate set of double doors a guard in civilian clothes stood waiting. He was a big man with a lantern jaw and active eyes. By Slaton's instantaneous evaluation—a learned habit—he looked quite competent.

Sorensen addressed Christine. "This is the visiting dignitary suite. The ambassador himself stayed here last year while his quarters were being renovated."

"Does that mean we have to act dignified?" Christine asked, looking warily at Davy.

Sorensen laughed. "Hardly. It's not scheduled to be occupied again until next month."

She introduced them to the guard, whose name was Nick, and who was almost certainly CIA. Everyone passed through the doors into a lavish suite styled in Old World decor. The floor was a patchwork of ornate carpets, the walls trimmed in gilded mirrors and oil paintings. Multiple chandeliers hung from the ceiling, giving the impression of a crystalline ice storm. There was a nice scent as well, something feminine that could only come from a sachet.

Ignoring it all, Slaton addressed Nick. "Any other entrances to the suite?"

"One window. It's bulletproof and not an exterior—overlooks the courtyard. Also a set of doors that leads to the embassy veranda."

"The window is okay, but I want two like you on each door, twenty-four seven, until I'm back."

Sorensen and the guard exchanged a look.

"I can make that happen," Nick said. His stone face then cracked into a smile, and he bent down to reach eye level with Davy. He beckoned him with a curled finger, and when Davy came near, the guard whispered something in his ear. Davy looked to the far end of the room and ran off.

Christine looked at the guard questioningly.

He said, "I told him he was allowed to play on the big couch."

Everyone watched Davy climb on a couch that had to be ten feet long.

Nick expanded, "I told him it was owned by a famous man a long time ago, back before Italy lost a big war."

"Who was that?" Christine asked.

"Benito Mussolini—at least that's the rumor."

"Must be priceless," Slaton said distractedly, his eyes still sweeping the room. He saw the window, and the doors leading out to the veranda. Beyond that a manicured garden blended into the embassy's interior courtyard.

Christine sided up to him and said, in a voice only he could hear, "Looks pretty nice."

"It's not a vacation. Remember, you can't leave the embassy."

She looked across the veranda. "Well, as prisons go, I give it five stars."

Satisfied with the arrangements, Slaton forged a smile for his wife's sake. "It looks solid," he said.

She didn't smile back. "It's not me and Davy I worry about."

"I'll be fine. It's just like we talked about—a little consulting work."

"Consulting. Did I ever tell you how bad you are at understatement?"

"A couple of days. That's all." He held up one of the phones he'd purchased that morning. "If anything here goes wrong . . ."

"I know," she said. "If the tea is cold, you'll hear about it."

She leaned into him for a moment, then Slaton broke away and went to the door with Sorensen. He stopped for one last look before leaving. His wife was chatting up the guard in what looked like an amiable conversation. His son was using Mussolini's couch as a trampoline.

Slaton left the embassy with Sorensen in a generic rental car. The traffic was Rome's usual, which was to say abysmal. While she drove, he helped navigate using her agency-issued smartphone. Once they reached the southern outskirts, he put the handset to other uses.

"What are you doing?" she asked as he typed and flicked across her screen.

"Research."

Sorensen nearly said something, but then relented and went back to the road.

For two hours they backtracked much of the route Slaton had covered with his family by train that morning. They passed through Cassino, the modern and vibrant version that had taken the place of the old city, which had been bombed to virtual ruin in 1944. Beyond the bustle of Naples they skirted Mount Vesuvius, at the base of which was the ill-situated ancient city of Pompeii. The sun was threatening the horizon when they arrived at Sorrento.

In further testament to Sorensen's efficiency, a police launch collected them at the municipal pier. Two amiable junior carabinieri, clad in orange life vests, began a guided tour as they struck out toward the channel. They pointed out the ferry terminal and the docks where tour operators, in high season, ran trips for gawking at the seaside. For the more adventurous, jet skis and kayaks were available to assault the local grottos.

It was a twenty-minute crossing to the Isle of Capri, and when they arrived the harbor seemed subdued in the fading light. Most of the shops were closed, and likely had been for weeks, while only a handful of cafés remained unshuttered. Their carabinieri guides regaled them with colorful accounts, from a policeman's perspective, of the rolling party that was summer in Capri. They told of the incognito celebrities who tried to hide among the crowds, and the legions of less famous who yearned to be seen, all against a backdrop of champagne baths and gold-plated madness. In the waning days of October, however, the beautiful people had moved on, and with them went their party planners, private chefs, and paparazzi stalkers.

The harbor soon fell behind, and in the distance Slaton saw their destination. Even from a mile away the yacht named *Cassandra* was impressive, her sheer size a testimonial to excess. Sleek and silky, resting effortlessly on calm seas, the ship looked like anything but the murder scene she was.

TEN

According to Sorensen, the inspector's name was Giordano, and he was waiting for them at a gangway on the yacht's leeward side. Slaton saw a modest man in height and build, yet noted a distinct air of gravitas in his deeply grooved jowls and furrowed brow. He wore civilian clothes, heavy trousers and a jacket with worn patches on the sleeves. A pair of round-framed wire glasses rested on a classically Roman nose, and beneath the jacket Slaton noted a subtle slope to the man's shoulders—as if the weight of Capri itself was resting upon them. Behind him were two uniformed officers, younger and more upright men who, in the time-honored way of Italian males, had their eyes pinned on the attractive blonde next to Slaton.

Sorensen took the lead, greeting Giordano in English, then introducing Slaton. "This is the man I told you about, Inspector. He's something of a specialist in what we're dealing with."

Giordano regarded Slaton for a moment, and when the two shook hands, he said, "I will not ask where you acquired your expertise. I only hope you can explain this mystery to me."

Slaton could have answered in fluent Italian, and would have done so were he a diplomat or a fellow policeman. Being what he was, he kept his linguistic abilities to himself—he never gave away anything cheaply. "I won't have every answer, but hopefully I can give you some direction."

Slaton was encouraged that the inspector seemed amenable to their involvement. He imagined an alternate scenario in which the man had been forced by a supervisor, on the request from some distant government ministry, to handhold a contingent of visiting busybodies. Such forced cooperation was rarely productive. As it was, Giordano appeared legitimately interested in getting help.

The inspector turned toward a stairway that led to the upper deck. The two uniformed officers stayed behind at the gangway. There was no issuance of booties or gloves, which told Slaton the scene had been well gone over for evidence.

As he fell in behind, Slaton studied the ship. He'd become a reasonably seasoned sailor in the last year, and what he saw impressed him. The boat was tidy, the crew keeping up with things. Lines were coiled, the radar antenna turning, and the few deckhands he saw appeared smartly uniformed. It implied a degree of competence and professionalism. More practically, it told him the crew were still getting paid. He wondered how long that would last.

Slaton asked, "Has the ship moved since the night Ivanovic was killed?"

The inspector wagged a finger in the air. "No, the captain has assured me the ship remains in the very same position. The scene you are about to see is precisely what Ivanovic saw that night."

They followed Giordano up a spotless teak staircase. The brass rails gleamed orange in the setting sunlight, and a brine-scented breeze swept in from the north. When they reached the upper deck, Slaton paused to take in the scene. Aft he saw a sprawling sitting area, and to one side a large wet bar. There was a covered hot tub that would accommodate at least ten people. What looked like a dance floor was surrounded by all-weather sofas. All the furnishings were outdoor contemporary, the frames brushed nickel, the upholstery the colors of the sea. Brilliant white lights were strung overhead in a decorative pattern, creating an atmosphere that was something between an operating room and a Christmas display.

"Has anything been altered?" Slaton asked.

"No. We secured this part of the ship immediately." Giordano led to the aft section of the starboard rail. "Ivanovic was standing here when he was struck in the chest by a single large-caliber round. He died almost instantly and tumbled into the sea. The body was recovered within minutes by the crew. Unfortunately, we uncovered very little physical evidence. A few traces of biological material were found here," the Italian said, pointing to a spot on deck that was marked with red tape and lettering.

Slaton looked over the rail and saw a twenty-foot drop to a choppy sea. "What about the bullet?" he asked.

"We've inspected the ship thoroughly, but it was not recovered. The post mortem report was very clear on one point—the round passed straight through the victim's body. Given the angle at which it struck, and where Ivanovic was standing, it almost certainly continued into the sea."

"Could it be recovered?" Sorensen asked.

"We considered a search. Unfortunately, *Cassandra* is anchored above a very steep drop-off. In the direction the bullet was traveling, the depth increases rapidly. There is no way to tell how far it might have carried before striking the sea."

"What kind of bullet are we talking about?" Slaton asked.

"We believe it was a fifty caliber."

"That's a big round. Very high-energy."

"Precisely. Which only further proves the point—any attempt to recover the bullet would require searching nearly one square kilometer of ocean floor, at depths ranging from fifty to seven hundred meters. To find something that size, under such conditions—it is beyond our abilities."

Slaton nodded. Everything Giordano said was true. "It might not help anyway. A spent round can be matched to a weapon, but by itself it often doesn't tell you much." He stared out across the water, and began roaming the deck. Beginning at the starboard rail, he circled slowly to port. Slaton looked forward and aft, then at the distant island of Capri. He estimated the nearest shore to be three miles away. He could ask for the distance to be measured precisely, but he was sure his estimate was good to within ten percent. That was all he needed.

Not a chance.

"You're *sure* this is where the ship was anchored?" he said to Giordano.

"The captain has shown me the electronic logs. *Cassandra* maintains a digital navigation record, and transmits the data regularly—insurance companies demand such assurances these days to protect their interests. The positions are accurate to less than one meter. The only variance at this moment involves the ship swinging on her anchor—which, of course, depends on the wind and the currents."

"So on the night Ivanovic was killed," Sorensen

surmised, "*Cassandra* had to be within a hundred yards of where she sits right now."

"Yes," said Giordano. "I even cross-checked the insurance company's data."

"Did the ship keep a radar log?" Slaton asked.

The inspector smiled for the first time, an awkward process in which facial creases deepened and the eyes behind the glasses narrowed. "You are wondering if there were other boats nearby."

"Yes."

"The ship's radar was active and being monitored—when anchored near a busy channel it is a standard safety precaution. The captain told me he checked the screen himself only minutes before Ivanovic was killed. He saw no other boats nearby."

"That's not exactly definitive."

"This was my thought as well. As it happens, there is also a radar system on the island." Giordano pointed toward Capri's highest hill. "The light is poor now, but the antenna is there, overlooking the main channel. There is a good deal of traffic between Capri and the mainland, particularly during the summer. The Guardia Costiera recently installed a radar unit to keep an eye on things."

"And they keep a record of the traffic . . . which you've already checked."

Giordano smiled to say that he had. He took off his glasses, held them to the light, and used a small cloth to clean an apparent smudge. "At the time of the killing, the only other vessel in the area was two miles from *Cassandra*. I was able to track it down rather easily—it turned out to be a local fishing boat. I have already spoken to the man who operates it."

"And?"

"I grew up with Mario. He was a lazy student, but

could always find the red mullet. I can tell you he is a threat to no one."

Slaton eyed Giordano. "You've been thorough."

"I have been desperate. I went as far as to check the record of air traffic. There were no helicopters or aircraft nearby."

Slaton grinned, wondering if even he would have gone that far.

Giordano was hailed from below by one of his men. He diverted to the stairs and began a discussion in Italian. Slaton caught a few words, enough to deem it harmless—something relating to another case.

Sorensen edged next to him and spoke in a hushed tone. "Well? Does what he's saying make sense? Did someone take out Ivanovic with a fifty caliber?"

"Hard to say. It's not a common weapon—especially outside the military. But it *is* the kind of gun a long shooter would use." His eyes remained fixed on the sea and the island beyond. He tried to come up with a scenario that fit what he knew. Try as he might, he couldn't. Apparently it showed.

"What's wrong?" she asked.

He turned a slow circle, taking in the horizon all around. After a pause, he simply looked at Sorensen and shook his head. "Everything," he said. "Everything is wrong."

ELEVEN

Slaton walked Sorensen through his reservations one at a time.

"On the way here I used your phone to look up the weather conditions for the night Ivanovic was killed."

"Is that important?"

"It's vital for a long-range shooter. It was clear that night, with good visibility, but also very windy—twenty knots from the west, with stronger gusts."

"So that would make for a tough shot."

"Tough isn't the word." Slaton put both hands on the starboard rail. "The longest sniper kill ever recorded was in Afghanistan, and the shooter used a fifty cal. It came in at around two thousand five hundred meters, roughly a mile and a half."

"Wow," she said. "I've missed on the range with my service weapon from twenty-five yards."

"So have some snipers. Long-range shooting is a different discipline. A different mindset. I don't know the specifics of that mile-and-a-half shot, but I can almost guarantee that the wind was calm and the target essentially motionless."

Sorensen looked out across the water. "How far is the island from here?" she asked.

"Three miles, minimum. At that range, on a windy night . . . a good shooter would do well to hit this yacht. But somebody managed to hit a human—and not only that, they hit him dead center of mass."

"So you're saying that whoever it was . . . they must have been closer somehow."

"No other possibility. Problem is, there are only two ways to get close on open water."

"A boat?"

"That's option one, but it introduces other complications. Thanks to the wind, any small boat would have been rocking hard—the seas were five to six feet that night. Even *Cassandra* would have been gyrating on swells like that. Which means the shooter would have been facing a grossly unstable platform, a target that was moving in two dimensions, and severe winds between the two. Not a realistic scenario. And besides, you heard what Giordano said—the closest boat was two miles away."

"Okay, strike the boat. What's the other way?" she asked.

"That's even more impractical. Imagine somebody using scuba gear to approach *Cassandra*. It fails on a number of levels. Six-foot seas alone would kill the idea—it would be like trying to shoot from inside a washing machine. And of course you'd have to cover two or three miles underwater to get close enough to have a chance. Two or three miles lugging a fifty cal through the ocean—it would be like hauling an anchor."

The sun touched the horizon, descending into its daily oblivion. The lights of Capri glimmered in the dusk, and to the left the Amalfi Coast was a deepening thread of amber.

"So where does that leave us?" she asked.

Slaton half turned and looked at her. "Absolutely nowhere." He blew out a sharp breath. "I'm sorry, but the facts as we know them—they make no sense. It's like somebody threw a stone and hit the moon."

"So this kill . . . you couldn't have done it?"

"Under the given circumstances—not a chance."

"But somebody *did*. Somehow."

Silence ensued, and Slaton looked once more over his shoulder at the island. He rubbed his chin and felt the coarseness of two days' stubble—he hadn't shaved since the Strait of Messina.

Sorensen watched him intently. "What is it?" she asked.

He shook his head. "Nothing. We're done here."

She frowned. "I hate to give up on this."

"Who says we're giving up? There's more we can work with."

"Like what?"

"You tell me. You said your people back at Langley were doing research. You told me there was more to Ivanovic's death than meets the eye. I still don't understand why the CIA is so interested in an uberrich Russian getting blown off his yacht. Square that in my mind, and maybe I'll see another angle. Something neither of us has thought of."

"Okay. The basics go like this. About a month ago we got some solid intel on a meeting in which Ivanovic joined up with three other men. We identified two right away: Vladimir Ovechkin and Alexei Romanov."

"I've heard the names," he said. "If I'm not mistaken, they're big-time oligarchs, guys in Ivanovic's league."

"Correct. The three of them are part of a very exclusive club—the friends of President Petrov."

"The chosen few who get rich while most Russians try to keep food on the table and stay warm in the winter."

"It's nothing new, but the divergence has been accelerating. Corruption in Russia has effectively been institutionalized—it's based on the model Petrov developed during his KGB days. State assets are stripped and handed over to a small group of kleptocrats. They cash out over time using various schemes, then move the money abroad. A portion is eventually 'gifted back' to the regime, most of which disappears into pockets. When anyone falls out of line, or in the rare instance when a private company actually succeeds on merit, the state intervenes. Everything is seized, and the whole cycle begins again."

"Wash, rinse, repeat," Slaton said.

"Pretty much."

"But this has been going on for decades. Three guys like that having a meeting? It hardly sounds like an intelligence coup. Which tells me it's the fourth person who's got your hackles up."

"Correct. But in order to explain the rest, I'll need to brief you on a few things. And to do that I need secure comm."

"Back to the embassy?"

"Back to the embassy."

"Good. My son gets cranky when I don't tuck him in."

Sorensen cocked her head quizzically.

"What?" he asked.

"You surprise me."

"How?"

"Well, the first time I saw you, during that mission in Lebanon, I'd never have figured you for the domestic type." Sorensen almost said something else, but then held back.

"Yeah, I know," he said. "To tell you the truth . . . neither did I."

TWELVE

If the early onset of winter was lamented on the Isle of Capri, it was received far more enthusiastically in certain enclaves to the north. Among the beneficiaries were some of the very same clientele whose hillside Anacapri estates were then being entombed with shutters and coverlets, wealthy individuals who had migrated to their winter chalets as predictably as any seasonal bird. Chief among the destinations was Davos, Switzerland.

The freak October storm that had stirred the Tyrrhenian Sea on the night Pyotr Ivanovic was killed was born of an anomalous polar weather pattern, an agitated air mass that gave rise, five days hence, to a second storm that buried the Swiss Alps in twelve inches of snow. Delighted ski resort operators sprang into action, and none more eagerly than those of Davos. Snow-making equipment was employed to deepen the base, and a handful of runs were quickly groomed for action.

Unfortunately, before webcams could be linked to broadcast word of an early opening, the town's chief, and only, meteorologist, a thick-skinned and dour Alpiner whose methods relied more on local lore than science, issued his glum follow-on forecast: temperatures would moderate quickly, and by the end of the week the mountain would be topped with nothing more than a foot-thick blanket of slush. After considerable hand-wringing, the hopeful resort operators relented, realizing that to open for a day or two, only to close again for a matter of weeks until winter took a firmer grip, would set an awkward precedent. It was announced that the resort would remain closed, although the ski patrol was given license to train for as long as the snow lasted. Within hours of that decision, Vladimir Ovechkin and Alexei Romanov sensed a unique opportunity.

The two Russians had been in Davos much of that month, and were spotted regularly about town in the aimless pursuits of the wealthy, albeit rarely in one another's company. Romanov was a fixture in the nightclubs, at the tennis resort and spa, and had been seen preparing diligently for the annual winter polo match in St. Moritz. Ovechkin kept a notably more low-key itinerary. In the afternoons he was often seen in the company of his exotic-looking young wife, frequenting the jewelry shops and clothiers along Promenade. In the evenings he'd settled into a rotation among his three favorite restaurants, often in the company of bankers and lawyers.

How either of them spent the rest of their time was left to speculation, and the locals knew better than to inquire. In what soon would become legend, however, the mismatched pair of Russians saw opportunity in the ski resort's brief and accidental window of uncertainty. They recognized a chance to do something their peers might never match: to rent a mountain for a day.

It was of course Romanov's idea. An avid sportsman still in his prime years, he relished a good down-hill run, and the idea of having an entire mountainside to himself, even if only for thirty hours, was nothing less than a dream realized. Notwithstanding the marginal conditions, there would be no need to suffer crash-prone beginners or packs of spike-haired snow-boarders. Ovechkin fell in with the idea, more out of ego than adventure, suckered into writing a check by Romanov's final prodding question: *How many of our friends can say they've had their own mountain?*

It was early evening when they got their first crack at the hill. Bundled in parkas and with ski gear in hand, the two men trundled to the lift station as the gondolas began moving under slopeside lights. The first car arrived, slowing beneath the massive cable, and a lone attendant ushered them inside. Ovechkin fumbled one of his poles getting into the gondola and it clattered to the metal floor. "Sorry," he said.

Romanov picked it up and held it until the rotund Ovechkin plopped onto the opposing bench. The gondola was built for six, leaving each man a wide seat on which to sprawl. When the door slid shut they were alone for the five-minute ascent.

Romanov handed back the pole. Ovechkin took it, but only at the cost of dropping a glove.

"Why has your wife not joined us?" Romanov asked.

"I invited her, but she had other plans."

"Sounds expensive."

"Yes, she does enjoy keeping the sales associates busy."

"Either that or she is having an affair with her masseuse."

"Go to hell. You should marry, Alexei, settle down a bit."

"Settle down? Is that what you call it? You're on your third wife."

"Estrella will be the last."

Romanov chuckled and looked out across Davos. The township sparkled in light, and tendrils of smoke curled from the occasional chimney. He glanced at the red gondola behind them. Five of his security men were inside, and six of Ovechkin's had bundled into the one behind that. "We're getting paranoid," he said. "In three minutes you and I will be alone at the top of a mountain, no one else within a vertical mile."

Ovechkin bunched his thick lips, a distinctly Slavic gesture. "I have survived a long time by being paranoid." In an obvious attempt to redirect things, he said, "Did you hear from *Argos* this afternoon?"

"The usual report. She is on schedule."

"What of the other two?"

"*Tasman Sea* and *Cirrus* are running as planned. Stop worrying. MIR Enterprises is running precisely as intended. And with military precision," he added, his voice rich in sarcasm.

Ovechkin worked his helmet into a more comfortable position. "Tell me, Alexei . . . do you trust the colonel?"

"Zhukov? What does it matter? We are married to him, for better or for worse."

"I have seen his new dacha outside St. Petersburg. It's not the kind of place a man buys on an army officer's salary."

Romanov laughed. "You of all people? Indignant over corruption?"

"My point is that we cannot forget who he works for. It is a departure for us to have someone between us and the president."

"That can only be in our favor. It makes us untouchable. The order of the world is changing, my friend. Russia is foundering, and no advantage can be left untapped to right the ship. I for one find it encouraging. In this new way of doing things, you and I have risen to the forefront."

Ovechkin sighed heavily. "Maybe you are right." A thin smile then etched his face.

"What is it?" Romanov asked.

"I was thinking about a conversation the colonel and I had during my last visit to Moscow."

"What was it about?"

"Mostly business—this mission, how to maintain secrecy. Yet seeing his dacha, I mentioned to Zhukov that if he had any money, I might know a few things about where to keep it."

"And what did he say?"

"He tried to convince me that he has nothing squirreled away—it was like talking to an old Soviet field marshal."

"Don't worry, after our upcoming venture he won't be able to deny it. Zhukov is no different from you or me. He was only invited late to the party."

"God help him, then," said Ovechkin.

Romanov's gaze turned thoughtful. "What would you have told him if he *did* have money to hide?"

Ovechkin chuckled, a rumble that came from deep in his chest. "Now there is the Alexei I know! The newest strategy is Cook Island trusts."

"I've heard of them. Tell me how it works."

"It is similar to the other shell companies our lawyers build, but with a wonderful legal twist. Anyone who wishes to file a lawsuit, or even inquire about your assets, can only do so in a Cook Island court. They have to be present for every filing."

"And where are the Cook Islands?" Romanov asked.

"That is the beauty of it. They are deep in the Southern Pacific, thousands of miles from any place you or I have ever heard of. I've never had the occasion to visit the place, but I keep thirty or forty million there."

"Give me the name of your local attorney. I should look into it."

Ovechkin's expression froze.

"What's wrong?"

"Nothing . . . it's only that Pyotr said precisely the same thing last week when I explained it to him."

The two exchanged an unsettled look. It was the subject they'd both been avoiding. This was their first private moment together since Ivanovic had been killed, and the undercurrent was undeniable. If there was one thing more important than money, it was staying alive long enough to enjoy it.

"His death," said Romanov, "it couldn't have had anything to do with MIR. Our ships haven't even played their part yet."

Ovechkin hesitated to respond. He found himself inspecting the interior of the gondola. His chalet was swept regularly for listening devices, but he and Romanov had entered dangerous new waters. "Could it have been the settling of an old score?" he wondered aloud.

"It's the only thing that makes sense," agreed Romanov. "No one can reach the heights we have without finding a few enemies. Pyotr admitted to me that he crossed a mafioso in Kiev. It was two years ago, maybe three."

"The one who tried to shoot a grenade through the sunroof of his limousine?"

Romanov laughed. "Then we have heard the same story. I think it was bullshit."

"He did enjoy his stories. But you are right. What happened to Pyotr . . . it was something from his past. He got careless."

Ovechkin looked up and saw the summit lift station approaching. He got his gear in order, and was soon panting from his exertions—the top of the mountain was more than nine thousand feet above sea level. When he'd first come here twenty years ago it had been as a fit young man, and even then he'd taken a day or two to acclimate. Today, having been in Davos for a month, he was as breathless as the day he'd arrived.

"You are going to have a heart attack," goaded Romanov.

"It's the damned altitude."

"You should take better care of yourself . . . for my sake."

"What do you mean?"

"With Pyotr's passing, you and I now own half of MIR. But that also increases our stake in whatever trouble it brings. I'd rather not face that alone."

"We knew what we were getting into. As did Pyotr."

The gondola reached the top of the mountain, and above them a huge wheel turned the cable back downhill. The door popped open and Romanov stepped outside. Ovechkin spilled out behind him in a tangle of skis and poles. The wind at the top was sharp, cutting through their thick parkas.

"It feels like Russia up here," Ovechkin spat.

Romanov laughed. "You are talking to a man from Norilsk. In Siberia this would be a lovely spring day. Now come, Vladimir, race me to the bottom!"

Ovechkin grunted as he jammed a boot into a binding. "Do that, and I will end up like Pyotr, only in more pieces. Go ahead—I will meet you there."

A victorious Romanov moved toward the slope.

Behind them, the two contingents of security men stood huddled in their respective groups. They stomped their feet to keep warm, gazes shifting between their principals and one another. When Ovechkin waved his men away, Romanov did the same. None of them had ski gear, so they all shuffled back to the lift station to go down the way they'd arrived—in the warmth of a gondola.

Romanov kicked off downhill, quickly gained speed, and was soon little more than a blur of blue on the floodlit slope. Ovechkin took a moment to gather himself. He was a decent skier, but didn't enjoy the slopes at night—the sharply angled light tended to play tricks on his eyes, not illuminating every trouble spot.

He looked out across Davos a mile below, now a pond of amber flickering in the bowl-like valley. It was a playground birthed generations ago by a privileged few, royal families and scions of Western industry. Now it had transformed into something else entirely. Realtors spoke Chinese and Arabic, and the Russians had all but invaded. They brought their money and their entourages, and made deals behind closed doors. Each January, during the World Economic Forum, the truly wealthy left for a month, receding into the shadows. They rented their homes for exorbitant prices to economists and politicians whose governments footed the bill, and to lesser industrialists whose companies they might soon target.

Romanov is right, Ovechkin thought. *The game is changing yet again.* He considered the three ships, and the ill-disguised soldiers who were on them. Was that really the future?

Ovechkin had no illusions—he himself was something of a legacy. He had risen under Yeltsin, and was one of the few who'd remained in favor when Czar Petrov took charge. He'd stood by quietly while languishing state companies, originally handed off to old Soviet cronies, were reclaimed by the state. Petrov issued them to new owners who wrung them for cash, and who paid one simple but unending price—absolute fealty to the new Russian president. Recently, however, under the burden of falling energy prices and a stagnating Russian economy, this new model of kleptocracy too was failing. In its place a new strategy was rising, one that went for the first time beyond Russia's borders. One that fused the country's lagging business interests with its last remaining strength.

Filling his chest with frigid evening air, Ovechkin pushed off and started downhill. He carved slow and sure turns with as much control as he could muster. Romanov was nowhere in sight.

Two miles away, at the base of the mountain, a young man stood in the shadow of a darkened ski school. He watched both skiers with a practiced eye, noting their form, which was divergent to say the least. More importantly, he noted their respective lateral tracks— how much of the mountain each man used from side to side. The observer was average in height, and a black ski parka made him look thicker than he was— the wiry frame beneath was the product of years of punishing exercise, augmented by the furnace-like metabolism of an active twenty-seven-year-old.

Nearing the bottom of the mountain, the streaking blue dot that was Romanov whisked to a finish. In a cascade of white his athletic frame disappeared behind the lift station, no doubt to catch the gondola for a return to the top. The visitor canted his gaze back uphill and saw the red-jacketed Ovechkin. Intermittently visible through stands of trees, he was carving wide turns at a far more judicious speed.

The young man heard heavy steps behind him. He tensed almost imperceptibly, recalling the scene he'd witnessed only moments ago: the two security details had departed the lift station for the warmth of the lodge. *Had one of them doubled back?*

The young man turned slowly, and a woman in a red ski patrol jacket appeared at the corner of the building. She had a set of skis over one shoulder, and her boots thumped over the frozen sidewalk. She looked surprised to see him.

"Can I help you?" she asked in German.

He understood the language perfectly, but elected to reply in English, adding a heavy accent that further belied his abilities. "Oh, I am sorry. The resort . . . it is open now?"

"No, not yet. It is still too early in the season. We had a few good days of snow, so the employees are undergoing some training. I think a private party also arranged access for the next two days."

"Two days skiing alone? How nice for them."

She smiled. "Yes. Unfortunately, warmer weather is expected soon. I'm afraid everything will be shut down again by the weekend."

"I understand . . . thank you."

"Come back in December," the woman said good-naturedly. "They say it will be a good season. Have you skied Davos before?"

"Oh, no. I am only a beginner." The visitor looked around, and said, "Tell me . . . is there a trail map?"

The woman pointed to a brochure box near the shuttered lift ticket office.

He thanked her again, and she went on her way, boots crunching over ice. He walked to the ticket kiosk and pulled a map from the box. Unfolding it, he looked up the mountain and easily correlated which run Romanov and Ovechkin had just used. He studied the surrounding terrain carefully, paying particular attention to the topography at higher elevations.

Satisfied, he made a mental list of what he would need. The young man then turned away and walked toward town.

THIRTEEN

The drive back to Rome was even more scenic at night, the same timeless sights set under a wash of white light and neon. So lost in thought was Slaton, he barely noticed his surroundings. Somewhere outside Naples, Sorensen made a stab at conversation.

"I recently bought a house in Virginia," she said.

"Sounds nice. Where exactly?"

"Woodbridge."

"Really? That's not far from Fredericksburg. Christine and I had a place there a few years ago."

Sorensen's eyes snapped back and forth between Slaton and the road. "*You* lived in Virginia?"

He grinned. "I guess that wasn't in my file."

"How long were you there?"

"Not as long as I would have liked." She kept looking at him, but if he was supposed to fill the gap with more details he failed miserably. He was rescued when her phone rang.

Sorensen looked at the screen. "It's the office. Hope you don't mind if I take it."

"Not at all."

Sorenson talked while she drove, and Slaton took the chance to regard her more closely. She really was a stunner, but to her credit, never once had he sensed her trying to leverage her looks. He turned away and found himself thinking about Virginia. He remembered the three-bedroom house with its pine fence, half-acre yard, and broad back deck. For him and Christine it had been their last grasp at normalcy, and for a time it had worked. But the interlude had also been dangerous for its tranquilizing effect—when the ghosts of his past returned, as they inevitably did, he'd been caught off guard. Ever since, they'd lived a whipsaw existence. The Caribbean and South Pacific, minimal contact with the outside world. That kind of isolation had both benefits and drawbacks. Chief among the lessons learned—seize a little civilization when it could safely be had. Today, apparently, that meant a guest suite in the United States embassy in Rome.

On the outskirts of the city Sorensen ended her call.

"Anything useful?" he asked.

"Maybe—I'll explain when we get to the embassy."

"Okay."

She eyed him again. "So tell me . . . where exactly did you go after Virginia?"

"If I tell you will it end up in my file back at Langley?"

She gave him a wounded look.

"Sorry. For what it's worth, I like you as much as any CIA officer I've ever met . . . even if that *is* a pretty low bar."

"Was that a compliment?"

"About as close as I come."

The city seemed to pull them in, as it had travelers for millennia. In the distance Slaton saw countless basilicas, and took particular note of the Archbasilica of St. John Lateran. He had toured the place once, many years ago, in the days before his post-Mossad career as a stonemason. He'd marveled at the mosaics, a virtual lecture in Cosmatesque style. Intricate inlays adorned seemingly every floor and wall, as well as the papal throne. He himself had never aspired to such artisanship, his work being of the more practical variety—garden walls and terraces, the occasional restoration of classic facades. Still, Slaton recognized talent when he saw it.

It was then—on the notion of recognizing talent—that his thoughts drifted curiously back to the waters of Capri. Try as he might, he could not come up with a workable scenario to explain how Ivanovic had been targeted. He himself was a product of the best training on earth, a distinguished graduate of the Israeli Defense Forces Sniper Course. A hundred thousand rounds fired from dozens of different weapons. Years spent in the field, shooting in countless tactical settings. At that moment, none of it helped.

How had the shooter done it?

Try as he might, Slaton couldn't come up with an answer.

It had been a quiet evening, and Franz Stoeckler surveyed the store he managed with his customary October glumness. For a retailer who sold outdoor gear, it was unfailingly one of the worst months of the year. Customers were not yet serious about skiing, and the fall clearance sales of hiking and camping gear were long wrapped up.

He saw two teenagers in his snowboard section, but they were only regulars from the neighborhood, boys who came to ogle expensive boards they would not be given for Christmas. Near the front an older woman was flicking through a skeletal rack of clothing on clearance. Stoeckler was considering closing a bit early when a young man walked in.

"Can I help you, sir?" he said in German, walking up briskly.

The young man gave him a blank look, and said, "Do you speak English?"

"We are the only full-service outfitter in Davos," Stoeckler said, making the switch. "All of our sales associates speak English."

The customer managed a thin smile. "Ah, very good. Then I would like to purchase some equipment for off-piste skiing."

"Off-piste, is it? Yes, of course. We have everything you might need."

As Stoeckler led to the correct section, his salesman's brain evaluated the man behind him. He was average in height, lean build, and moved with a distinctly athletic carriage. His hair was light brown, cut short, and a thin growth of whiskers roamed across his face. The heavy accent on his English suggested an origin to the east and north. Probably Russian, but perhaps a Pole or a Latvian.

"Have you skied our backcountry in Davos before?"

"No."

"We like to say it is the birthplace of off-piste. In 1894 Sir Arthur Conan Doyle was among the pioneers of the discipline. He honed his skills right here in Davos. Do you know who he was?"

A blank look on the customer's face was his answer.

"Conan Doyle was the Englishman who wrote books about Sherlock Holmes, the famous detective." Still the customer showed no reaction. Stoeckler abandoned his story. "How will you be climbing—Telemark or touring skis? Or perhaps a traditionalist who prefers snowshoes?"

"Alpine touring skis."

"The most practical choice."

They reached the skis, and before Stoeckler could make a recommendation the young man pulled a set of carbon fiber skis from a rack. He knew precisely what length he wanted, and within ten minutes a full set of equipment was lined up. To Stoeckler's delight, there was no apparent concern for price.

"Will there be anything else?" he asked.

Yes, the young man replied, there would be a good deal more. As quickly as they could navigate the aisles, he selected a single ensemble of high-end ski clothing, a large backpack, energy bars, and a water pack. He also picked out a set of compact binoculars. Stoeckler was nearly out of breath by the time they massed it all at the checkout counter.

"There is one more thing," the young man said. "I require a topographical map of the local mountains."

"But of course."

Stoeckler went to a glass cabinet and reached for an expensive GPS device.

"Actually," the young man said, "I would prefer a simple paper map, laminated if possible."

"*D'accord,*" said Stoeckler, diverting to a different cabinet. He pulled open a wide drawer and extracted a hiking map. "Is this what you had in mind?"

The customer took the map in hand and studied it for some time. "Yes, this should be accurate enough."

"Accurate enough? It is issued by the Swiss Federal Office for Topography. There is none better."

The young man seemed about to argue the point, but relented. "It will do nicely."

Stoeckler began scanning the merchandise. "Will

you wait here in Davos for the season to begin?" he asked.

"I thought I might train a bit tomorrow."

"Tomorrow? The snow is thin in places—it won't last more than a few days."

"Yes, so I've been told. But it is always best to test new gear in mild conditions."

With a nod to his customer's show of good sense, Stoeckler summed up the purchase. The total came to over three thousand Swiss francs. His customer produced not a credit card, but a wad of cash. It was curious, but not unheard of.

"Can I help you carry your purchase to your car?" Stoeckler offered once the transaction was complete.

"No, I will manage, thank you."

He watched the young man walk outside with both arms full. He seemed to pause for a moment, then turned away from the parking lot and disappeared into the night. Stoeckler gave a slight shake of his head, then happily shut the cash drawer and began closing out the register.

FOURTEEN

When the embassy came into view, Slaton felt like a weight had been lifted. The complex looked different at night, luminous and festive, belying the vital work being done within the bastion-like walls.

He went straight to the visitors' quarters, and at the entrance were two security men he hadn't seen before. They both spotted him immediately, and one said something into a throat mic. The pair seemed alert and competent, no quarter given for the fact that they were already established in what was effectively a fortress. Once vetted and sent through to the suite, Slaton saw two guards outside in the courtyard. His wishes had so far been respected. Security was tight.

He found Christine in the bedroom. She was chatting up the housekeeper, a woman of roughly sixty whose name was Bella. Slaton was introduced, and Bella began talking. She was full of good humor and authentic Italian recipes, and claimed an encyclopedic knowledge of the embassy. She professed to be the longest-serving embassy employee, and it might have been true. She knew the history of the building and who worked in what department, and claimed to be privy to scandals going back to the Reagan years. She said it all with openness and enthusiasm, as well as a judicious lack of details that bolstered her case.

It was nearly Davy's bedtime, and in the burst of energy all children display at that hour, he'd taken to running circles around an ornate oval rug as though it were a track in a stadium. Slaton played along and began giving chase. Soon the two women were cheering, and in a flurry of giggles Dad lost the race despite his rampant cheating. There was a brief wrestling match on the floor, followed by a well-orchestrated chase with a toothbrush. Bedtime rituals took fifteen minutes, and soon after Davy was fast asleep on a daybed. In happy disarray on the floor around him were makeshift toys acquired from the embassy kitchen: plastic bowls, wooden spoons, and a colorful assortment of nested measuring cups.

"All is well on the home front," Slaton said, having caught his breath after the whirlwind.

"Is that what this is?" Christine responded as she pulled off her shoes.

"For one night, at least. I've got to go back upstairs. Anna wants to show me a few things."

"I'll bet she does." A wry smile. "Guess I'm not invited?"

"Not specifically. But I'll ask if you want."

"Actually, I've got plans." She tipped her head toward the bathroom. "There's a claw-foot tub in there that looks glorious."

"Okay, enjoy."

"After a month at sea—are you kidding? How long will you be?"

"Not very."

She looked at him doubtfully.

"I promise."

* * *

Slaton found Sorensen in a briefing room that was every bit as high-tech as the visitors' suite was antiquarian. There were banks of computers and monitors, and a technician whose name was Mike—Sorensen professed him to be a magician with information.

Slaton shook his hand, and Mike the Magician began working a keyboard while Sorensen talked.

"You asked me back in Vieste why we considered Ivanovic's death important. The first reason, as I alluded to then, was that the FSB seems to think it is. The latest message traffic suggests they still think an assassin-for-hire is responsible."

"Yours truly."

"From what we've gathered, you seem to be the primary suspect."

"Maybe that's what they want you to gather."

She stared at him quizzically. "Care to expand on that?"

"My name has come up in some high-profile incidents in recent years. That said, I doubt the FSB has any hard evidence that I'm still alive."

"I'll grant you that—what they know about you is probably more speculation than fact."

"So there's my point. What better way to divert attention from the real assassin than to point your finger at a ghost?"

"Meaning what? That the FSB itself is responsible?"

"The FSB? Not necessarily. Let's just say someone on the Russian side of the fence."

Sorensen shrugged her shoulders. "It's a theory. But the FSB's involvement could be a natural response.

One of the president's friends was murdered. That's personal."

"Did Ivanovic have a close relationship with Petrov?"

"Nobody in Russia amasses the kind of wealth Ivanovic did without the president's seal of approval. Petrov dresses his little gang of crooks in a cloak of sovereignty, and they effectively control Russia. It's gotten so brazen, we actually have a new desk dedicated to tracking these oligarchs—only a few dozen have real influence in the Kremlin, and it's helpful to know who they are. Ivanovic was close to Petrov for a number of years, but according to our analysts their relationship had cooled recently. There was a dispute over development rights to a gas field in the Arctic."

Slaton took a seat at a small conference table. The chair was comfortable and artfully designed. It had probably cost a thousand dollars. He leaned it back on two legs. "Okay, so there's no way to be sure why the FSB is interested in Ivanovic's death."

"No . . . not really."

"Then fill me in on the other side—why is the CIA interested?"

Sorensen nodded to Mike, and a photograph appeared on the front-and-center monitor. Slaton studied the image in silence. Four men stood together on the deck of a large house. The forest at the margins of the shot implied a remote location, deep woods and steep terrain. It did not escape Slaton's notice that the picture had been taken from a very high angle, implying an aerial shot. The resolution was spectacular, leading to two possible conclusions: it had either been sourced from a drone at medium altitude, or U.S. satellite surveillance had come a long way since his last Mossad briefing. A time and date stamp in the lower right corner had been electronically redacted, and in the lower left was another blacked-out field, most likely lat/long coordinates.

"Where was this taken?" he asked.

"Russia."

Slaton leveled a hard look on Sorensen.

"Sorry, but I can't be more specific. The level of classification is very high."

He studied the faces of the four men. Slaton recognized Ivanovic immediately. Sorensen had already briefed him on two of the others, but he didn't know which was which. "Who's the one on the right?" he asked.

"That's Alexei Romanov. He's in Ivanovic's league in terms of wealth. He owns the biggest mining company in Siberia, a telecom, and substantial natural gas holdings. He keeps a high profile, which is probably why you recognized his name earlier. He recently bought a second-division soccer team in England, and owns choice real estate in both London and New York. Next to Romanov, of course, is Ivanovic. I've already given you his background. The older man on the far left is Vladimir Ovechkin."

Slaton saw a paunchy man in his fifties. He was pink-skinned, going bald, with a pronounced stoop in his posture.

Sorensen continued, "Financially, he's nearly on par with the others. Interestingly, Ovechkin is one of the few surviving players from the nineties. He was at the front of the line when the old Soviet state-held companies were parted out to Yeltsin's cronies. Today his corporate profile is centered around oil and gas infrastructure—a pipe and pump guy."

"Okay. And the fourth man, center-left?"

"That's the kicker. He had us stumped for a while. We ran his facial profile through every matching database we have. At first we assumed he was a businessman like the others, maybe a new guy Petrov had brought in to take over a company that got reclaimed from someone who'd fallen out of favor. That's how it works these days. The president giveth, and the president taketh away. It keeps everyone in line."

"I'm sure it does."

Mike zoomed in on the fourth individual. Slaton saw a man in his mid-forties with a regulation haircut, lean build, and square features. In the captured frame he was practically standing at attention, spine rod-stiff and chin tucked. He was wearing what looked like khaki trousers and a dark polo shirt—a virtual uniform for soldiers when they were off duty.

"He's military," Slaton said.

"We eventually came to the same conclusion. But that's a wide net to cast. And unfortunately, when it comes to the facial profiles of Soviet military personnel, our database is pretty limited."

Slaton pinned his gaze on Sorensen. "But you figured out who this guy is."

"We got lucky, the old-fashioned way. A sharp-eyed analyst recognized him."

"Recognized a soldier? What are the chances of that?"

"Pretty high in this particular case. You asked me why the CIA is interested. Well, this guy is the reason. When I found out who he was . . . that's when I booked the next flight to Rome."

FIFTEEN

"His name is Viktor Zhukov," said Sorensen. "He's a colonel in the Russian army."

"Forgive my skepticism, but there's got to be a hundred thousand officers in the Russian army. Are you telling me you have some savant analyst who can pick out one guy from a roster like that?"

"Hardly—and it's actually closer to two hundred thousand. As it turns out, Zhukov is something special."

Slaton's gaze narrowed questioningly.

"He's not just any colonel—he's a senior officer in the 45th Guards."

"Spetsnaz?" Slaton remarked, using the common moniker for the Russian Special Forces.

"Yes. He's been a fast burner, saw action in Chechnya, Georgia, and the Caucasus. More recently Ukraine."

Slaton looked once more at the man standing left-center in the photo. He was probably close to fifty years old, pale face and sturdy build, distinctly high Slavic cheekbones. The photo wasn't tight enough to register the man's eyes, but they could only be blue. In the captured image Zhukov was talking and the three oligarchs listening. This in itself seemed an odd contrast—a hardened Special Forces predator addressing a congregation of vultures.

"Okay," Slaton said. "But even Special Ops isn't that big a deal. What put Zhukov on your radar to begin with?"

Sorensen gestured to Mike, and a different series of photos began cycling on the monitor. There were five in all, but it took only one to understand. Zhukov was standing between a limousine and a large building, and he was talking animatedly with a man Slaton recognized immediately: the president of the Russian Federation.

"It began roughly eighteen months ago," Sorensen said. "Zhukov began popping up regularly with the president. We do our best to track Petrov through official and unofficial channels. As far as we can tell, these two have been meeting at least once a month."

The same five pictures kept cycling like a fragmented movie. All at once, Slaton was struck by what they *didn't* show. In all five images only two people were present—Zhukov and the Russian president. Every setting appeared private, although not necessarily secretive. In one the two men stood together on the balcony of what looked like a government building. In another they were walking across a field, both shouldering shotguns on an obvious hunting expedition. "What I'm seeing looks unofficial, almost personal."

"We noticed the same thing. Petrov of course holds regular meetings with his military command staff. Zhukov has never been seen at one of those official gatherings."

"So while establishment generals give briefings, the favorite colonel gets a quail hunt."

"Something like that."

"Is it possible they're just old friends?"

"That would be the simple answer," she said. "We've looked into Zhukov's background. He's the son of an army officer, attended the best military schools. He's got a wife and two daughters whom he rarely sees."

Sorensen spun a finger and Mike pulled up a new screen. A close-up of Zhukov flashed to the monitor, a photo that looked like it had been pulled straight from a military personnel file. Slaton didn't ask how the CIA had acquired it. The colonel was in uniform, same taut lips and high cheeks, although the haircut was a bit loose for a full colonel, barely within regulation. Slaton recognized this for what it was—a bit of Special Ops bravado, typical for a breed of soldiers who set themselves apart wherever possible. And yes, he thought, the eyes were definitely blue.

Sorensen said, "As far as we can tell, Zhukov and Petrov never crossed paths until a couple of years ago. There's a record of the colonel receiving an award for valor from Petrov, probably something involving the Ukrainian campaign. Medals for operations like that have to be issued outside the public eye. We think this might be where they first became acquainted."

"You make it sound like they're dating."

"I'm guessing Colonel Zhukov was handpicked by Petrov to run a special project. Something important, based on the frequency of their meetings. And I think these three oligarchs are involved."

Slaton's eyes skipped away from the monitor and landed on Sorensen. "You just changed pronouns, Anna. *We* became *I*."

She dipped her chin like a kid caught cheating on a test. "The Agency has been monitoring this relationship between Petrov and Zhukov for over a year. There's interest, but not what I would call concern."

"You think it deserves more attention."

"The tie-in worries me—Petrov's favorite Special Ops guy meeting with three men who are as corrupt as any in Russia. Nothing good can come from that. I've been doing what I can with the resources I have. I run a minor desk back in Langley, and we've been digging. We approached it from the corporate side. These three oligarchs have extensive holdings—that's something concrete, with records and finances that can be tracked. My team is trying to find out what's changed in the last year, uncover any business venture that ties them all together."

"Not a bad angle."

"Honestly . . . it's a bit overwhelming. We produce so much raw information these days, it's hard to sift through and extract what's important. When Ivanovic was killed, my suspicions only hardened, but I couldn't convince my section supervisor to put more man-power behind it. Then I heard that the FSB believed a high-end assassin was responsible. They were trying to put the blame on a former Mossad operator who's long been whispered about. At that point, I have to admit . . . I decided to use you."

"Use me?"

Sorensen and Mike exchanged a glance. It was clearly a signal—Mike excused himself abruptly, something about working his magic elsewhere.

When they were alone, Sorensen said, "I jumped a few levels on the organizational chart. Director Coltrane knows me, and he saw you work in Lebanon. I got word to him that the Russians were accusing you of being responsible for Ivanovic's death. That piqued his interest, and I was given two minutes to lay out what I had."

Slaton stared Sorensen down. "Let me be clear about one thing—I don't want the director of the CIA taking an interest in me. Not in any way."

"Relax—I didn't get very far. Coltrane thought it was speculative. He wouldn't allocate extra resources to pursue it. About that same time I discovered you were in Italy."

"You had your people track me down."

"I did . . . and I don't blame you for being angry about it."

"I was at first. But honestly, you've shown me some gaps in my off-the-grid scheme."

"No harm, no foul?"

"Something like that," he said, then looked at her pensively. "So tell me, when you found out I was in the vicinity of Italy—did you really think I might have killed Ivanovic?"

"I considered it."

"And?"

"You had the opportunity. Certainly the ability. Money could have been a motivation. But no . . . something told me you would never take that path."

"That doesn't sound very analytical. You put too much faith in your instincts."

"Do I?"

"You approached me in Vieste. If I *had* been a killer for hire, it might not have ended well for you."

"It didn't end well. You shot my brand-new dinghy."

Slaton couldn't contain a grin.

"Anyway," she said, "that's what brought me here. I came to Italy because I thought it was my best chance to uncover what's going on with these Russians. And I came to you because I thought you might be able to help."

"Okay. But I've tried and it didn't work out. Does that mean we're done here?"

Her pretty face fell downcast. "You really don't know how Ivanovic was killed?"

Slaton chose his words carefully. "Given what I've seen so far, no."

She looked dejected, but seemed to accept his answer.

Slaton looked at the picture on the screen one last time. He said, "For what it's worth, I think your instincts are good. I've been where you are before. You have a hunch about something, but the facts are thin and you can't get backing to pursue it. Sometimes you just have to move on."

"Move on? Is that what you would have done in your days with Mossad?"

He gave her a circumspect look, but didn't answer.

"All right. I'll arrange for a car in the morning to take you and your family back to Amalfi."

"Don't worry about it. We'll make our own way back."

As Slaton stood to go, he noticed that Sorensen went straight back to work, combing through emails on a laptop. He had a fleeting urge to put a supportive hand on her shoulder, to say something conciliatory. Having been in her position, he knew how empty either gesture would be.

He left the room in silence.

Back at the suite Slaton discovered the main room dark. Davy was sound asleep on the daybed in the corner. He paused for a moment to watch his son.

Aside from the slow rise and fall of his chest, he was completely still. Calm and unaffected by the world around him.

Slaton wished it could stay that way, yet he knew the currents of his son's life would one day grow more turbulent. Today he viewed his father as a virtual blank slate. He knew that Dad was always around on the boat, and made a mean grilled cheese sandwich. Knew that he was a fast runner when they played chase. *Can I ever tell him the truth?* Slaton wondered. *Tell him what I once was? How can I not?* He and Christine had time to work it out. But all the same, that day of reckoning, the likes of which few parents faced, *would* come.

He found Christine in the bedroom. The only light was a dim shaft spilling from the steam-shrouded bathroom, and she came out drying her hair with a plush white towel. She beamed an effervescent smile when she saw him. "That tub was great. And here I had the impression you took up in squalid apartments when you went off on missions."

"Yeah, it's like this every time."

She looked at him questioningly. "Something wrong?"

"No, it's all good," he said, putting on a smile. "I'm glad you like the place."

"I could get used to it."

"Better not. I think we're leaving tomorrow."

She gave him a mock pout. "Maybe we can get a room in town and stay for a few days. This *is* my first time in Rome."

"I'm not sure if that's a good idea."

She took him by the hand and led him to the bed. They sat on the edge, and she said, "Can you tell me what Anna said?"

He was surprised by the answer that arrived. He *could* talk about it, no worry about security clearances or compartmentalization. Without intelligence services or directors to answer to, he could set his own flow of information. Then and there, Slaton decided that his wife had a "need to know." He explained what he'd found on *Cassandra*, and covered what Sorensen had told him. When he was done, he waited to see if Christine's take on it all matched his own.

"This involves the president of Russia?" she said cautiously. "Am I cleared to know that?"

"About as much as I am. Mind you, this is only one intelligence officer's speculation. But I think Anna is onto something. I wish I could have been more help. As it stands . . . her investigation has hit a wall."

"Okay. So what happens next? We go back to *Windsom*?"

Slaton met his wife's gaze. It was soft and open. So much so that the cast of characters in his head—covert photos of hard Russian faces—dissipated as readily as the steam drifting in through the open bathroom door. He heard soft jazz playing in the background, something he knew she enjoyed. Christine had once told him she'd acquired a taste for it during medical school—she said it helped her concentrate.

For Slaton the genre had always brought a different response, and one he'd never tried to explain. Jazz, in fact, was the music of safe houses. It was played in them because, at reasonable volume and hours, it was the genre least likely to raise complaints from neighbors. So too, the aural backdrop was an effective countermeasure, masking hushed conversations and delicate phone calls. Under the right circumstances, it could suggest someone was in residence when they were not. Instrumental tracks were preferred, since lyrics could be an indicator of the listener's language preference. Miles Davis' horn—that was the same in Germany as it was in Armenia. After Slaton had parted ways with Mossad, he'd avoided jazz for a time for the memories it brought back. Thanks to Christine, however, his aversion was ebbing. What he heard tonight he liked, something soft and melodious that belonged on a stage in a small club.

"Actually," he said, "maybe you're right. A couple of days in Rome could be educational for Davy."

"I don't know about educational. He'll remember any playground more than the Coliseum."

"So will I."

She smiled, then leaned forward and kissed him on the cheek. She was wearing a nightshirt he'd never seen before, a silken blue item. It had narrow lapels and diamond-shaped buttons running down the front. "Did you go shopping?" he asked.

"Not yet. There were some clothes in the closet."

"Whose are they?"

"The duchess of something-or-other. Apparently she stayed here last month and got carried away on her shopping excursions. She left a lot of what she bought behind when she returned to England. Bella said she was my size, and that I could keep anything that fits. This caught my eye."

"Okay."

She looked at him with mock anticipation.

"It's nice," he said.

She kept staring.

"The color suits you?" he added hopefully.

Christine sighed. She got up and went to a tray that held a bottle of gin and an ice bucket. "Sometimes you are a romantic challenge."

"We're married."

Her eyes snapped up, but then softened when she saw his grin.

"You are the *most* vexing man."

"But I can be useful too."

She came at him with two full tumblers and held one out. Slaton took it.

"I'm glad you do that now," she said.

"Drink?"

She giggled. "I'm glad you feel secure enough to let down your guard now and again. When we first settled down you wouldn't touch alcohol."

"It dulls the senses."

"Most people don't mind a social drink now and again."

"Most people don't have to worry about—"

She jabbed a rigid index finger in the air, cutting off what he was about to say.

"Sorry."

"Not tonight. Let's forget about all that."

He put his tumbler on the nightstand, already half-empty, and felt the warm burn in his throat. "There—my guard is officially down." He moved closer and put a hand behind her neck, drawing her gently toward him. He reached up with his free hand and felt his way to the highest diamond-shaped button. From top to bottom, he unfastened them ever so slowly.

SIXTEEN

Anyone watching Colonel Viktor Zhukov walk through the halls of the Kremlin Senate might have thought he was marching in a parade. His stride kept time to some private cadence, and he took every corner at a sharp ninety-degree angle. Anyone who knew him would have forgiven it. He had simply never known any other way.

Zhukov himself, however, felt a degree of distraction in his step. A longtime officer in the 45th Guards, Russia's elite Special Forces unit, he had seen some of the nastiest fighting in Chechnya and Ukraine. Syria was a bloodbath all to itself. In light of the difficulties of those campaigns, he thought it peculiar that his stomach had rarely knotted the way it did on this front—during his one-on-one meetings with the president of Russia.

His escort was a severe and officious woman named Olga, a longtime member of Petrov's personal staff. Wearing what looked like a drab housedress, she was Mother Russia herself, a babushka taken straight from Tolstoy's Siberia. Ambling ahead of him, she kept a running commentary on their surroundings. She pointed out the room where Lenin and Trotsky had argued over the need for trade unions in a "workers' paradise," and paused briefly at an overdone canvas tribute to the Battle of Stalingrad. Zhukov, an ardent student of Russian history, did not appreciate being treated like a tourist, but he kept his opinions to himself. Having never before been inside the Kremlin—his other meetings with Petrov had been in more understated venues—he thought it best to allow the staff their rituals.

Olga ordered him to wait at a predictably ornate set of double doors. Zhukov stood motionless at the presidential threshold, the hallway still and quiet. While not a man prone to introspection, he could not escape the idea that his career had reached a crossroads—and the door before him represented a highly untraditional path.

As a lifelong military officer, he'd served the Russian Federation for twenty-five good and honorable years. Yet his most recent assignment, working directly for the president, fell outside the usual chain of command. No, he corrected, it fell outside any relationship whatsoever with the Russian army. In private moments he sometimes wished he still reported to a general. Wished that his only worries involved fitness reports and jockeying for the next promotion.

At some point in recent months, Zhukov realized, he had crossed a line of sorts. This new mission was something dark and unpredictable, yet it wasn't without perks. Petrov's unashamed attempts to procure his loyalty had at first surprised him. The dacha was comfortable, even if he'd done nothing to earn it. So too the sporty Jaguar that had shown up in front of his house one day, key fob and registration papers, already written in his name, dropped through the front door mail slot like a holiday greeting card. It seemed superfluous for a colonel in the Russian army who was simply serving its commander in chief, albeit in an uncharacteristically direct manner. Zhukov had tried to write it all off, reckoning that was how things were done in these halls.

The problem he saw was in defining a path forward. He could envision a scenario in which he was made a general next week. Another where he was forced into retirement. Many of his peers had already hung up their boots, moving to Cyprus or the Black Sea, places where pensions went further and where finding one's feet in the sand guaranteed a view of the sea. A few were hanging on, battling for promotions the old-fashioned way. Zhukov, by no design of his own, had found himself on a third course. And one that increasingly occupied his thoughts.

The president had alluded to his future with more than a dash of palace intrigue: *A man of your talents, Colonel . . . you could do well in business. I am always on the lookout for dependable individuals, steady hands who can run things. An oil company, perhaps. Or a platinum mine or rail line. Success breeds success.* It had been broached in a decidedly offhand manner, both men on horseback during a long weekend in the Urals. Zhukov was sure it had not been mentioned carelessly. The rest of his exchange with Petrov had reflected so many others. Never lies, but never quite the truth—always an oily middle ground.

He'd done his best to not dwell on the idea, but Zhukov increasingly found himself consumed. And if such implausible suggestions were fulfilled? He realized it would make him no different from the men he'd been assigned to oversee—the ones so integral to his assigned mission. On the other hand, he saw a chance to leave behind the cutthroat army promotion ladder for something of far greater potential. In the end, Zhukov relented to one certainty—his future now depended on the man on the other side of this door.

His musings ended abruptly when Olga reappeared and ushered him inside.

The president of the Russian Federation was seated behind his desk. Sergey Petrov was not a large man, but short-boned and sturdy, like the pit bull that he was. Of course, behind the most important desk in Russia, physical stature was irrelevant. His background was KGB, as was that of most of his governing clique. Spies who'd gone imperial and become their own masters.

Olga disappeared, closing the doors behind her, and Zhukov stepped smartly across the room. His boots thumped together when he reached the desk, and he stood neatly at attention. He resisted an urge to salute. Petrov had set him straight on that during their first meeting—the president had grown weary of such customs, and Zhukov was to render them only if cameras were nearby.

Petrov seemed to ignore him for a time. He straightened papers on his desk, and scribbled a note on a pad. Then, with the slightest of hand gestures, he directed Zhukov to take one of the two chairs opposite the wide desk. There would be no small talk about sports or the weather. The latter would have been natural—the first Arctic gust of winter was at that moment flogging Moscow with a vengeance—but nothing Petrov did was designed to make a man feel at home.

"Have you uncovered any new information regarding the death of Pyotr Ivanovic?" the president asked.

"No sir, nothing since we last spoke. I think your suggestion of a professional assassin is right on the mark. Unfortunately, such individuals are necessarily elusive."

Petrov nodded understandingly. "I realize you are a busy man, and I know I have asked a great deal of you. With that in mind, I yesterday ordered the FSB and SVR to make identifying this killer their highest priority."

He was referring to Russia's internal and foreign intelligence services. Zhukov recoiled at the idea of Russia's two most feared intelligence agencies interlacing with his own work. "Have they made any progress?" he asked cautiously.

"I received an initial briefing only this morning," the president continued. "They originally came up with four killers-for-hire who could have had a hand in something like this." He referenced a paper on his desk. "One was a Venezuelan, a man who hasn't been seen in years. As it turns out, we discovered he was recently made a guest of the state in Guatemala— something about putting a bullet in the president's mistress. There was a South African, but he is getting old and is rumored to have gone to New Zealand for cancer treatment. Then there was a Belgian, a very gifted marksman. An SVR man was dispatched to track him down and found him quite easily in Amsterdam, drunk and in the company of two prostitutes. Not completely disqualifying in the matter of Ivanovic's death, but by all accounts the man is tireless in his pursuits and has been in Holland for some time."

Here Petrov paused, and Zhukov was obliged to fill the silence. "Which leaves but one remaining suspect. Of course, one has to consider the chance that—"

"I know what you are thinking," Petrov said unnervingly. "Our mafia here at home can be troublesome. Yet I find such a scenario unlikely. Any attack on Ivanovic is effectively an attack on me. No one in the brotherhood would be so foolish."

"So then . . . who is it we are concentrating on?"

"They say he is Israeli, although a few claim him to be Swedish. His name is David Slaton, although even that seems uncertain. He once worked for Mossad, but is rumored to have gone rogue, perhaps even become a hired gun. Whoever he is, his exploits are legendary."

"I think I've heard the name," said Zhukov. "But was he not killed a few years ago in Geneva?"

"And more recently in Lebanon. He's been implicated in assassinations across the continents, going back over a decade. The man seems an apparition, yet comes to life with startling regularity."

"Assuming he exists, do we know where he might be or who he could be working for?"

"Not yet. But we are watching closely. We've quietly shared our suspicions with the Italian police, not that they'll make any progress. It's rather like giving eyeglasses to a blind man." Petrov curled the fingers of one hand as if to inspect his fingernails. "But enough of that—it's something for the intelligence services to worry about. Tell me about our little mission."

Zhukov undertook a mental shifting of gears. "The ships remain on schedule, and our assets in the region are planning accordingly."

"Good. And the proceedings in Morocco?"

"According to Tikhonov, the testing has been mostly successful."

Petrov's chin lifted ever so slightly. Tikhonov was the project's chief engineer.

"He tells me it is nothing unexpected—especially given the accelerated timetable and logistical complications." They both knew this was the most precarious part of the plan. Critical work was being done by civilians far from the security umbrella of the Russian state—and correspondingly far from Petrov's oversight. Yet it was that very remoteness, the combination of location and deniability, that demanded its inclusion.

"You should take another trip there," said the president. "I hear it's lovely this time of year."

"I'll make the arrangements."

"Actually . . . let my people take care of your travel. Anything I can do to ease your burden." Petrov looked at Zhukov pensively. "I should mention something about Ivanovic . . . as it turns out, he owned a majority stake in Primatek. Those shares will have to be reallocated."

"To his heirs?" Zhukov said, trying to recall what Primatek was. *Natural gas,* he decided tentatively.

Petrov chuckled. "Heirs? If Pyotr had any children they are certainly not legitimate." He locked his dead eyes on Zhukov.

The man was ruthless in his lack of expression, and the descriptive tag that had come to Zhukov on their first meeting remained intact—he was looking at the world's most accomplished gambler. How many men had received similar inducements? he wondered. How many had abandoned their principles from the very chair in which he now sat?

Petrov said, "You have done well, Viktor. Very well. See this mission through, and we will all be better for it."

Zhukov said that he would, and for five minutes more he briefed the president on the specifics of the three ships owned by MIR Enterprises. The next meeting was arranged, and with business concluded, Petrov averted his attention without comment to the papers on his desk. As an officer who'd stared death in the eye on battlefields across Asia and the Middle East, Zhukov was not easily unsettled. Even so, it was with no small relief that he beat a hasty retreat.

When he reached the hall again, a corridor where Stalin and Lenin had once roamed, he breathed more freely. Olga was nowhere in sight, but he was sure he could find his way out. Navigating the baroque passages, Zhukov had a great deal on his mind, yet one curious thought rose to the front: it occurred to him that the true history of this place was likely far different from what he had learned as a schoolboy.

In the office he'd just departed, the president didn't look up until long after the door was closed. Alone after a busy morning, Petrov pushed away the papers on his blotter and spun his chair to face the window. He took in a panoramic view of Red Square under a dark pewter sky. Through wind-spun flurries he saw Lenin's Tomb, and in the distance the Moscow River. The river appeared unseasonably bleak and lethargic, well ahead of schedule to its ice-clad winter stillness.

His eyes drifted across the city, and everywhere he saw light and motion. The streets were full of cars and delivery trucks, and office buildings blazed bright in the dim morning light. But for how long? he wondered.

The spring had not been bad, energy prices holding up nicely in expectation of robust summer demand. Then things settled in Nigeria and Venezuela, and the Americans had gone back to their shale fields. By August the forecast was damning. Oil and natural gas prices, Russia's lifeblood, were in full-scale retreat.

He'd been down this road before: shaving pensions, postponing road work, shorting long-neglected military accounts. Stopgaps at every turn to buy time. As long-term policy, he knew, it was entirely unsustainable.

His ministries were doing their best to spin news feeds and block troublesome internet sites, and the FSB cracked down unrelentingly at any hint of coordinated protest. For a time distractions had been useful. The campaigns in Ukraine and Syria had brought a resurgence of nationalism, fleeting as it was. Yet Petrov's drumbeat of renewed Russian greatness was losing its cadence, faltering on the disharmonies of food shortages, stunted health care, and aging demographics. Unless something changed in that refrain, his greatest fear might soon be realized.

Petrov had long understood that no one person, nor even any small group, could threaten his hold on power. Pockets of resistance would always exist, and there would be scandals to tamp down, the odd whistleblower to eliminate. Yet he knew that ultimately there was but one real threat to his endless grip: the collective will of the Russian people.

It had nearly come to pass once before, after the last election he'd so painstakingly controlled. The protests had nearly gotten out of hand. Petrov knew a revolution when he saw one, and he'd issued the necessary orders. The FSB had clamped down, rounding up protesters and threatening activist leaders. The most troublesome were shunted to labor camps. That had kept the opposition off balance, but just, and in those days the economy had been in far better shape. Oil and gas prices had been more than twice what they were now. More unnervingly, twice what they were projected to be in coming years.

And without those revenues to support so many budgetary demands . . .

Unsustainable.

His attention still outside, Petrov wondered how many eyes were at that moment looking the other way, gazing up at the most important window in Russia. The pane was constructed from special glass, proofed against bullets and eavesdropping and whatever other incursions might be attempted. He supposed it was all necessary, and he was glad to have it. More so each day.

And if this new scheme didn't work out?

Then the glass before him, Petrov knew, would not be enough.

SEVENTEEN

On that same morning, as an awakening winter was lashing the Moscow River, Slaton sat in the courtyard of the Rome embassy enjoying an early coffee with Christine. A lifting sun bathed the veranda in warm light, and they watched as Davy played in the grass with Bella's three-year-old grandson.

Their idyllic moment was ruined when Sorensen appeared.

"We've found something you should see," she said, her eyes on Slaton.

He deferred to Christine for guidance. Her face was tense, but she nodded all the same. "It's all right, go ahead."

Slaton followed Sorensen to a small, simply furnished office he'd not seen before. She removed a photo from an attaché and set it on the desk. Slaton saw an overhead picture of what looked like a freighter. It was making passage through a narrow canal between strips of tan desert.

"It's a boat," he said.

Sorensen frowned.

"Suez Canal?"

"Yes. Her name is *Argos*. My team in Langley were able to build one solid link between Ivanovic, Romanov, and Ovechkin. About four months ago they formed a corporation named MIR Enterprises. It's a classic series of shell companies, but we were able to unravel enough to figure out that they bought three ships. *Argos* is one of them."

"Okay. So three really rich guys put together a shady company and bought some old freighters. I don't mean to invalidate your team's work, but what could be more in character? That's what guys like that do."

"We have concrete evidence linking these men to the Russian president."

"No. You have one photograph of them with a colonel who's on the president's A-list." Slaton waited for Sorensen's counter. Whatever it was, he guessed she'd already made the same argument unsuccessfully with her superiors back in Langley. When nothing came, he felt a twinge of sympathy.

"Any idea where this ship is going?" he asked.

"No. We know she left Sebastopol seven days ago, en route to Mumbai."

Slaton stood straight and conjured a mental map in his head. "When was this photo taken?" he asked.

"A few hours ago."

He paused to make calculations. "Did she make any stops since leaving Crimea?"

"None that we know of, but we've just figured this out. Why do you ask?"

"You're telling me she took seven days to get from Sebastopol to the canal. That's what ... maybe a thousand nautical miles? I'd say she either stopped along the way, or she's moving at minimum speed."

"You're right," Sorensen said. "That's good. It's something we can dig into."

"You said they bought three ships. Can I assume you're looking for the others?"

"We are. There's commercially available satellite data on virtually every merchant ship these days. The ones that don't participate we're pretty good at isolating and tracking."

"Tell me about it."

"Right—I guess you've seen that firsthand. Anyway, we think one called *Tasman Sea* departed Cam Ranh Bay last week, a westbound course. The other ship owned by MIR is named *Cirrus*, but we're having trouble locating her. All are of the same general class and configuration—dry goods carriers, around two thousand deadweight tons. Between two and three hundred feet in length, they're basically coastal freighters. And it might be a coincidence, but each ship is fitted with a deck crane like this one." She pointed to the picture of *Argos*, and he saw a loading crane mounted amidships.

Slaton rubbed a hand on the back of his neck. "And let me guess—you've run this all by Langley, but it didn't change anyone's mind. Still no backing."

"They'll come around. What else should we look for?"

Slaton regarded her closely. "You know, I've got to admit, Anna, in terms of sheer tenacity—you may have even me beat."

She kept staring at him.

"Any idea what kind of load they're carrying?"

"I've got my team looking into it. We watch the Black Sea ports and Cam Ranh pretty closely, but it takes time to access the files and sort through."

"Okay. And if you get images, I'm assuming the CIA can analyze what's been loaded onto a freighter?"

"We have a few tricks. Even after it's loaded we can sometimes tell the general class of what's being carried. Only—"

"Only the assets that do it are either aircraft or satellite-based, which makes them very expensive. Not having high priority, you don't get access."

"Not yet."

He looked away and worked through her problem. "Crews. Try to find out if they hired new crews."

"Why?"

"You're operating on the assumption that they're doing something illicit, and you know these boats have new owners. If they interviewed new crews, it implies a long-term venture. If they kept whoever was on board, it suggests they're in a hurry. That would be good to know in the near term."

"Good—we'll work on that."

"It should keep you busy for a while."

"Definitely. And thanks for your input."

"Anytime."

Slaton turned to go.

"David," Sorensen said, forestalling his departure, "I know what you're thinking—that this probably all amounts to nothing."

"Actually," he said after a long pause, "that's not what I was thinking at all. You may be onto something here, Anna. But you need to prove it."

The loading crane Sorensen had pointed out in the satellite footage looked quite different from the vantage point of the ship's deck. It was Captain Zakaryan's habit to make one round each day across *Argos*, from stem to stern, seeking trouble spots and making assignments for the day's maintenance detail. This morning he noted little. A bit of rust and some chipped paint, a frayed cable to be replaced on the main windlass.

His inspection ended at the fantail, and there he

paused and looked out to the horizon. In what was a peculiar scene for a sea captain, he saw brown desert on both sides. The Suez Canal was at its narrowest here. To port was the unsettled Sinai, and to starboard greater Egypt. He'd once frequented the nearby harbors, Alexandria and Port Said, but the troubles of recent years had curtailed those runs. In a reflection of the new Middle East, the Egyptian government was besieged by insurgencies, various Islamic groups vying for territory and power. Gone were the tours of the great pyramids and dinner along the Nile. The main roads were overrun by armored personnel carriers and checkpoints, the urban alleys beset by secretive gatherings. Egypt was not alone. From *Argos*' aft rail, there wasn't a shore within five hundred miles left untouched by the violence.

A wistful Zakaryan made his way aft, and found himself drawn to the main cargo hold. The hatches were secure, yet he paused all the same and peered down through a gap into the darkened space below. He never heard the footsteps behind him.

"You will find out soon enough," said an all-too-familiar voice.

He turned and saw Ivan the Russian.

"I could lose my master's license if we are carrying anything illegal."

"You could lose far more if you don't follow my orders to the letter."

Zakaryan held the man's stare, which likely surprised him. Ivan had brought three of his own men on board. Zakaryan had a crew of twenty who mostly followed his orders. It was fantasy, of course, to imagine mutiny—the Russians were well armed, and obviously trained soldiers. Still, it felt good to keep the man on guard.

"Are we on schedule?" Ivan asked.

"So far. We had to wait a bit longer than expected at the head of the waterway." He explained that traffic on sections of the canal were one-way, and that the morning southbound convoy had gotten a late start. "The time can easily be recovered," Zakaryan added.

"I'm glad to hear it. Did you find anything requiring maintenance on your morning walk?"

The captain paused. "Only a few routine items."

"It is good that you keep ahead of things. But just to give you warning—I suspect significant repairs may soon be required."

Zakaryan kept staring at the man, but could think of no possible reply. In the end, he only turned on a heel and headed aft.

EIGHTEEN

It was nine o'clock that same morning when Romanov and Ovechkin reached the top of the mountain in Davos. The hour was out of character for both men, neither of whom habitually kept early appointments—Romanov due to his penchant for late nights in the clubs, and Ovechkin because he enjoyed lingering over breakfast and a newspaper.

"We have the mountain all day," Romanov remarked.

"I might keep up with you now," said Ovechkin. "The weather is warming." He unzipped the front of his jacket.

"That will only slow you down."

"We'll see."

Ovechkin watched Romanov speed off, no turns whatsoever to govern his speed. He kicked downhill himself, more aggressive in the bright daylight. He felt the strain come to his thighs, and soon wind was snapping at his face and the front of his open jacket. Ovechkin had to admit that it *was* invigorating. He was enjoying himself. Gaining confidence and running faster.

Halfway down the mountain he rounded a sharp curve, and fought a brief bobble when he hit a patch of ice. He'd no sooner righted himself than he spotted Romanov's red-jacketed figure sprawled in the middle of the run ahead. He was completely motionless, his arms and legs splayed at odd angles. One ski was still attached, the other trickling away far down the slope. Ovechkin angled toward him and cut to a stop. The impression up close was shocking—the snow beneath Romanov was red with blood.

He looked all around, left and right into the trees, and then downhill. There was no one in sight. Ovechkin looked up toward the summit and saw one of his security men staring down from the upper lift station. He waved his pole in distress, and the man pulled out his phone and began talking and gesturing frantically.

Ovechkin took out his own phone and called the emergency number.

"There has been a terrible accident!" he said. "Send help quickly!"

The ski patrol did exactly that. They arrived in five minutes, in no small part because they'd been practicing rescue procedures when the request for help arrived. Fifteen minutes after Ovechkin's call, Romanov was on a stretcher at the bottom of the mountain. A pair of EMTs stood shaking their heads. Everyone could see it was no use.

The police were nearly as prompt, not because they'd been undergoing training, but because organization is a deeply ingrained Swiss trait. Within an hour the scene had been declared safe and completely cordoned off. Soon after, a detective, a bookish man named Ottinger, was assigned to what was clearly a murder case.

Here the local efficiencies began to falter, and by

midafternoon poor Ottinger was as much at sea as the despondent Inspector Giordano had been in Capri. As was customary in murder investigations, he issued a brief initial report to the national police soon after arriving on scene. National, in turn, relayed the preliminary dispatch to a host of law enforcement agencies across Europe—a forwarding list that the CIA, through a well-embedded bit of computer trickery, had copied itself into. The name of the deceased, Alexei Romanov, flagged instantly with a particular Langley desk that had been performing searches on the Russian. At the speed of light, the dispatch from Davos' chief inspector boomeranged back across the Atlantic.

It landed on the virtual desk of a man named Mike in the United States embassy in Rome.

"It's Romanov this time!"

Slaton was on the floor building a Lego car with his son. He looked up and saw a visibly agitated Sorensen. Christine was also in the room, and looks were exchanged all around. What resulted was a single nod.

Minutes later Slaton was with Sorensen in yet another briefing room, causing him to wonder how many existed in the embassy's maze of corridors. This space was more contemporary than the others he'd seen, and he sat in an ergonomic chair, an artful blend of brushed nickel and leather. Sorensen was too excited to sit.

"It happened in Davos," she said. "Romanov was skiing, and halfway down the mountain he was shot."

Slaton skipped past the disconnect of skiing in October. "Shot," he repeated.

"I don't have many specifics yet, it's only been a few hours. There was apparently one wound from a large-caliber projectile. He died almost instantly. We have a good relationship with the Swiss, so the police should be helpful. If you and I go up there and—"

Slaton held up a hand to cut her off.

"What?" she asked.

He averted his eyes to a blank wall, and silence ruled for a time. With those few critical pieces of information, his private landscape shifted yet again. Would his name be tied to this crime as it had been to the last? It seemed likely. At the very least, inspectors in Capri and Davos would soon be comparing notes. The thought of showing his face to yet another homicide investigator did not sit well.

"That's not going to happen," he finally said.

A look of defeat spread across Sorensen's face. A kid whose team just lost the big game. "You mean you won't go to Davos?" she said.

"No . . . I mean you're not going with me."

She eyed him critically.

"If I go, it has to be solo. Sorry, but that's nonnegotiable."

"Why?"

"I won't explain my reasoning. You want my help, it comes with my rules of engagement."

She stood straight and seemed to weigh it. A part of him hoped she would turn him down. She didn't.

"All right," she said. "What do you need?"

"Right now? I need to convince my wife this is a good idea. If that goes well, then I need you to take a picture . . ."

NINETEEN

Slaton was officially a CIA contractor early that afternoon. He was given a passport in a fictitious name—the photograph was thirty minutes old, the date of issuance backdated five months. He'd been correct in assuming that a big CIA station like Rome would have a supply of blanks—perfectly legitimate passports that came preloaded, ready to be issued on short notice. There was also a sat-phone that looked curiously like a standard iPhone, and next to that on the dining table in the suite was a stack of five thousand euros in various denominations, along with a credit card issued in the same name as the passport. As false identities went, it was both comprehensive and efficient.

Christine eyed the cash and docs with an unease that was all too familiar—she knew such benefits came with a price. "You're getting pulled into something, David. I don't like it."

They were having lunch at the table, Slaton cutting up pizza for Davy, who was on his second slice. "It shouldn't be any different from Capri. I go up and have a look, then tell Sorensen what I find."

"But she's not going."

"No. I wanted to go alone—I figured you'd be less jealous that way."

A hard stare.

"I've got to cross a border this time, and I want to stay under the radar. The more people involved, the more difficult that gets. Anna will be more useful here, coordinating things."

His wife regarded him thoughtfully. She wasn't second-guessing or being critical. She was trying to understand. "David . . . tell me why you're doing this."

He slid the plate in front of Davy, who instantly began shoveling in chunks of authentic Italian pizza. With his son preoccupied, he drew in a long breath and said, "The FSB has already tried to tie me to one killing. Stands to reason they'll do it again. Somebody out there is gunning for these Russians. Somebody like me. Not many tears will be shed for the people who are being targeted, but Sorensen has one thing right—there's a larger agenda here, with at least a loose connection to the Russian president. What happened in Davos today might not be the end of it."

She kept her eyes on his, unwavering.

"I know what you're thinking," he said. "You're thinking this isn't our battle. But as long as my name is getting thrown into the mix, I really don't have any choice."

"I understand that." Christine calmly refilled their son's cup with juice. "But what happened to Ivanovic in Capri—I think it bothers you that you can't figure it out. Or maybe . . . maybe you're worried there's someone out there who's better than you."

He blew out a laugh. "Really? You think this is some kind of ego trip on my part?"

"I don't know what to think. In all honesty, and for reasons I don't understand, I actually agree. I think you should go to Davos."

He looked at her with something between surprise and admiration.

"Just promise me one thing," she added.

"What's that?"

"The minute you figure out what's going on—you tell the CIA about it, and we get the hell out of here."

News of Romanov's demise swept into Moscow by a number of paths. The intelligence services regularly scoured police reports for incidents involving Russians abroad. Of these there was no shortage, although entanglements with prostitutes in Thailand and banking violations in Liechtenstein were far more prevalent themes than finding a dead oligarch on the side of a mountain. On an official level, the Swiss Ministry of Foreign Affairs immediately notified its counterpart agency in the Russian Federation, as per diplomatic protocol, of the murder of a Russian citizen.

As usual, however, it was the informal networks that ran the quickest. In the case of Romanov, such a thread began when the deceased's suddenly unemployed chief of security notified an old friend in army intelligence of the tragedy. This instigated a water-cooler gabfest inside the GRU's halls along Grizodubovoy Street, one that ultimately bubbled up to its leadership.

The ultimate end user, of course, was President Petrov, who was notified of the calamity by a whisper in his ear during a closed-door meeting with senior Duma members. By all accounts, the president appeared little moved by the news.

Yet of all those informed, the one who perhaps

showed the most interest was a guest in the process of checking out from Moscow's Four Seasons Hotel. Colonel Zhukov studied at length an email on his phone, which described what could only be another sniper attack. On finishing, he internalized the same two questions he'd been pondering for a week.

Could Slaton really be alive?

And if so, who had hired him to kill two of the three principals of MIR Enterprises?

Zhukov was helpless for answers as he stepped outside, leaned into a fierce wind, and boarded a taxi that would deliver him to the ongoing calamity that was Sheremetyevo Airport.

If there was compensation for the burdens of Rome's Fiumicino Airport, it was convenience of schedule. On being dropped at the departures level, Slaton booked the next available flight to Zurich—a mere thirty-minute wait for a one-hour journey on Alitalia. The passport and credit card he'd acquired only hours earlier worked seamlessly, and by four o'clock that afternoon he was standing in a rental car queue in Zurich.

He selected a boutique rental company that dealt in specialty vehicles, and there he requested the most rugged vehicle available. It turned out to be a Mercedes-Benz SUV, and came at a substantial premium, but if there were expense reports to file, he reasoned, Sorensen would be the one filing them. Slaton knew he was heading into the Swiss Alps on the cusp of winter, and he wanted no complications that could be avoided.

He was intimately familiar with Zurich, having visited a number of times in recent years. As with so many of the places he'd been, however, the memories were not kind ones to be dwelled upon, and so he felt little nostalgia as the bustling skyline faded in his mirror.

The Mercedes whisked him effortlessly through farmland for a time, and then the terrain began to make its demands. Straight stretches of road were lost to curves, gentle at first, and later the kind for which guard rails were requisite. Hills became mountains, the peaks invisible in mist and broken clouds, like curtains to the sky itself. The townships became gradually smaller, many set on lakes whose darkened surfaces belied crystalline Alpine water.

Slaton should have thought it all appealing. Should have recorded it as a place where he might take his family one day. As it was, he only hoped the Alpine canton around him wouldn't fall into the same category as Zurich: a once-charming backdrop tainted by memories of violence.

The next twenty-four hours would tell.

Slaton waited until he was just outside Davos before calling Sorensen on his new faux iPhone. She'd told him it was a secure device, but he no longer gave allowances to any such technology. At the moment, it hardly mattered anyway—what he wanted to know was of minimal intelligence value.

There were perfunctory greetings, and when Slaton inquired about his family he felt like some kind of traveling salesman. Once that was settled, Sorensen asked, "Have you reached Davos yet?"

"I'm still en route, but getting close. Do you have any more details about Romanov's death?"

"It took some work, but one of my people talked to the detective in charge, a guy named Ottinger."

"How did you—"

"Don't ask. The important thing for you to know is that Romanov was killed by a single high-caliber round, probably a fifty cal. It struck center of mass."

"Just like Ivanovic."

"Almost identical."

"Almost?"

"Yeah, there was one difference. The bullet very clearly entered his back—he was shot from behind."

"Okay. What else?"

"My guy asked the detective if they'd found the round—I figured you'd want to know."

"And?"

"The detective laughed, and said they'd work on it in the spring. Since Romanov was shot from behind, the bullet would have kept going downslope. Because it was such a big round, and depending on the angle, it could have gone another thousand yards in almost any direction. The mountainside is covered in a foot of new snow."

"I'm starting to see a pattern."

"Me too—Ottinger's investigation is headed for a ditch, just like Giordano's in Capri."

At that moment the mountain they were talking about came into view in Slaton's windscreen. He saw ribbons of snow cutting through the tree line on a massive rising slope. It looked stately and imposing, yet amid that grand scale Slaton sensed something peculiarly comforting. A feeling that it could be made much smaller.

"I don't know," he said. "Maybe it's not so hope-less after all."

TWENTY

Slaton pulled into Davos as the sun left the day behind, halfhearted shafts of light casting their closing palette across the peaks. He drove directly to the ski area, and left the Mercedes in a remote corner of a broad and nearly empty gravel parking area. On the other side of the lot, near the Alpine-themed lodge and ski lifts, a half dozen police cars and vans were parked in a cluster. None of them had their lights rolling, signifying the passage of the crisis stage on the mountain above.

He set out on foot and surveyed the scene. Halfway up the slope he saw a group of men and women in ski jackets, three idle snowmobiles around them. The snowmobiles were parked in a triangle, their headlights converging on the point in the snow that was the center of everyone's attention. He noticed that the gondola lift was running, two uniformed policemen standing watch at the entrance.

Slaton veered away from the lift station toward a group of condominiums, a three-story affair near a motionless chair lift whose seats were covered in snow. At the base of the condos he saw a handful of people, including two young men in ski instructor jackets who stood gawking at the tragedy uphill.

He traversed the bottom of the mountain cautiously, his eyes sweeping across the high slopes. From the spot where the investigative crowd had gathered, he walked his gaze upward, estimating loosely how far it would take for a skier who'd been shot to fall, tumble, and come to rest. The precise answer, of course, depended on how fast that skier was moving. From where he stood, Slaton noticed that the section of run leading uphill from Romanov's final resting place was a relatively straight track. Once his mid-mountain estimates were firm, he scanned upward and outward, glad to have arrived before the light completely faded.

Altogether, the scene before him was completely different from the one he'd seen yesterday on a yacht in Capri. Here a sniper could easily get close to his target, become lost in the trees in a hundred places. A close-in shot would render irrelevant many of the usual complications. Wind, air density, temperature, elevation—all were inconsequential for a trained sniper at a hundred yards. Unfortunately, as convenient as all that was, Slaton knew he wasn't looking at a short-range shot. He knew because, just as in Capri, the round had been described as very large caliber. Slaton thought it likely that the shooter had used the very same weapon, and nobody lugged a fifty cal into the woods for a hundred-yard shot. More to the point, working in such close proximity with a heavy gun complicated a sniper's ultimate end game—to escape to shoot another day.

Yet if all that extrapolation was correct—if the shooter had again used a fifty cal from long range— one mind-numbing complication emerged. In Capri, Ivanovic appeared to have been engaged at extreme distance, and while he was standing on a yacht that was rolling on heavy seas. Here the range could well have been less, but the target had been rushing downhill—judging by the slope, and depending on Romanov's abilities and mood—at something between twenty and fifty miles an hour.

And there was the logic-shattering disconnect. Same gunman, same weapon, outrageously different circumstances. Each impossible in its own right. Yet the results spoke volumes. In each case, one shot giving a clean, center-of-mass kill.

But how?

It was then, as Slaton stood puzzling beneath a setting sun, that he was struck by another commonality between the shootings. It involved not a known fact, but a glaring deficiency. In both cases the bullet had disappeared, and was essentially unrecoverable.

This brought pause. In Capri the vexing issue had been excessive range. Here it was a target moving at high speed. Was there a common solution? Slaton was among the most experienced technical shooters on earth—not the competition variety who practiced by firing thousands of rounds from the same position, but the belly-in-the-mud, wait a full day for a half chance type. Whenever possible, his geometry and calculations were finalized beforehand, in briefing rooms using models and surveillance photos, then amended as necessary in the field. The high-end assassin, which was what he was dealing with, must have known Romanov would be here. He knew his target would be moving fast across the side of a mountain, and made a plan that was within the capabilities of his weapon. He would also have designed a convenient escape.

Combining Capri with what was before him, Slaton put himself in a briefing room. He looked across the base of the runs and saw a shuttered ski school.

Next to that an equipment-rental barn was locked down tight. The two ski instructors were still to his right, and he walked in that direction. One was a thirtyish man, the other younger. It was the younger one who nodded amiably.

Slaton nodded back. "I heard someone died up there this morning," he said in English.

"Unfortunately, yes," the younger man said.

"Perhaps he could have used another lesson or two."

The Swiss looked at him uncertainly. There was a chance the man didn't appreciate black humor, but Slaton suspected his reaction was more an appraisal. The ski patrol would have been first to reach Romanov this morning. Rescuers who were accustomed to collisions with trees and other skiers, and who typically dealt with sprains and broken bones, would have seen something very different. Word about the shooting would have spread like wildfire among the staff. Yet Slaton was an outsider here, and therefore might not be trusted with such intimate knowledge.

"Actually," said the young man, "I saw him making runs earlier. He was a very good skier—fast, but always in control."

"Bad luck then," Slaton said, adding a shrug of indifference.

In truth, he was encouraged by the answer, because it gave him more to work with: *Fast, but always in control.* Unfortunately, in the falling light, this new information could not be applied until morning. The idea percolating in his head was speculative, the least plausible of his implausible theories. But it was the only one that fit every fact, so he decided to run with it.

If I had come here with a long-range rifle, intending to kill Romanov under such circumstances . . . how exactly would I have gone about it?

The first concept that came to mind was curiously straightforward. He edged back toward the man in the red jacket. "Sorry to bother you again, but can you tell me if there is an outfitter in town?"

The Swiss smiled, and said helpfully, "Why, yes. There is only one, but they are a good shop—they will have anything you need."

Slaton smiled back. He got directions, thanked the man politely, and with darkness finally blanketing the peaks, he headed into town.

"And you never heard a gunshot?" asked Ottinger.

An irritated Ovechkin shifted in the hard plastic seat. "There was nothing. I was headed downhill, wearing a helmet and a knit cap. What could I hear? Have you talked to Mikhael, my security chief? He was at the top of the mountain, in a much better position to see or hear something."

He stared at the detective, a hound-faced man with sad brown eyes, who said, "Yes, we have talked to him."

Ovechkin looked overtly at his watch. He had been at the station for three hours, most of it in this barren interview room. He'd had enough. "Inspector, I wish I could help you. What happened to Alexei is a terrible thing. Believe me when I say I very much hope you catch who did this. My own safety is clearly at risk. Did you make the inquiry in Capri as I suggested regarding the death of Pyotr Ivanovic?"

Ottinger nodded to say he had. "Thank you for that. I discussed the case with an inspector there"—he referenced his notes—"Giordano was his name. There do appear to be similarities between the deaths."

"Similarities?" Ovechkin grumbled. "They are

identical—my business partners have both been shot by a sniper. My life is at risk, I tell you. The minute we finish here, I am leaving Davos for some place more secure."

The inspector looked at him severely. "You expect to leave?"

"I do. And before you trouble yourself by suggesting otherwise, I should tell you I have already consulted my attorney in Bern. He assures me that by the laws of your canton there is no justification for my detention."

The policeman seemed to consider arguing the point, but finally relented, perhaps imagining the army of lawyers Ovechkin could bring to bear. "Very well. But will you at least do me the courtesy of leaving a contact number?"

Ovechkin took a pen and a notepad from the table, and wrote down his mobile number. He got up and headed for the door, trying not to grimace as he did so. His quadriceps were feeling the effects of last night's battle on the mountain—it was the most exercise he'd gotten in months.

He found Mikhael waiting in the lobby, and soon they were on the road. Ovechkin considered stopping at his chalet on the low slopes to pack a few clothes, but decided a quick exit would be better. Anyway, there was nothing there he couldn't live without. He would call Estrella later and explain that business matters had necessitated an early departure.

"Straight to the airport," he ordered, "before they change their minds."

Mikhael steered toward Samedan Airport, a small airstrip tucked in a bucolic valley outside St. Moritz. There his private jet would be waiting, fully fueled with the crew ready. As the snow-covered peaks fell obscured in thin evening light, Ovechkin knew what had to come next. From the back seat he fired off a text to Colonel Zhukov.

Romanov dead. I am very worried. Leaving Davos. We need to meet, somewhere safe. Suggest the same venue as last month.

He waited, but got no immediate reply. He wondered where the colonel might be.

TWENTY-ONE

For the second night in a row Franz Stoeckler surveyed the sales floor with his usual seasonal pessimism. For the second night in a row he was saved by a man he'd never seen before.

He came through the door and spoke briefly to a cashier, who pointed toward the back of the store. Stoeckler intercepted him at the camping aisle. "Can I help you, sir?" he asked, something telling him to go straight to English.

"Possibly. I am here in Davos to meet a friend. We're planning to go into the backcountry, but he arrived before I did—I think he might already have purchased his gear."

Stoeckler immediately thought of last night's customer. He racked his brain for a name, but realized the man had never given one. "Yesterday evening, perhaps? There was a younger man with an accent—I thought he might be Russian, or perhaps Latvian."

The customer smiled congenially. "Yes, that would be him. You helped him?"

"Indeed. He knew precisely what he wanted."

"I fear we've gotten our signals crossed—his phone is failing. He didn't mention where he was staying, did he?"

"No, I'm sorry. He said he was here for some off-piste skiing, and purchased everything he would need."

The customer seemed to consider it. "Well, he is something of an expert . . . perhaps I should buy the same gear. Tell me, would you have an exact record of what he purchased? I don't want to forget anything."

Stoeckler nearly scoffed, but reminded himself that this customer was not a countryman, and therefore not necessarily acquainted with the Swiss obsession for records. "I can certainly help you with that, sir. Please come with me."

Stoeckler led the way to an unused checkout stand and logged into the register. He called up last night's transactions, and a list was displayed on the monitor. There were few to choose from, and he quickly highlighted the record in question. "Here we are," he said, turning to find the customer already looking over his shoulder.

"Yes," the man said. "That does look comprehensive. I see he paid in cash."

For the first time Stoeckler hesitated. The man he was looking at was slightly older than last night's visitor, taller and more strongly built. His English came with an accent Stoeckler couldn't quite place. Combined with the fair hair, he thought perhaps Scandinavian.

"Can you help me find everything?" the man said.

Any reservations brewing in Stoeckler's head were lost in that moment. "But of course." He made a show of studying his customer. "I think an extra large for the jacket?"

The gray Nordic eyes smiled.

* * *

It took fifty minutes to fulfill the list, everything sized and fitted and ready for use. Slaton watched the salesman scurry around the store pulling skis and boots from racks, estimating and adjusting, unfailingly keeping to the most expensive brands. Several times, as Herr Stoeckler was otherwise occupied, Slaton studied the sales record from last night he'd printed out. He saw nothing of use, the entire customer information field being blank. He knew the store had a surveillance system that monitored the registers—he'd been doing his best to avoid a ceiling-mounted camera since coming inside. He suspected that last night's star customer had done the same. Try as he might, Slaton could think of no reasonable explanation for asking the clerk to give him a look at the video.

He obliquely learned a bit more as the process ran. He asked the colors of his companion's jacket—gray—so as to choose something different, and discovered that the man was between a medium and a large in clothing, and wore size nine shoes. All useful, but hardly telling. The most intriguing purchase was a laminated topographical map, and Slaton requested his own copy without hesitation. His purchases ended up in a mountainous pile on what had become his private checkout stand.

Stoeckler began the math, and asked, "Will there be anything else?"

"I hope not," Slaton replied in good humor. "But if my friend and I come up short, we'll know where to come."

"Of course. I can tell you he may have gone out today—he seemed eager to test his new gear."

"As am I," Slaton said.

He paid with the credit card, not wanting to dent

his cash cushion so severely. Stoeckler began putting everything into a shopping cart.

"Is this how my friend took his gear to the parking lot?"

"Actually, no," Stoeckler said. "It must have been quite a workout, but he carried everything by hand. He must have been staying nearby."

"Probably," Slaton said, as he thought, *But he's not here anymore.* "What makes you think I wouldn't do the same?" he asked good-naturedly.

"It is quite simple, sir. I saw you drive up earlier."

Slaton looked outside. His Mercedes was parked in the front row. The smallest of mistakes, but a mistake all the same. He didn't dwell on it.

The two exchanged wishes for a pleasant evening, and Slaton headed outside feeling he'd made considerable headway. And completely unaware he was making his second mistake.

As he walked out of the store, Slaton had no way of knowing that three blocks away, from the fourth-floor window of the tallest hotel in town, a wiry young man stood watching him closely. He used binoculars, indeed a pair exactly like the ones Slaton was at that moment loading into the back seat of his Mercedes rental.

The watcher was transfixed. He would very much have liked to take a photograph of the man standing behind the SUV, but the lights in the parking lot were feeble, and he had no equipment for long-range night imagery.

Could it really be him? he wondered.

Only yesterday it had seemed little more than fiction. The whispers about David Slaton to begin with, planted by the FSB and SVR, he knew to be no more than *maskirovka*—a bit of deception to keep the authorities in Italy and beyond guessing. It served to keep his own name from being added to any suspect list, not that it likely would be.

As a sergeant in the Russian Special Forces he'd often performed work abroad, although it had always been in a military capacity, embedded in units operating largely inside combat zones, and always with the utmost of discretion. Places like Chechnya and Ukraine, where generic, sanitized battle dress was the uniform of the day, and where identity cards were little more than nostalgic remembrances. It was a notable reversal of classic military norms: the avoidance of attribution for a mission. For the units in which he typically operated, to be recognized for battlefield success, and by extension for Russia herself to be credited, was tantamount to failure. Obfuscation was the new primary objective. Medal ceremonies became private affairs, unit citations closely guarded secrets.

And now? the sergeant mused. *Now we have taken things to the next level.*

He had become part of a new shadow army—in his case, a unit of one. His clothes were strictly civilian, his identities forged by the finest craftsmen in the FSB. His weapons and tactics were the only vestige of his military heritage. In bygone days, during wars between great nations, such subterfuge would have labeled him as a spy—the most grievous of offenses, and, if he were captured, punishable by death.

But who bothered to declare war anymore?

Irregular warfare—that was the new normal, and he had put himself at the forefront. So confident was the sergeant in his cover, he'd not given a second thought to the fact that the police in Capri were searching for a hired assassin. Now he sensed an error.

His first warning had been the call that came yesterday: a man had shown up on *Cassandra*, in the company of an American woman who was almost certainly CIA. They were looking into Ivanovic's death. The man was tall with slate-gray eyes, and had asked knowledgeable questions. That was how *Cassandra*'s captain had reported it—the skipper had been retained to keep an eye on more than just his boat. Now, the very next day, a man of vaguely the same description had appeared in Davos, and only hours after the strike on Romanov.

Coincidence?

The sergeant had first spotted him an hour ago at the bottom of the slope. He'd watched the man blend casually into the meager crowd that was gawking at the proceedings mid-hill. He seemed no more than a curiosity in those first moments. Then something about the way he moved, the way he surveyed the mountain, seized the sergeant's attention. He'd noted the watchful manner in which he approached a ski instructor, and the way he'd taken directions into town. Then—most incredible of all—the man had walked straight to the outfitters. Through the tight angle of the storefront window, the sergeant watched the same salesman he'd dealt with last night collect a pile of equipment for the newcomer. As far as he could tell, a purchase identical to the one he himself had made.

No, he decided. There could be no doubt. *Someone* was tracking him. But . . . could it really be Slaton?

He watched the Mercedes pull out of the parking lot and disappear into a maze of buildings. He couldn't tell where it was headed.

The sergeant weighed his options. He was tempted to go back to the outfitters. He was sure he could manipulate the salesman into talking about this new customer. He reckoned the man who was tracking him had done much the same. *I think my friend came in last night. I'd like to buy the same gear.* Whoever he was, he was clever.

In the end, the sergeant decided it wasn't worth the risk. He was already on a tight schedule, and it was time to leave Davos. The local police might be plodders, but they weren't stupid. In time they would make connections, discover that a man with a heavy East European accent had been at the store last night buying climbing gear. When that happened, he needed to be far away. To the positive, they now had a second suspect to track down, a man who'd probably claimed to know the first.

That would confuse things nicely.

He collected his few possessions and headed into the hallway, closing the door of his prepaid room quietly behind him. The more he thought about it, the more he was convinced—it might very well be Slaton. Quick-stepping down the main stairwell, he tried to remember what Mossad called their assassins. Every service had their monikers, and it came to him on the first-floor landing. *Kidon.* Hebrew for bayonet.

His midsized Audi was in the basement parking garage. His gear, including the weapon, was already secure in the trunk. He fired the car to life, and moments later the big garage door lifted to present a serene Davos evening. He surveyed every sidewalk and road before pulling out, his attention more acute than at any time since he'd arrived. It wasn't the police he was looking for.

As the sergeant set out at a measured pace toward

Zurich, he gave the new developments considerable thought. When the road began to straighten, and with Zurich on the horizon, he placed the expected call.

It was answered immediately.

"I am leaving Davos," he said in Russian. "But there may be a complication . . ."

TWENTY-TWO

Slaton woke well rested, having taken a room in a small and peaceful rooming house on the outskirts of town. The prices were reasonable, the staff pleasant, and when he went downstairs in search of coffee that morning he encountered a full breakfast buffet in the homespun dining room.

He had given thought to shunning a room altogether to spend the night in the Mercedes, whose rear seats reclined. It would have made sense had he been on the run, but in that moment he remained in the clear. For once the pursuer instead of the pursued. After a good night's sleep, followed by a full meal, he was sure he'd made the right choice.

He settled his account, and on stepping outside discovered that the promised break in Switzerland's early winter had not yet come to pass. The temperature hovered near the freezing point, and a drifting mist had claimed the mountains. The steel October morning gradually took its grip on Davos, turning black silhouettes to gray and slowly adding angles to muted shapes. The one bit of good news—there was no new snow. Had that been the case, his morning's work might have been greatly complicated.

Slaton had spent the previous night mapping out a

route on his new topographical map, and he set out in the Mercedes with a particular road in mind—by no coincidence, the one that led farthest up the mountain. He found the road easily, and was encouraged to find pavement for the first half mile. At that point it digressed to a gravel service road, but one that was well maintained. Two months from now it would all be impassable, but today the snow was thin, the patches of ice few. A frigid stream was intermittently visible on his left, wending through a forest that had been caught in the middle of its annual defoliation.

The Mercedes climbed ably, its four-wheel drive put to good use. Where the gravel road came to an end he found a locked gate, and beyond that, as promised by the map, was the head of a hiking trial. Slaton pulled the Mercedes into a small level area, a makeshift parking apron likely cleared for summer hikers.

He went to the tailgate and collected his gear. Heaving the backpack in place, he put his skis over one shoulder and set out on the trail. There were two general schools of off-piste skiing. One involved purists who invariably started at the bottom of a mountain and climbed every step. Having no need for self-validation, Slaton took the more practical approach—he started with the highest traversable road, then added as much elevation as possible using prepared surfaces. Only where man-made paths ended did the skis and poles come out.

He climbed at a steady pace, his breath going to vapor in the still morning air. The trail was wet, but there was little ice, and footing was not a problem. After thirty minutes he encountered a scenic overlook, and using the map, Slaton took a moment to orient himself. He looked down toward the ski area and easily spotted the point on the lower run, still marked with yellow crime scene tape, where Romanov had met his end.

He shifted his gaze upward to his objectives. He had discerned three, all chosen yesterday during his dusk survey of the upper mountain. The first would be the easiest to reach: roughly two thousand yards from where he stood, a gray-granite outcropping of boulders situated well below the upper lift station. The other two points involved more climbing: a pair of rock ledges near the summit, spaced roughly five hundred yards apart. By Slaton's estimate, any of them might have concealed the killer who'd struck Romanov.

Of course, there was no guarantee of success. If he didn't find what he was after, he would undertake a second survey from high on the mountain and try again tomorrow. It was all little more than conjecture and analysis, meaning there was a fair chance he would fail.

The only way to know for sure: climb a mountain and start searching.

Where the trail became lost in snow, Slaton donned the touring skis. He climbed at a steady pace, his heart rate and respiration accelerating. Halfway to the first objective his legs were burning, and his lungs strained in the thin air. When he finally reached the field of boulders, he paused, leaning heavily on his poles.

He looked downhill, and as expected saw a clear line of sight to the spot where Romanov had come to rest. By his shooter's eye, nine hundred yards. More telling, however, was what he did not see. Snipers invariably set up shop long before their targets were expected to appear. Patience was requisite when hours, even days, had to be spent concealed in wait. After any engagement, successful or not, the general rule was to clean up, leaving as few traces as possible of one's stay. Spent casings, food wrappers, water bottles, flattened grass. To the greatest extent possible, the hide was to be put back to its original state—except in the rare case when a shooter was advertising his presence. To erase the evidence left behind was not merely a defensive measure, but part of the greater psychological war. It enhanced the sniper's mystique.

But while a sniper might hide his presence from a casual observer, or even a trained detective, it was far harder to conceal from a peer. Slaton knew every nuance, the signs that were hard to erase. As he evaluated this potential hide, he was struck right away by one glaring disadvantage. Without cover overhead, there was no way anyone could have approached the outcropping, let alone remained here for hours, without leaving marks in the carpet of snow. And once those marks had been made, nothing short of a fresh three-inch snowfall would put things back to a natural state. Which hadn't happened.

He surveyed the field of boulders carefully, and the terrain all around. He saw not a single boot print or ski trail. There were no impressions or detritus in the various granite nooks. Wanting to be sure, he spent twenty minutes going over the area, and in the end he was satisfied—no one had been here yesterday.

He looked up the mountain toward the other two conceals he'd identified. They were roughly the same distance from where he stood, both a climb of perhaps two thousand vertical feet. One of the ledges would be significantly more difficult to reach, the terrain below steep and rugged. Yet in that site Slaton saw one notable advantage—proximity to a snow-covered run that offered a quick escape.

That's the one I'd have chosen, he thought.

The mist was thinning, the day getting warmer. Slaton looked down over Davos, then out across the Alps. It was a magnificent view, snow-capped peaks in the distance brilliant against a deep blue sky. He took a water bottle from his pack, drained half, and set out uphill. His neck craning upward, he dug his skis hard into the fast-softening snowpack.

The air distance from Moscow to Ouarzazate, Morocco, is twenty-five hundred miles. Zhukov felt as though he'd been transported to another world.

His transition had begun in Casablanca. He'd arrived there the previous afternoon, and spent the night in a hotel that had been arranged by Petrov's staff. It was called Hotel Le Doge, sixteen rooms in Casablanca's bustling Art Deco quarter. He'd been told it was a five-star property, and Zhukov found no reason to doubt it. His room had been spacious and clean, with furnishings that might have been brought straight from Paris. The walls were trimmed in royal blue, complemented by veils of silk that billowed around a four-poster bed. For a Special Ops grunt who'd long been happy for a dry sleeping bag, and nothing short of ecstatic for a tent, it necessitated a degree of adjustment.

But adjust Zhukov had.

The posh treatment ran through the morning, a sumptuous breakfast brought by a waiter who refused to let his coffee cup go dry. Then, finally, reality had intervened. Zhukov packed his bag, bid an attractive concierge goodbye, and returned to the airport. For his connecting flight, the previous day's business-class seat on a Boeing was supplanted by a decidedly more narrow space on a dusty thirty-seat turboprop. For the first time in his life he had asked a ticket agent if an upgrade was available, only to be told that the airplane was small and therefore offered but one class of seating. Zhukov, who'd grown up under Communist rule, smiled and told the agent he understood. He'd of course endured far worse in military transports. All the same, yesterday *had* been nice.

Am I going soft? he wondered.

After a bumpy forty-minute flight eastward, his two-day conveyance was complete. The chilly terminal buildings and jetways of Sheremetyevo seemed barely a memory as he descended a wobbly set of stairs to a tarmac baking in unseasonable heat. Gone were the snow-covered sidewalks and sunless Moscow sky, in their place only barren red desert and a hammering sun.

Is there any temperate place in this world? he wondered.

With the airplane unloaded, twelve passengers ambled en masse toward an earthen terminal building. In terms of size, the place wasn't much bigger than the first army barracks Zhukov had called home, and he was struck by its unusually thick walls and decorative turrets. He thought it a conspicuously defensive architectural style, and wondered what narrative that suggested about the people who lived here.

The passengers around him wore an eclectic mix of clothing, casual Western brands layered with traditional shirts and colorful vests. Zhukov himself wore a casual jacket and trousers. He could scarcely remember the last time he'd donned a proper uniform—one more degree of separation from his previous existence.

Immigration had been endured in Casablanca, and with no luggage to claim, his passage through the terminal building took less than a minute. He had been here twice before, and outside he pulled to a stop along the familiar red-and-white striped curb—as far as he knew, every paved street in Ouarzazate was lined in similar fashion, some vestige of French colonial oversight. Looking up the only road—there was no need for separate arrival and departure lanes—Zhukov saw but one vehicle.

The beaten Toyota Land Cruiser was parked a hundred meters away and began moving immediately. It might have been either red or brown, but dust had muddled the issue, and when the SUV pulled to a stop directly in front of him Zhukov peered through the open passenger-side window. He recognized the driver right away—the same young man who'd collected him on his last visit, five weeks earlier.

"Hello, Colonel," said Muaz in English.

Zhukov dropped his rollerbag in the back, then took the front passenger seat. "Good morning, Muaz. Thank you for being prompt."

The young Moroccan smiled, and steered toward the main road. He was a spindly kid of Berber extraction, with walnut skin and a mop of unruly black hair kept in check by a maroon fez. No more than twenty-five years old, his knobby limbs were the perfect complement to the perpetually crooked grin that attested to Muaz's most prominent trait—his unfailingly positive nature. It had always been a mystery to Zhukov how the poorest people in the world often seemed the happiest. He decided his own experiences had denied him a valid statistical sampling—the non-Russians he'd dealt with overseas, particularly in recent years, often regarded him as either protector or paymaster.

"The traffic is not a problem today," Muaz remarked.

Zhukov looked up the street. He saw one other car moving. He glanced at Muaz and saw the grin. "Yes, very funny," he replied in a monotone. Zhukov idly regarded the Toyota's interior. It had once been refined, but the color of the leather seats had faded and there was a side-to-side crack across the dash. The sun and heat doing their relentless best.

"Have there been any visitors to the airfield since I was last here?" Zhukov asked. This had been his parting mandate to Muaz, a request to keep an eye on things—reinforced with a healthy wad of euros.

"Only one group from India."

"Engineers?"

"No, I think not. They talked about building a hangar of their own and performing test flights—a project that would take many years."

This made sense to Zhukov, and he wrote it off as harmless. It was, ostensibly, the reason the place was here. The airfield had been carved from the desert, high on a plateau overlooking the Sahara. It had been given the name Tazagurt in honor of a kasbah, long gone to rubble, that had once stood sentry on the nearby twin peaks. With a ten-thousand-foot runway, one hangar, and three support buildings, the facility was three years into a five-year plan. Russians, Zhukov knew, always loved their five-year plans.

The Tazagurt project had been specially licensed by the Moroccan government, and was funded as a joint venture between the Russian Office of Technology and Development and its corporate overseer, RosAvia. A relatively new aerospace design bureau in Russia, RosAvia was fast rising to join the likes of Sukhoi and Tupolev. The sales pitch behind the undertaking had been part politics, part business. Russia, under president Petrov, was doing its best to establish footholds in new corners of the world, competing with the traditional Western powers and a newly emergent China. In this case, as a practical matter, the weather in Morocco was fair almost year-round, offering test pilots and engineers relief from harsh Russian winters. Also, because Tazagurt's main runway had an elevation of four thousand feet above sea level, it was an ideal location for the certification and testing of airframes in high-altitude, high-temperature conditions. This was the basis of the slick PowerPoint presentation that had been given to Moroccan authorities: Tazagurt was an eminently logical location for an aerospace design and test facility.

Zhukov's reasons for being here, however, were far more oblique.

Muaz drove south through the town of Ouarzazate, and it was much as Zhukov remembered, the dominant color being a ferrous red-brown hue. This was yet another universal theme taken from his travels: in underdeveloped countries, the hue of buildings was invariably the same as the earth upon which they were built. The geometry of the structures here, however, seemed less in harmony with their surroundings, rounded architectural edges that contrasted with the jagged mountains beyond.

The township soon fell behind, and in no time they were swallowed by the desert. Zhukov saw a landscape that was nothing less than lunar. He was not the first to notice it. Had they taken the main road from Ouarzazate in the opposite direction, they would have encountered Atlas Studios. By land area, it was the world's largest film studio, and had served as a backdrop for the likes of *Lawrence of Arabia* and *Game of Thrones*. Atlas' sets were favored for scenes demanding one overriding characteristic—absolute desolation. Zhukov could see what lured the directors here. Brown dirt and rocks ran to the horizon on either side, barren topography that showed no sign of civilization, the only marks being those drawn by water and eons. Indeed, the only human element in sight was what stretched out before them—a lone ribbon of asphalt reaching into the hills.

Twenty minutes later the RosAvia hangar appeared on the horizon. Soon after, the main runway came into view, its grooved concrete shimmering like a mirage in the rising heat. The entire complex was surrounded by a fence, which seemed superfluous in such a remote place. Zhukov told anyone who asked it was meant to keep the hyenas off the runway.

Nearing the main gate, he took one last look at the Anti-Atlas Mountains beyond. They looked raw and untouched, the colors and textures vivid. No different from what had existed for a million years. It was that desolation that had brought him here, every bit as much as it had the Hollywood moguls. The primary difference—Zhukov intended to leave no record whatsoever of his work.

TWENTY-THREE

The climb took nearly two hours. Slaton countered the frenetic terrain with a steady pace, as unrelenting as an incoming tide. When the temperature began to rise he removed his jacket, the Alpine air refreshing in its crispness. Even so, as he neared the crest his body began to protest. He was straining with each step and his form faltered, skis dragging and edges catching. His heart seemed on its redline, pounding from the combination of exertion and altitude.

When he was roughly a thousand feet below the summit, the snow deepened noticeably. In months to come, as the base became thicker and less stable, the possibility of avalanches would have to be considered when moving off trail. Fortunately, that wasn't yet an issue.

He rounded a thick stand of trees, and the ledge he'd spotted from below finally came into view. Right away Slaton was encouraged. He noticed subdued chevron impressions in the snow, much like the ones he was making now, only less fresh, having gone through one day's cycle of heating and cooling and wind. Closer still, he recognized a single set of ski tracks leading down to the nearest groomed run. This could be what he was after. On the other hand, it might only be the signs of an adventurous ski instructor who'd gone off trail.

On reaching the outcropping, he removed his skis and walked across rocks to the shadowed ledge. The most substantial overhang covered twenty feet from side to side, and was high enough for a man to stand beneath. He studied the ground carefully, and saw a spot where strands of summer grass, gone brown and stiff, had been flattened. He inspected the area closely, and noted the muted impressions of boots on wet ground. There was no trash, and of course no fifty-cal casing. It didn't matter. He was convinced this was the place. Roughly twenty-six hours ago, the shooter had been here. Lining up Alexei Romanov in his sight.

He looked down along the slope of the mountain, and his conviction was further strengthened—not only was Romanov's final resting place in clear view, but from that reference point Slaton could see clearly five hundred feet uphill. A long enough interval for tracking and aiming, followed by a thoughtful pull on the trigger.

Yet satisfying as it all was, the mechanics once again failed. He estimated the range to be between twelve and thirteen hundred yards. A long shot under ideal circumstances. Probably manageable with one condition—a stationary target. Yet Romanov had been moving fast. By all accounts, he was a highly accomplished skier, and the section of hill where he'd been hit was steep. Depending on his aggressiveness at that moment, he would have been traveling in the vicinity of forty miles an hour. That combination of range and target speed had but one sum: an utterly impossible shot.

Just as in Capri, Slaton stood stumped. Whoever

this shooter was, he'd now succeeded twice. In each instance, a single shot taken under unthinkable geometry.

So how did he do it?

His eyes went back to the shadows of the hide. He was ruminating on the twin unlikelihoods of distance and target movement when something new caught his eye. Roughly ten feet from where the shooter had likely lain prone, he noticed two small indentations in the soft ground. He went closer, bent down, and saw a pair of identical impressions, each the size of a playing card. They were perfectly rectangular, roughly a quarter inch deep. On closer inspection, Slaton saw a third imprint in the matted grass. The spacing was perfect. *A tripod.*

But to support what? The fifty cal?

He kept looking, but saw nothing to give an answer. Then the oblique thought he'd discarded in Capri returned. He pulled the backpack from his shoulder and removed his binoculars—the same make and model the assassin had bought and used from this very place.

Slaton trained them downhill and focused on the spot where Romanov had come to rest. He tried to estimate how far the Russian would have tumbled after his near-instantaneous death. Accounting for a variety of speeds, Slaton reckoned between thirty and fifty feet. He walked his circular field of view uphill accordingly, and studied beyond that point, imagining a straight line from his present position to the snow bank beyond. He saw what looked like a broken tree branch nearby, and ten yards to the right of that an aluminum snow-making pole rose from the forest's edge like some great robotic arm. Slaton recorded a half dozen other reference points, including the police-taped accident scene itself. He consolidated all of it into a single mental diagram.

He didn't know if what he was contemplating was even possible. But there might be a way to find out.

Slaton spent another ten minutes going over the sniper's den. He found nothing more of interest. With the sun nearing its apex, he packed his gear and donned his skis. A climb that had taken most of the morning would be reversed in a matter of minutes. He downed the last of his water, kicked into the snow, and in a flurry of shallow turns he accelerated downhill.

The speed put a breeze across his face, biting and cool. The only sound was the coarse grating of his skis through powder, rhythmic and smooth. It was the smallest taste of freedom, and Slaton enjoyed it while it lasted.

He knew it would end abruptly halfway down the mountain.

Argos' anchor splashed into the shimmering sea fifty miles south of Sharm El-Sheikh. It sank nearly a hundred feet before hitting bottom. To the east, easily seen under the bright midday sun, were the high slopes of Tihamah, Arabia's wide coastal plain that shelved unremittingly down to the Red Sea. To the south and west, lost in the marine haze, were the sun-infused shores of Egypt.

"Now what?" asked Captain Zakaryan.

Ivan, who was standing next to him on the bridge, said, "Now? Nothing—we wait. You should broadcast a message on the VHF radio. Tell whoever is listening that you've anchored to make minor repairs. If anyone asks, assure them no technical assistance is required—your chief engineer has things well in hand."

"We are in international waters," Zakaryan said. He pointed to the distant tan shore. "The coastlines here are among the most remotely populated in the Middle East. I doubt anyone will hear us, let alone offer help."

"All the better."

"How long will we be anchored?"

Ivan shrugged. "Our repairs should be done by tomorrow morning, I think. But tonight we will be busy. Expect a welcoming party—a few boats."

"We will offload our cargo?"

"A good portion of it."

"And where do we sail next?"

"That I will keep until the morning," Ivan replied. "Now . . . have your crane operator meet me on deck. He and I have a few things to discuss."

The Russian disappeared, and in an increasingly familiar response, Zakaryan's irritation went to relief. He found himself revisiting his original decision—difficult job market or not, it might be time to find a new employer.

As he looked out toward the distant arid shores, he could not know that at that same moment two other captains were looking in the opposite direction, one south and one west across the Arabian Peninsula. Nor could he know that the masters of *Cirrus* and *Tasman Sea* were having very much the same thoughts.

The hangar Zhukov approached wasn't particularly large, at least as such structures went. It would never have held a widebody airliner, although a midsize commercial transport might have fit inside. The half dozen MiG-21 fighters sheltered at that moment? Those were no problem at all.

He entered the hangar through a gap in the massive main doors, and right away saw the old jets. If they'd ever been state-of-the-art machines it was long before he had entered the army. Even so, he knew a handful were still flying above the world's second-tier stages. It was an iconic airframe, stout and cylindrical, with a tail and wings that were heavily swept. The nose was little more than a massive air intake upon which was centered its signature nosecone. The MiG-21 was simple, robust, and plentiful—indeed, it was the most-produced supersonic aircraft ever built. It was also a design nearing the end of its service life. As if to validate the point, all six of the jets before him were painted dull gray with orange tails. The bright fin flashes signified that they'd been adapted for test work—much like a facsimile gun with an orange plastic tip.

The hangar wasn't air conditioned, but large floor fans worked hard to stir the thin desert air. One of the MiGs was unbuttoned from front to back, various panels hanging open for servicing and maintenance. Another was surrounded by test equipment, everything umbilicaled like life-support equipment to a critically ill patient in a hospital. This was where Zhukov found the man he was after.

He was seated behind a test stand, typing on a laptop computer. His name was Boris Tikhonov, and for three years he had served as the lead engineer on Ros-Avia's pioneering project. Zhukov was intimately familiar with the engineer's background. His brilliance had been recognized early on—it was one of the few positives of the plodding Soviet era that mathematically gifted children were systematically identified. Unfortunately, recognition in itself was not enough. The chosen few were separated into schools that would drill them relentlessly on rote memorization of theorems and spewing back equations. Left unaddressed was academic adventure, the risk-taking and innovation so essential to scientific breakthrough. More recently, the ruling kleptocracy had hampered things further, viewing research and entrepreneurship as little more than a threat to their wholly owned, if noncompetitive, industrial establishment. Altogether, it created an intractable and burdensome atmosphere for Russia's most promising minds. A ball and chain on creativity from which few escaped.

Young Tikhonov, however, had refused to be so bound. As a teen he'd been shunted through a series of special schools, and in quick succession was expelled from no fewer than three of Russia's top engineering universities. His professors used terms like "brilliant" and "impossible" in equal measure, but there was no denying his potential. Unable to conform long enough to obtain an advanced degree, and wholly unsuited to life in academia, Tikhonov gravitated to a series of entry-level engineering jobs. That was where Zhukov had found him: frustrated, underpaid, and by Russian standards, a middling-grade abuser of alcohol. Most important of all—Boris Tikhonov was a man eager to prove his genius to the world.

Zhukov approached across the broomed concrete floor, and not for the first time wondered if he'd made the right choice. Having spent a career in the military, he was accustomed to dealing with men and women who kept a certain standard of appearance. Tikhonov was, to say the least, cut from a different vein. He was grossly overweight with unkempt dark hair, the style of which seemed inspired by a lightning strike. He wore a bushy beard, either because he was too lazy to shave, or to hide an excessively florid complexion. Zhukov knew the man was a heavy drinker, not to mention a heavy eater and smoker. In sum, a man who had little use for the word "moderation" in any arena. Yet he also knew that on the days when Boris Tikhonov was sober, he was among the most pioneering minds in Russia.

Tikhonov hovered over his keyboard, parked on a stool that looked far too small for his massive frame. When he saw Zhukov coming, he forced a smile.

"Boris!" said Zhukov brightly.

Tikhonov stepped away from his computer and the two exchanged a handshake. Neither carried forward to an embrace, which would have implied true friendship.

"I was not expecting you so soon," Tikhonov said.

"My schedule has been unpredictable lately."

"Thanks to you, mine has been completely predictable—nothing but work."

"Good! And how goes our project?"

"Well enough. I have isolated the reason for our recent setback." Three weeks ago the seventh MiG in the hangar had crashed on a proving flight.

"Did the problem relate to the guidance system?" Zhukov asked.

"Definitely not. Our telemetry was solid all the way to the ground. It was nothing more than an engine failure—the first stage turbine, as far as we can tell."

"Is that not a problem?"

"No more than it ever was," Tikhonov replied. "There is a reason the MiG-21 was built in such great numbers—to account for attrition. And I'm sure the designers never expected they would still be flying after fifty years. These aircraft in our little squadron are not maintained to the usual Air Force standards. If I had more money, more personnel . . ." He let his complaint trail off.

Zhukov had heard it all before. His expression fell serious, his tone certainty itself. "As I told you from the beginning, our project is very important. Staffing must be kept to a minimum to maintain secrecy."

"Secrecy? Is that why my private design bureau has been exiled to the steppes of the Sahara?"

"You are being paid handsomely to bring success."

Tikhonov opened his mouth, a rude comment rising, but Zhukov cut him off with, "You've done well, Boris. But only when the concept is proven can we expand to a larger scale. Finish things here, and I guarantee RosAvia will be given another contract soon."

"With increased funding?"

"Without a doubt. I see countless applications for your work—not only in the training environment, but on the front line as well. What you are creating represents the very future of tactical aviation." He watched the engineer's wide frame straighten ever so slightly. "When is the next test flight scheduled?" Zhukov asked.

"Tomorrow. Can you stay for it?"

"I wouldn't miss it. I very much want to see the system in action."

"Then you shall."

Tikhonov went back to his workstation.

Zhukov looked through the hangar and saw a half dozen workers. Only a few were Russian, and there were no soldiers among them. He himself had been

responsible for that—some vestige of honor that
seemed almost nostalgic. His attention was caught by
a parachute hanging near the ceiling, one of the red-
and-white "drag chutes" used to slow the fighters after landing. It billowed in the wake of the circulation
fans, reminding him of the flowing bedside curtains
at Hotel Le Doge. Zhukov blinked away the distraction.

*What curious intersections my thoughts find these
days.*

He turned his eyes back to the jet in front of them.
It seemed bizarre that his country's future depended
on such an obsolete airframe. The Russian Air Force
had retired its squadrons of MiG-21s at the end of
the Cold War. For a time, thousands had sat derelict
on bases around the country. It was that inventory
from which the jets had been drawn—scrap metal
until the day Tikhonov had presented a paper to Ros-
Avia executives on how they might be resurrected.
His idea was not unique—indeed, the Americans had
been doing something similar for decades. But Tikhonov's twist to the old concept was inspired—or so
thought a certain army colonel who'd been sitting in
the back row.

Now, three years later, Zhukov was astonished at
how far they'd come. More incredible yet: the way in
which it would all soon be brought to bear.

TWENTY-FOUR

Slaton set a hard turn to break his descent down the mountain. He coasted to a stop in the trees on the northern side of the main run, a recess with a commanding view of the spot where Romanov had gone down.

A man and a woman, both in ski gear, were taking measurements at the scene. The woman stood near the small cordoned area, while the man had climbed forty yards uphill and was standing next to a flag that had been planted in the snow. Using some kind of optical measuring device, he took readings and called them out to his partner, who dutifully recorded them in a book. It was all very organized. All very Swiss.

Unknowingly, they were doing much of Slaton's job for him. The two were clearly calculating where Romanov had first been hit. It was likely a guess based on where he'd fallen, referencing the first tumbling gouges in the snow, although it was possible they'd obtained some kind of camera footage of the event—Slaton supposed ski resorts maintained surveillance to fend off liability. Whatever the source, he allowed that the position of the uphill flag was based on known facts.

Soon the man and woman, who could only be police, packed up their gear and disappeared downhill. There was no one else in sight. Unsure how long that would remain the case, Slaton seized the moment and kicked off toward the higher of the two points.

Slowing as he approached the flag, he rounded the spot and then continued downhill. His speed and direction were governed by the mental diagram he'd created at the granite ledge far above. Slaton skidded to a stop and looked uphill. He assumed the police had plotted the pertinent details of the crime—where Romanov had been shot, and where he had come to rest—with a reasonable degree of accuracy. He alone, however, knew the most critical point: where the shot had originated.

He lined up the high ledge to the point where Romanov had been hit, and from there drew a line straight downhill. He extrapolated the path the bullet would have taken after passing through its target. Because the police had no starting point, they would be relegated to searching acres of snow-covered mountain for the bullet. Slaton hoped he could narrow things down to something far more manageable.

He glanced briefly at the base of the mountain. If his pause near the accident scene had drawn any interest, he saw no sign of it. A few staff and ski patrol members were milling about, and a police evidence van was parked nearby with its rear doors ajar. There was no sign of the man and woman who'd just departed with their measurements. All the same, Slaton knew his time was limited. He had no good reason to be here, and sooner or later he would be confronted.

Along the trajectory he'd calculated, he eased very slowly downhill. With his skis carving wide, slow turns, he plowed ever so cautiously in search of the telltale mark.

The images arrived early that afternoon, and Sorensen was alerted by Mike.

"Two of the three have anchored," he said, shuffling satellite pictures between two monitors in the embassy comm room.

Sorensen studied the God's-eye views, and was not surprised by their clarity. The CIA kept its best birds over the Middle East. She saw anchor lines angled off the bow of each ship. *Argos* was distinguishable by her uniquely situated deck crane, *Cirrus* by a pair of large lifeboats mounted astern.

"What about the third ship?"

"*Tasman Sea* is still moving. She's in the Persian Gulf, nearing the Straits of Hormuz."

"Can you give me a map that shows all three?"

Mike typed, the screen flickered, and soon a map was presented with Saudi Arabia at the center. The three data points were clearly marked. *Argos* was stationary off a remote section of the Saudi coast in the northern Red Sea. *Cirrus* lay in the Gulf of Aden, off the shores of Yemen near the Omani border. *Tasman Sea* was skirting the narrowest channel in the Persian Gulf, and a small vector arrow showed her heading.

"The two that are anchored," she said. "Can we tell if they're in international waters?"

In a decidedly untechnical maneuver, Mike pulled the swizzle stick from his coffee cup, set it over the scale on the electronic map, and used a fingertip to mark off twelve miles. He gauged the positions of the two anchored ships to the nearest coastline. "Looks like both are just outside the limit. You think that's important?"

Sorensen thought about it. "If it was only one of them, maybe not. But both having taken up identical positions, and at the same time . . . it's too much of a coincidence."

"Should we run it past the front office?" he asked, referring to Langley.

Sorensen pondered it. On appearances there was nothing damning, just two freighters that had thrown down anchor hundreds of miles apart. It was curious because they were owned by the same company. And unremarkable for the same reason. "Maybe their corporate controllers told them to lay up," she speculated. "I've heard that oil tankers often do it as a business strategy. They'll drop anchor outside a port to delay delivery if the owners think the price of crude is about to go up."

"Could be, I guess. But we don't know what they're carrying."

"No, not yet." Sorensen thought about it long and hard, then shook her head. "I can only play my director card so many times. This isn't enough—we need to keep watching."

"Okay, I'll stay on it."

Mike went back to his coffee, then began typing.

Sorensen moved toward the door, yet before she left the room she turned and looked at the screen one last time. From a more distant vantage point, the big picture on the map left a more unsettling impression. From where she stood, it looked very much like Saudi Arabia was being surrounded.

TWENTY-FIVE

Slaton's hands were going numb. He was wearing ski gloves, but after ten minutes of digging through snow and ice, enough frozen moisture had invaded the cuffs to leave the inner linings permeated.

He'd found what he wanted within minutes of beginning his search of the hill—a cavity in the snow the width of a one-euro coin. Slightly larger than the diameter of a fifty-cal round, but that broadening could be due to any number of factors. The bullet might have flattened after striking Romanov, and probably wobbled as its ballistic energy died. Or the increased diameter of the hole could indicate the snowpack had melted slightly, then refrozen overnight. Whatever the reason, Slaton was confident of one thing—the bullet that had struck Romanov lay very near the spot where he was digging on hands and knees.

He'd done his best to trace the hollow path, which ran on an acute angle along the slope of the mountain. In no time he cleared a five-foot-long trench. It was perfectly feasible that the round might have penetrated the frozen earth as well, but that would leave telltale marks of a different kind. He had to be getting close.

He glanced toward the ski lift, and noticed a pair of men staring up at him. They didn't look like police

officers, nor the ski patrol, and he pegged them as resort workers—perhaps lift operators or hotel clerks.

Slaton dug faster, his frozen fingers clawing through
the wet insulation of his gloves. He saw a glint of
metal and felt a surge of adrenaline, only to be disappointed when he recognized the shaft of a shattered
ski pole. He tossed it aside and kept going, ripping
away snow and ice until the tunnel intersected the
ground beneath.

He heard a shout from the bottom of the mountain.
A female police officer was waving him away. Slaton
heard an engine roar to life, and he saw a young man
in a ski patrol jacket astride a snowmobile.

He pulled off his gloves and tore into the soil with
his bare fingers. He discerned a spot where the dirt
looked freshly turned, and he clawed into the frozen
earth. He found it not by sight but by feel—something
smooth and hard and cylindrical. He wedged his fingers beneath and pried, trying to get a grip on something that definitely felt metallic. The snowmobile
began revving up the mountain.

Finally, the object in the dirt flipped free. Slaton
picked it up, hoping his guesswork had held together.
It was mostly covered in mud, but the when he wiped
one side clear it became shiny and sleek. Menacingly
thick. Surprisingly undamaged. It was like nothing
he'd ever seen. But it *was* what he was after—a spent
fifty-cal round.

Slaton pocketed his find, jumped to his feet, and
locked his skis into their bindings. The snowmobile
was a hundred meters away, closing fast. Leaving his
gloves on the snow behind him, he set off straight
downhill. Accelerating quickly, he began an arcing
turn toward the tree line to his right.

Over his shoulder he saw the snowmobile alter its

path, an attempt to cut him off. Yet the driver veered toward the middle of the hill—he was waiting for Slaton to shift in the opposite direction, the second half of an S-turn that would repeat to the bottom of the mountain. That turn never came.

Slaton flew headlong into the wooded glade. The world turned to a blur, foot-thick tree trunks flashing past left and right. One of his skis struck a snow-covered rock, and Slaton nearly lost control, but with windmilling arms he righted himself and kept going. He slalomed left and right, giving mature trees and saplings equal respect. He couldn't avert his eyes for an instant, cutting continuously left and right in a path that had likely never been taken. More importantly—one that even the most experienced snowmobile driver would never try to mirror. With his eyes riveted to the forest ahead, his only inkling of what was behind him came from sound. He tuned out the rhythmic swishes of snow and ice, and heard the snowmobile engine go to idle.

He was forced to slow where the slope steepened and boulders predominated. He planned each turn in a split second, and went airborne over a patch of ice. Three frenetic minutes later Slaton burst clear of the forest, ending on the road where he'd begun.

The Mercedes was parked somewhere uphill. He tore off his skis and bindings, threw them in the forest, and retrieved his hiking boots from his backpack. Knowing that some kind of response would already be organizing at the base of the mountain, he took off uphill on a dead run.

There was indeed a response, but it was slow in coming. The local police first trundled up to the mid-mountain crime scene, trying to determine if evidence had been corrupted by the stranger they'd seen. That question went largely unanswered, although they did discover one alteration to the slope: near a pair of wet ski gloves, a freshly dug trench in the snow.

Within the hour two inspectors from the national police arrived, a pair of men who'd been assigned to the case late yesterday. Their involvement had been ordered by the foreign ministry when it was realized that the shooting victim who'd gone careening down a Davos mountainside was a prominent foreign national.

On being informed that a stranger had been meddling at the scene, the pair from national quickly took charge and surveyed the area. They surmised correctly that the man had been trying to locate the unrecovered bullet from yesterday's murder. Whether or not he'd found it could only be speculated upon, but their thinking soon coalesced on one sensational possibility—that the individual seen digging might have been the shooter himself. A spirited search was launched of the adjacent glade, continuing until nightfall. The evidence recovered was minimal, but not inconsequential: two skis, two poles, two bindings, and two sets of fresh tire tracks on the nearby road—one led up the mountain, the other down.

The most useful detail, as it would turn out, was that the ski gear appeared to be new. The investigators considered that it might have been purchased recently, and, in a swift victory, they confirmed it had been sourced the previous day from the main outfitting store in Davos. It was here, however, just as momentum was rising, that the wheels fell off their investigative chariot. Not one, but two suspicious men, both fitting the general description of the stranger seen on the mountainside, had purchased nearly iden-tical sets of gear in the last two days. The inspectors presumed a bit too quickly that the pair had been working in concert to eliminate Romanov—indeed, the second man to visit the outfitters had admitted to the sales manager that he was an associate of the first.

The inspectors from national canvassed local ho-tels, asking every desk clerk, housekeeper, and pro-prietor if a room had recently been rented by a pair of young men. One might have been from Eastern Europe, the other perhaps Scandinavian. Getting nowhere, they scoured CCTV footage from across town, looking for two men plotting an assassination. The results were ambiguous at best.

In the weeks that followed the detectives from na-tional would gradually sort things out. They would revert to the basics of tire tracks, climbing gear, and eventually even identify the ledge high on the moun-tain where the shooter had perched to target the Rus-sian. Unfortunately, by the time they established that accurate big picture, other events would have oc-curred to render their progress moot.

Events that would unfold very soon, far from Davos. Events that would doom any chance of the police ever determining who had killed Alexei Romanov.

TWENTY-SIX

Slaton drove nonstop for two hours, happy to have had the foresight of keeping the Mercedes' gas tank full. When he finally pulled onto a gravel siding, he had a sharply angled overlook of Lugano, Switzerland, just north of the Italian border.

For the last hour he'd weighed how much longer to keep the rental Mercedes. He decided it would soon be linked to Davos, making it a poor option for crossing into Italy. His identity papers were almost certainly still clean—he'd paid cash at the rooming house and checked in under a throwaway name. He had also done his best to avoid cameras, and doubted any high-quality photographs were circulating, although these days one could never be sure.

The greatest uncertainty: How serious were the police about finding him?

He'd been seen nosing around a crime scene, and fled when confronted. Suspicious, but on its face no more than a minor offense. He supposed that, at the very least, it would make him the Swiss equivalent of a "person of interest" in the inquiry into Romanov's murder. The police would ask questions around Davos, but no nationwide hunt would be instigated for a man in a dark blue ski jacket.

Not yet.

The natural escape from Davos would have been north toward Zurich, with its people and airports and trains. By going south, Slaton knew he'd made an unexpected move. Yet that wasn't why he'd done it.

His ski jacket was resting on the passenger seat. Slaton pulled it closer and sank his hand into the left front pocket. He removed the spent round he'd recovered, snapped on the interior light, and inspected it closely for the first time. He'd seen many a fifty-cal round in his time, all the lethal variants: standard ball, tracer, armor piercing, and the ever-popular explosive incendiary. What he held now was none of those.

The projectile appeared extremely well machined, not a standard metal jacket but high-grade steel that had undergone minimal deformation after passing through a rifle barrel, half a mile of air, one human, six feet of snow, and a final deceleration through ten inches of Alpine mud. Yet there was one distinct aberration in the finely manufactured projectile—the tip had been completely crushed, and beneath the remnants of its thinly capped nose he saw something other than burnished metal: a tiny wafer, now mangled, that shone almost mirror-like in the reflection of the SUV's dome light.

Slaton sat mystified.

After a long period of thoughtful silence, he returned the spent bullet to his jacket pocket. From another he retrieved the phone the CIA had given him. He turned it on and placed a call.

"There you are," Sorensen said, picking up immediately.

"I'll assume that's only a turn of phrase and that you don't have my position nailed down right now," Slaton replied.

"I'm not trying to find you, but apparently others are. We got word that the police in Davos are looking for a guy who was seen tampering with their crime scene today. They say he was on the tall side, and a very good skier. They suspect he's one of the two men responsible for killing Romanov."

"Two men? That's what they think?"

"It's a theory."

"So is Castro ordering the hit on JFK." Slaton noted a slight intermission between their exchanges, an oddly comforting sign that told him the call was encrypted. "Did you learn anything else?" he asked.

"The police interviewed Ovechkin. As soon as they ran out of questions, he bolted from town."

"Any idea where he went?"

"No, but I'd say he's running scared."

"Can't say that I blame him. With his two business partners dead, he's the last man standing."

"It causes me to wonder what's in the articles of incorporation of MIR Enterprises. His ownership stake might have gone up two hundred percent in the last week."

"You think Ovechkin is behind these shootings?"

"It has to be considered."

Slaton thought about it. There was a certain interdependency among Russia's kleptocratic elite, but they were also a cutthroat lot. He remembered how Anton Bloch, the former Mossad director, had once characterized the breed: *They exist like crabs adrift in the ocean on a plank of wood. In heavy seas some are invariably swept away, a few perhaps with a nudge.* "It's possible," he said. "But I'd still give odds that Ovechkin is getting fitted for body armor right now. And as for those articles of incorporation, good luck tracking them down."

"Obscured ownership?"

"You'll find more shells around MIR than in the Red Sea. Speaking of which, are you still tracking those freighters?"

"We've got a bead on all three. *Cirrus* and *Argos* have both anchored, one off the Saudi coastline and the other in the Gulf of Aden, near the Yemen-Oman border. Both are just outside the twelve-mile limit."

"Any idea what they're doing?"

"As far as we can tell, just sitting there. We did get some message traffic—it was captured by one of our missile cruisers near the Gulf of Aden. Apparently *Cirrus* reported on VHF that they were having minor technical problems."

Slaton didn't reply right away.

"I know," she said, "it sounds suspicious that both would break down at the same time."

"It sounds impossible. What about your third boat?"

"*Tasman Sea* is moving through the Straits of Hormuz as we speak."

"Same bad neighborhood," Slaton remarked. "So what do you think the chances are that *Tasman Sea* will anchor for a technical stop somewhere in the southern Persian Gulf tonight?"

"Pretty high. We're going to watch them all closely. What about you—other than stirring up a hornet's nest at the scene of the crime, have you made any headway?"

Slaton eyed his jacket. "Maybe. I've got some research to do."

"Research?"

"I'll explain when I know more. In the meantime, I think it's important to find out where Ovechkin has gone."

"That may not be easy."

"I'm sure your agency is up to it."

"I don't have an agency behind me—not yet, anyway. I'm still on a manpower budget . . . but I'll see what I can do."

"Are you at the embassy?"

"I am."

"How's my family?"

"They're great. Want to talk to them? They're just down the hall."

Slaton did, and for the next twenty minutes he suffered not a single thought about dead oligarchs or suspicious freighters. Christine and Davy lifted his spirits, and he assured them he'd be home soon. Only after he ended the call did it occur to him how obscure that concept was. Where *was* their home at that moment? A guest suite in the United States embassy in Rome? A docked sailboat in Amalfi?

No, he realized. It had nothing to do with cities or residences. *It's wherever my wife and son are.*

He turned the phone off, cranked the Mercedes to life, and pulled out into thin traffic. It was time to advance his primary reason for turning south from Davos. It was time to visit an old friend in Milan.

TWENTY-SEVEN

The number of assassins on earth whose reputations were in Slaton's league could be counted on one hand. Every one of them would tell you unreservedly that Pietro Vittorio, whose field of expertise was very much affiliated, was a man without peer.

He had been born on the island of Sardinia, the product of a man with good hands and a sharp eye, and a woman for whom food was a religion. The elder Vittorio ran a small tool and die shop, making pipes until the start of World War II, then gun barrels during and after—during because the fascists had demanded it, and after because rifle barrels proved far more profitable than threaded pipe.

Signori Vittorio's talents with lathes and grinders were reflected clearly in his only son. Young Pietro skipped school in the seventies to learn how to drill, and skipped marriage in the eighties to build the business his aging father had begun. In the early nineties he finally married, a guileless woman who knew nothing about guns but everything about authentic Sardinian cooking. It was then, with his belly full and his clientele growing, that Pietro Vittorio's comfortable life had come undone.

His troubles began when he signed a minor contract

with a Serbian militia at the outset of what would become an ugly war in the Balkans. Vittorio's contribution was a mere handful of modified, high-end sniper rifles that proved devastatingly effective. From a financial standpoint the venture was but a minor supplement to his established accounts, no more than a few dozen highly accurate guns. As a business strategy it was a disaster.

The Balkan War played out in all its viciousness. Truces were declared, breached, then awkwardly reinstated. The world watched from a distance, and with more than its customary revulsion. When the Adriatic dust settled and details emerged, the world stood aghast. From soft chairs in the Hague, lawyers of the United Nations did their best to catalogue war crimes and bring charges to bear. Among the least egregious, but most provable, offenses involved a registered arms contract between a certain Sardinian gunsmith and a ruthless Serbian strongman.

As the lawyers of the International Criminal Court began to debate matters of temporal and personal jurisdiction, the Italian government decided to take the lead in soothing the collective conscience. They instigated their own proceedings against anyone who could be proved to have aided and abetted the worst of the Balkan criminals. Among the first to fall under their magnifying glass: a boutique armorer from a tiny village in Sardinia.

Vittorio claimed, in a classic armorer's defense, that he could have no way of knowing that the end users of his weapons were targeting schools and churches. He tried to distance himself, claiming he was no more than a simple gunsmith. It was all to no avail—he, or more accurately his business, was among the first sacrifices. While not held criminally responsible, his license to manufacture arms in Italy was permanently revoked. So stung, a bitter Vittorio sold his building and most of his machinery and let go six employees. To make his exile complete, his good wife, shamed by her husband's illicit dealings, left him and went back to cooking for her mother.

With no small amount of bitterness, Vittorio packed up a few of his best machines and moved to Milan, a location that was both central to Europe and far removed from his troubles. There he set up a one-man shop and embarked upon a new business plan: His license to sell guns commercially had been revoked, but he was not banned from working with private parties. Over time his reputation quietly grew, and his client list became thick with shadowed men and women who sought the very best—and who, more importantly, never quibbled over price.

Within five years he was doing modifications for Delta Force, the SAS, and a handful of lesser-known but equally lethal operators. Among them: a certain Mossad assassin who was destined for legend. To these select individuals, Pietro Vittorio was known not by his given name, but simply by his trade.

He was *l'Armaiolo*.

The Armorer.

Slaton had ditched the Mercedes on a residential street in Lugano, reasoning that it looked perfectly at home amid the rows of well-kept hillside residences overlooking the lake and a brooding Monte San Salvatore. He crossed into Italy by train, his passport never challenged, and reached Milan by mid-afternoon.

There he wasted no time. Not wanting to use his

CIA-issued phone, nor compromise the handset pair he shared with Christine, he took the time to purchase a new throwaway device. As he activated the burner, Slaton wondered what nuances of electronic tradecraft might now escape him. Communications intelligence was a fast-moving discipline, and he'd spent most of the last year at sea. Were burners still secure for one-time use? Could he use it more than once to call the same number? Should he limit his call to a set amount of time? It was all of course unanswerable, and he felt a distinct unease at having been away from the game for so long.

Slaton departed the Milano Centrale station toward Porta Nuova, Milan's primary business district. There the streets were clean and busy, lined with modernist facades representing a virtual who's who of global commerce. As he walked, Slaton was reminded of yesterday's climb—his legs felt as though he'd spent the entire day doing lunges at a gym. He knew he was in good shape, aided by the occasional masonry job, yet if life at sea had its charms, it also ruined the pursuit of any serious training regimen. Slaton decided that once this affair was behind him, it would be time for a serious self-appraisal: fitness, marksmanship, Krav Maga. Knowledge of the latest technologies. He could permit no weaknesses.

He addressed the burner phone, dialing as he walked. There were roughly ten phone numbers in the world Slaton had committed to memory. The Armorer's was one of them.

Vittorio answered on the second ring, his Sardinian accent, with its core resonance of Latin, clear on every word.

"*Ciao*," Slaton said, keeping with Italian. "It's your friend from Stockholm."

A pause, then, "It's been some time."

"Three years, but who keeps track? I have need of your expertise."

"But of course."

"Are you available this evening?" Slaton asked.

"Certainly. I am in the middle of a project, but the deadline is well off. Come around seven."

"All right. Are you still at the same address?"

"I am. However, if this is only a consultation . . . perhaps we might meet for dinner."

Slaton weighed this proposal on two levels. Vittorio was inquiring if Slaton would be carrying a rifle to be modified. If so, fine dining was hardly an option. He also knew the armorer's wife had abandoned him, and that he desperately missed her cooking. "I have something to show you," Slaton said, "but nothing to draw attention."

"Good. Do you know Risoelatte?"

"No, but I'll find it."

"It is long one of my favorites. They have discreet tables, and the waiters are among the slowest in Milan."

Slaton could not suppress a grin. "Seven it is."

TWENTY-EIGHT

Risoelatte was situated in the center of town, south of Parco Sempione and easily accessible by the Cairoli metro station. Slaton arrived early enough to circle the block once. He had no specific reason to suspect a threat, but his guard had been high since stepping off *Windsom* in Amalfi.

More concerning than anything on the streets was what he saw on entering the establishment. The restaurant was a multilevel affair, three floors connected by a haphazard series of stairs sided by hip-high wrought-iron rails. The waitstaff, enduring a floor plan that could never have been designed with a restaurant in mind, shuttled up and down the precarious staircases, and hesitated wisely at blind corners with full trays of food. *Now I know why they're slow,* he mused. From a security standpoint the place was nothing less than a trap. There were too many physical obstacles, too few exits, and the haphazard seating layout seemed a recipe for innocent casualties. But then, few customers would view the restaurant's layout with such admittedly black optics.

In truth, Slaton saw why the place had so captured Vittorio. The blinding array of colorful chairs and tablecloths might have been taken from kitchens across

Italy, and probably had been, via estate sales and secondhand stores. Risoelatte, in all its charm and frills and soothing textures, was a lonely man's vision of home and hearth.

Slaton found Vittorio seated at a table for two. On top of the table were flowers and a candle, all of it framed by a window dressed in curtains with a blue and white checkered pattern. He was a small man with thick dark hair going gray at the sides. High cheekbones were split by a prominent nose, the kind of features that projected a degree of character in an aging face—an aspect of worldliness and experience that in Vittorio's case was not unearned.

They shook hands warmly, and Slaton took a seat across from the armorer.

Theirs was an established professional relationship, yet without the pretenses that might be expected of bankers or salesmen. There was no mention of shared acquaintances, which they certainly possessed, and neither man asked if business was good for obvious reasons. A basket of bread and a plate of fruit were already on the table, politely untouched. Vittorio asked for a bottle of wine and two glasses, and flinched only slightly when Slaton ordered tap water as well.

"Three and a half years," Vittorio said. "I checked my records."

"Then you must be right."

"You look very fit. Life has been treating you well."

"More or less." Slaton nearly added something about marriage agreeing with him, but recognized the pitfall. "I'm effectively retired."

Vittorio raised one eyebrow before reaching for the bread. "A man of leisure? Now there is something to which I can aspire."

"You enjoy your work too much to give it up."

The Sardinian cracked a roll and dipped it into a plate of oil. With a shrug, he said, "Yes, I do see your point. My end of things is rather more sustainable."

The waiter came with the wine, then presented the daily specials. They agreed to share a plate of salmon tartare, after which Slaton selected wholemeal pasta, Vittorio veal with asparagus. The waiter whisked up a half staircase and disappeared. Still, the two men at table twelve did not immerse themselves in business. They instead succumbed to the time-honored flow of Italy: the natural progressions of food and conversation.

Slaton explained that he'd been away from Europe for some time, and gave an enthusiastic account of cruising the world's oceans. Vittorio countered with vigor, updating him on the two mainstays of all Italian debate: politics and soccer. Slaton chased tiny meatballs around his plate and found that he was enjoying himself. As happy as he was with his family on *Windsom*, the isolation of living at sea, together with their self-imposed communications blackout, was a departure from social norms.

The meal was exquisite, and only at the end, with a well-constructed tiramisu in front of him, did Vittorio take the final turn. "So tell me what has brought us together."

"I'm doing a bit of detective work for a friend. I recovered a spent round that's got me mystified. It's not like anything I've seen, and I'd like your opinion."

"What caliber?"

"Fifty, most likely, but possibly twelve-seven." The latter referred to the Russian fifty-cal equivalent, a 12.7mm round. The Russian round packed punch, but was primarily intended for anti-materiel use—

employed not on people, but rather against helicopters and big-block truck engines.

Vittorio was clearly intrigued. "I will help if I can."

Slaton took his napkin from his lap and reached into a pocket. He wrapped the spent round in the soft cloth and pushed it across the table. He watched the armorer closely.

Vittorio uncovered the round but left it bedded in the half-folded napkin. His eyes went narrow, and he reached into his jacket for a pair of readers. Balancing them on his long nose, he dragged the round into better light. He looked up once at Slaton. Then a second time. He said nothing for a full five minutes, his craftsman's hands turning the bullet as a jeweler would a rare gem.

"Do you know what it is?" Slaton finally asked.

Vittorio hesitated mightily. "It's very unusual. Not like any fifty I have ever seen."

"But?" Slaton prodded.

Vittorio folded the napkin to cover the round. "I would like to take a closer look, perhaps make some inquiries. Is this something that might be considered evidence by the police?"

"If it were in their possession . . . yes."

Another look. "Then I should be discreet in my inquiries."

"That *would* be best."

"Can you tell me anything about the circumstances of how it was employed?"

Slaton had been expecting the question. "I can and will. But I don't want to color your evaluation. Once you've had a good look, I'll explain the rest."

Vittorio seemed to understand. "Very well. To study it properly, I would have to take it to my shop."

Slaton nodded in agreement.

"Let us meet again . . . say noon tomorrow?"

"Done. Can I ask what you're going to do?"

"I will begin by trying to determine the metallurgy. That might narrow down the manufacturer, or at least the country of origin. I also have a good customer who is a dentist."

"A dentist?"

"The man is an avid hunter, big game. I've done a fair amount of work for him. As it happens, he keeps an advanced X-ray machine in his office and lets me use it on occasion."

Vittorio discreetly pocketed the round, then attacked his tiramisu with vigor.

Slaton sipped coffee, and at the end he reached for the check. When Vittorio protested, he gave the armorer an explanation that was in equal measure satisfying and informational.

"Don't worry, our meal will be expensed to the United States of America."

"In that case," the armorer said with a thin smile, "perhaps a touch of amaretto would be in order . . ."

TWENTY-NINE

Captain Zakaryan woke at two that morning to take in the proceedings. While he was not directly involved, Ivan had been forced to tell him the schedule since Zakaryan was the one who would issue orders to the crew: an unloading operation was to take place in the small hours of that morning, essential personnel only, under cover of darkness.

Given the circumstances, Zakaryan wanted to be present. The unloading of a freighter at sea, he knew, was a delicate undertaking, and for that reason exceedingly uncommon. To begin, the weather had to cooperate, and here, at least, fortune was on their side. The Red Sea air was still and warm, and a scimitar moon gave a bit of illumination to the proceedings. The greater problem, and the reason that open water transfers were a highly irregular maneuver, was the matter of placing two ships in close proximity to one another.

Standing on the bridge shortly before 3 a.m., Zakaryan made his case to Ivan. "It is exceedingly dangerous for ships of *Argos*' class to rendezvous at sea. If at any time I feel the safety of my vessel is compromised, I *will* intervene."

The Russian glanced at him dismissively. "There

is no need to worry, Captain. The risks you envision will not come to pass."

Ivan was proved correct ten minutes later. Not one, but three boats appeared on the radar screen, and soon after materialized on the murky marine horizon. The largest was no more than fifty feet long, on appearances a light fishing trawler. The other two were no more than large dhows, open-deck merchant boats with both a mast and an engine—the kind of coastal traders that were endemic to the region. In the lightest of breezes, and in single-file formation, the little fleet pulled near *Argos*' leeward port side like remoras to a shark.

Zakaryan watched intently as the trawler came in tight, tied on, and took the first load. The two smaller boats idled in wait fifty yards seaward. *Argos*' deck crane was run by his best man, a wiry Indonesian who could move crates with a deftness to rival any symphony conductor. Three men on the trawler's deck guided the crate the final few feet, muscling it into place and lashing it down. Over the next thirty minutes, seven more loads were lowered over *Argos*' port rail. The dhows proved a quicker operation, each having deck space for only two crates. Within an hour, all three receiving boats were under way, fast blending into the black horizon. None displayed navigation lights, and as they faded from sight the captain referenced the radar. He watched three unmarked blips diverge on separate courses toward the Saudi coast.

Zakaryan descended a ladder to the main deck, and walked amidships. At the lip of the cargo hold he looked down. An even dozen crates remained. He didn't know precisely what was in them, but he harbored few illusions. *Argos* was hauling some manner of military hardware, and now, under his watch, she had injected it into a highly unstable part of the world. He tried to imagine the number of laws and regulations they were violating, but was quickly over-whelmed. Then again, having come this far did instill a certain sense of commitment going forward. What was it the British said? *In for a penny, in for a pound.*

Zakaryan noted a presence behind him. He didn't have to turn to know who it was.

"What now?" he asked.

"Now," Ivan said, "we pull anchor and sail south."

Zakaryan felt like a getaway driver leaving the scene of a crime. Which, in essence, he very much was. "Speed?"

"We are still in no hurry, Captain. But I can tell you one bit of good news . . . rest assured, you and I will soon part ways."

The satellite trained on *Argos* did its job admirably. It was called USA-245, a curiously opaque name for a device whose every facet of design was intended for clarity. The primary mirror was nearly two and a half meters wide, not coincidentally the same diameter as the mirror in the Hubble telescope, the essential dif-ference being the direction in which it was trained—not toward the heavens, but instead at one of the most embattled regions on earth. It was established in an elliptical polar orbit as part of a tightly managed constellation, and once each day USA-245 passed over the Red Sea where it recorded, and instantaneously relayed, highly accurate visual and infrared images.

These files were downloaded initially to the Na-tional Reconnaissance Office. NRO analysts screened the results first for quality assurance, and then ran the raw images through an initial digital enhancement. At that point, they routed the data through well-established channels to various agency departments and desks. Before any detailed analysis took place, interesting first-look footage was shared with sister intelligence agencies—in this case, a section at Langley who'd made a specific request for coverage of the coastal waters around Saudi Arabia. Specialists there quickly sorted through hundreds of images, and extracted a handful that fit certain narrow criteria. These were forwarded by a secure link to the Rome station.

Which was how, over her morning coffee, Anna Sorensen was flicking back and forth through images that had been captured only hours earlier from roughly two hundred miles above the Saudi Peninsula.

She had never been an imagery analyst, but one hardly needed to be to see *Argos* surrounded by three small boats. Successive photos showed the ship's deck crane extracting crates from her main hold and depositing them onto the smaller boats. Orbital mechanics being what they were, USA-245 did not capture the entire dubious show. Sorensen knew that other birds might eventually fill in the blanks—most pertinently, where the smaller boats had gone after taking on their loads. They would also likely confirm what was a near certainty—that *Tasman Sea* and *Cirrus* were engaged in similar mischief along other shores in the region.

With hard evidence finally in hand, Sorensen decided it was time to push things up the chain. She refilled her coffee cup from a distressed break-room machine, and set out toward the embassy communi-

cations room rehearsing her impending call to headquarters.

What Sorensen could not know at that moment
was that USA-245 was not the only satellite to have
recorded the festivities. Twenty minutes behind, and
in a marginally different orbital path, was the Israeli
satellite known as Ofeq-11. Its sensor suites and communications platform had a number of technical differences from the NRO bird, and Ofeq-11 did not
have the luxury of being backed up by overlapping
coverage. What was very much the same, however,
was the grim aura of concern its data stirred in headquarters buildings around Tel Aviv.

The unrest began at the Ministry of Defense, which
operated Ofeq-11. With little delay, news of a men-
acing incident in the Red Sea reached Mossad headquarters at Glilot Junction. There, lights in executive
suites began flicking on in the very small hours of the
morning.

THIRTY

Zhukov woke at first light, shortly before the alarm on his phone was set to go off. Sun streamed through the window of the trailer on the edge of the RosAvia complex. It was where the entire corporate contingent lived, a tiny prefabricated neighborhood that had been wheeled in behind trucks, along with two community trailers—one serving as a dining hall, the other a makeshift recreation room. There were thirteen employees in all, aside from Tikhonov, the minimum number of mechanics and technicians necessary to keep a small fleet of ancient MiGs and their attendant equipment running.

Zhukov found Tikhonov, all too predictably, in the dining trailer behind a massive plate of eggs, sausage, and bread. A half dozen team members were seated at nearby tables, but there was little interaction at such an early hour.

Spoiled by recent stays in five-star hotels, in both Casablanca and Moscow, Zhukov viewed the cafeteria-grade offerings—which he would have been delighted with as a lieutenant—as thoroughly unappetizing. He went to a pot on a burner and filled a Styrofoam cup with something black and bitter-scented that might have been coffee. He slid into a bench seat across from Tikhonov.

"We should go into town tonight," the engineer said through a full mouth.

Zhukov stared, amused that Tikhonov had the gastronomic resolve to plot dinner while gorging himself at breakfast. He had, however, anticipated the suggestion. It had actually become something of a ritual—on each of Zhukov's previous visits, he'd taken Tikhonov into Ouarzazate for dinner at the only viable restaurant in town. The place served a decent mutton with apricots, and reasonably good local wine—all of which escaped Tikhonov, who invariably gorged himself silly on the heaviest special available and swilled wine like it was water. On their last outing Zhukov had needed help getting his tablemate in the car when they left. This, at least, was familiar ground for the colonel. No Russian army officer could run a unit effectively without the core skill of managing stumbling drunks. Indeed, without it, there would be no Russian army.

"Yes, by all means," he said, "dinner tonight on RosAvia. Now—tell me about the schedule."

"Ach, the schedule again. All is going according to plan."

"This afternoon's flight?"

Tikhonov tapped his wristwatch. "Two o'clock."

"What are the proving points?"

"Test points," the engineer corrected. "Today we will expand the flight envelope to assure controllability at maximum speed."

This drew Zhukov's interest. "I read that the MiG-21 can fly at twice the speed of sound."

Tikhonov laughed out loud, a rich bellow that

echoed through the pre-fab building. "Mach 2? Hardly. That is what books will tell you, but these old crates of ours would disintegrate at that speed. One point three, perhaps one-four in a dive."

"That's still fast."

"Fast enough to meet the project specifications."

"What about the infrared?"

"We've been bench-testing the pod every day, and have undertaken two successful flights using the chase aircraft as a target."

"So the system is working?"

"The results are nominal, no aberrations noted. Which is only to be expected—all the hardware we are using is proven, taken from other airframes. That was an integral part of my proposal from the beginning, to use off-the-shelf technology. If we tried to modify these airframes from a clean sheet of paper, make them do what we want—it would have taken years. The live-fire exercise will be key. I expect it to fully validate our baseline data."

"And when will that be?"

"Barring any setbacks, the day after tomorrow."

"You've cut the timeline close."

"I don't know why this timeline of yours is so important, but I have done all I can with the resources available. You can't imagine the technical obstacles that have arisen. The first target drone arrived a month ago, but the air force idiots who shipped it neglected to include the software package. It's like sending a car without the keys."

Zhukov suppressed a twinge of anger. As a career military officer he was not used to those lower in rank speaking their minds. He reminded himself, not for the first time, that dealing with civilians was different.

"But now everything is ready."

"Of course," Tikhonov said, stuffing half a sausage into his mouth. "Two o'clock this afternoon. Now, be a good colonel and go get me some more coffee."

Zhukov stiffened, but before he could lash out the big man broke into a fit of laughter. Tikhonov flapped his hand in the air dismissively, then got up and went for his own coffee. Having had enough of his lead engineer's antics, Zhukov got up and went outside.

He walked into the new morning. The air was cool, the high desert at the bottom of its daily thirty-degree temperature swing. He veered away from the Ros-Avia complex and ended on a hill near a stand of brush. His eyes panned across the distant mountains, and once again he was struck by the divergence of his surroundings in recent days. Most unnerving of all: his uneasy visit to the Kremlin.

He was increasingly troubled by the path Petrov was carving. Like everyone in the military, Zhukov had watched with detachment over the years as the president shaped a new Russia. He'd begun with a core of former KGB associates from St. Petersburg, the so-called *siloviki*, then branched out to absorb elements of the mafia and a handful of political elites. From that base, and as the sole arbiter of the nation's wealth, he had generated over a hundred new billionaires. The lucky winners were chosen exclusively by Petrov, a process guided by one attribute—complete and absolute loyalty.

In return for that, the oligarchs were granted wide latitude in their operations. Factories, gas fields, and mines fell virtually unregulated. The plundered wealth flowed freely, unhindered by accounting principles or reporting guidelines. Whatever rule of law remained fell to little more than nostalgia for Russia's chosen few.

Yet that abandonment of order was not without consequences. The kleptocrats invariably moved their money to Zurich and their families to London, ill-disguised insurance against any fall from the Kremlin's good graces. They'd all seen it happen before. The warning signs came first in the form of visa bans and travel restrictions. Those who didn't fall back in line suffered asset clawbacks and disappearing accounts. Trumped-up charges were the final red flag, civil or criminal depending on whose toes had been trod upon and how heavily. At that point, the smart ran west. The unfortunate few who ignored the pattern ended up with one of three fates: work camps, psychiatric institutions, or in the most egregious cases, outright assassination. Czar Petrov, flanked by his princes of the moment, recognized but one law—that of absolute power.

From his relatively comfortable existence as an army officer, Zhukov had long viewed the regime as most Russians did—an undeniably corrupt bunch, but one that had reignited a long-lost nationalist fervor. For a time there had been collective patience, a belief in the oft-repeated promises that the tide so obviously lifting the oligarchs into the stratosphere would eventually bring along the rest. Yet the drumbeat of new Russian greatness had clearly lost its cadence, faltering under food shortages, deficient medical care, and pension cuts. Further rounds of "reallocation" ran their course, and still Russia waited as the wealth gap between rich and poor became the highest of any developed nation on earth. Now the one-legged economy was teetering as energy prices fell. Unrest was on the rise.

And there, Zhukov knew, was where he had come into the picture. Petrov had turned to the last untapped resource in Russia, a card that had long been in his hand but one he'd never had the nerve to play. Now the president had taken that course, and with schemes that were nothing short of audacious.

Crimea was annexed boldly, and no sooner had the Russian standard been raised over Sebastopol than the president's gang of elites pounced, setting upon her valuable Black Sea ports like jackals to a warm carcass. Spurred on by a surprisingly muddled Western response, Ukraine was next, little green men flooding across the border to "advise" local rebels— and more importantly, to seize and reallocate vital energy infrastructure. When Russia's air force was leveraged to further unbalance Syria, the president's cronies were in tight formation with its squadrons of fighter-bombers. They contracted to expand the port facilities of Tartus with outrageous kickbacks, and went to the head of the queue for new oil and mineral leases.

A wistful Zhukov turned away from the jagged mountains. The Russian military—*his* military, the once proud and brave protectors of the Motherland— had fallen to little more than a global thug squad for the ruling kleptocracy. A state-sponsored protection racket. He knew he should have felt bitterness at the degradation of his calling. Could the heroes of Stalingrad, and their brothers who'd overrun Berlin, ever have imagined such manipulation? Regiments of soldiers acting like spies. Avarice usurping honor.

Zhukov turned and set out toward RosAvia's little trailer park. As he did so, he yielded to that most Russian of reactions: resignation. Driven by Petrov's thirst for power, the appropriation of Russia's military was running headlong into unknown territory. A train that one army colonel could never stop.

That being the case . . . *Who am I to turn down the chance of heading up a rail line? Perhaps I'll even be good at it.*

THIRTY-ONE

Slaton spent the night in small hotel on the east side of Milan, an address that was chic and restful, and likely tested the limits of his CIA credit card. He enjoyed a leisurely breakfast under a patio awning, and later spent thirty minutes on the phone with Christine. Ten more he spent watching a video stream of Davy doing somersaults in the embassy's grassy courtyard. It was the longest he'd been away from either of them for months.

At half past eleven he set out for the modest shop in the Brera District where Vittorio both lived and worked. Slaton began with an excursion along Via Montenapoleone. There he saw the designs of Versace and Gucci displayed in windows along the street, and those of Ferrari and Lamborghini cruising between them. It was haughty and ostentatious, and no different from a dozen other streets in a dozen other cities where the beautiful people ran. Not so long ago Slaton had himself been a billionaire, the accidental consequence of a Mossad mission that had imploded to his benefit. At the time that wealth had seemed as empty as it was unearned, and he'd had neither the time nor inclination for spontaneous consumption.

That being the case, when the money evaporated as easily as it had come, he felt not a trace of remorse.

On arriving in Brera he diverted into the municipal park and performed a rudimentary countersurveillance scheme, made easy by rows of hedges and intricate walking paths. He still had no specific cause to be on edge, but old habits were old habits for a reason.

Having been to Vittorio's shop twice before, he was familiar with the address, and he made one loop around the building upon arriving. Slaton knocked on the door two seconds before noon. No one appreciated precision like a gunsmith.

Vittorio opened the door promptly, probably having had the reverse thought. The two shook hands, and the armorer led Slaton down from the first floor living quarters into the basement where he ran his shop. Nothing had changed. It was a small and cramped workspace, a makeshift office in front and a machine shop behind, the two divided by a cheap bamboo partition. The smell of machine oil weighed on the air.

"It pains me to remind you," said Vittorio, taking a seat behind his desk, "but I must ask for your complete discretion in anything we discuss. I have recently been reissued a limited license to modify arms, but the carabinieri have been dogging me lately. I show them antique weapons I've brought gloriously back to life, and they accuse me of using hacksaws to saw off shotguns for the underworld down south."

"Do you?"

"Certainly not. A die grinder with a diamond cut-off disc gives a far superior product."

Slaton grinned as he took a seat across the desk.

Vittorio began by reaching into a drawer and removing the round in question. It was wrapped in a fresh piece of oilcloth. He set it on the table between them, exposed the bullet, and adjusted a trainable work light. "First I should thank you—you have tested me. It's good to find a challenge now and again."

"And did you come up with an answer?"

"I will let you be the judge." Vittorio pointed to the bullet. "The jacket is unlike anything I've seen. I could not specifically identify the material—it shows signatures of an advanced alloy, but also retains characteristics of a composite. It appears perfectly machined, but keeps an unusual degree of pliability. I also noted three slightly altered belts that circle the round's midsection."

Slaton looked more closely, and he did see three barely discernible rings. "What would those be for?"

Vittorio raised a pointed finger to tell Slaton his question had to wait. "Also," he picked up, "we must consider the damaged tip. Beneath this crushed composite is a reflective wafer which could have few possible utilities. And as I mentioned yesterday, I thought it might be useful to have a look inside."

The armorer opened the same drawer and removed a printout of an X-ray image. *From a dentist's office,* Slaton mused. Vittorio placed the evidence between them.

In the ghosted picture Slaton saw electrical circuitry, and, at perfect intervals along the longitudinal axis, what looked like dense ribs of metal. A bright circle near the shank of the round got his attention. "What's that?" he asked.

Looking pleased, Vittorio leaned back in his chair. "That, if I am not mistaken, is a battery."

Slaton stared at the armorer. Vittorio only stared back in silence, allowing him to work it all out.

"Are you saying what I think you're saying?" Slaton asked.

"Don't tell me you haven't had your own suspicions. The battery, optics of some kind, the dense masses around the waist. This is something that I fear might put you out of business, my friend. What you have here is a steerable bullet."

CIA director Thomas Coltrane sat in his office wearing gym attire. Even so clothed, he cut an undeniably dapper figure. He worked out nearly every morning in the headquarters gym, and the regulars there knew better than to interrupt him as he went through his paces—thirty minutes of free weights, followed by cardio. It kept him trim and fit. What few in the building realized, however, was that it was less a matter of self-improvement than an outlet for the stress of his position. Proving the point this morning, and as typically happened at least once a week, events had cut his workout short.

He used his fingers to comb back damp and mussed silver hair as he stared at two messages on his desk. Both were marked urgent, were highly classified, and had been delivered in tandem as he was loading a squat rack. Now in private, he looked at them in disbelief, not so much for what either contained, but simply because they had arrived in such serendipitous unison. One was an internal flash message, sourced from a recently promoted department head whom he knew quite well—Anna Sorensen. She was in Rome, delving into the matter of a recently assassinated Russian oligarch. That very fact—that she'd gone to Rome to pursue a lead he'd already told her wasn't worth chasing—struck Coltrane on two fronts. He was pissed she hadn't taken his advice. He was also impressed by her initiative.

As it turned out, the second message implied she'd been right. An urgent dispatch from the Israeli ambassador to the United States had been forwarded through the State Department. In spite of that circuitous routing, the Israeli version was nearly identical in content to Sorensen's report.

Coltrane picked up the messages, one in each hand, and read them carefully a second time, trying to discern any differences. There were few. Last night, the two intelligence services had independently, and nearly simultaneously, detected an offload from a freighter in the northern Red Sea. Three small boats had taken on crates and run fast ashore to ports along the Saudi coast. Sorensen's version suggested that two other freighters, one in the Gulf of Aden and another in the Persian Gulf, were undertaking parallel operations.

Having seen Sorensen in action, Coltrane knew she was competent. More to the point, he had to admit that her instincts, which he'd discounted only days ago, had proved dead on. Right then the director made his first decision. Anna Sorensen would take the lead on this. His second choice proved more problematic. Israel was already involved, with an apparent threat on their regional doorstep—something they never took lightly. Against that, Saudi Arabia, Yemen, Jordan, or even the Gulf Arab states could also be facing some degree of risk. From such a combustible cast of characters, who should he share the information with?

His problem was mitigated by a quick analysis of the evidence. Odds were, the cargo was nothing more than small arms, or possibly explosives. Of course, other possibilities had to be considered. The worst case was always some manner of WMD. Could the crates contain the precursors of chemical weapons, a makeshift laboratory for biological agents? Even nuclear material? Coltrane thought it unlikely. The sheer quantity of material involved, along with the fact that it was being dispersed to different geographic points, shouted that they were looking at conventional weapons. Even so, it *was* quite an arsenal.

"Enough to start a small war," Coltrane thought aloud in the confines of his office.

He touched a button to call his deputy into the office, thinking a strategy session was in order. As he did, Coltrane had no idea how prescient his mumblings would prove.

THIRTY-TWO

"Something like this," said Vittorio, with perhaps the trace of a smile, "it might even make me obsolete."

Slaton sat motionless, the armorer's words resounding in his head ... *a steerable bullet.* He'd heard rumblings of it for years, and knew the idea had been experimented with. Now, with the results on the desk in front of him, concept leapt to reality.

"Is it U.S. or Russian?" he asked, knowing these were the most likely suspects to take the lead on such technology.

"In a sense, both," the armorer hedged.

"Both?"

"I took precise measurements, and this is definitely a fifty-caliber round. I'd say it was fired from a Barrett, which of course is an American gun. But it might not be so simple. The bullet exhibits certain signatures—the curvature of the shank and milling characteristics—that lead me to believe it was of Russian manufacture."

"So where does that leave us?"

"Here, I think, is where you might provide the remaining answers. Now that we know *what* it is, please tell me the circumstances of the engagement."

Slaton did. He began by telling Vittorio about the

first shot that had presumably been taken from extreme range, and in which the bullet couldn't be recovered. "The target was three miles from shore on a very windy night, and he was standing on a boat that would have been rocking on heavy seas. A guided round makes sense. It makes the scenario realistic." He then explained how he'd come across the spent round on the desk in front of them. Without mentioning Davos specifically, he covered a ski slope and a high ledge—a more manageable shot in terms of range, but taken against a fast-moving target. He also told Vittorio about the young man who'd visited the only outfitter in town.

After a reflective pause, Vittorio said, "Going back to your question, then—I would say your shooter is Russian, most likely Special Forces, but certainly a trained marksman. He probably used a Barrett. I can't tell you why the Russians designed this round for a fifty caliber as opposed to their twelve point seven millimeter standard."

"Maybe they stole the engineering diagrams and didn't want to change anything. This weapon was always going to be highly specialized, essentially unique. And there's nothing difficult about acquiring a Barrett—particularly the M82 civilian version."

"I agree, although I think the word *weapon* is not sufficient. You and I are looking at but one part of a new weapon system. I have given a great deal of thought as to how such a bullet might track toward its target—truth be told, I was up half the night thinking about it. Was there any evidence that this shooter, or perhaps his spotter, had some kind of secondary targeting device?"

Slaton nodded. "In the hide on the mountainside—I saw what looked like the footprints of some kind of tripod. Based on what I saw, I'm convinced there was only one person under the ledge. Our shooter was operating alone."

Vittorio nodded, deep in thought.

"Do you have any idea how it could work?" Slaton asked.

"The tracking itself is not so complicated. Given the wafer evident in the crushed nosecone, I would bank on one of two possibilities. First would be some kind of designator-tracking system, likely using reflected laser energy. The second is that both the bullet and targeting system have infrared sensors. Targets might be acquired using the pod, with an initial picture and perhaps even GPS coordinates transmitted to the bullet. Once airborne—generally referred to as the terminal phase—the bullet would transition to autonomous tracking. Both techniques are long established in military armaments, and miniaturization is an ongoing trend. The far greater problem, though . . ." The armorer's voice trailed off.

"Spin," Slaton said, finishing the thought.

"Precisely. Bombs and missiles use fins for stabilization, yet they can also be steered by them. Bullets, on the other hand, are stabilized in flight by their tremendous rate of spin. The round you've given me clearly contains some kind of perimeter weighting. It must function to either create a shift in mass, or perhaps alter the round's aerodynamic shape. It is also likely that the gun's twist rate has been modified to reduce spin. Either way, the challenge must have been to make it all work with respect to bullet rotation."

"Is that possible?"

"There are some very clever engineers in this world, and I think the results speak for themselves. Whatever trick they've come up with, it seems to work."

Vittorio leaned back in his chair, and pointed toward the round. "I would love to keep this, but I suspect you want it back. There are intelligence services and manufacturers who could learn a great deal from studying it."

"I do have to keep it," Slaton said. He took the bullet and wrapped it tightly in the oilcloth. "Thank you for your help. I owe you more than last night's dinner."

Vittorio rose and shook Slaton's hand. "Think nothing of it. You are, after all, a regular customer."

Slaton turned to go, and as he did Vittorio said, "It is not really any of my business . . . but I recall reading about some recent ugliness down in Capri. Then another tragedy two days ago in Davos. Both Russians, I think."

Slaton turned back toward the armorer, but said nothing.

"I trust that going forward you will use great caution."

Slaton nodded to say that he would. Moments later, as he struck out into a bright Milan day, the armorer's parting words seemed trapped in his head.

Zhukov watched the ancient MiG roll obediently behind a tug, its nosewheel connected by a heavy tow bar. Tan whirls of dust swept across the runway, the usual atmospheric confusion of early afternoon on the high desert.

The tug pulled onto the runway and soon had the jet positioned with its nose pointed down the ten-thousand-foot concrete strip. The driver disconnected the tow bar and left the jet where it was, lifeless and lonely against the bleak high plains backdrop.

"Run the prestart checklist," Tikhonov ordered.

The engineer occupied the only available chair on the elevated, open-air control station. Standing behind him, Zhukov looked all around. He thought it was the most comical setup he'd ever seen. The two men were perched on the rooftop platform of a highly modified Sprinter van. Above them a great yellow beach umbrella fluttered under the midday sun. In the interior of the van beneath them were racks of radios and equipment, and heavy cables snaked away toward a second vehicle a hundred yards distant—a forty-foot-long refrigerated truck that had been converted into a mission control center. Tikhonov had assured him the umbilical was only a redundancy—the two vehicles were perfectly capable of operating great distances apart. Indeed, this was an essential part of the greater concept.

The van was positioned roughly at midfield, fifty yards clear of the northern edge of the runway. The mission truck was farther back, centered in a clearing in the scrub. Zhukov thought it an awkward way to go about things, yet Tikhonov had assured him it was a tried and true process.

Everything was driven by one unique characteristic of the jet sitting before them: taking the place of the pilot in the cockpit was a box of control and telemetry equipment. In essence, the MiG had been converted into a drone. From his perch on the Sprinter, Tikhonov would fly the airplane off the runway using a joystick and throttle on the control panel in front of him. He had explained to Zhukov that having eyes on the drone was essential during takeoff to correct for crosswinds and gusts—the delay in transmitted data was simply too slow, the naked eye having an advantage of critical milliseconds. Once the aircraft was airborne, at a safe altitude, control would be handed off to a pilot in the mission truck who ran things for the bulk of the flight. On recovery, the same process ran in reverse, Tikhonov taking over from the van's rooftop to land the MiG—the most delicate maneuver of all.

Zhukov watched a pair of crewmen with headsets walk up to the jet.

"Gear pins," Tikhonov challenged.

"*Removed,*" came a voice over a speaker.

"Panels."

"*Closed and secured.*"

Step by step, the final checklist was run. Battery, generator, fuel pumps, auxiliary power unit.

Minutes later the MiG's engine was idling, the technicians trotting away. Zhukov knew things would happen quickly now—the MiG-21 was a gas hog, and time spent on the runway with the engine running was time lost in the air.

Tikhonov ran through a series of control checks, and Zhukov saw the jet's ailerons and rudder move in concert with his inputs. Finally the power was advanced, and the turbofan began spinning up. Even at mid-level thrust it brought a dull roar, drowning out every other sound and scattering a flock of sand grouse nearby.

"Brakes released," Tikhonov said.

The jet began moving, tentatively at first. Then the engine throttled to full power and the afterburner was engaged, dumping torrents of raw fuel aft of the turbines. Commercial airliners, Zhukov knew, had engines designed to minimize noise, a neighborly gesture to the busy cities above which they operated. The MiG was not so constrained. It barreled down the runway with a roar that was raw and unrefined, tearing apart air as it accelerated, beating the desert silence into submission. As the jet passed the control van Zhukov felt its sound more than he heard it, a low-frequency thrum that shook him to the core.

Yet it wasn't the noise that made the greatest impression. Over so many years in the military, he'd seen many fighters take flight. Never had he seen one thunder past without a pilot in the cockpit. It seemed robotic and cold, a machine without a soul.

Soon the raucous noise faded, and the MiG became little more than a dot as it clawed into a flawless blue sky. He looked at Tikhonov and saw something close to glee. He was like a teenager behind the joystick of the ultimate video game.

"Prepare for transfer," Tikhonov said into his microphone.

"Ready to accept control."

"On my mark. Three . . . two . . . one . . . execute."

There was a moment of uncertainty, a technical pause as circuits closed and switches activated. It reminded Zhukov of a handoff in a track relay race—a few doubtful seconds in which the baton might be dropped.

"I have the aircraft," said a remote voice from the truck behind them.

Tikhonov pushed back in his chair. "Clockwork, I tell you! Come, Colonel, we will watch things unfold from the mission truck."

"How long will the flight last?"

"Thirty minutes of actual test work. Then we run the recovery sequence."

"That doesn't seem like much."

"Fighters are designed for speed, not endurance— they are the thoroughbreds of the sky."

Tikhonov backed onto the ladder that led down past the Sprinter's rear doors. As Zhukov followed, the big umbrella above them fluttered in a gust, its edges shimmering like the petals of a giant yellow flower. Once again he thought the whole arrangement looked ridiculous, but he set the notion aside. If their plan succeeded, no one would be laughing.

Zhukov reached ground level, and side-by-side the two men walked toward the mission truck. It was a slightly uphill grade, in unseasonable heat, and he noticed the engineer was sweating profusely—in truth, he looked not far from a heart attack.

They encountered a section of ground that appeared charred, and Zhukov paused. The grass was burnt to its roots, and even stones and rocks had been blackened. "Was there a fire here?" he asked.

"Yes, we lost a jet here last month. It crashed during landing."

Zhukov looked over his shoulder at the Sprinter fifty yards behind them. "You were on top of the van . . . and it crashed so near?"

"It wasn't that bad. One of the landing gear collapsed and the jet skidded off the runway. It was nearly out of fuel, so there wasn't much of a fire."

The two began walking again, a subtle grin beneath the engineer's beard. "Do not worry, Colonel. Because of the mishap, I decided to incorporate a change. Each aircraft now carries a modest explosive charge. If control is lost, I can flick one switch and . . ." Tikhonov touched all ten fingers together, then spread them wide in an instant. "Boom!" He laughed robustly.

"That sounds like a fix an army general would order," Zhukov said.

"I suppose it does. But the contingency will likely never be used. You know what they say . . . lightning never strikes the same place twice."

THIRTY-THREE

"Something has come up," Sorensen said as she sat with her hands on the car's steering wheel.

Slaton stared at her. In his years in the field, he'd developed a private theory that the more banal an intelligence officer's opening line, the greater the impending doom. If it held here, it did not bode well for his near-term well-being.

He'd taken the first available flight from Milan, and on his request, she'd picked him up at Rome's Fiumicino Airport. They needed to talk, and instead of wasting an hour in a cab, he'd reasoned this would be more efficient—at least from his point of view. Sorensen had commandeered a generic sedan from the embassy motor pool, and they were at that moment stalled in the usual afternoon rush in the heart of Rome.

"*Argos* performed an offload in the Red Sea last night," she said. "Three smaller boats arrived and crates were transferred."

"And you find this surprising?"

"I guess not. The smaller boats delivered whatever it was to various points along the coast—all in Saudi Arabia. Since then, we've learned that *Cirrus* did pretty much the same thing from the waters off

Yemen. *Tasman Sea* is a little behind, but she just dropped anchor north of Al Jubail in the Persian Gulf."

"Okay, so we have a coordinated smuggling effort on the Arabian Peninsula. Tell the Saudis and let them handle it."

"That may not be an option."

"Why not?"

Sorensen didn't respond right away, her eyes fixed on the bumper of a motionless truck ahead.

"*Why not?*" he asked in a manifestly level tone.

"There's a complication."

There it was again, he thought. Ominous understatement. His eyes bored into her, and she finally met his gaze.

"We weren't the only ones who noticed *Argos*," she said.

"Who else would be looking—" Slaton locked up midsentence. "Israel."

She nodded. "They have satellites too, and watch their backyard closely. There's been a flurry of back-and-forth today at the highest levels—it began with the Israeli foreign ministry contacting our state department, and ended with CIA director Coltrane having a lengthy discussion with his counterpart at Mossad."

"Director Nurin."

Traffic began moving ever so slowly. "I know the two of you have a history," she said.

"That's putting it lightly."

"Nurin thinks highly of you, as does Director Coltrane."

Slaton felt like a fighter watching a big glove coming toward his face. No time to duck. "You know why I don't like platitudes?" he asked reflectively.

Sorensen didn't respond.

"Because people give them right before they dump something lousy on you."

"Are you this cynical with your wife?"

"Ask her."

"Like I said," Sorensen picked up, "there was a lot of back-and-forth. No one knows what was in those crates. Conventional weapons seems the most likely answer, but WMD can't be discounted. Israel is adamant about pursuing this. *Argos* has moved farther up the coast toward the Gulf of Aqaba—she's anchored southwest of Sharmaa, still in international waters."

"But closer to Israel."

"I'm afraid so. Mossad has a tactical team on standby. They intend to go in and determine what the cargo is."

"By force?"

"Surreptitiously would be preferred, but whatever it takes. And that's where you come in."

"Where *I* come in?"

"Director Coltrane told me to emphasize that participation on your part is strictly voluntary."

"How considerate of him—notwithstanding the fact that I don't work for the CIA and never have. I'm not even an American citizen."

As if not hearing his protest, Sorensen said, "I briefed him on your situation. I told him the Russians are circulating that you might have murdered two of their citizens—as it turns out, two men who had an ownership stake in these ships."

"I'm sure *that* coincidence wasn't lost on the director."

"No. And he mentioned something else—something I didn't know. He said you worked with Mossad not long ago, a joint operation in the Golan Heights."

Slaton felt like he was again streaking down the mountain in Davos—only this time instead of skiing he was tumbling, caught in a kind of private avalanche. He *had* done a cross-border exfil mission with a Mossad tactical team eight months ago. The objective had been to retrieve an ISIS defector, and it had ended as a qualified success. Now it was just another operation coming back to haunt him.

"Coltrane doesn't need me," he argued. "If the CIA wants a hand in this, they have plenty of operators."

"True. Unfortunately, it's Mossad who are being problematic. You're the only one they're willing to work with. It was something worked out personally between the two directors."

"And if I decline?"

Sorensen was silent for a time. "I don't know," she said. "Nobody seems to have thought things through that far. I'm pretty sure Israel is going to go forward, with or without you." She eyed him thoughtfully. "Honestly . . . it looks to me like they're backing you into a corner. Maybe you should tell them all to go to hell. The world will go on."

He nodded appreciatively. "Thanks for that."

"I mean it. I've gotten to know Christine and Davy, and I'd totally get it if you walked away right now. Set sail on that boat of yours and never looked back."

He sat in silence.

"But whatever you decide," she continued, "I need to know soon. They want an answer."

"All right. I'm guessing it can at least wait another hour."

"Another consultation with your wife?"

"Something like that."

Sorensen acquired a thin smile.

"What?" he asked.

"It just struck me that when most guys ask for a kitchen pass, it's to go golfing or watch a game at a bar."

"Guess I'm not most guys."

She looked at him with something he couldn't place. The road opened up ahead, and she accelerated on a freeway.

He said, "Regardless of what I decide, there's something I need from you."

"Shoot."

Slaton eyed her. The grin was still there. He said, "Vladimir Ovechkin is the last surviving member of this little group of Petrov's. I'd really like to know where he went after Davos."

"I've been doing my best with that."

"With all due respect, I want more. I want Director Coltrane to do *his* best. A full court press from Langley."

"Okay, I'll pass it on."

"And there's something else you should tell him."

"What's that?"

"It has to do with what I learned in Milan . . ."

THIRTY-FOUR

Vladimir Ovechkin was sweating profusely as he got out of the car in front of the villa. He'd been sitting inside for thirty minutes while his security team went over the place, and the car's air conditioner wasn't keeping up. Finally, Mikhael, the team leader, had given the all clear.

It hardly seemed necessary.

The villa could not have been more isolated. Sitting alone on a bluff, it was a ninety-minute drive south of Casablanca. The vistas along the ribbon of coastal highway had grown increasingly desolate. Long gone were the resorts, the beaches here too rocky for a decent brochure picture, and what little shopping and dining existed would be a shock to European sensibilities. The adjacent valleys were correspondingly barren, too arid to be farmed, too inaccessible to be populated. The only occasional visitors, Ovechkin had been told, were roving bands of surfers who sought perfect waves by day and lit bonfires in the coves by night. And even for them, October was a low month.

Amid that seclusion, the residence in front of him was an outlier in its own right. The nearest neighbor was a mile distant in either direction, and the main coast road could barely be seen. To make Ovechkin's solitude complete, his wife had gone to Paris. It had been his idea, and he already regretted it—curiously, not due to the shopping bill that would invariably result. As he got older, Estrella was increasingly a comfort, and Ovechkin found himself having thoughts lately he'd never before entertained—chief among them being that this marriage, his third, might be his last. The notion of hiding out here, with no one to talk to but his security team—who were as thick in the head as they were in the shoulders—was positively anesthetizing. Ovechkin pushed his lamentations away, realizing how ridiculous it was to feel sorry for himself.

Romanov and Ivanovic would certainly trade places with me, he thought.

He walked inside the villa, and was disheartened to find that the air conditioning wasn't working. The doors and windows were shut tight all around, and there was a musty odor in the main room—he knew the place hadn't been used in many months. It wasn't a particularly big residence—five rooms, or so he'd been told. The villa was owned by an acquaintance, a second-tier Siberian timber magnate who was looking to climb higher in President Petrov's hierarchy of largesse. The man had offered the place to Ovechkin graciously, no doubt hoping to curry favor with someone who was higher in the pecking order. Russia was full of such men—desperate to climb, and willing to contort in any way to make it happen. In truth, the villa's owner was doing much what Ovechkin himself had done so many years ago. Translating favors and loyalty into a lucrative lifestyle. Unfortunately, the poor bastard who owned the villa, and a hundred others like him, were missing one vital piece of the puzzle: they didn't realize that the rules of the game were about to change.

"Why isn't the air conditioner on?" he asked Mikhael.

"There is no air conditioner, sir. I've been told it's generally quite pleasant along the coast, especially this time of year. Apparently it's been warmer than usual lately. It might also have to do with the generator—the unit I saw would never support such a heavy electrical load."

Ovechkin closed his eyes for a moment, then strode to a set of wide French doors. He pushed them open, and was instantly enveloped by a cool ocean breeze. Sheer white curtains billowed like luffing sails from either side of the entryway, the air sweeping up the cliffs as if to embrace him. He strolled out onto the broad seaside patio, and could almost feel his blood pressure—which tended toward the high side—fall to diastole. "Maybe this won't be so bad after all," he murmured to himself.

His thoughts of relaxation were interrupted by Mikhael. "I should make sure we have enough fuel for the generator. There is also the matter of bringing in food. Can you tell me how long we will be staying?"

"Plan for a week," Ovechkin said.

Mikhael grunted and disappeared into the villa.

Ovechkin took a seat on a lounger, his bulk crushing the long cushion. The patio swept outward in broad curving lines, and tiered down on the north side where an aqua-blue swimming pool stood in wait. The Atlantic beyond appeared unusually calm. Taken together, the effect was positively tranquilizing. Ovechkin let his eyes drift up and down the coast, and he decided he'd chosen well. It was as if he'd stumbled upon the most pleasant of all the earth's ends.

"I recovered the bullet that killed Romanov," Slaton said.

Sorensen glanced away from the road. "How did you manage that?"

He explained his private investigation in Davos, how he'd tried to guess where the shooter had holed up. "I saw a few good options," he said, "but they were way up the hill. Reaching them would have required climbing gear, and I guessed that our shooter didn't have any going in. Chances are, he didn't know how he was going to set up against Romanov aside from the weapon he was lugging around. Turns out, there's only one outfitter in Davos—one place where he could have gotten what he needed to climb the mountain."

"So . . . you went there too?"

"I was one day behind him, and I got a little lucky—I talked to the same clerk."

"You actually talked to someone who's seen this guy? Did you get a description?"

"Not a very good one, but yes."

"We should tell the police to check the store—it must have cameras. They need to know Romanov's killer was there."

"Actually . . . I'd rather we didn't take that route."

After a brief hesitation, she saw the problem. "Right—because you were there too."

"It was the night after the murder, but yes. I also might have mentioned to the clerk that the guy who'd been there the previous night was a friend of mine.

On top of that, I showed up in Capri six days after Ivanovic was killed. The police will piece all that together eventually, but I'd rather not give them a head start."

He went on to explain how he'd discovered the shooter's hide, and then used that location, along with a little geometry, to recover the bullet. "I was prying it out of the ground when the authorities got suspicious and came up the mountain after me. I got away, but this is all just one more link chaining me to the whole affair. By now they'll have found my gear, and maybe the SUV I rented—which, by the way, I put on the company card you gave me. I'm not sure how the CIA pays its bills, but at some point the Swiss gendarmerie will try to track that charge, along with what I bought at the outfitters."

"Okay, thanks for the heads-up. We'll make it disappear before there's any blowback."

"Good."

"What did you do with the bullet?"

Slaton had anticipated this question. The spent round was, at that moment, in his suitcase in the back seat, wrapped in soft cloth. It was no longer of immediate use to him, but he knew the technology sections of both the CIA and Mossad would love to get their hands on it. Having not yet made his choice as to who was more deserving—and with both agencies theoretically prominent in his near-term plans—he decided it was a bargaining chip to hold in reserve.

"It's in a safe place," he said. "But I did make a stop in Milan—I wanted to show it to an old acquaintance."

"What kind of acquaintance?"

"A man who knows more about guns than anybody I know. He's the best in the business."

"And did you learn anything?"

"I did. To begin, I figured out how the shooter managed such remarkable accuracy. It's a guided bullet."

"A *what*?"

"It's been on drawing boards for years—a round that can alter its path in flight. I heard your Sandia National Labs had a project, and I'm sure the Russians were trying to keep up."

"I've never heard of such a thing. How does it work?"

"I don't know—not exactly. It either gets a reflected signal or takes some kind of guidance cues. There aren't any steerable fins, but the jacket seems pliable, and there appeared to be carefully crafted weights inside."

"Inside?"

"My friend put the spent round under an X-ray machine. Whatever the mechanism, the bullet is somehow able to change direction to track a target."

"Which means you could shoot someone on a boat from an island three miles away."

"Or a skier rushing downhill."

The embassy came into view, and Sorensen steered toward the heavily guarded side entrance.

She said, "So who's behind it?"

"Hard to say. My gunsmith thinks the gun used was a Barrett fifty cal, which is made in America. But he's pretty sure the round is a Russian item."

"Based on what?"

"Based on design characteristics only a gunsmith would understand. I tend to agree with him based on my own findings. The salesman I talked to in Davos mentioned that our shooter had an accent—according to him, either Russian or Latvian."

"So our shooter is Russian."

"Almost certainly. I'd guess he's either current or former Special Forces. And we know he's carrying a unique weapon system, strictly military grade. No private operator would have access to technology like that."

"So he's Russian-sponsored."

"I can't see it any other way."

Sorensen weighed it all as they sat parked behind a van at the security gate. She said, "It strikes me that this assassin, whoever he is, is part of a bigger operation. He's killed two of the three men who own a small fleet of ships—ships that are right now smuggling something into Saudi Arabia. This *must* all be connected."

"I agree."

"And whatever is going on . . . it can't be good."

"No. It's not good at all."

THIRTY-FIVE

"Tell me about the second shot," asked the man, who was on the left. He wore thick glasses and was nearly bald, a horseshoe of close-cropped hair above his ears. His mouth seemed set in a terminal pout, and his accent was eastern, probably Irkutsk. The sergeant had never liked Siberians.

Having spent much of his life waiting for targets to appear, he was an inordinately patient man. Indeed, the trait had been integral to his meteoric rise in the army. Regrettably, when it came to suffering post-mission debriefings with engineers, his forbearance was more akin to that of a hyperactive child. Today there were two to deal with, the man joined by a woman—a severe-looking matron wearing what looked like a burlap housecoat. *God help me,* he thought, as he said curtly, "The range was roughly twelve hundred meters. I estimated the target to have been moving at roughly sixty kilometers per hour. Right to left at a fifty-degree angle across the slope of the hill."

"Exactly fifty degrees?"

The sergeant quelled an impertinent response for, "He was *skiing*. It is a fluid act, not a straight line."

"How much higher was your position?" asked the woman.

"I had no way to calculate the precise elevation. I can tell you the tracking unit displayed a declination of twenty-one point three degrees—I remember that much."

"Did you not write these numbers down?" she asked.

The sergeant held steady. "Twenty-one point three degrees."

They asked more questions. Atmospheric conditions, the serial number of the gun he'd used, the tracking performance of the targeting pod. With each answer the Siberian scribbled on a diagram he'd been building. From where he sat, the sergeant could see the man had not drawn the mountain, but rather variables and vectors and angle measurements. The three of them had done this dance once before, after the kill in Capri. That had taken four hours. The man began scrawling equations, and referenced a calculator. The housecoat watched him and nodded.

In that computational interlude, the sergeant lost any regrets for his poor academic showing as a schoolboy. Growing up in the wilds of Kamchatka, the business of putting meat on the table had always taken precedence over algebra. Ammunition was not to be tested and experimented with, but utilized as a means to forestall hunger. *How simple it had all been then.*

As he sat in silence, a discomforting thought recurred. If this new weapon was perfected, would it not undermine the very qualities that had brought him here? With a gun stock on his shoulder the sergeant was the best in the Russian army—a raptor's eye and steel coolness had lifted him above his peers.

Yet could this new gun not be used just as well by the two engineers facing him? Might their technical adeptness and analytical minds prove superior behind the new superbullet? He smiled inwardly, knowing the answer.

No. They could never do what I do.

He forced his attention away from the man with the pencil. The room they'd chosen for the debriefing was essentially a laboratory. He saw benches and test stands, and a chart with the periodic table of elements adorned one wall. The adjacent room was the industrial end of the operation—machines for milling and production, and freshly rifled gun barrels lined up for testing. The entire building seemed tainted by an acrid smell, something between electrical solder and burning plastic. The facility was nested coyly in an industrial park on the western outskirts of Moscow. Its parent company was a well-known arms manufacturer, yet this particular outpost was perhaps its most secretive subsidiary, an off-the-books operation that existed in some administrative eddy between the state and private sectors.

The calculations ended. "Yes," said the man, "very impressive. Can you tell us where the projectile struck its objective?"

The sergeant groaned. In his own view they were talking about a bullet that was damned good. To them it was a rocket aimed at Mars. "Somewhere fatal. He didn't get up."

The man looked crestfallen.

"Enough—you are all geniuses! The damned thing worked, and I can't tell you any more. Now give me what I came for!"

His flare of temper had the desired effect. The man and woman pressed back perceptibly in their cushioned chairs. A look was exchanged. "Of course," said the Siberian cautiously. He nodded to his partner.

The woman got up and went to an industrial safe on the far side of the room. She typed a code into a keypad, and after a mechanical clunk she pulled open the door and removed a metal ammo box.

She brought it to the table. "Here you are. The last three cartridges of the prototype production run." She presented it with something near reverence. The sergeant noted that the box itself looked as though it had never been used—most ammo boxes he'd seen in his day had more dents than a Moscow taxi. Inside, he knew, were the last three special cartridges, each cradled in foam and a custom-fit plastic case. When he'd seen those trappings with the first batch, it had struck him as a ridiculous way to pamper a bullet.

"As you know," the man interjected, "our project is in a precarious position at the moment. The initial bench tests did not perform as expected. There were spin and stabilization issues, and the guidance software showed faults in certain atmospheric conditions. But you have brought renewed success." He smiled a Cheshire smile. "Two-for-two. Should these final rounds succeed, we'll have a good case for having fixed the problems. Continued funding would be almost guaranteed. But I implore you . . . *please* record every condition. Altitude, humidity, temperature, light conditions. Write everything down."

The sergeant took the plastic case. "I'll be sure to bring my sharpest pencil." He departed the room without further comment. No one offered best wishes until they met again.

He made his way through the utilitarian halls, and was ignored entirely by at least a dozen workers on his way out. No one had any idea who he was, nor that the future of their employment in this place rested completely on his proficiency with the contents of the box in his hand.

He reached the exit and paused in the portico between the inner and outer doors. The exterior doors were glass, and he saw a nasty winter blow outside—snow was sweeping sideways in a fierce wind. In the long Russian dusk he saw a young woman scurrying in from the parking lot. She was practically skating over the sidewalk. He set down the box and reached into his pocket. Pulling out his phone, he turned it on and checked for messages. The one he'd been waiting for had finally arrived:

Target #3 arrived as expected. Proceed Casablanca.

He put away his phone and donned his gloves. He pushed open the door just as the woman arrived, and she came inside in a rush, a gust of bitter air swirling through with her. The door closed and they exchanged a cordial smile. The sergeant thought she might have been pretty, although it was hard to say with her hair disheveled and her face furrowed against the cold. But she did smell nice—that much he knew. Something light and floral that somehow overpowered the maelstrom. The sergeant wanted to say something, but before any clever words came together the woman was gone.

He stood there for a moment, still and dispirited. He then picked up the ammo box, tilted his head down, and reached for the door a second time.

Casablanca.

It sounded warm and wondrous.

* * *

Slaton reconnected with his family for the best part of an hour. He began by making only passing mention to Christine of his digressions in Davos and Milan, explanations that must have come off as stilted and rehearsed. He was silence itself on the matter of what was brewing on the Red Sea. Only when Davy was sitting on the courtyard patio, engrossed in a box of toy cars and trucks Bella had brought in, did Christine force the issue.

"What's wrong?" she asked.

He looked at her over the round patio table that separated them, on it a sweating ice bucket and bottles of water.

"What makes you think something's wrong?"

She stared at him.

"Right."

In trying to consolidate his scattershot thoughts, Slaton knew his only refuge was honesty. He told her what he'd learned in the last day, including the events on the Red Sea. Much of the information was likely classified at the highest levels in Langley and Tel Aviv, but once again Slaton enjoyed the freedom of his own system. As had been the case regarding Capri, his wife had a need to know. He left nothing out, and ended with the invitation, jointly issued by the CIA and Mossad, to become involved. It took nearly twenty minutes. In that time Davy never lost his focus—he had the toy cars set up in static lines on the stone terrazzo that reminded Slaton of the traffic from the airport. It was all done with remarkable precision, the bumpers of the cars lined up perfectly. Slaton wondered if he had been so exacting as a child, but quickly drove the thought away for the extrapolations it introduced.

"They want to bring you in on this operation?" Christine asked.

"Yes."

"Will it be dangerous?"

"On the face of it, there's no reason to think so. We're not talking about an interdiction. The objective is simply to get a look. That said, I'm not sure what this ship is carrying—there's always a degree of uncertainty."

She seemed to consider it. "I remember once you explained a term to me—mission creep. I feel like that's what's happening. First Capri, then Davos, now this. With each incremental move you get more involved."

"Yeah, I'd say that's a fair label. But I haven't committed to anything. I told them I wanted to talk to you first."

"My opinion aside—do you want to do it?"

"*Want to?* Hardly. But I can't ignore the big picture. My name is still getting linked to these shootings. Anna mentioned today that Inspector Giordano, the policeman in Capri, called this morning asking about me. He wanted to know who I was and why she'd brought me into the investigation. He's heard rumblings that a Mossad assassin gone rogue might be responsible for Ivanovic's death."

"Any idea where that came from?"

"I don't know the exact channel, but the network had to be Russian."

"Which only gives a thicker smokescreen to whoever *is* responsible."

He nodded. She was looking at him intently now, trying to read what he was thinking. He kept to the truth.

"To answer your question," he said, "yes, I'd go. I think something dangerous is on the horizon, and I'm in a good position to do something about it. Maybe a unique position. What's going on in the waters around Saudi Arabia, the death of these two wealthy Russians . . . it's all connected."

"When we talked about this earlier, I made an accusation. I said I thought your involvement, at least in part, was ego driven. I implied you were bothered by the idea that there might be somebody out there who's better than you."

"I remember."

"That's not the case anymore."

He looked at her questioningly.

"Don't you see?" she went on. "You figured out how he did it—this guy cheated."

Slaton couldn't contain a grin.

She remained serious, and her next words were delivered with the caution of a technician defusing a bomb. "This may surprise you . . . but I think you should go."

His head tipped ever so slightly. "You're right, I am surprised. And your reasoning?"

"For one thing, because Israel is involved now. In spite of the rough relationship you and I have had with Mossad, there's no denying it's your homeland. I think you're right that something ominous is going on, and that you're in a better position to uncover it than anyone. Also, as much as I hate to say it . . . you're good at this kind of thing. There's also the fact that the Russians keep pushing your name into this mess. The only way to put a stop to that is to figure out what's going on. Figure out who's really responsible."

He nodded.

"But when all is said and done," she said, "there's one reason that's more compelling than any of those others."

"What's that?"

"If I asked you to drop it right now . . . I know that you would."

THIRTY-SIX

The small town of Eilat is a representative micro-cosm—in essence, it is a reflection of the Jewish state itself within the greater Middle East. A community effectively surrounded by hostile factions, it lays bracketed on two sides by Jordan and Egypt's unruly Sinai, and on the others by the sea and forbidding terrain. Across the deceptively calm waters to the south, Saudi Arabia can clearly be seen, and Israel's more cosmopolitan regions lay far to the north across the desolate Negev Desert. Yet Eilat's isolation is also its greatest virtue, and at vital junctures in Israel's history it has served as the country's lifeline, offering vital access to the Gulf of Aqaba and the Red Sea. That importance was proved soon after the establishment of statehood, when Egypt closed the Suez Canal to vessels destined for Israel's Mediterranean ports. Eilat, waking from its dust-covered slumber, emerged as the nation's lone foothold for trade with the east.

As a consequence of this strategic lesson, the facilities of the Port of Eilat have since been deliberately overbuilt, providing far more capacity than necessary to support a seasonal tourist town of fifty thousand residents. In the event of a crisis, the seaport can be transformed into a shipping hub capable of supporting a nation. On this particular late October day, Eilat was Slaton's destination for reasons that were not unrelated. He, in concert with Mossad, needed access to the Red Sea.

With time being critical, Slaton was whisked from the Rome embassy back to Fiumicino Airport—this time not to the passenger terminal, but to a more sedate corner of the airfield where a sleek Learjet stood waiting. The aircraft wore generic markings, giving Slaton no hint as to whose little air force it belonged—Mossad's or the CIA's. That question was answered when he was greeted in Hebrew by the captain, and then a flight attendant.

The jet was built for speed, and with a seasonal tailwind the flight took slightly less than three hours. For much of that time Slaton slept in a plush leather seat, and by the time the wheels were lowered for landing, evening had made its arrival. Through the oval side window he saw the distant glow of Eilat, a wash of shimmering amber in the gathering desert night.

The Lear came to rest near a midsized building where a half dozen other jets waited for well-heeled owners. Slaton recognized the place as an FBO, or fixed base operator—effectively, a terminal for private and corporate aviation. Inside he encountered a cursory display of customs and immigration, a man and a woman who were actually waiting for him, and who spent less than a minute going over his documents. That done, he walked outside and immediately spotted a familiar face. Anton Bloch was standing next to a small Kia SUV—among the most commonplace cars in Israel.

"Hello, Anton."

"It is good to see you, David."

"I keep thinking you might actually retire some-day."

"You should know better by now. For me there can be no retirement—only sporadic periods of rehabilitation."

Bloch was Slaton's original mentor, indeed the man who'd recognized his talent, and handpicked him to become what he was—something that over the years, the protégé had still not decided whether to forgive. Bloch had served as Mossad director for much of Slaton's time there, and since "retiring" had become something of a special projects manager for the new director, Raymond Nurin. For all their turbulent history, Slaton's relationship with Bloch today was distilled to one event: the man had once put his life on the line for Christine. That he would never forget.

He threw his small suitcase in the back, and took the passenger seat as Bloch drove. This in itself was a curiosity—former Mossad directors were generally given drivers, and always warranted protection.

"Where's your detail?"

"I am, as they say, working without a net. This business in the Red Sea came up quite suddenly, and Nurin asked for my help in facilitating things. Security would have been an unnecessary complication."

Slaton felt a response rising about the complications of having no security, but let it pass. Instead, he said, "Facilitating? Because I'm involved?"

"And there is something I'd like to know—how *do* you manage to insert yourself so regularly into Israel's affairs?"

"Trust me—I ask myself that very same question."

The two exchanged status reports on their families, and as they did Slaton regarded his old boss, thinking he looked surprisingly fit and relaxed. Surprising because he never imagined that any former director of Mossad could find health, let alone peace, given the gallery of death and misdeeds they'd spent a career both arranging and suffering.

The only real stunner in their exchange came from Bloch. "My daughter has decided to enter the service."

Slaton stared at his old boss. "Mossad?"

Bloch nodded.

"The last I heard she was at university."

"I argued against the idea as best I could. I assured her it would lead to nothing but a lifetime of pain and misery. She seems to have inherited my stubbornness."

Slaton looked out the far window to conceal his grin.

"We've been setting up shop since this morning," Bloch said, clearly changing the subject.

"Where?"

Bloch reached into the back seat and retrieved a hardhat with an ID attached by a small metal clip. He handed it across and Slaton saw a poor quality picture of himself, probably taken years ago. Under his photograph was the certainly fictitious logo of something called CSR International.

"What am I?" he asked.

"Make something up. A welder. Our base of operations is in a very quiet corner of the port complex. It's a trailer, hasn't been used since our naval interdiction campaign of 2002."

"Sounds cozy."

"We swept out the vermin only this afternoon."

"We?"

"You'll find out soon enough. For now, expect a thirty-minute drive. I'd suggest you relax. It may be a very long night."

In spite of the sleep he'd caught on the Lear, Slaton didn't argue. Bloch knew more than he did about the timetable for the next twenty-four hours—and rest was among the most important of preparations for any mission.

He reclined the seat and closed his eyes.

THIRTY-SEVEN

Slaton was nudged awake by Bloch. He opened his eyes to see a gate with a guardhouse a hundred meters ahead. Bloch drew the SUV to a stop at the checkpoint. While a port security man studied their IDs, which seemed to pass muster, his partner, a woman, went around the outside of the vehicle with an undercarriage mirror. It was a cursory inspection, suggesting there had been no recent breaches or terror alerts. Whatever threat scale was used here, it had sunk to its lowest level.

They were cleared to proceed, a simple railroad gate lifted, and Bloch steered into the vast port complex. They passed row after row of factory-fresh automobiles awaiting trailers that would disperse them across Israel. In the distance Slaton saw a small cruise ship, and the festive lights strung across the superstructure reminded him of those he'd seen on Pyotr Ivanovic's yacht. The cruise ship was the only thing in sight that wasn't industrial in nature. Tall loading cranes hovered over the wharves, looking like great birds, and container trucks were being loaded under bright lights. A rail yard was active on the shoreward perimeter, and a new thoroughfare leading north was in the initial stages of construction. Altogether, a busy place that aspired to one day be busier.

They eventually reached an isolated tract far from the piers, a little-used stretch of gravel along the perimeter fence. Bloch parked in front of a dilapidated double-wide trailer that was resting on concrete blocks—it actually appeared to lean slightly to one side. Equipment tugs and cargo containers were rowed on either side of the trailer, some of them rusting and discarded, a few pieces looking operable. The fence behind was twelve feet high, the top laced with razor wire, and on the other side was a wide cleared area washed in bright security lights. Beyond that Slaton saw barren desert stretching into rising terrain, the shadows of rough-edged hills evident in the gloom.

Bloch pulled the Kia up to the trailer and parked next to two other vehicles—one a generic sedan, the other a white work van. On the side of the van was the same CSR International logo that was stenciled on his ID. It struck him that the vehicle was resting low on its suspension, implying a heavy load inside. Clearly the groundwork for this Mossad venture had long been in place. He wasn't surprised. Top tier intelligence agencies kept a ready supply of corporate facades: papers in order, licenses granted, tax records current, facilities rented or purchased. All waiting for the day when they were required on short notice. Or the night.

Bloch hadn't been kidding about the vermin—near the steps that led up to the trailer's only door Slaton saw the carcasses of three dead rats, all of which looked to have suffered small-caliber gunshot wounds. No doubt silenced weapons.

He followed Bloch up a set of loose wooden stairs

and through a dented metal door. The interior of the trailer was a hostage to overdone fluorescents, and in the harsh light he saw three familiar faces. Slaton shook their hands in turn. Tal, with intense dark features; Matai, whose shaggy black mane perpetually begged for a haircut; and the leader, Aaron, whose strong build was nearly a match for Slaton's, and who exuded a commander's confidence.

"You look no worse for wear," Slaton said to Tal. They'd all worked together on a mission in the Golan earlier that year, and Tal had suffered a minor gunshot wound—if there could be such a thing.

The commando rolled his right arm like a baseball pitcher in warm-ups. "No issues. The surgeons did a nice job."

Bloch intervened. "You can all reminisce later. Time is critical."

The four operators took seats around a cheap plastic table, the kind typically used to hold grocery store hors d'oeuvres at office parties. Bloch launched into a ten-minute mission update, and little had changed. "The bottom line, gentlemen . . . we *must* find out what this ship is carrying."

"What's the general plan?" Slaton asked.

"To begin, Matai has acquired a boat," Aaron said.

"What kind of boat?"

"Nothing military," Matai replied. "From here, we can't reach the spot where *Argos* is anchored without traversing both Egyptian and Saudi waters. That means we need a cover. I've done a lot of diving down here, and I have a friend who owns a small dive boat. It's a six-pack," he added, meaning it was sized for six divers.

"Is it fast?" Bloch asked. "You have a fifty-mile crossing to reach *Argos*."

"If the seas are calm, which they're forecast to be tonight, she'll do thirty knots, forty in a crisis."

"I'd rather not go there," Slaton said.

"Me neither, but it's a good thing to have in your back pocket."

"What else?" Slaton asked.

Aaron smiled. "I'm glad you asked."

Aaron led Slaton outside to the van. With a quick look over his shoulder to ensure the coast was clear, he pulled the rear doors open. The back of the van was so full of gear it blocked the view of the driving compartment.

"Tal got a little carried away," Aaron said.

"That's not necessarily a bad thing. I like having options." The first thing Slaton saw was transportation. "Nice DPDs." It stood for diver propulsion device, and there were three of them. The DPDs looked like a cross between a jet ski and a torpedo, and Slaton noted that they were made by Stidd Systems, an American company specializing in military-grade nautical accessories.

"Top of the line," said Aaron, "and of course modified. Sonar, autopilot, extended-range lithium-ion batteries. Almost six knots at top end."

Slaton was impressed. Six knots didn't sound like much in the fast-paced terrestrial world, but for a fully geared diver in open ocean it was the equivalent of skydiving. He looked at the sidewalls of the vans and saw the rest. Three full sets of dive gear, including tanks, wetsuits, and monocular underwater night-vision goggles. The masks were full-face units with comm ability, which would be critical given what they were attempting. On the more tactical side, he saw enough guns and explosives to conquer a small town.

"What kind of mixture?" Slaton asked, pointing to the scuba tanks.

"Enhanced gas rebreathers. We can go all the way to the bottom in the area we'll be working, no exhaust bubbles to give us away."

Slaton eyed it all thoughtfully. "Most of this will look right at home on a dive boat," he said.

"That's the idea. This stuff gives us a lot of options, but we still haven't finalized a strategy for how to approach *Argos*."

"Strategy?" Slaton repeated. He slammed the doors shut. "Who needs strategy with firepower like that?"

THIRTY-EIGHT

The debate in the trailer was necessarily hurried—the team had a tight timeline in which to concoct a mission. The good news was that if all went well they were looking at no more than a surveillance op, and everyone involved was experienced and accustomed to fluid tactical situations. The biggest worry was the limited intel they were working from.

To begin, Aaron drew a comically amateurish map on a wall-mounted whiteboard: scrawled in different colors were a squiggly coastline, *Argos*' position, and four viable ports from which smaller vessels might be expected to sortie sometime in the next eight hours. This was the most damning variable—there was no guarantee *Argos* would even perform another offload tonight. Given what they knew, it seemed probable, but if nothing happened, the consensus opinion was that they should return to Eilat and take another day to prepare.

Aaron's artistry was heckled unreservedly as the work of a grade school dropout. It was the kind of levity born of stress, and tonight predictably short-lived.

"We should begin with our preferred outcome," said Bloch. "Our primary objective is to discover what's being brought ashore in these containers. Secondarily, we would very much like to avoid any knowledge of our presence."

"That might not be easy," said Tal, who was tipped back perilously in a molded plastic chair. Everyone was seated around the big table, and for the first time Slaton noticed a large brown stain in the center. He hoped it was coffee.

Bloch put everyone on notice. "The last thing we want is to get into a firefight. Headquarters has gone over last night's footage intensively. We think *Argos* is crewed by civilians, but we've distinguished a small security contingent that look professional—between four and six men."

"That's only *Argos*," Slaton said. "What about the receiving boats?"

"That requires a bit more speculation. To begin, there is no guarantee the same transfer boats will be used. Even if not, it's probably safe to assume that if another offload takes place tonight, we will at least see the same types of vessels and crew. The boats last night were clearly working boats, locals most likely, who'd been hired out for the evening. We suspect they were operated by their usual crews, but each boat carried one or two armed men, most likely from one of the regional militias."

"Which militia?" Aaron asked.

"There's no way to tell from a few satellite shots. You can make that your third objective—take a few pictures if possible to help us identify the boats and crew. Along this stretch of the Red Sea coast, there are any number of characters who might be involved."

"But this isn't happening only in the Red Sea," Slaton argued.

The three commandos lasered in on Bloch, clearly

not having been briefed on *Cirrus* and *Tasman Sea*. The former director filled them in on two other ships anchored off distant shores of the peninsula. "*Argos* is the nearest to Israel, so she is our greatest concern. For the same reason, she is also the most accessible. Find out what this ship is delivering, and we can reasonably extrapolate the results to the other two."

"Okay," said Matai, "so how do we go about this?"

"Boarding *Argos* would be my last choice," said Aaron. "We could manage it, and we'd learn what's in the crates—but to do that without being seen would be difficult. It also raises the chance of fireworks exponentially."

"Agreed," said Tal.

"Based on what you've seen," Slaton said, addressing Bloch, "does the cargo being transferred look uniform?"

"I'm not sure what you mean."

"I'm wondering, if we get a look at what's on one of the smaller boats—would that be representative of what the others are carrying?"

"From the imagery I've seen so far, yes. But it's a good point." Bloch scribbled a note on a small pad. "I'll put the question to our analysts." He went to the white board and used tape to post a half dozen high-resolution images from Ofeq-11. Four showed *Argos* during last night's offload, and the other two depicted later shoreside operations with the smaller boats docked in port. That done, he looked expectantly at his hastily assembled team. "You, gentlemen, are the experts. How do we go about this?"

Aaron said, "To begin, we follow the cargo through its entire journey—we can't discount any opportunity. It begins in *Argos*' main hold. As discussed, getting on board for a look without being seen—that would be high risk. Once the cargo has been loaded onto the smaller boats, the same problem is magnified. It would be even harder to get aboard and have a look undetected."

"We could sink one of the smaller boats," Tal suggested.

"How deep is the water?" Slaton asked.

Aaron referenced a nautical chart on the main table. "Right now *Argos* is anchored on the thirty-meter line. As you get closer to shore things gradually shallow out."

"That's doable," said Tal. "Sink one, and with our dive gear and scooters we do a quick salvage operation at less than a hundred feet."

Silence ensued as the four commandos weighed it.

Slaton was the first to call out the plan's weaknesses. "That still leaves a lot to go wrong. Attaching explosives to do the job—that wouldn't be easy. If the blast takes place alongside *Argos*, everyone knows something is up. We might get a look at what hits bottom, but it raises too much suspicion."

Aaron came up with a modification. "If a charge sinks one of the transfer boats on the way back to shore, you limit suspicion to the few guys on that boat. There would be a hell of a lot of scrambling while it went down—maybe they would only think they'd hit a reef."

"Or maybe they would all drown," Slaton argued.

"Are we worried about casualties?" Aaron asked.

"We're talking about smugglers," said Bloch, which was a clear enough answer. "But if an entire boat and crew disappear—once again, it raises a warning."

Tal added, "It would be tricky to set a timed charge anyway. Without knowing the speed or the course the boat will take, there's no way to tell exactly where it will go off. Any minor miscalculation, and we could end up searching for a shipwreck in open ocean."

"In the middle of the night," Slaton added.

"What if we do it close to shore?" Matai suggested.

"We don't know where that is," Slaton argued. "We can't assume these boats will necessarily return to the ports they launch from."

Everyone sat staring at the white board.

Slaton stood slowly. He walked over and studied one of the satellite images.

"What is it?" Aaron asked.

Slaton tapped the photo that had gotten his attention. "We said we should follow the cargo all the way to shore. I think we missed one part." He looked at Bloch. "I need a little information."

"About what?"

Slaton told him specifically what he wanted. It wasn't particularly technical in nature—more logistical.

Bloch picked up his phone. As he did, Slaton glanced up at an old analog clock on the wall. It was running ten minutes slow, which could have been due to old batteries. More likely—someone's attempt to ease the time crunch.

"It's evening," Bloch said as his call ran to the right department. "Most of our researchers have gone home."

"Meaning?"

"Meaning I'll have to curse more loudly than usual."

Captain Zakaryan found Ivan in *Argos'* officer's mess. He was sitting with two of his men, three empty food trays on the table. Each man had a coffee cup, and a nearly empty bottle of vodka was between them. An hour ago there had been two full bottles.

"What time will your festivities begin tonight?" Zakaryan asked.

Ivan scowled.

As a sea captain, Zakaryan knew a good deal about men and drinking. In his experience there were two kinds of drunks: those who turned giddy and light-hearted, and those who tended toward belligerency. The underlings were both grinning stupidly, but there was no question into which category Ivan fell.

"Same as last night," he said, his speech surprisingly unslurred.

"Will tonight be the end of it?" Zakaryan asked.

"Maybe so."

"I'll have the loading crew ready."

"Good. I hope they are in better form than the cook. The beef tonight was crap."

All three Russians seemed to wait for Zakaryan's retort. He wasn't going to give them the satisfaction of losing his temper. "Where will we go next?"

"Out to sea. Back toward the Mediterranean, I think. I hear the south of France is lovely this time of year."

"France? Perhaps we should send a message to the owners to see if they agree."

"No message is necessary," Ivan growled. "Your orders are to go where I tell you."

"And in the meantime," one of the other men said, more drunkenly than his superior, "take away these trays. They are attracting flies like a pile of shit."

The two junior men burst out laughing.

Zakaryan turned toward the companionway and left the Russians behind. He took solace in the idea that he would soon have the chance to revisit his decision to stay on as *Argos*' captain.

Soon this will be over, he told himself. He tried to remember in what computer file he'd stored his old résumé. The other shipping lines might or might not be hiring—but it was time to move on.

Bloch had answers twenty minutes later. He walked to the photograph Slaton had zeroed in on, and referenced his notepad—he'd been scribbling constantly during the phone call.

"The crane on *Argos* is a standard jib configuration, with a weight rating of twenty-five tons. The main cable is most likely eighteen-millimeter braided steel, ending in a hook block. From there you have a double sling made of a high-tensile composite fabric. It cradles the load at four attach points."

Slaton said, "And the load is essentially a square crate the size of a standard pallet. Weight unknown, but presumed heavy."

"Correct," said Bloch. The former Mossad director waited a few beats before asking, "Have I answered your questions, David?"

"You have." He explained what he had in mind, and everyone took a few moments to wrap their heads around the idea.

"It solves pretty much every problem," Aaron agreed.

"But do you think it's feasible?" Tal asked. "Can we do that?"

"I can't speak for you guys . . . but I'm pretty sure I could manage my part."

THIRTY-NINE

By ten o'clock that night everything was loaded on the boat. Slaton increasingly saw the wisdom of Matai's choice—the dive boat was thirty feet long and wide-beamed, with three big outboard motors and a decent radar and nav suite. The deck was open, built for divers lumbering in their equipment, and there was a custom-built platform with a ladder near the stern to bring everyone back aboard. The air tanks were slotted into PVC holders along each side, the valves retained by bungees, and long benches gave a stable base for gearing up in rough seas.

"The weather is holding," said Aaron. "It should take about two and a half hours to get to the general area."

"I like the dive boat theme," Slaton said, "but isn't this an odd hour?"

"Not as much as you'd think," said Matai. "They actually do a fair amount of night diving down here. The bigger problem is the narrow waterway. We're in Israeli waters for less than ten miles. After that, our choices are either Egyptian or Saudi territory. Both run patrols, but the Egyptians are far less active these days—they've been cutting back because they don't have the money for it. Their boats are pretty slow too—we could outrun them if it came to that."

"How encouraging. Don't they have deck guns?"

Aaron answered, "I don't expect any problems. It's the lesser of evils to keep to the right on the way out, and once we hit the Red Sea proper we'll be back in international waters."

"Okay," Slaton said, "but all the same . . . let's not get stopped." He surveyed the deck and saw it covered with equipment. The DPDs were lashed down in the open, but modifications aside, these too could be part of a normal dive excursion. Less easy to explain were the weapons and explosives, which were all below deck.

Matai fired up the motors one at a time, and the big outboards churned to life. Slaton looked across the pier. The only person in sight was a distant figure wearing a night watchman's uniform. Slaton looked at Aaron and nodded toward the man.

Aaron said, "Don't worry, Bloch has already made arrangements with him. We've thought of everything."

The comment begged for a comeback, until Slaton looked at Aaron and saw the wry smile.

"Yeah," he said, "I'm sure you have."

Dinner was taken at the usual venue, La Kasbah des Sables. Because Tikhonov was a regular, he and Zhukov were given a prime table at the edge of the decorative indoor pool. Like most buildings in Ouarzazate, La Kasbah was nothing special on the outside, an old Glaoui mansion of earth-tone walls that looked little rehabilitated from the streetside. Inside, however, the restaurant was an appeal to the senses.

The floor plan was open with high ceilings, the lighting thoughtfully set to highlight ornate rugs and wall-mounted spice jars. Rich fragrances from the kitchen filled the place, enhancing the naturally sweet desert air. The pool was the architectural highlight, a free-form blue pond backlit by a wall of brass oil lamps. Romantic as it all was, ambiance was not why Tikhonov frequented the establishment.

With some relish, the engineer had told Zhukov the story on their initial visit together. The first time Tikhonov had walked into the place, he'd been warned by the waiter that the nightly special was spicy lamb, and that it was served in large portions. The waiter suggested politely that since he was not a native, he might prefer one of the less zesty European selections. Tikhonov, a man unaccustomed to gastronomic moderation, had responded by ordering the plate and consuming it, then ordering it again, complaining that the first serving had been lacking in both size and heat. After the third iteration—a full pound of lamb nearly buried in pepper and cumin and cayenne—an uneasy truce was declared between the Russian and the chef. Now, each time Tikhonov returned, their relationship had fallen to something of a contest.

"The only problem with this place," Tikhonov remarked, "is that they do not serve vodka." For the third time he tipped a cask of Moroccan red to charge his wineglass. Tikhonov never needed an excuse to get drunk, but this afternoon's successful test flight was as natural a cause as existed for celebration.

Zhukov was still nursing his first glass. "I will send you a case soon, the Swedish brand you like."

"You promised that last time."

Zhukov said, "Forgive me, but I've been busy," while he thought: *If I'd sent a case of vodka we'd be three days behind schedule.* "So tell me what you learned from today's flight. Were the test points realized?"

"Every one! We exceeded six Gs, which meets the baseline requirement. We also managed to attain one point four Mach, but had to go into the forties to do it."

"Forties?"

"Above forty thousand feet."

"I am an army officer—what does that mean for the project?"

"It means the supersonic requirement was met, but we validated at a higher altitude than would normally be used operationally."

"You mean the jet won't go supersonic at low altitude?"

"Certainly not. Few in the world can, at least not sustainably. It matters little—the program parameters have all been met."

"Then a toast is in order."

The two raised their glasses and tapped them companionably. Right then the waiter approached with a covered tray—he appeared to be struggling. Not without ceremony, he lifted a great silver lid to present Tikhonov with a mountainous portion of beef tagine over couscous. The meal would have defeated any normal table of four, and was served not on a plate but a massive platter.

Tikhonov roared with laughter. "Tell Didier he has outdone himself! Bravo!" He wiped his mouth with a wrist as a kind of warm-up, then tucked a napkin into his collar to prepare for the assault.

A second waiter arrived with a red snapper fillet for Zhukov. As they began the meal, Zhukov said, "I look forward to the live-fire test the day after tomorrow. It must be satisfying for you, the culmination of three years of work."

Tikhonov made a sweeping gesture with an empty fork. "There will be no problems. It is among the most simple of scenarios. I have been meaning to ask why you chose such benign conditions. Low altitude, low speed, a non-maneuvering target. It is hardly a challenge."

"Perhaps, but we cannot afford failure. Those above me must be assured we are spending wisely."

Tikhonov stopped chewing for the first time since the food had arrived. He swallowed heavily and said, "You bring something else to mind. I have been meaning to ask about the account you had me set up."

It had begun six months ago. At the end of their first dinner here, Zhukov had instructed the engineer to establish an unusual bank account, ostensibly for the deposit of operational funds.

"What about it?" Zhukov asked.

"This Russian bank is one I've never heard of. And the amounts deposited—they seem to change significantly, higher every month."

"Is that a problem? Consider any overages a bonus."

The engineer's eyes narrowed. "I am not accustomed to such generosity from our government."

Zhukov reached for the wine as he pondered how to say what came next. He needed a facial expression to fit the situation—a degree of manipulation he'd rarely had to conjure in regimental staff meetings. He went with stoicism. "Actually, I'd like you to become comfortable with it. I have initiated changes to the project's accounting methods. Later today you will see an even larger deposit arrive."

Tikhonov put down his fork softly. "How large?"

Zhukov told him.

The engineer's eyes widened.

Zhukov remained impassive. "I am in the process of setting up my own account, Boris. I think if one-third of this deposit were to be forwarded there, perhaps in a week or two, we might find ourselves in a mutually beneficial arrangement. One, I dare say, that could continue for some time. You should set up another account, in a quiet place. I could tell you a few things about tax havens, but I expect a man of your abilities would prefer to manage things on your own. Keep enough in the main account for operations, then do what you think is best with the remainder."

Zhukov waited. This was the moment of truth, the point where any indications of shady dealings, which he'd been alluding to for months, crossed the line into collusion.

The engineer reacted predictably. He dug into his beef with gusto. "Why not?" asked a beaming Tikhonov.

The colonel watched his tablemate relax into a predictable rhythm, extended periods of gorging punctuated by gusts of good humor. Zhukov relaxed as well, and tried to suppress a smile. *How easy it had been,* he thought. After so much careful planning and cautious manipulation, in the end Tikhonov had barely blinked at the suggestion of a tainted windfall. The colonel wasn't really surprised. Corruption in Russia was endemic these days, having metastasized into every thread of society. Legions of individuals in important positions would, for a regular and substantial consideration in either cash or property, make virtually any accommodation. Corporate managers, small town mayors, policemen. And, apparently, engineers working on secret military projects.

Zhukov had long held himself to be above such

failings. He was a product of Russia's finest military academies, places where honor and creed and faith in the Motherland were ingrained to the core. Where service to country put one on a higher moral plane. Now that view seemed suddenly quaint, like an old-fashioned propaganda film where every man was brave and every woman virtuous. The truth of it all struck Zhukov with alarming suddenness: He was at that moment acting on direct orders from the president of the Russian Federation. Zhukov, a decorated soldier who had bled for his country, had been reduced to being nothing more than Sergey Petrov's con man. Of course, it would not be without compensation. The Jaguar and the dacha to begin. *And one day?* he thought. *Perhaps the platinum mine instead of the rail line.*

It was then and there, in a quirky Moroccan restaurant behind a fine fillet of snapper with cilantro and lime, that Viktor Zhukov's long-held fortress of duty and honor suffered its terminal breach.

While Zhukov and Tikhonov were perusing the dessert menu at La Kasbah des Sables, twenty miles away a large airplane was landing at the Tazagurt airfield. The transport was a regular arrival, although not on any fixed schedule—it came on an as-needed basis to deliver whatever components were necessary to keep RosAvia's research moving.

While Tazagurt was not an official port of entry for international flights, special accommodations had been made. This fell under the auspices of the negotiated joint agreement between Russia, Morocco, and the RosAvia Corporation: In exchange for the expenditures involved in building an airport and its associated research facilities, Morocco allowed Ros-Avia to import direct shipments to the airfield with expedited customs and immigration handling.

The jet was an Ilyushin Il-76, a four-engine strategic airlifter operated by a minor, and very discreet, subsidiary of RosAvia. The pilot brought the big jet to a stop using half the available runway, and from there he steered toward the hangar. A ramp worker with lighted wands guided the jet to its regular spot, and there the aircraft commander set the parking brake. Only after the chocks had been installed did the aircraft's integral stairs begin to lower.

The first person to deplane was an athletic young man dressed in plain khaki pants and a dark green shirt. He went immediately to the back of the aircraft, and stood waiting on the tarmac while the rear loading ramp was lowered.

As if on cue, a customs inspector, who'd been forewarned of the arrival, and who was a regular overseer of RosAvia's shipments, stepped smartly across the ramp from the small administration annex near the hangar. Dressed in a neatly pressed uniform, he too went straight to the rear loading ramp. There the Ilyushin's captain was waiting with two manifests: one for crew and passengers, the other for cargo.

The inspector took the manifests in hand, but didn't look at either. Instead he waited patiently while the young man walked up the inclined ramp. From the great cargo bay he retrieved two suitcases. One was a hardened case, four feet long and two feet wide, and of a weight and sturdiness that implied some kind of tools or equipment. Which, in a sense, it very much was. In his other hand was a simple roller bag.

The young man carried both off the aircraft and presented himself to the customs inspector. He handed over his passport, and observed, as he'd been briefed, what was a well-practiced drill. The document was returned within seconds, minus five bills, each of the one-hundred-euro denomination, that had been folded inside. The inspector nodded once, then watched in silence as the young man lifted his suitcases, set out across the tarmac, and disappeared into RosAvia's administrative offices. Only then did the customs man address the manifests in his hand.

Five minutes later the sergeant reached the street-side parking lot. He set his luggage next to the trunk of a nondescript sedan, the key to which he'd collected from a receptionist in the RosAvia building. He lifted the trunk open to find a second equipment case, similar to the one he was carrying but of a slightly different shape. He pushed it to one side, and with a bit of maneuvering everything fit. Closing the trunk, he took up the driver's seat. After one look at the map on his phone, he started the car and set off on a two-hour journey to the seaside south of Casablanca.

FORTY

A moonless night on the Gulf of Aqaba is a very dark place. No night, however, is dark enough for four operators on a hastily planned mission.

The ersatz dive boat pounded through three-foot swells. They were making good time, with Matai at the helm, but the ride was punishing. Slaton would have preferred calm seas—not because he minded the discomfort, but for more practical reasons. The DPDs, the dive computers, the guns. How many times had he seen missions fall apart because equipment had failed under harsh conditions?

As they beat a path southward, Slaton used the time to plan for contingencies. What happened if they had only two operable DPDs to begin? What if one failed midway through the mission? Did they need a rendezvous plan in case someone lost their GPS signal, an old-school backup based on dead reckoning and light signals? If everything went to hell, could they swim to the shores of Saudi Arabia?

They'd covered half the distance to their target, and in an hour *Argos* would begin to show up on radar. Aaron was in constant communications with Mossad headquarters, and he relayed the disappointing news that their mission would have only partial drone coverage—the Israeli Air Force was leery of encroaching on Saudi airspace.

The three men going in the water—Slaton, Aaron, and Tal—would have full facemasks with comm while they were submerged. Even so, coordinating an underwater assault at night required extensive planning. To begin, they studied information Bloch had provided regarding currents in the designated area. The team spent twenty minutes hanging on to a bulkhead and going over comm protocols and visual signals. A precise course between the drop point and *Argos* was loaded into everyone's GPS unit, and it was agreed that no high-intensity lights would be used—a dead giveaway in the crystalline Red Sea waters—but that chemical glow sticks would be mandatory in the initial approach.

Sonar on the DPDs could be used to approach *Argos*, which would stand out like a mountain against the otherwise barren seascape. Sonar would also be critical on egress to rendezvous with the dive boat. On one point everyone was in agreement—given what they were attempting, nothing would lead to disaster more quickly than three divers floating twelve miles out to sea, out of air and ideas, and trying to find their ride home.

The team coordinated how they would stay together using signals with the light sticks, and how to rejoin if they became separated. They covered the rules of engagement if they were seen or attacked, and how to respond if one of them was captured. On this last point there was no argument, nor any request for direction from headquarters—either they all came back, or none of them did.

Matai, who would stay with the boat during the underwater approach, gave a heads-up that they were ten minutes from *Argos*' position. On that cue, everyone began gearing up. Wetsuits were donned, scuba rigs checked, and each DPD was powered up and put through a system test cycle.

"Battery is eighty percent on number one," Aaron said.

"It showed one hundred back in port," Matai responded.

"Is that enough?" Slaton asked.

"Maybe," said Tal. "If things go as planned, we can run slow on the egress."

"And if they don't," said Slaton, "we've already briefed how to handle it. Two men on whichever sled has the better charge, and we sink the bad DPD."

Nods all around.

The engines slowed abruptly, and the boat settled on the sea.

"I've got a hit on radar," said Matai.

All four men went to the helm and looked at the screen.

"Right where she's supposed to be," said Aaron.

"All right," Slaton said. "I think this would be a good time for one last sit-rep."

The Red Sea mission was being overseen by Mossad's headquarters operation center. Deep in a bunker in the Glilot Junction complex, sixteen sets of eyes—intelligence chiefs, analysts, and sensor operators—were watching both *Argos* and a small dive boat in real time. A drone was giving maddeningly intermittent coverage as the operator did his best to navigate the latticework of airspace at the mouth of the Gulf of Aqaba. It wasn't a particularly busy area in terms of air traffic, but the skies were monitored closely by suspicious neighbors all around—the never-ending "Game of Thrones."

Also under watch at the ops center was the Saudi shoreline, and it was activity there, near a place called Gayal, that generated the first outbound message of the night. The town lay behind a spit of sand—the outline of which vaguely resembled a shark—that reached seaward to form a natural harbor. Just after midnight, three small vessels, between twenty-five and forty feet in length according to analysts, set out from the docks. Everyone in the ops center watched the tiny flotilla round the edge of the peninsula, and within minutes two salient points became clear. First was that the boats appeared to be staying together, an amateur convoy of sorts. Second was that they'd set a course that led straight toward the freighter *Argos*.

FORTY-ONE

Christine waited until Davy was fast asleep—he'd had a rambunctious night, and stayed awake later than usual. She covered him with a blanket and went to the doors that led to the veranda. She already knew that Nick, the guard she'd gotten to know best, was one of the two on duty there.

She went outside. "Hi, Nick."

"Evening, ma'am."

"Are you on duty much longer?"

"Two more hours," he replied.

"I wonder if you could do me a favor."

"If I can."

She explained what she wanted.

"That's not how it's supposed to work," he said.

"I know . . . but I won't leave the embassy. It's just down the hall."

"Your husband would have my ass if anything happened."

He looked inside at Davy—he was obviously fast asleep. Christine gave Nick her most heartfelt look.

He said, "I'd have to clear it with Miss Sorensen first—explain what you want to do."

Christine knew it was a reasonable request, and she'd half expected it. "Sure."

"Hang on." Nick walked a few steps into the courtyard and had a hushed conversation on his lapel mic. After he stopped talking, there was a thirty-second pause. He finally turned back to Christine.

"Okay," he said. "Go ahead."

She couldn't stop herself from hugging the man. Seconds later Christine was out the front door—the security team there was expecting her. As she walked away down the hall, she looked once over her shoulder at the two burly guards. She'd never seen such intimidating babysitters in all her life.

"Okay, we're on," said Matai, who was the first to see the message. "We have three boats fifteen nautical miles northwest of *Argos*. They're holding a dead-on course for an intercept."

A brief debate ensued about whether there was any possibility of this not being the predicted rendezvous. Tal said, "We need to be sure. Once we get wet, we're committed. If these boats make a turn and go fishing, we have no choice but to come back on board. At that point we'll have spent air and battery power on the DPDs that we can't replace without going back ashore."

The rest knew he was only playing devil's advocate.

"Waiting and watching isn't an option," Aaron argued. "If these are the receivers, which is highly likely, they'll be here in an hour, maybe less. It'll take at least that long for us to maneuver close without drawing attention, get in the water, and make our approach to *Argos*."

After a brief pause, Slaton said, "There's really no choice. We drive as close as we can, prep to go, and in twenty minutes get one last update from the ops center."

He looked all around.

There was no dissent.

The tiny armada never wavered in its course. They were making a beeline for *Argos*.

The DPDs were in place near the aft platform and all three divers suited up. Weapons were secured to each DPD, but if everything went as planned only one would be used.

The three men in wetsuits looked to Matai for guidance. He was standing at the helm with a night-vision scope. The ocular wavered as he steadied it to his right eye against the rocking boat.

"Thirty-two hundred meters," he finally said. "We shouldn't get any closer."

Slaton and Aaron had already agreed that two miles was the minimum closure. With the receiving convoy approaching, *Argos'* crew would be watchful. Only minutes ago Matai had used a new device from the technology section, an off-the-shelf diagnostic tool that had been tweaked by Mossad's engineers. They called it a poor man's RWR, or radar warning receiver—an allusion to the more complex devices on fighter aircraft that sensed enemy radar emissions. Built to detect specific radiofrequency bands, the unit would tell them if *Argos'* radar was painting them. Not surprisingly, it was. There was no information about range or azimuth, which a more expensive device might have managed, but it gave confirmation on one point: they were being watched.

Matai put *Argos* dead on the port beam. He would steer a meandering course for the next hour, but barring emergency contingencies, this was as close as he would take the dive boat to the ship they were targeting.

"Fishing boats are more common than six-pack dive boats in these waters," Matai said. "We should have brought something, a few deep sea rods or nets."

"I doubt they have surveillance gear that can see us two miles away," Tal argued. "All they'll see is a small boat on their radar that isn't getting any closer."

"Probably," Slaton intervened, "but while we're gone you might gather up some mooring lines and hang around the transom. Try to look busy."

"A longline fisherman," Aaron seconded. "That's good."

"I'll do what I can," Matai said. He then referenced the navigation display. "This is the spot. Everybody ready for an update on waypoint one?" The three divers each addressed their wrist-mounted nav devices. When he got three nods, Matai said, "Mark!"

From that moment forward, the coordinate set for that position, an invisible symbol in the middle of the Red Sea pinpointed by a satellite constellation thousands of miles above, would serve as the primary reference point for their very small universe.

Three splashes followed. Then, one by one, Matai shoved the DPDs off the stern and into the water.

FORTY-TWO

To be submerged in the ocean at night is akin to drifting in outer space. With neutral buoyancy, there is an impression of weightlessness, the body floating in a spherical void. The visual impression is even more disorienting, absent any background of distant stars. The darkness, particularly on a night without moonlight, is effectively absolute, giving no sense of up or down. On an entirely different level, there is the matter of large marine predators, the likes of which thrive amid the shallow reefs of the Red Sea. Such uneasy circumstances, once combined, create a devil's playground for the imagination. But then, as the old joke went, it was the sharks who had to worry when Special Forces operators were turned loose in a shared ecosystem.

Slaton cracked the chem light that was strapped to his forearm. A dim glow came to life, and within seconds he saw two others, vague points of light in the pitch black sea. Each man had been assigned a unique color: Slaton was green, Tal red, Aaron blue. With visual coordination established, a successful comm check came next—they'd performed one on the boat, but systems had a way of degrading under twenty feet of seawater.

By design, the lights on the DPDs were easily managed—their controls were lit in a subdued green hue for night work. Slaton took up position on the lead unit and adjusted the rheostat to give the minimum illumination for a readable display. There had been considerable debate about the depth at which they would traverse the two-mile gap to *Argos*. Going deeper offered better cover for their scant emissions of light, but shallow depths were slightly advantageous in terms of power and air use, allowing for a deeper and more lengthy dive if necessary—even using advanced gas mixtures, the human body had saturation limits. In the end, they'd compromised on a depth of thirty feet for their ingress.

With all checks complete, they began their descent. Slaton heard the dive boat above them as Matai gunned the motors, low frequency vibrations that conducted strongly through the water. Matai's plan was to initially angle away from *Argos*, lessening any attention they might already have drawn. He would not, however, divert more than a mile from their waypoint for extraction.

Within minutes the team was at thirty feet and under way. Slaton took the lead of a wedge formation, one man on either side. After the pulse of the outboards faded, the only remaining unnatural sound was a faint hum from the DPDs—their electric motors and ducted propellers had been designed for auditory stealth.

It was an otherworldly sensory environment in the open ocean at night. Slaton heard lobsters clicking, and occasional grinding noises as reef creatures went about their nocturnal business. It struck him that the water seemed unusually warm—for all the problems they might face tonight, hypothermia wasn't among them.

He kept a steady course toward *Argos*, checking occasionally over either shoulder to ensure Tal and Aaron were in position. As they glided together through the ebony sea, he felt confident—everything was going according to plan.

It was an intractably troubling thought.

From the wing of the bridge Captain Zakaryan watched the three boats. It was a dark night, and most of *Argos'* lights had been extinguished, but there was enough starlight to make out the receivers as they neared. The contingent varied only slightly from the previous night's showing—this time there were two broad-decked fishing trawlers and a single large dhow.

Ivan was somewhere below deck, probably giving orders to crewmembers that might or might not be contrary to those Zakaryan himself had issued. He could have intervened, but the idea of confronting the Russian held little appeal—even less so given the condition he and his goons had been in earlier. He tried to take solace in the fact that there had been only minor missteps last night. Tonight the crew would be familiar with their tasks. Everyone knew their jobs, and being an experienced sea captain, he knew that interfering in a smooth operation often brought nothing more than mistakes. Mistakes, in turn, brought delays. *The sooner this is done,* he thought, *the sooner we can make for port and throw these Russians off our ship.*

To that same end, Zakaryan had meandered into the hold earlier and spoken quietly to his senior deckhand, a Romanian. He'd not bothered to ask the man what was in the crates, because he probably didn't know. But he had asked how many were left, to which the Romanian provided a definitive answer: twelve. Exactly one half the original count. The implication was obvious, and he'd seen his own relief reflected in the deckhand's expression. Tonight would put an end to the entire dreadful affair.

Zakaryan watched the lead trawler pull alongside, and thought, *Thirty more minutes.*

He contemplated whether to wait for daylight to weigh anchor, and visualized the westbound midday schedule for transiting the Suez. Unfortunately for the captain, his forward thinking was premature. He had no way of knowing that one hundred yards to port, in the warm night waters, three commandos were preparing an assault that would alter his plans considerably.

FORTY-THREE

For the team in the water, there had been no mistaking the arrival of the three boats—everyone heard their screws churning and motors rumbling.

The three divers paused at a staging point one hundred meters west of *Argos*. There each man took to his preset tasks. Slaton and Aaron removed weapons from their respective DPDs. Each carried a Heckler & Koch MP7, which met every requirement: reliable, compact for handling underwater, and fitted with proven sound suppressors. The H&Ks were not long-range weapons, but for what Slaton envisioned they would be more than adequate.

Tal's job was to corral the DPDs, manage them for neutral buoyancy, and keep all three in the right place while Slaton and Aaron made their final approach. In a worst-case situation, Tal could make a dash toward *Argos* to assist if necessary.

Slaton referenced his wrist-mounted GPS, then backed it up with a compass heading. Both he and Aaron slid their chem lights beneath the sleeves of their neoprene wetsuits. That done, they left Tal and the DPDs behind to cover the last hundred meters. They kicked in unison through the pitch black sea, each with an MP7 in their outside hand. While no one in the world could see it, the two highly trained killers set out in the absolute darkness with their free hands clasped together like preschoolers walking to the first day of class.

As foreseen by her captain, the scene on board *Argos* was more organized than it had been the night before. The concept of an offload at sea had been new to the crew then, and it was with no small amount of seamanship, and perhaps a bit of trial and error, that they'd managed to swing twelve crates over the side without damage or loss. Tonight the process was more familiar, and everyone knew what to do.

Two of the three receiving boats were the same as last night, and the third retained two crewmen who'd manned the replaced dhow—that boat had faced engine trouble on arriving back in port. So it was that, within ten minutes of the rendezvous, one of the receivers lay secured to *Argos*' port side, and the deck crane had the first load poised overhead.

Captain Zakaryan took in everything from a vantage point on the forecastle. He saw the heavy crate hovering high in the work lights, and deckhands laboring to stabilize the load. Ivan was somewhere on the bridge—the reason Zakaryan had gone forward. *Argos*' skipper didn't like the essence of what was taking place on his ship. It was illicit, and he had no control. But he was pleased that the operation was going smoothly—because that meant the end was in sight.

Slaton was the first to surface, and he did so with one shoulder grounded to *Argos*' hard steel hull. He was treading water, his buoyancy compensator set slightly negative—stop the gentle bicycling of his fins, and he would fast disappear beneath the surface. The big ship herself was serving as cover—effectively, he had his back to the biggest wall in twenty miles.

With nothing more than his dull black mask exposed, he surveyed the scene. He and Aaron had positioned themselves near *Argos'* stern, abeam the twin propellers—it was the farthest point from where the loading would take place, amidships near the deck crane. Slaton immediately saw the three smaller boats. Two were laying off to port, in holding patterns to the west—nearly right over Matai's head. The third boat was in a loading position, lines secured fast to *Argos.*

There was virtually no illumination on Slaton's position, the curvature of the hull giving a shadow from *Argos'* work lights. The smaller boats displayed only low-intensity deck lights that threw off a muted glow.

Slaton reached behind his back and gave an underwater OK signal.

Aaron surfaced right behind him.

"As advertised," Slaton said quietly into his mask-mounted mic.

"Do we wait?" Aaron asked.

Slaton weighed the pluses and minuses. The receiving boat was moored securely alongside the bigger ship. Sixty feet above her, the first load was being lowered. "I want to see at least one transfer. Then we make the call."

"Agreed."

Together they watched the crate descend. Based on the effort expended by the deckhands manning the guidelines, it was quite heavy. As the load neared the receiving boat, the crew guided it as far forward as possible, until the crate thumped conclusively to the wooden deck. Slaton watched closely as the hook-and-cradle assembly was disconnected, then lifted back up for the next load. The crane's boom rotated away, out of sight from where Slaton and Aaron were treading water. Just then, Slaton noticed a man looking over the rail well forward of their position.

Slaton instinctively went still, although there was little chance the man could see them. Something about him seemed different from the other crewmen on deck. He was no ordinary seaman, but more of an overseer whose duty, apparently, was to scan the sea with a cautious gaze. He was built like a bulldog and had Slavic features. His hair was cut by a stylist whose work Slaton recognized—a bunkmate with electric clippers, number three guide on the top, number one on the sides.

He nudged Aaron and nodded toward the man.

"Yeah, I see him. Security?"

"Must be."

The man suddenly backed away and disappeared.

"Next load?" Aaron suggested.

"I see no reason to wait," Slaton replied.

He widened his fins to steady himself. Light seas lapped rhythmically at *Argos*' hull. In ten minutes they would have their answer as to what was in the crates. And they would have it with no explosives, and hopefully no casualties—at least none that wouldn't appear accidental.

Slaton reached to the side of his vest and unclipped the MP7. Very, very slowly he lifted it clear of the water and trained the barrel upward.

Christine watched the surreal scene on the big-screen monitor before her.

Sorensen had mentioned earlier that she was going to try for a feed from Langley to watch the mission in real time. If it worked out, she'd promised to tell Christine how things had gone soon after the fact. That had gnawed at Christine in unexpected ways, and when Davy fell asleep she finally relented. With the help of Nick, she'd been cleared into the embassy comm room.

She'd seen her husband at work before—indeed, in the days after they'd first met there had been little else as they'd run across England like fugitives. Yet that had been a firsthand observation in which she'd been at his side. This was altogether different.

"Is there a delay in what we're seeing?" she asked.

"A small one," Sorensen replied. "Ten, maybe twenty seconds depending on how it's routed and filtered."

"And this is taking place off the coast of Saudi Arabia?"

"Yes—but I can't tell you exactly where."

Christine let that go, not wanting to press her luck. *What does it matter?* she thought.

"Can you zoom in on the aft waterline?" Sorensen said to Mike.

The scale of what they were watching changed.

Christine's eyes combed the scene for details. The feed was from a drone, apparently Israeli, that was circling nearby. She knew little about such things, but the resolution seemed excellent. Sorensen had told her the ship's name was *Argos*, and that the smaller boats around her were expected to take on cargo of some kind. The entire scene was monochrome, the sea nearly black and *Argos* outlined in white. Everything else was drawn in muted shades of gray. She

could discern crewmen scurrying on deck, and saw
tackle and machines in action.

"A team of four was sent in," Sorensen said. "I see
two of them now."

"Where?"

She pointed to a spot along the big ship's aft
waterline, and Christine saw two tiny figures bobbing
in the sea. Mike did something, and the tiny blobs
once again enlarged, becoming humans in diving
gear. They also acquired on-screen designations: the
numbers 1 and 2.

Sorensen explained, "They're all wearing signal lo-
cators the drone can sense."

"Is one of them David?"

"I can't say for sure. This mission was a scramble
from the outset. According to the Israelis, the plans
were changing right up until the moment the team
left port in Eilat. Even then there were variables
in play. I can tell you that their objective is pretty
straightforward—they're trying to find out what's inside those crates."

Christine thought, but didn't say, that Sorensen
had it wrong. There was nothing straightforward
about the scene before them. That thought was confirmed when one of the two figures in the water lifted
a short-barreled weapon and appeared to train it on
the nearest small boat.

FORTY-FOUR

As smoothly as he'd raised it, Slaton lowered his gun back into the water.

"What's wrong?" Aaron said at a whisper.

"Bad platform," Slaton said. He was facing, in essence, a variant of the problem he'd described to Sorensen regarding the shooting of Ivanovic in Capri. Light waves that had seemed inconsequential all night were suddenly problematic. The three-foot seas collided with *Argos*' steel hull, creating a roil of choppy water along the ship's waterline. To make the problem worse, occasional trails of wake from the two boats churning in the distance added to the hydrodynamic chaos. The rough water alongside the ship was ideal for cover—their hooded wetsuits and masks, all a dull black, blended perfectly into the irregular backdrop—but what was good for concealment didn't translate to a stable shooting platform.

"Should we move away from the ship?" Aaron asked.

"No. If we get too far from the hull we'll be exposed, catch light from the main deck."

Slaton looked up and saw the second pallet being lowered. He decided to try a second time. Anchoring his shoulder hard against the hull, he raised the gun and tried to train the scope on his target. It was better, but then a second problem arose—with his head so close to the ship, waves splashed across his facemask, obscuring his vision through the scope.

"Dammit!" he muttered. He was only looking at a seventy-meter shot. Unfortunately, his target was only three inches wide, and he anticipated having to hit nearly the same spot with multiple rounds in quick succession.

The second load was complete now, the sling and hook rising for the next pallet. Opportunity missed.

Slaton pulled his mask down around his neck, twisting it to keep the comm unit in a usable position.

He tried a third time, testing things by putting the scope on the radar dome of the fishing boat. Aaron tried to help, wrapping a supporting arm across Slaton's free shoulder.

Slaton lowered the weapon. "It's still not stable."

"If I had a good handhold on the boat I could wrap you up," said Aaron.

Both men looked up and down *Argos'* long steel waterline. They saw nothing but flat steel plating.

Then Slaton had an idea. "What about the limpet?"

Aaron considered it. "Might work."

Tal, who'd been listening in, realized what they were getting at. "On my way," he said.

"What the hell are they doing?" asked Mossad director Raymond Nurin.

He said it in Hebrew, which was understood by everyone in the headquarters operations center. Perhaps because he was the director, or perhaps because no one could think of an answer, there was not a single reply from the two dozen staff around him.

Two thousand miles away, in the basement of the U.S. embassy in Rome, Anna Sorensen repeated Nurin's words verbatim, albeit in English. She, not surprisingly, got a response from the woman who knew the shooter better than anyone.

"He's improvising," Christine said.

Slaton and Aaron remained submerged in place as they waited for Tal. Slaton surfaced long enough to see another crate get lowered, then watched as the receiving boat cast off and was replaced by another.

Tal arrived four minutes later, and although it was impossible to tell because he was wearing a rebreather, Slaton suspected he was huffing from his undersea sprint. Tal handed over what they were after.

The limpet mine had been included in their arsenal almost as an afterthought. It was a weapon created before World War II: an explosive charge integrated with a powerful magnet that could be attached by a diver to the hull of a ship. It was a simple concept, and had been used in combat with varying results, most famously in a foiled attack by Argentina against a British warship in Gibraltar during the Falkland Islands War. Slaton's team had brought one tonight not because their goal was to sink a ship, but as an option for unseen contingencies. Perhaps a blast to serve as a distraction, or a method of destroying evidence—a few pounds of explosives had a way of fueling an operator's imagination.

Aaron took the mine from Tal, who immediately swam back toward the DPDs—left untended long enough they could drift and become lost, greatly complicating a stealthy egress.

Slaton and Aaron surfaced again.

"Whatever you do," Slaton whispered once his mask was back around his neck, "don't arm the damned thing. If we put a big hole in *Argos* it might raise a few questions."

"You think?"

The utility of the mine at that moment had nothing to do with the explosives it contained. More important was the powerful magnet, and the solid handle that was integrated in the limpet's frame.

Aaron attached the mine to *Argos*' hull at the cost of an audible *clunk*. Both men remained motionless for a moment, but the sound was drowned out by the loading operation nearby—the crane in action, shouts from deckhands, lines being dropped on deck. The second boat was now moored in place, and the crane's boom appeared, a new crate swinging high overhead.

"Let's do this," Slaton whispered.

By tilting his head sideways, he found that he could hook his right wrist through the handle of the mine and keep the MP7 in a firing position. Aaron did his best to help, grabbing the handle as well and using long, steady strokes with his fins to stabilize Slaton's free shoulder.

The waves were unrelenting, but when Slaton looked through the gun sight he liked what he saw— not a motionless picture, but a manageable one. He trained the crosshairs on the crate, which had not yet started to lower. He then walked his reticle up one of the four risers. The sling was made of a composite fabric—extremely high tensile strength, but easy to manage when not bearing weight. At that moment, the four taut bands were likely supporting tons. Each band was roughly four inches wide, and Slaton selected a spot halfway up the most seaward strap. He paused his reticle where the word *LIFT* was stenciled. His finger began the pressure.

The first round fired with a metallic clank—with the suppressor, there was little sound beyond the gun's mechanical action, and that was lost to the ratcheting of the crane. Slaton saw right away he'd scored a hit—one nine-millimeter hole, center-right from his aim point on the heavy strap. He'd already calculated it would take more than one. He fired again, at the moment the whole assembly began to lower. Hit. The crate was sixty feet above the boat now, descending slowly. The deckhands helped Slaton unknowingly by stabilizing the rig's spin as it was lowered.

His third shot was a miss, a wave striking his shoulder at precisely the wrong moment. His wrist was getting numb from pressuring the limpet mine's handle. His fourth shot was a hit. The strap now had three holes, clustered in a three-inch grouping. It was the fifth round that gave the desired result.

Slaton never saw where the bullet hit, but there was a sharp bang, almost like an unsuppressed gunshot. The crate seemed to hesitate for an instant, as if making a decision. A gentle rotation came next. Then a calamity of physical forces began as the rig's remaining bands failed. One snapped free like a cracked whip, and the load swung violently in the opposite direction. This caused the two remaining bands to fail simultaneously.

Poised fifty feet above the fishing boat, the crate dropped like a five-ton anvil. To his credit, the lone crewman on the fishing boat's deck saw it coming and threw himself into the sea.

Against the ship's backlights, and with crewmen screaming in the background, the crate hurtled toward the boat like a freefalling train.

FORTY-FIVE

Captain Zakaryan heard the great bang, and it put his sailor's instincts on high alert. Loud noises, sudden and unexpected, were never a good thing on a ship. Failed rigging, bent propeller shafts, shifting cargo. More alarming yet was when such noises were accompanied by rapid motion. And that was what registered next—an explosion of action along the port beam.

It came so fast Zakaryan couldn't comprehend what was happening. He ran to the port rail amid a chorus of shouting, and there he looked down over the side. He saw the boat that was being loaded, and had the distinct impression that a giant shark had taken a bite out of its port beam. He saw a man sliding across her shattered deck, and flotsam arcing out across the water. The boat was foundering, listing badly to starboard. Water washed over the gunnels like waves on a gentle beach. His years at sea allowed the captain to extract the most important elements of the scene before him. First priority: the lines connecting the damaged boat to *Argos* were taut as piano wire.

"Cut those lines free!" he shouted. The smaller boat was going to sink within minutes—there was nothing to be done about that—but mooring lines under such tremendous strain were a danger to both *Argos* and her crew.

He saw a quick-thinking deckhand produce an ax and cut the lines fore and aft. Zakaryan's gaze swept over the sea. He counted three men in the water, and began shouting orders to collect them. He was surveying the wheelhouse of the sinking boat when his thoughts were interrupted.

"What the hell happened?"

He turned and saw Ivan. "Something failed in the lifting rig—one of the crates dropped."

The Russian turned apoplectic. He looked down over the side, then up at the boom of the crane. "Can you fix it?"

"Fix it?" Zakaryan repeated, following Ivan's gaze to the tangle of limp loading straps. "First I'm going to make sure everyone is alive! We can talk about what to do later."

Ivan's expression grew dark, but he said nothing.

Zakaryan began moving along the rail, bellowing orders as he went.

Ivan went the other way, up toward the bridge. Minutes later he was in the communications room sending a message.

"What just happened?" Christine asked.

"I don't know," Sorensen replied. She too was left staring at the screen.

They'd both seen the disaster play out in a flash, but it all happened so fast it took time to decipher what had occurred. The crate getting lowered was gone, and *Argos'* deck looked like a kicked beehive—men were swarming and spotlights crisscrossed the

sea. The small boat next to *Argos* had nearly cap-
sized, its hull rolling to the sky like an upended turtle.
A lifeboat had been launched from *Argos* and men
were being plucked from the water.

"I don't see them anymore," Christine said. There
was no need to mention whom she was referring to.
Just as there was no need to question responsibility
for the scene before them.

"Whatever happened," Sorensen surmised, "I think
the job is done."

Christine couldn't take her eyes off the chaos.
"But . . . how?"

After a moment, Sorensen said, "Tell me something. Have you ever known David to miss?"

"Miss? As in . . . ?"

Sorensen nodded.

Christine thought about it. "Yes. He was snorkeling
once in the Philippines, and I saw him spear a jellyfish
when he was aiming for a grouper."

"Don't tell me he brought that home for dinner."

She shook her head distractedly, her eyes still glued
to the monitor. "No. Without even surfacing, he retrieved the spear and shot the grouper on his second
try. It was like he refused to even breathe until the job
was done."

"So there you are." The two finally locked eyes.
"With any luck, they'll all be back in Israel in a few
hours."

Eight minutes after the event, and one hundred and
five feet directly below *Argos*, three divers arrived at
the coral sand bottom. The man in the lead looked
upward repeatedly, referencing the riot of lights on the
surface above. Some were steady, while others swept

as if searching. Slaton was certain none was looking for them.

Confident in the distractions of the mayhem above, not to mention the optical diffusion granted by a hundred feet of seawater, he turned on his diving light and began sweeping it across the bottom. It didn't take long to find what they were looking for. It was strewn over an area the size of a swimming pool, an explosion of evidence scattered across coral outcroppings and sea fans and pristine white sand.

Wanting to be methodical, one of the men produced a small underwater camera. A flash was of course necessary, but ten quick strobes later they had the proof they'd come for. Soon after that, the three divers were gliding west toward their rendezvous point at top speed.

FORTY-SIX

It took an hour for *Argos*' crew to regain control of the situation. One boat had been lost, and the trawler that had been loaded successfully departed for the Saudi coast. That left one empty receiving boat, broken rigging on the crane, and a shaken crew on *Argos*—not to mention four men on the dhow who seemed less than enthusiastic about coming alongside.

It was here that Ivan stepped in. He engaged in a heated debate with Zakaryan, and only when two of Ivan's backups appeared in the company of machine pistols did the captain submit to the inevitable—the remaining crates would be transferred. It was the first time the Russians had brandished weapons, although it didn't surprise Zakaryan that they'd come prepared. Or perhaps they'd raided one of the crates to make their point. At least that ill-kept mystery was definitively answered: Before the doomed trawler had gone down, Zakaryan had seen assault rifles strewn across her listing deck like candy from a broken piñata. It left no question as to what was being smuggled.

He reluctantly gave the orders, and soon his crew was back in action. If any mistake was made, it was that the failed sling was not inspected—in the haste to clear the deck and get things moving, a crewman simply detached the shredded rig from the hook and threw it overboard. The crane was then fitted with a backup sling, and everything was double-checked.

The last boat took on the remaining crates, and set off just as the sun was breaking the horizon. Under the orange eastern glow, *Argos* weighed anchor.

Before the engines could be engaged, Ivan appeared on the bridge and addressed Zakaryan. "I have received new instructions regarding our next port of call."

"From who?"

"The ship's owners—I can show you the message if you like."

Zakaryan bristled, but said in a level tone, "I assume the south of France is no longer on our itinerary?"

"Correct. Set a course to the Bab al-Mandeb Strait."

The captain's eyes narrowed. This was to the east, where the Red Sea merged with the Gulf of Aden, the narrow throat between Africa and the southern Arabian Peninsula.

Ivan said, "Our next port of call will be Djibouti."

Zakaryan was not entirely dispirited. Djibouti was on the Horn of Africa, no more than two days' sail. Far less than France. He would be rid of his unwanted guests sooner than expected. He issued the order to his executive officer without comment, but then his mood darkened again when he considered what awaited in Djibouti. What if Ivan and his squad didn't leave there? Would more guns be loaded? Some other illicit cargo?

Argos accelerated quickly, its lone funnel churning

out black smoke that was not misaligned with her captain's mood. She'd been under way no more than twenty minutes, a chevron of wake building astern, when the Russian named Ivan went to the comm room and sent another message.

Sorensen and Christine were in the embassy's in-house café. At three in the morning there were no meals available, but the coffee machine never slept. They each had a full cup as they sat together at an institutional table.

"Thanks for letting me sit in on that," Christine said.

"No problem."

"It seemed like it went okay." She looked at Sorensen as if begging for confirmation.

"I'm no field operative, but yeah, I'd say it went well. Of course, we had a very restricted vantage point. I'm guessing there were some tricky moments."

A silence fell, and Sorensen was cutting her over-brewed coffee with cream when her phone rang. She took the call.

Christine noticed she didn't try to move away for privacy. She caught enough to know it was an update from Langley. The call lasted two minutes.

"Good news," Sorensen said as soon as she hit the end button. "The team are nearly back in Eilat. They called ahead with a preliminary report, but so far it sounds like a home run. Everyone is accounted for, and both Mossad and Langley are convinced that no alarms were raised on *Argos*—the loss of the crate and one boat are apparently being written off as an accident. I'm not sure where it will all go from here, but the director is happy—apparently the scheme was David's, and it seems to have worked perfectly. We have the evidence we need, and whoever is operating that ship doesn't realize what really happened."

Christine stared at her cup, ruminating over it all.

"That had to be terrifying," Sorensen said.

Christine looked up and saw Sorensen staring at her thoughtfully.

"I mean, to see your husband in a situation like that."

"Actually . . . it was kind of enlightening."

"In what way?"

"I guess I saw how good he is at what he does . . . or what he used to do."

"I've seen David work once before. The mission was far more complex, but the end result was every bit as effective." She thought about it, and said, "I have a lot of interaction with cops in my line of work, and I know their basic rule when it comes to using force: you use the minimum amount necessary to get the desired outcome."

"Which is what David did tonight."

"Exactly. Although, in his particular specialty, it's not so much a moral or legal imperative. Avoiding unnecessary casualties is generally in his own best interest. Tonight there was no response whatsoever. The team got in, got out, and no one ever knew they were there."

The two sat in silence for a time, until Christine said, "I remember one guy in my med school class—he went on to become a really top-flight surgeon. It was no surprise. We all noticed him in our first year of school, when we were dissecting cadavers. It's a grim business, and most of us muddled through to get the job done. But this one guy, he could uncover a nerve or a tendon better than any of the second-years who were teaching us. He was a prodigy, just had a gift for it." Christine turned her cup in her hands. "I'm no expert, but what I saw tonight . . . given what they were up against, and the way it turned out . . ."

"You're right . . . David's a natural. He operates in situations most people can't imagine. And I've never seen anyone do it any better."

The results of the raid on *Argos* were quickly shared between the CIA and Mossad. After independent analyses of the underwater photographs, as well as surveillance footage of the other suspect ships, *Tasman Sea* and *Cirrus*, the affair ended where it had begun—in a conference call between the two directors.

"Things went as well as could be expected," said CIA director Coltrane.

"The team is still in debriefing," replied Raymond Nurin, his Mossad counterpart. "In the photographs we have identified AK-47s, PKM machine guns, RPG-7 grenade launchers, Spandrel anti-tank missiles. All worrisome equipment, and a lot of it, yet nothing that isn't already endemic in the region. I was concerned we might find worse—stockpiles for some kind of chemical attack, or perhaps lab equipment suggesting the manufacture of a biological weapon. If something like that had been brought to Israel's back door, we would be having a very different conversation."

Coltrane was seated behind the desk in his office, perusing the same high-resolution underwater photos that Nurin likely had spread across his own desk. His eyes were locked on the most spectacular image: wedged against a large stand of brain coral was the only recognizable section of the shattered crate, and next to that thirty rifles lay stacked like cordwood amid a school of curious snapper.

"I agree," he said, "conventional arms is the best we could have expected. But this is a significant cache. Given what we now know about *Argos*, we can only assume these other two ships, *Cirrus* and *Tasman Sea*, are distributing similar loads."

"We have reached the same conclusion," Nurin said.

"I really don't see any option here. We have to tell the Saudis what's going on."

There was a pause on the Tel Aviv end as calculations were run. Finally, Nurin said, "I won't argue otherwise. Perhaps when you do, you could mention that we were involved in uncovering this intelligence, and that it comes with our blessings. For the good of the neighborhood, one might say."

Coltrane's somber grin could not be seen an ocean away. "I suppose Israel does deserve something out of it. But this all begs one greater question: Why did three Russian oligarchs, two of whom are now dead, put together a shipping company and use it to smuggle an arsenal into Saudi Arabia?"

Nurin, clearly at a disadvantage, asked, "What exactly are you referring to?"

In their original conversations, the two had concentrated on the immediate crisis of *Argos*. Thinking the backstory less critical, Coltrane had not gone into detail about MIR Enterprises, nor the suddenly abbreviated life expectancy of its principals. He now explained the rest as he knew it.

"This cannot be a coincidence," Nurin said.

"Certainly not," agreed the head of the CIA. "Two of the three owners of this company have been murdered—by a very capable sniper, I might add. The FSB are quietly promoting the idea that Slaton is responsible."

"Slaton?"

"I know. He's is certainly capable, but he's no hired gun. One of my case officers was actually with Slaton when the second man was killed. Because the Russians are trying to implicate him, Slaton did some detective work on his own. He uncovered a bit of evidence from the second shooting. I don't know the specifics, but I'm told it suggests the shooter is Russian. Which makes sense, in a twisted sort of way."

There was a heavy pause, and Coltrane imagined that as soon as their call ended, Nurin would be making a follow-up connection to Eilat.

"Do you know the name of the surviving owner of this shipping company?" Nurin asked.

"Vladimir Ovechkin. He's been a favorite of President Petrov for some time. Oil and gas—been around since the mid-nineties."

"Do you know where he is?"

Coltrane gave a muted laugh. "Funny—Slaton has been asking that same thing. It appears Ovechkin is laying low."

"Very low, would be my guess."

"I can tell you we've been looking for him."

"Any luck?" Nurin asked.

The director's eyes drifted over a message that had reached his desk only minutes earlier. "I think we might have something soon . . ."

True to his word, Coltrane wasted no time in alerting the Saudis. Within minutes of ending the call with

Mossad director Nurin, he arranged a second to his counterpart at Saudi Arabia's General Intelligence Directorate, or GID.

His name was Bandar al-Fahd, a first-tier prince who'd been on the job less than two months. Coltrane had spoken with al-Fahd twice before, and thought he seemed capable, if a bit overwhelmed. As he waited for the prince to be pulled from a meeting, Coltrane weighed how best to impart his information. He decided that in this initial call he would defer mention of Israel's involvement in the affair—that could be hashed out later. By doing so he would keep suspicion to a minimum, and perhaps muddy the fact that the CIA had been monitoring the impending smuggling operation for the best part of three days.

While his call ran, Coltrane found himself staring idly at the wall—in particular, his graduation photo from college. His degree had been in chemistry, and not for the first time he was surprised by the odd applicability of his old studies. He'd taken to envisioning the CIA's vast network of ties with foreign intelligence agencies as a variant of the periodic table of elements. Every box on his private chart represented a particular foreign service, each with its own structure and orbit and spin. Times of crisis brought isotopic variants, subject to decay and varying levels of toxicity. His musings were interrupted when Prince al-Fahd finally came on the line.

With all the force he could muster, Coltrane told his Saudi colleague that tons of conventional arms were at that moment metastasizing through the Kingdom. He promised to back up the warning with hard information, and gave his personal assurance that the CIA would do its best to help.

When the call ended, Coltrane followed through. His staff forwarded photos of *Argos* over established secure lines. Three floors down, teams of analysts began scouring raw data for anything to help track the weapons that had come ashore. Photos of wharves were pored over, road traffic monitored, and enough information was shared with regional offices to press human sources for answers.

As the hunt for the missing weapons expanded into an agency-wide undertaking, Coltrane assigned a second working group to track down Vladimir Ovechkin. The Russian had long existed as a minor file in the CIA's database, but with one verbal directive, an obscure oligarch became the agency's second-highest priority.

Ovechkin's existing profile was gone over for possible aliases, travel habits, and business interests. The most simple theory was that he was hiding out in a property he already owned. Unfortunately, his only known residence was outside St. Petersburg, and given that the elusive assassin was very possibly Russian, consensus opinion was that Ovechkin would not venture there. It was a virtual certainty that he owned at least one overseas residence—as the oligarchs knew better than anyone, money left in Russia was money left at risk. It was equally likely that any such property would be held within a maze of trusts and shell companies so baffling it would not be uncovered on short notice.

In the course of its rushed inquiries, the CIA learned that Ovechkin was registered with Air France's frequent flyer program, was a season ticket holder of the Chelsea Football Club in London, and had recently placed a down payment for a new personal jet with the Canadian company Bombardier. Enlightening details one and all, but nothing to establish his whereabouts in that moment. As it turned out, the most alluring hit for the newly created "Ovechkin desk" came in the early hours of that morning.

FORTY-SEVEN

Slaton allowed one hour for debriefing after they docked in Eilat. At that point, he shut the interview down and was given a room in a quiet hotel. The other members of the team took rooms in the same wing.

Exhausted after the all-night mission, he slept for six hours, to be awakened just after noon by the sound of a jackhammer. He went to the window and saw a work crew battering a hole in the sidewalk directly outside his window. The noise was insurmountable, but the sleep had done its work—he felt much improved. Yet if his body was reinvigorated, his thoughts remained in disarray.

The mission to reveal what was being carried on *Argos* had been a success. Unfortunately, that truth did nothing to lighten his own dilemma. He still faced the matter of an assassin running amok with a revolutionary weapon. And Slaton remained the prime suspect in two of his shootings. *Argos*, along with the arms she'd been hauling, was inextricably linked to the deaths of Ivanovic and Romanov. Unfortunately, Slaton was no closer to revealing what that link was.

He looked at two phones on his nightstand: one a simple landline provided by the hotel, the other a secure CIA device. He knew what he had to do. His first call was to room service for a sandwich and coffee. His second utilized the mobile, and involved ten minutes of connections, security protocols, and just simple waiting. In the end he got what he wanted—the ear of CIA director Thomas Coltrane.

"You did well last night," Coltrane said.

"It worked out. Now that we know what was on board, how are you handling it?"

"I can't go into specifics, but we've informed the Saudis—they'll have to take the lead on the response."

"Have any of these shipments been interdicted?"

"A handful. We're hoping to find more soon."

"Hoping," Slaton repeated.

"We're dealing with it," said the CIA director, irritation creeping into his voice.

Slaton suspected he might have gotten more sleep than Coltrane in the last twenty-four hours. "Where are the ships?" he asked.

"All three are under way, headed in the general direction of the Horn of Africa. We believe they're empty."

"Could they be going to pick up another load?" Slaton wondered aloud.

"Possibly, but it hardly matters. We're watching them closely. By the time they reach any port, we'll have a solid case built—there's already more than enough evidence to shut down MIR Enterprises. The more pressing concern now is to help the Saudis track down these shipments. It might take a week or two, probably longer for anything that went through Yemen—but we'll catch up."

"That might be too late."

"Too late for what?"

Slaton hesitated. "I don't know. Something about

this seems too simple, too obvious. We're talking about a significant influx of arms. The Saudis have always had their share of domestic enemies—there's a restless Shiite minority, Al-Qaeda and ISIS elements. Houthi militias are right across the border in Yemen. We're talking about a country where one-third of the population are immigrants. And, of course, Iran would be happy to throw fuel on any fire."

"The Saudis also have a competent National Guard who've dealt with this kind of threat before. Their first and foremost mission is to protect the royal family, and they generally do it well."

Slaton knew Coltrane was right. The House of Saud spared no expense in assuring their own safety. There had been no WMD on *Argos*, no secret weapon. Only large caches of guns and ammo. It was enough for a minor revolution, but the kind of thing the king and his princes had stamped out before. He looked out the window and saw the port of Eilat, the high sun glistening on Israel's southern playground. It was time for the question. The real reason he'd called.

"What about Ovechkin? Have you found him yet?"

Coltrane answered without hesitation. "No. But we are making headway."

The CIA was indeed making progress. Their first lead in the search for Ovechkin, as was increasingly the case these days, came by way of the internet, and from a source no analyst could have predicted: one photograph, taken the previous evening and posted online, of a charity gala in Paris. Standing atop a red carpet in a stunning Dior strapless was none other than Ovechkin's wife, Estrella.

Among the few verifiable truths in Ovechkin's file, and in divergence with many of his nightlife-loving peers, was that he generally traveled in the company of his wife. It was simplicity itself for the CIA's data-trackers to confirm that Estrella Ovechkin was checked into the same five-star hotel in central Paris that had hosted the charity event.

At first light that morning a surveillance team was dispatched from the Paris station, among them a stunning young woman whose French was nearly perfect and whose curvature was unquestionably so. She had little trouble prying from a bellman that Estrella, who was a frequent guest, had in fact not arrived in the company of her husband. To the contrary, free from the watchful eye of his overbearing security team, she had spent the last three days shopping with abandon along Avenue Montaigne.

The initial disappointment at Langley that they'd not found Ovechkin was fast forgotten as new leads were chased. Signals intelligence seemed the best bet, and it was here that an improved operational relationship with the National Security Agency proved invaluable. By chance, the NSA had for weeks been busy at the same hotel on an unrelated matter: tracking the phone calls and internet traffic of a deposed African strongman who was in the process of recharacterizing billions of dollars of U.N. aid into a comfortable retirement plan. Already having extensive coverage on the property, NSA quickly determined that Estrella's phone, provided by her husband, was quite secure. Yet the phone was not her sole channel of net access.

Either bored or exhausted from her exertions on Avenue Montaigne, Estrella had taken to amusing herself on Instagram and Facebook. Better yet, apparently in need of an improved platform for her browsing, it was discovered that she'd recently purchased a tablet device from the Apple store on Rue de Rivoli, and thereafter set up a string of accounts in her true name. The NSA knew all of this because she freely utilized the hotel's Wi-Fi, and because she ignored entirely VPN software. Such open networks were commonly referred to in the tech community as "plastic colanders"—nicely pliable and full of holes.

With a weakness identified, the NSA took up a fight that was hardly fair. In precisely seventeen seconds they cracked Estrella's tablet password: *vladimir* had been their second choice, after *password*. From there, the pursuit of Vladimir Ovechkin began in earnest. It was an increasingly common blunder among criminals, and consequently a vein often pursued by data miners, that as diligent as they might be in securing their own communications, they too often, and too carelessly, associated themselves with amateurs. Neckless thugs, buxom mistresses, Bahamian lawyers—all were engaged regularly, but few effected stringent internet safeguards.

So it was, as Ovechkin's third and best wife woke that morning and began exchanging shopping selfies with her friends, NSA analysts were hard at work sifting through her iPad. Files were downloaded, prioritized, and decrypted. As hoped, a string of emails with her husband was isolated, and that cyber address became the new target. Because Ovechkin himself was more security conscious, the subsequent trail took longer to follow. Yet he too had made mistakes.

Once the outer walls of Ovechkin's account were breached, the real work began. His messages were scoured for any leads on his present whereabouts. The contents of his inbox were largely business related, although one with a subject line titled "Men's holiday next February in Manila" was flagged for later follow-up. Disappointingly, the most recent email proved to be over a week old. This meant all activity predated the deaths of Ivanovic and Romanov, backing the idea that Ovechkin had indeed gone to ground in both an electronic and physical sense. Not to be defeated, the NSA did what they always did in such situations: they followed the money.

A link to an account with PVD Bank in St. Petersburg was extracted from a months-old email. As a rule, brick-and-mortar banks in Russia were a paranoid lot, and quite serious when it came to physical security. Guards stood in front of shored-up buildings to discourage armed gangs, and vaults were unusually solid. For the most part it worked.

More vexing, however, was the cyber back door. Banking regulators in Russia had become virtual bystanders, helpless to forestall online intrusions—an inevitable consequence of a government that turned a blind eye to, and at times even encouraged, hackers who wreaked chaos across the internet. This meant banks were on their own to fill online security gaps, and indeed they made a valiant effort, spending inordinate amounts of time and money to keep computer networks safe. By most accounts they were reasonably good at it.

The NSA, however, was better.

The firewall of PVD Bank was breached with little difficulty, and done in a way that left no evidence whatsoever of the intrusion. Ovechkin's accounts were combed for leads, and based on certain large transfers, it was clear that he kept accounts in other countries. All were flagged for follow-up when time was less critical. The NSA easily identified a handful of transactions relating to MIR Enterprises, and it became clear that Ovechkin's investment in the concern had so far been a one-way street—all expenses, no income. This wasn't unusual for a fledgling corporation, yet given what the CIA knew about MIR's business model—illegal arms shipments to high-risk Middle East neighborhoods—they strongly suspected that any profits were being piped elsewhere.

The most incisive find came near midmorning when Ovechkin was linked to a credit card. Hacking that account proved a challenge, but was eventually successful. The statements were a gold mine.

Teams pored over credit card transactions, and found charges from restaurants in Davos, Switzerland, and a spa in nearby St. Moritz. Ten days before that was an entire page placing Ovechkin in Moscow. At the top of the statement, however, were the two most telling purchases, both made within the last forty-eight hours. One was at a grocery store, the second a gas station. Finally, the bank's transaction log evidenced an hours-old balance inquiry from Ovechkin himself, and this led to a new IP address. The IP address could not be pinpointed, but it arrived via an internet service provider whose geographic coverage was narrowly definable. This, in turn, correlated perfectly with the gas station and grocery store. More would undoubtedly be discovered in time, but seven hours after beginning its quest, the CIA had what it wanted.

Vladimir Ovechkin was holed up somewhere along the southern coast of Morocco.

FORTY-EIGHT

While the CIA working groups tracking down Ovech-kin were having a productive morning, those hunting arms shipments in Saudi Arabia were making far less progress. Of the five caches that had reached the Red Sea shoreline, two were tracked to Duba, and one each to Gayal, Al Wajh, and Umluj. In what was thought to be a matter of atrocious bad luck, all the cargo was confirmed to have arrived ashore but subsequent movements proved untraceable due to gaps in satellite coverage. Embarrassing as it was, Langley could not track a single shipment beyond the docks.

Acting on the CIA's warning, the Saudis did their best to forestall whatever trouble was brewing. They inspected warehouses and delivery trucks in each of the identified ports. In a rented shed in Gayal, two crates were discovered that seemed to match the provided satellite images. Unfortunately, both had been emptied of their contents, and a witness reported that a group of men had loaded everything into a pair of trucks hours earlier. A description of the vehicles was quickly circulated, and one was found abandoned with a flat tire, still laden with its load, along a wadi outside town. The inventory discovered was exactly what the Americans had described—a dense collection of basic small arms. Another crate was discovered in a commercial garage in Duba, four men scattering to the wind minutes before the authorities arrived.

In National Guard headquarters in Riyadh, the influx of weapons was discussed at length during a hastily convened meeting of the security council. Everyone agreed that the smuggling operation was problematic, yet there was consensus that the Americans were exaggerating the scale of the operation. Many also expressed irritation that they had not been advised of the threat sooner—timely intervention as the boats came ashore would have been a showstopper. Their pique heightened further when a senior CIA man let slip that Israel had been helpful in uncovering the plot. The Saudi foreign minister in particular, who kept a seat on the security council, was nettled that Israel had inserted itself into the matter, no quarter given for their claim of "the good of the neighborhood."

Farther afield, the shipments sourced in the Gulf of Aden had by all accounts disappeared into the wilderness of Yemen—this to no one's surprise. Due to competing American surveillance commitments, the destinations of the shipments along the northern shores of the Persian Gulf had never been nailed down.

Up and down the Saudi establishment, everyone went through the motions. Detachments along the northern frontier were given vague orders to keep an eye out for possible weapons shipments, although no one could say just where or when they might take place. Police along both coastlines were ordered to look for suspicious vehicles. At various levels, the Saudi reaction vacillated from annoyance to caution to disbelief.

What those involved in the search—including the Americans—did not know was that leaders at the highest levels of the Saudi establishment were monumentally distracted by a wholly separate concern. It was not based on any specific threat, but centered around an event that had been on the books for months, and whose arrangements were proving a logistical nightmare.

For good reason, only a handful of princes and generals knew the full details. Among them, not a single one ever imagined that the two events could be linked.

Slaton's CIA phone rang as he got out of the shower. He answered with wet hair and a towel around his waist. The number wasn't familiar. The voice that greeted him was.

"We know roughly where Ovechkin is," said CIA director Coltrane.

"Roughly?"

"We've narrowed it down to fifty square miles of a certain country."

"Okay. Which miles in which country?"

"Before I tell you . . . I'd like to know why you're so interested."

Slaton hesitated. Only minutes ago, under a stream of hot water, he'd been asking himself the same question. He hedged with, "Because I don't think the CIA is going to pursue him."

"Ovechkin's involvement in this scheme won't be forgotten, I promise you that. But for the time being, he is not a priority. The situation in Saudi Arabia takes precedence. I'm sending Sorensen to Riyadh. She uncovered this threat, and the Saudis always respond better face-to-face—they're funny that way."

"You're taking her out of Rome? What about—"

"Don't worry, she told me about your arrangements. I issued the order myself—your wife and son will remain secure at the embassy."

"Okay . . . thanks for that." He decided that with Coltrane's backing, security for his family would only get tighter. He also didn't question the wisdom of sending a woman to deal with the House of Saud's exclusively male leadership. All things considered, he liked the idea of having someone he trusted inside that fence.

Coltrane said, "Since you didn't answer my question about your interest in Ovechkin, let me put it a different way. Is it him you're after, or this mysterious assassin?"

"I think one leads to the other. And sooner or later, both need to be reckoned with."

"For whose sake?"

Slaton didn't reply.

"You really want to chase this," said Coltrane, more an accusation than a question.

"I don't like loose ends. Right now I have an advantage, and I don't want to lose it."

"I'm not so sure about that advantage. Miss Sorensen briefed me on the bullet you recovered. It sounds like a revolutionary system."

"That remains to be seen. Every weapon has its weaknesses."

"So does every soldier."

An impasse developed, the faint hiss of static carrying in both directions. Coltrane broke it. "Begin in

Casablanca. Hopefully I can fine-tune your search by the time you arrive."

"Casablanca," Slaton repeated. He weighed it for a moment and thought it made sense. Some co-processing part of his brain began drawing maps and calculating distances in the background.

Coltrane gave Slaton a special phone number to reach him directly.

"And if I find Ovechkin?" Slaton asked.

"I can't tell you what to do. But if he stays alive long enough . . . we'd like very much to have a word with him."

At 12:35 that afternoon Sorensen learned she was booked on a 4:10 commercial flight to Riyadh, Saudi Arabia. Traffic on a Sunday would not be particularly bad, but all the same she rushed her preparations. With her bag packed and an embassy car being called up, she diverted to see Christine. Sorensen found her on the patio having juice and sweet bread with Davy.

"Care to join us?" Christine asked.

Sorensen thought she looked weary, but decided that was as it should be—she'd stayed up half the night watching her husband on a mission. "Wish I could," she said. "They're shipping me off to Saudi Arabia."

"When?"

"I'm leaving in ten minutes."

Christine's tight visage remained unchanged. "Does this have to do with—"

"Yeah, it does. The front office wants somebody on the ground who knows the situation."

After a few beats, Christine said, "I just got a call from David. He said he'll be gone a few more days—that he has one more thing to do."

"Did you ask what it was?"

"No. I only asked him to please come home as soon as he could."

"He will," Sorensen said. "I know it."

Christine locked eyes with her, deconstructing the answer. Wondering if it was based on insider knowledge or blind hope. Sorensen did her best to smile, and probably failed. She turned away abruptly and headed for the door.

FORTY-NINE

With the game shifting to Saudi Arabia, Slaton's status sank like a stone. He'd had the support of two of the world's leading intelligence agencies only hours earlier, but with everyone now busy tracking down arms shipments, he was no longer a priority operator. Which was why, for his journey to Morocco, he was relegated to flying commercial.

Bloch volunteered to drive him to the new Ramon International Airport north of Eilat. The desert swept past the windows in a tan blur as Bloch pushed the speedometer on a road with little traffic. The two forced a bit of small talk about Israeli politics, and then their respective families. There was no mention of the previous night's mission, nor any reminiscing about missions past. The former had been covered in debriefs and was ready for filing. The latter was left untouched because that was the custom of their relationship—certain memories were better left unsalvaged, like old shipwrecks whose ghosts ought not be disturbed.

Slaton checked in thirty minutes early for his Air France flight to Casablanca, with a mandatory connection in Paris. He and Bloch were still together upon reaching the boarding area—the former Mossad director might be retired, but he retained enough clout to bypass airport security.

"You have told me where you are going," Bloch said. "But I'm not clear on *why* you're going there."

"Neither am I," replied Slaton.

"Aaron and the others asked me to pass along that they would be happy to assist if needed. It couldn't be anything sanctioned, you understand . . . but I suspect Director Nurin might give them a week's leave to relax on the Atlantic."

"Tell them thanks, and that I'll keep it in mind. But hopefully that won't be necessary."

"Will the CIA provide you help?"

"Probably—they gave me the intel I'm working from. But you know how fickle intelligence chiefs can be."

Bloch might have grinned.

"Anyway," Slaton went on, "the Americans are pretty busy right now hunting down these shipments."

"From what I hear, they are so far having little success. The Saudis are good at certain things. They have advanced airplanes and hardware, and funding is never an issue. Are you aware that they have the third biggest defense budget of any country in the world? They actually outspend Russia. Unfortunately, money does not always buy safety. There comes a point when one must get one's hands dirty. Developing human networks on home ground, battering down doors in the middle of the night, inserting spies into neighboring capitals. These things have never been a Saudi strength—and that's what it takes in our little corner of the world."

Slaton nodded cautiously. "Honestly, Anton, I don't really consider this my corner anymore. In fact, the world would be better off without corners."

Bloch's lips went to an upturned U. "Dear God, next you'll be telling me you're a social democrat."

"Hardly."

"Be that as it may . . . do you have my number in case you need assistance?"

"I do, and thanks for offering."

"It's not just me. The director asked me to express his personal appreciation for your work last night. He feels as though he owes you."

Slaton reached into his pocket and presented Bloch with a heavy object wrapped in cloth. "Now he owes me more."

Bloch turned the cloth to uncover the damaged fifty-caliber round. "Is this what I think it is?" Slaton had alluded to its existence earlier.

"It is. I think the CIA would be interested as well. After you've had first look, please share it with them."

"I will forward your wishes. Nurin and his Technology Department will be happy to have it."

"That's not who I'm giving it to."

Bloch nodded. Slaton knew he understood.

"In that case," Bloch said, "the State of Israel thanks you."

The sergeant found the key to the small house under a weed-filled plant pot near the front door. Who had put it there he had no idea, but the logistics were as reliable as ever. Cars, air transport, safe houses, cash—all were his for the asking. He thought it would be a nice way to go through life.

He went inside and saw a living area with a low box-beam ceiling, a combined kitchen and dinette, sided by one small bedroom. To say the place was dated would be putting it kindly—this from an army enlisted man who'd grown up in a farmhouse built before the rule of Lenin. The walls were some kind of stucco, and appeared unpainted. The furniture was simple and fusty, the flower-print curtains on the windows serviceable but worn. A lone shelf on one wall held a row of paperback mystery novels, English language versions all dog-eared and yellowed with age. Add a seventy-year-old widow, he thought, and the picture would be complete.

He went through a door with squeaking hinges and climbed a short set of stairs to a pergola-topped patio. He walked to the edge and was rewarded with a stunning view of the sea. The shack overlooked a beachfront cliff, and was set back coyly in a narrow ravine. He looked straight down and saw the seaward foundation supported by a half dozen timbers that looked as old as the rest. *If they've held up that long*, he reasoned, *they'll last a few more days.*

He scanned the horizon and saw one house to the distant north, another to the south. The latter was the closer of the two, a mile away at the base of a minor peninsula. An unseen gull cawed, and he heard the hum of a distant car passing. The coast road was far behind him, the long setback ideal for privacy.

The sergeant went back inside. In the kitchen he found groceries in the cupboard and a few basics in a small refrigerator. Tea, bread, canned meat, milk. Two tomatoes sat on the shelf by the window. He set a pot of water on the stove, lit the burner, and went back outside. From the highest point on the patio he strained to see south along the cliffs. Five miles further on, he knew, was another villa, yet there was no line of sight. The coastline ribboned away in that direction, and all along its length was a two-hundred-foot drop to the narrow beachhead below.

A *challenge,* he thought, *but nothing insurmountable.*

He went back inside, then out front to his car. He retrieved his luggage and brought it all to the bedroom. Setting the heaviest case on the bed, he flicked open the latches and lifted the lid. He left the Barrett where it was, but removed the targeting unit and its power cord. The battery was nearly dead, and he located the only electrical outlet in the room and plugged in the charger. He realized he should have mentioned that to the engineers: battery life in the field had been lacking, especially in the cold of Davos. He'd managed the issue so far, but it ought to be corrected.

He checked his satellite phone and saw nothing new. No changes in the schedule, nothing about his target. Best of all, nothing about his pursuer. That was something the sergeant couldn't ignore. The man he'd seen in Davos, who might or might not have been Slaton, had been close on his heels. Might he still be? He dwelled on the question for only a moment.

He set the big case on the floor next to the rollerbag— there was no luggage rack in the doorless closet. He resisted an urge to make use of the three coat hangers provided. He wasn't going to be here long, and leaving his clothing packed seemed the best choice. Like so many places he'd stayed over the years, the business of settling in was performed with departure in mind.

He went to the kitchen, set his phone on the small table. He strolled to the bookcase and ran a finger across a row of bonded spines. Making his selection, he pulled an old techno-thriller from the shelf and settled onto a couch with wayward springs. He cracked the book open and began to read.

FIFTY

Captain Zakaryan prided himself on being a master who kept the pulse of his ship. He knew when the cook was slacking, when engineers smoked below deck in prohibited areas, and when a good drunken shore leave was in order. Early yesterday, the mood aboard *Argos* had been the foulest he'd ever seen, south of resignation but not quite to mutiny. Now, one day removed, with *Argos* running fast under a bright midday sun and the shores of Djibouti on the distant starboard rail, the atmosphere was nothing short of buoyant.

He sat with two of his officers at a table in the mess hall. The cook had prepared a zesty Thai dish that was going over well, and Zakaryan had ordered that a case of beer be distributed among those not on duty—the second shift would be treated later. His executive officer was in the middle of an off-color joke when Ivan appeared at the mess hall entrance. He said nothing, but simply stood in the passageway and stared.

A frowning Zakaryan excused himself before his second reached his punch line.

"What is it?" he asked, stepping through the water-tight door to face Ivan.

"A meeting must be called."

"What kind of meeting?"

"The kind that everyone will attend," Ivan said.

"*Everyone?* I can't muster the entire crew—someone has to mind the ship!"

"How many?"

"Four is the minimum on watch—three on the bridge and one on deck."

"Very well. But spread the word that every other man must be present—twenty minutes." The Russian turned and strode away.

Zakaryan wasn't surprised. Not really. They'd assembled a similar meeting in Sebastopol before setting sail, and the entire crew had been in attendance. Everyone listened for ten minutes as Ivan had explained how he and his men were on board as representatives of MIR Enterprises. Zakaryan tried to imagine what the subject would be this time. His best guess was that Ivan would put on his most threatening tone and warn everyone against discussing their voyage in the wharfside bars.

Yes, he thought, *that's got to be it.*

Minutes later his crew began filing into the mess hall.

The CIA operations center was tracking *Argos* closely. For thirty hours the ship traversed the Red Sea southward, and by midday local time, the day after her offload, she was clearing the narrow Bab al-Mandeb Strait. This put her in the Gulf of Aden, with the limitless Indian Ocean stretching out ahead.

It was here, slightly north of the port of Djibouti, that *Argos* began to slow and maneuver. The senior watch officer in Langley was the first to notice. "What's going on?" she wondered aloud.

Any of the ten people in the room might have ventured an answer. Not surprisingly, it was the maritime specialist in a corner-pocket workstation, a retired Navy commander, who said, "I don't think she's headed into port after all. She's steering north, away from Djibouti."

The significance was lost on no one. Everyone's eyes went to the other two square symbols with data tags that were no more than twenty miles distant. *Cirrus* and *Tasman Sea* were both steaming south.

"Whatever's happening, I don't like it," said the watch officer. "I'm calling the boss."

Director Coltrane's instructions had been clear: he was to be notified of "any appreciable change in the situation." The alteration of *Argos*' course apparently qualified, because five minutes later the director was standing at the head of the room looking at the sea of monitors. As they all watched, the brazen arms smuggling operation they'd been tracking for days took a new and unexpected turn.

"Are they doing what I think they're doing?" Coltrane wondered aloud.

In fact, the picture before them was increasingly clear. *Argos* had slowed on a northerly course, while *Cirrus* and *Tasman Sea* were on intersecting southerly courses. In effect, MIR Enterprises' entire fleet of three vessels was executing a rendezvous at sea.

"What could they be up to?" asked the watch officer, posing the question in everyone's mind.

"What's our source here?" Coltrane asked, pointing to the main monitor.

"Right now satellite—we may hit a gap soon."

"Can we get a drone on station?"

Everyone's eyes went to the coordinator who managed such requests. He typed furiously for two minutes before announcing, "Air Force is the best option. They can divert another mission, but it will take forty minutes to get overhead."

"Do it!" Coltrane ordered, sensing that forty minutes was about to seem like a very long time. "What about the Navy? Any ships in the area?"

Another pause, then, "*Decatur*. She's an Arleigh Burke–class destroyer . . . sixty miles north."

"Send a message that we need eyes on this. Ask nicely—the Navy has been a pain in the ass lately."

Everyone watched what seemed like a slow-motion dance on the primary screen. The squares representing the ships had nearly merged. When they were four miles apart, the point of convergence seemed assured.

"Is there something special about that spot?" Coltrane asked. "Whose territorial waters are we talking about here?"

The technician who ran the banks of monitors added territorial lines to the display—an invaluable overlay when it came to operational decisions.

"All three ships are outside twelve miles," said the watch officer. "Djibouti, Yemen, Somalia—they're free and clear in open water."

"So why *there*?" Coltrane muttered.

What seemed a rhetorical question was actually answered, again by the technician who ran the displays. He said, "Maybe you should take a look at this, sir."

The central monitor altered, and the overlay that was added took a few beats for everyone to comprehend—it was a bathymetric chart, the contours of the sea floor and associated depths presented. Right away everyone saw the significance.

"God Almighty . . ." Coltrane said.

As the ships closed to within three nautical miles

of one another, they were positioned perfectly over the deep marine trough that ran parallel to the Saudi peninsula. With over eight thousand feet of water beneath their keels, the tiny fleet was joining up over the deepest trench in the Gulf of Aden.

"Is everyone present?" Ivan asked.

"Yes," Zakaryan replied, having just completed a head count. "Now tell me what this is about."

The crew, minus the four on duty, had filed into the mess room. Every table was full, and a few were left standing near the door leading to the galley. The prevailing look on their faces was one of strained patience—to a man, everyone wanted to get this cruise over with and dump their Russian passengers.

"We will begin in a moment," Ivan announced. He went to the mess hall entrance and stood at the threshold. Less than a minute later, the four crewmen who were supposed to be on duty came through the passageway, the last in line stumbling from a shove. Behind them were two of Ivan's thugs, each with a machine pistol leveled.

"*What are you doing?*" Zakaryan demanded. "The boat is running untended! We can't leave—"

Zakaryan was silenced when Ivan lifted a handgun and pointed it at his head. The captain stood frozen.

Without another word the Russian stepped backward through the watertight door that doubled as the mess hall entrance. He disappeared, and the door immediately clanged shut. Somewhere behind them, deep in the galley, it happened a second time—the sound of a flood door thumping into place.

"What's going on?" a crewman asked nervously.

Everyone heard heavy noises outside, and the door's

twin bolting handles dropped into position. Zakaryan rushed to the door and tried to open it. The handles were jammed. He turned and ran for the galley—it was the only other way out of the joined compartments. Another man beat him there, only to find that the galley exit, which led to the aft quarterdeck, had also been immobilized.

Zakaryan rushed back to the mess hall. His crew looked at him expectantly. He was contemplating what to say, something calm and authoritative, when *Argos* was shaken to her core by a violent explosion.

"What just happened?" Coltrane bellowed.

The closest thing to an answer came from the sensor technician. "Switching to infrared."

The image of *Argos* on the screen altered to a different spectrum, and the problem could not have been more clear—blossoming from her aft port side was a massive heat signature, enough to warm the surrounding sea.

"That would be an explosion," said the watch officer.

"A big one," the Navy commander remarked. "She's already starting to list."

"Sir!" said the watch officer, pointing to a different screen.

Coltrane shifted his gaze and saw *Tasman Sea* presenting a nearly identical picture. Then, as the entire room watched, *Cirrus* disappeared momentarily in a flash of light and smoke.

"Sweet Jesus," Coltrane remarked. "They're all being scuttled."

"What about the crews?" the watch officer asked. "Each of these ships must have twenty or thirty—"

"Look!" a technician nearly shouted.

On the periphery of one screen a small boat came into view. It was dagger-shaped and moving fast—heading straight toward *Tasman Sea*. Everyone watched in silence as the fast-mover closed in on the bigger ship. The image was magnified as the boat slowed suddenly, and four men could be seen leaping from *Tasman Sea*'s slanted deck into the water. The sleek boat picked up all four survivors. It then set out at high speed in the direction of *Cirrus*.

"There have to be more crew than that on board," said the watch officer.

"Oh, there are," Coltrane responded. He whipped around to the coordinator. "Where's *Decatur*?"

"Sixteen miles north. She should arrive on scene in . . . roughly thirty minutes."

"Tell the Navy to push it up—flank speed or whatever the hell they call it! This is an emergency!"

Over the next ten minutes everyone watched as the speedboat collected four men from each of the three sinking ships. It then sped off, at a computed speed of fifty-two knots, toward the lawless frontier that was the coast of Yemen. In that time, *Cirrus* disappeared beneath the waves. The other two ships were nearly submerged, minutes from joining her. Aside from those rescued by the cigarette boat, not a single survivor was apparent on the foundering decks or in the water.

"Do we have *any* assets in the area that might be able to intercept this fast mover?" Coltrane asked pleadingly. "If that boat reaches Yemen we're going to lose her."

"I've already checked," said the coordinator. "Nothing that could catch up. The only chance would be *Decatur*. She has a decent angle—at top speed she might be able to intercept the smaller boat. But if she does that—"

"I know what the choices are," said an exasperated Coltrane. "We can either chase down that boat or search for survivors. But we can't do both."

It was the easiest decision Coltrane had faced on that day. Unfortunately, he was quite sure where it would lead. For the next two hours the U.S. destroyer *Decatur* executed a by-the-book search pattern, amid oil slicks and debris, over the deepest trench in the Gulf of Aden.

Not a single survivor was found.

FIFTY-ONE

Slaton realized he'd been spoiled as of late when he had to suppress disappointment at not having a private jet for his journey to Morocco. His welcome back to the real world had been finalized the previous night when his connection to Casablanca from Paris Charles De Gaulle was canceled at the last minute.

He was forced to wait until the next morning, and spent the night at an airport hotel. During that layover, he'd called Christine to give her an update on where he was headed. Their conversation could be condensed to its final exchange.

Are you sure you want to do this? she'd asked.

No, Slaton replied, staring out a broad window at an airliner lifting from a runway. *But I'm sure it needs to be done.*

Christine had not argued, and first thing this morning he was back in the airport security line.

He arrived in Casablanca on the stroke of noon. The arrival queues were surprisingly busy, and it took nearly an hour to clear customs and immigration. That, at least, went without a hitch, and minutes after his CIA-furnished passport was returned, he was cutting through the terminal crowds like a deer through forest.

He saw rental car counters in the distance, but before going that route Slaton decided to make a phone call. He dialed the direct number Coltrane had provided. No one picked up after ten rings, and there was no voice-mail option.

So much for my private line, he thought, ending the call. He tried not to take it personally—the man *was* director of the CIA, and presumably had other issues on his agenda.

He diverted outside, and steered away from the busy curb where taxis and buses were doing a brisk business. At the end of the sidewalk he looked out across the far reaches of the airfield. A handful of small aircraft were parked in line at a flight school, and beyond them he saw a modest air cargo building. With minimal contemplation, Slaton placed a call to his backup source.

Anna Sorensen picked up immediately.

Slaton said, "I just tried to reach your boss, but he didn't answer."

"I'm not surprised. There's a crisis right now."

"When is there not?"

"Hang on . . ." There was a thirty-second pause, and Slaton heard a series of clicks on the line. Sorensen's voice returned. "All right, encryption is verified. You probably haven't heard about *Argos*—she just sank off the coast of Yemen."

"Sank?"

"There's more." She explained what had happened to MIR Enterprises' other two ships, and that a speedboat had rescued four men from each. "We had a Navy destroyer on the scene within minutes, and two merchant ships have joined the search. There don't appear to be any survivors."

"There had to be fifteen, maybe twenty men on

the ship I saw," he said, recalling the busy crew he'd watched from the shadows of *Argos*' hull. He also recalled the one man who'd struck him as something other than a typical sailor. *Number three guide on top, number one on the sides.* Slaton had mentioned him in his debriefing with Mossad, as had Aaron. They'd both pegged him as some manner of "security," and suspected he wasn't alone. Yet neither could have imagined this. Not a security team, but rather executioners in wait. A team of four on each ship. Waiting to destroy evidence in the most comprehensive way possible. "Were you able to track these guys who ran?"

"No, the boat they boarded was fast—it headed straight toward Yemen and we lost track near the shoreline. We're trying to pick up a trail, but I wouldn't count on it—our networks in Yemen aren't the most reliable."

"Which is why they chose it. This whole operation looks more professional by the minute. It's almost certainly state-sponsored—and the guy I saw looked Russian."

"That keeps coming up, doesn't it?"

"Yeah . . . it's beyond coincidence."

"Way beyond," she agreed. "These ships got scuttled and the crews were murdered."

"Aside from trying to locate these kill squads, how is the CIA responding?"

"We're continuing to press the Saudis—we think there should be a stronger response to these arms shipments. Since I'm up to speed on what's happening, Coltrane sent me to Riyadh."

"I know."

A brief pause. "You do?"

"He mentioned it when I last talked to him. He

said the Saudis tend to be more forthcoming in person."

"True enough. So do you have any better news? Any luck finding Ovechkin?"

"I just got to Casablanca—flight delays. I called your boss a few minutes ago hoping he'd have more for me to work with. The search box he gave me is a little overwhelming—I've got to narrow it down somehow."

"So since you couldn't get hold of him, you called me?"

"Something like that."

"Wish I could help," she said, "but I haven't heard anything new. If I talk to the director, I'll tell him what you want. But as you can probably understand—Ovechkin isn't the priority right now."

After agreeing to keep in touch, Slaton ended the call. He pocketed the phone and looked at the rental car counters in the terminal.

He wondered how he was going to find Ovechkin in a fifty-square-mile area. He once again swept his gaze across the greater airport. His eye was caught by a sign in the distance, and a new idea took hold. It would be, without doubt, an extravagant option.

It would also be the quickest way to cover a lot of ground.

FIFTY-TWO

"Excuse me . . ."

Rayan Omar turned with a start, banging his head on an engine cowling as he did so. A man he'd never seen before was standing behind him. He was rather tall, with a strong build and light hair. The eyes, an unusual shade of gray, held him amiably.

"I'm sorry," the man said, "I didn't mean to startle you. Do you speak English?"

Omar nodded. "Sure, a little bit." He rubbed the sore spot on his scalp, and wondered why he hadn't heard the man approach over the hangar's hard concrete floor.

"Are you a mechanic for the air service?"

"Mechanic, pilot, refueler. Whatever is needed today."

The visitor looked surprised, but was still smiling. "Pilot and mechanic?"

"No airplane is better maintained than the one flown by a man who is both."

"Yes . . . I see your point. My name is Ericson." A hand was offered. Omar wiped one of his own with a greasy rag and the two shook.

"You are Norwegian?" Omar asked, trying to nail down the man's accent.

"Swedish, actually. I'm a real estate developer. I flew in today for a business meeting, and while I'm in the area I wanted to scout out a few properties. I'd like to inquire about chartering an aircraft for an hour or two."

Omar tipped his head noncommittally to one side. Not because he was uncertain about the prospect, but to avoid an appearance of eagerness. "Where precisely do you wish to go?"

"South along the coast. Thirty, maybe forty miles."

Omar straightened a bit. "Yes, that might be possible." He mentioned how busy things were this time of year, hoping the man hadn't seen the empty parking lot out front. He also remarked on the recent price rises of aviation fuel, perhaps with some exaggeration. Only then did he put forward a ruinous hourly rate.

The Swede never flinched, suggesting to Omar that the man was operating on a deep expense account. In truth, it was a more accurate assessment than he might have imagined, although he could never have guessed the source of the funds backing the credit card in his pocket. Omar was thinking about properties to the north as well, when the Swede said, "There is one catch—today is the only day I'm free."

Omar winced. He turned and gestured toward the twin Comanche behind him. "All three of my fleet are in the shop. This one might be ready tomorrow, but no sooner."

The Swede turned circumspect. He looked out through the hangar door, and Omar hoped the sign on his competitor's building wasn't in view: Fly It Again Sam Tour Flights and Charters.

Feeling the deal slipping away, he quickly said, "There might be one possibility . . ."

He led the real estate man to the hangar's rear door, then out into the torrid midday sun. There, grilling on the black tarmac, was a Bell Jet Ranger. It had been a sleek helicopter in its day, even if that day was forty years ago. The red paint had faded to something near ochre. One of the skids was bent—not by any fault of Omar's, but from an unfortunate towing incident—and the two rotor blades appeared to rest at distinctly different pitches. On the asphalt beneath the chopper was a puddle of something blue. It certainly wasn't his showcase aircraft—but as far as he knew, she was airworthy.

"Can you fly it?" the customer asked.

Omar grinned broadly, and said that he could.

Colonel Zhukov was not a happy man. He stood rigidly in the big mission truck, the air inside cool and dry to support banks of electronic gear. He was hovering behind a very busy Tikhonov.

The test flight had been scheduled for noon, but difficulties with telemetry links had forced a delay. It was not unexpected. The mission control truck was thirty miles from the RosAvia complex. Parked on a remote gravel service road, it cut a lonely figure in one of the most remote regions of Morocco—this in a country that served as threshold to the Sahara. Today that remoteness was entirely the point.

The live-fire exercise could only be performed over unpopulated desert. This morning two of Tikhonov's men had scoured the "shoot box" using ATVs just to make sure no wayward goat herders or adventurous European hikers were at risk. So too, the airspace above them had been cleared by Moroccan air traffic control. Taken together, it made the area an airborne firing range, twenty square miles of sky and earth sanitized of all bystanders. And, from Zhukov's point of view, all witnesses.

It was nearly two thirty when the engineer finally had his electronic kinks straightened out.

"The MiG is airborne," Tikhonov announced from his workstation.

A still simmering Zhukov said nothing.

The takeoff was being performed by one of Tikhonov's technicians, who would at that moment be under the umbrella on the roof of the Sprinter van. Zhukov listened to the same sequence he'd heard two days ago, albeit from the opposing radio.

"*Prepare for transfer.*"

"*Ready to accept control.*"

"*On my mark. Three . . . two . . . one . . . execute.*"

"I have the aircraft," Tikhonov announced from his soft swivel chair.

Zhukov stared at the radar display and saw two white dots, both sided by data tags. One was the MiG, closing in fast from the west. The other had been orbiting overhead for fifteen minutes. That aircraft was a modified M-143 drone, originally designed for the Russian military as a target for testing air-to-air and surface-to-air missiles. At twenty-six feet long, and with a narrow wingspan, it was smaller than most aircraft, but had a fighter-like top speed of over five hundred knots. Powered by a small turbojet engine, the M-143 had been launched from a truck just outside the aerial range. Tikhonov commanded it to fly wide circles as they awaited the MiG.

"Twenty-five miles and closing fast," Tikhonov said. "I am going to activate the MiG's targeting pod. As soon as that feed is verified, the drone will be released into its maneuvering run. Everything will happen quickly from that point."

"How long do I have?" Zhukov asked.

"Five minutes. If you wish to go outside, now is the time. Remember where I told you to look."

It was Tikhonov who'd suggested that he watch from outside. The "full effect," he'd called it. Everything on the monitors would be logged for further analysis, and could be gone over later frame by frame. The spectacle in the sky above them, however, would not be recorded. Not in any way.

Zhukov weaved between consoles in the darkened control center, and when he opened the door the bright midday sun hit like a Taser. He squinted severely, but his eyes quickly adjusted. He walked clear of the big truck and scanned the horizon to the west. He picked out the distinctive mountain, miles away, that Tikhonov had given him as a reference point. From there Zhukov looked up. He removed a water bottle from the thigh pocket of his cargo pants, took a swig, then snugged it back in place. He lifted the binoculars hanging round his neck and, like the tank commander he'd once been, surveyed the flawless blue sky.

He swept the optics back and forth for a full two minutes before spotting the loitering drone. It was roughly three miles away, a tiny silhouette enhanced by its bright orange paint job—the same shade as the MiG's tail. He followed the aircraft through two lazy circles, then saw it veer suddenly into a hard turn.

Zhukov knew the profile because he had dictated it: the target drone would descend to two thousand feet above the desert floor, then take up a straight and level path at two hundred and fifty knots. There would be no evasive maneuvering, no countermeasures of any kind. The one thing he'd not dictated was the course, and when the drone rolled out of its turn it seemed to be rushing straight at him. Was Tikhonov aware? Had he planned it this way? Zhukov recalled with unease the pool of charred earth he'd seen where one of the jets had crashed.

He pulled his eyes away from the glasses and tried to spot the MiG. The problem was that he didn't know from which direction the jet would come. It had to be near, and flying far faster than the target—this too was in the profile. Zhukov began to alternate, scanning the sky with his naked eyes, then using the binoculars. The target drone was getting bigger, no longer simply an orange silhouette, but an aircraft with wings and a top-mounted engine. When it was inside two miles, still headed straight at him, the binoculars were no longer necessary.

Was there a technical problem with the MiG? he wondered. A failure of some kind?

Then it came out of nowhere.

In an explosion of noise the fighter rushed no more than fifty feet over Zhukov's head. The jet was going so fast, he would later realize, that it was nearly outrunning its own sound signature. A shock wave hit, an incredible wall of noise. Caught by surprise, Zhukov instinctively stepped back, and in doing so stumbled on a rock and ended up on his ass. His water bottle bounded from his thigh pocket and splattered him with water.

Even so distracted, Zhukov never let his eyes waver from the MiG. He watched the two forms merge with a nearly head-on aspect. Watched the distance between them close in a blur. *Hitting a bullet with a bullet.* That was how Tikhonov had described it, but it didn't do justice to what he was witnessing. The MiG tipped one wing in the final instant, a last desperate correction, and then the predestined end: an incredible midair collision.

Zhukov recoiled at the sight of what looked like two meteors colliding. Orange flames burst outward in a ragged sphere, a release of energy that for an instant overpowered the midday sun. The sound wave was next, and even half a mile away Zhukov felt the conflagration's heat as it spread across the desert. When the nova of bright orange flames receded, it was replaced by smoke and spinning fragments of wreckage. He heard skittering sounds in the desert all around, and knew instantly what they were: bits of fiery shrapnel finding their everlasting homes.

The explosion dissipated gradually, like a wave on the beach backing into the sea. Zhukov pulled himself to his feet, his burst water bottle in one hand, the binoculars still in the other. The desert in the distance was littered with smoldering wreckage, and a few final pieces of debris fluttered to the ground, tracers of white smoke marking their path like so many sputtering fireworks. The next thing Zhukov heard was rolling laughter behind him. He turned and saw Tikhonov at the top of the steps. He had one hand on the door of the control truck, and the other pointed a finger as he laughed.

Zhukov looked down. The front of his pants were sodden—surely from the open water bottle. He let the engineer have his moment.

Tikhonov suddenly fell distracted. He reached out and removed a jagged piece of metal that had embedded in the outer wall of the truck. The engineer studied it for a moment, then tossed it aside. "That was perhaps a bit too close," he said. Without waiting for a response, he descended the stairs. "Come, Colonel, let's have a closer look."

They walked across hardpan desert to the smoldering debris field. On arriving, both men meandered amid the bits of twisted metal, avoiding stands of scrub that had caught fire. The acrid smell of jet fuel laced the air.

They paused near the largest section of wreckage, the MiG's vertical tail, which was largely intact. The engineer looked at him triumphantly. "And there you are. We now have proof—the system works. I have done everything you've asked."

Zhukov's eyes narrowed, and he responded in a sulfurous tone, "Not quite, my friend. You have done everything I've asked so far. But now I can tell you the rest—the one thing that remains."

"What are you talking about?" asked Tikhonov.

Zhukov explained the project's final test. Then he explained why Tikhonov was going to perform it. When he was done, the engineer was no longer smiling.

FIFTY-THREE

The helicopter did indeed fly.

As a rule, Slaton trusted things mechanical—snipers, after all, bet their lives on well-machined levers and bolts. The contraption in which he was riding, however, was a stern test of that conviction. It clattered and rumbled, and every buffet from the turbulent midday air seemed to translate directly into his seat. He was riding up front, at the right-hand copilot's station. The flight instruments before him vibrated to a blur, needles bouncing chaotically inside gauges trimmed with red-and-green arcs. Most of them, thankfully, remained in the green.

Slaton had ridden in his share of helicopters, usually advanced military models that whisked him across borders on moonless nights. On those flights he was invariably weighed down by weapons and gear, not to mention the attendant trepidation that came with such equipment. The mission he was conducting now—a sightseeing excursion over sunsplashed coastline, perusing seaside hotels and mansions—was a new line for his résumé.

"We'll be clear of town soon," said Omar. "The coastline you wish to see begins a few miles ahead."

Slaton heard Omar loud and clear through the

noise-canceling headset he'd been given, a necessity against the din of the engine and *whump whump* of the rotor blades. On Slaton's request, they were cruising a thousand feet above the water and half a mile offshore—distant enough to not draw attention, but keeping a clear view of things.

"There is the property I would choose!" said Omar. He pointed to a particular villa along a beach that was thick with them. Slaton saw an expansive pool, and on the adjacent deck a young woman was sunbathing nude, oblivious to the passing helicopter.

"I don't see a for sale sign," he said.

"Too bad. Perhaps she could be part of the bargain."

Slaton contemplated a number of responses, taking into account his budding relationship with the man, Islamic moral standards, and guys being guys. In the end he could think of no reply that would advance his mission.

A mile farther on, Omar pointed out a midsized hotel on a bluff overlooking the sea. "This place was recently sold—it was owned by one of the richest men in town. I suspect it is quite profitable. I can tell you it does a good wedding business." As if to prove the point, a large group of well-dressed people were mingling on a broad terrace. Tables with catered food had been set up to one side, and white curtains billowed beside flowered trellises.

"I prefer to invest in private residences," Slaton said. "They're easier to manage from a distance."

They were fifteen miles from Casablanca's airport, skimming southward at a hundred knots, when the trappings of civilization began to fall away. Sand beaches and man-made breakwaters yielded to stone tide pools and natural escarpments. Hotels and condos gave way to private residences. There were grand new villas and old cabins, at first shoulder to shoulder, then spreading farther apart as the city faded behind them. Slaton thought most of the homes looked unoccupied, meaning this seafront was no different from any other—as more of the world's wealth coalesced in fewer hands, the lucky winners were increasingly spread thin. They rotated between beaches like these and marinas in Capri. Mountainsides in Davos.

Yes, Slaton thought, *this is just the kind of place Ovechkin would run to.*

Omar maneuvered toward a promontory that jutted into the sea, a thousand-foot-high finger of stone presiding above rough-hewn shores. As they neared the crest, an updraft caught the chopper, and Omar fought the controls momentarily as the aircraft lurched sideways. The old Jet Ranger seemed to groan in protest, and something behind them clattered to the floor. Omar seemed not to notice.

"The coastline is rugged for the next twenty miles," he said. "There are many cliffs and coves. You'll see fewer villas here, but some are very nice, very private. I can fly closer to any that catch your eye."

"Thanks, I'll let you know."

Omar was right—as the coastline became more isolated, Slaton saw great stretches of barren cliff between residences. Unfortunately, even if things remained the same for another twenty miles he would be looking at hundreds of possibilities. He was struck by a sudden sense of futility, and began to doubt his strategy. The premise of renting a chopper had seemed a good option. Ovechkin was likely hiding somewhere along this thirty-mile stretch of shoreline. But even so, that left too many possibilities.

He checked his phone and saw a good connection. Disappointingly, there were no new messages. He was never going to find the Russian this way. Slaton tried to put his doubts aside, and soon began to think more positively. The tour flight wasn't a waste of time—he was learning the lay of the land, getting a feel for coves and terrain he might soon have to negotiate.

He was watching the ever-changing shoreline whisk past when Omar said, "We are now thirty miles south. Do you wish to go farther?"

Slaton hesitated. "No," he finally said. "Let's head back."

"Along the beach?"

He looked inland and saw a narrow valley nestled between banks of brown hills. Not wanting to rely too heavily on his assumptions, he said, "Let's turn ashore. Fly up the first valley."

The pilot did so, and soon the Jet Ranger was cradled between the gentle slopes of opposing tawny ridgelines.

It would be another day before Slaton realized his mistake. Had he asked Omar to continue another four miles southward, rounding one last wall of cliffs along the coast, he would have encountered a sight to behold. And a sight that would have changed his thinking entirely.

The vital thread of intelligence that put the CIA back on track came not from the usual sources. For an agency that prided itself on the efficacy of satellites, listening posts, and cyber intrusions, it was a flashback of sorts, and a victory for the few remaining hands of the Cold War, that they were saved that day not by technology, but rather a human source. Or more concisely: a Yemeni garbageman with a fondness for good Scotch.

The agent's handler was an Omani-American, a deep-cover CIA officer who traveled extensively through Yemen's coastal regions under the guise of selling bulldozers—a shockingly lucrative trade in a country that was continuously either demolishing war-torn buildings or erecting their replacements. As both a rearranger and collector of dirt, the CIA officer had long come to realize that municipal garbage workers were among the most useful of spies. They were natural visitors to every corner of a city, and notoriously poorly compensated. They also handled all manner of discarded trash, a long established source of valuable intelligence. Best of all—trash collectors were among the most unseen and unremembered individuals on the planet.

The recruit in question was particularly useful thanks to his route—he collected refuse every Monday from bins around the international airport in Aden. At the outset the handler paid cash, on a pro rata basis, for whatever intelligence the Yemeni could dredge up. The agent dead-dropped information to the CIA via false bottoms in select garbage cans around the city, and he proved consistently productive. Quite by accident—a spontaneous re-gift during the holiday season—the handler discovered that even better results could be inspired when the usual retainer was supplemented by a fifth of Macallan double cask Scotch. So incentivized, the agent put on display an extraordinary new show of industry. In short order, his code name was changed to Macallan, and his communication links were upgraded from trash can bottoms to a satellite phone.

It was through this device, during the course of his regular rounds, that he proved his worth once again that afternoon.

Macallan had received an urgent, and very specific, message to keep a lookout around the airport. He'd no sooner pocketed his phone to dump a can into his truck than he spied something very near what he'd been asked to look for: a large contingent of non-natives arriving in a rush. Telling his partner he needed to pee, Macallan disappeared around the side of a small aviation repair shop. He took two pictures and sent them immediately. He could never have imagined the audience they would find thousands of miles to the west.

"The airplane near the hangar is an Embraer Legacy," said an analyst at a central console in the Langley operations center. He was referencing an overhead image, refreshed every few seconds, of a parking ramp on the airfield in Aden—they'd wasted no time in getting drone coverage. "Macallan's picture shows eleven men getting on board, all carrying equipment."

"It doesn't look big enough to hold that many," remarked Director Coltrane, who'd just arrived and was being brought up to speed on the development.

"Standard crew of two, up to thirteen passengers in a normal configuration. It'll be cramped, but under the circumstances I suspect our hijackers will squeeze in."

Coltrane looked at the second jet on the drone feed before them. "And that one?"

"A Citation X, much smaller. One man got on board."

"Are we sure these are the men who scuttled those ships?"

"It's only circumstantial," said the duty officer. "We suspect that twelve individuals, at least one a non-Arab, were responsible for the sinkings. That's how many were plucked out of the sea by a fast boat and run ashore. Three hours later, twelve non-Arabs show up at the nearest airport and board a pair of private jets. That's all we can say for sure. There's a chance they could be something else—oil workers, maybe construction laborers."

Coltrane didn't bother to respond. The duty officer had made his point, but no one was buying it. "Can we find out where these jets are going?"

"We're working on it," the duty officer replied. "They look ready to depart, which means they'll have flight plans in the system."

"Do airplanes need flight plans in Yemen?"

"They do if they want to enter anybody else's airspace without getting shot down."

"Here it is," announced a voice from the back of the room. "One jet filed to Kubinka Air Base, just outside Moscow."

Moscow, Coltrane thought. *Why am I not surprised?* "Which jet is going there?" he asked, exchanging a glance with the duty officer.

"The Embraer," said the technician. "The other is filed for a different destination. A place called . . . Ouarzazate."

Coltrane tried to meet the technician's gaze, but he was somewhere behind a bank of monitors. "Where the hell is that?" he called out.

"Eastern Morocco. Pretty much the middle of nowhere, except . . . there is some kind of industrial park there, one big runway and a couple of hangars. I'll see what we have on the place."

Coltrane nodded, then said in a reflective low voice, "So we know where these guys are, and we know where they're going. But what do we do about it?"

Apparently not sure if the question was rhetorical, a new voice added her two cents. Connie Stine was from the Office of General Counsel—at least one lawyer was always on duty in the ops center. "Not much," she answered. "There is no immediate threat to U.S. interests, and it's not our airspace. Not to mention the fact that our sole source here is an alcoholic garbageman."

"We could do a quiet intercept," the duty officer said. "*Reagan* is in the Persian Gulf . . . we could have a pair of Hornets shadow them."

Coltrane shook his head. "To what end? As soon as they hit Iranian airspace we'd have to call it off."

The ensuing silence was an answer in itself. Their hands were tied.

"All right," said the director. "Let's keep an eye on them as long as we can—especially the one headed to Oraz . . . whatever the hell it's called."

"Anything else?" the duty officer asked.

The director thought about it. "Yeah. Send Macallan a case of his favorite, my compliments."

FIFTY-FOUR

Langley got its second break soon after the first. In the twenty-four hours since nailing down a suspect IP address, the NSA had kept up the pressure. As was often the case in the cyber realm, success came not in black and white, but as a carefully assessed series of probabilities.

For years the NSA had been vexed by the use of burner phones by terrorists. Such devices were maddeningly difficult to track, particularly when used by individuals moving inside a big city. Nailing down where Vladimir Ovechkin had holed up, however, was a somewhat more level playing field.

For an agency that records the whereabouts of more than a billion phones a day, the filtering of large amounts of data is of paramount importance. Algorithms are leveraged to map calls, extracting from the cellular noise certain intersections of suspicious users. In the case of Ovechkin, whose geographic whereabouts were already narrowed down, the strategy taken to pinpoint his location involved burner phone clusters.

In effect, the local mobile network was monitored, and when any new phone was activated, its position was crosshatched to other numbers that had recently fallen off the grid near the same location. Over time, the method highlighted specific addresses where the use of throwaway phones flourished. Ovechkin was known to keep a sizable security entourage, along with support staff, and he himself would have to maintain contact with distant bankers and lawyers. Altogether, they could be expected to operate a minor constellation of limited-use handsets. For its part, the NSA knew the technique would work—the only variable was time. What surprised even its own analysts was how quickly the results came.

Within twenty-four hours of approximating Ovechkin's location, they identified three distinct burner clusters. One, a farmhouse five miles inland, was quickly discounted when an intercepted call revealed a hashish smuggler coordinating a series of deals with northern distributors. Brief consideration was given to alerting local authorities, but that was put on hold on the advice of the CIA's regional desk: seventy percent of Europe's hashish was sourced from Morocco, resulting in both a significant trade surplus and a government that habitually turned a blind eye.

A second location was put down almost as quickly—the five-story walk-up outside Zemamra turned out to be a rooming house that was a waypoint for migrant laborers from sub-Saharan Africa, dozens of whom purchased prepackaged phones each day.

By default, the third address showing a spike in burner activity became the NSA's focal point, a modest villa along a remote stretch of coastline. Over the course of that morning, the agency isolated and recorded three calls sourced from the villa. None offered particularly damning content, but they all displayed one highly unusual commonality—in each conversation the language spoken was Russian.

* * *

Slaton received the update from Langley within seconds of the Jet Ranger's skids touching down. While Omar tended to the helo, its rotors spinning down and its turbine ticking with heat, Slaton veered from the flight line into the relative quiet of the hangar. He listened for a full two minutes.

"How sure are you about this?" he finally asked.

"It's not a slam dunk," said the Langley duty officer, who'd been instructed to pass on the news. "All we know for certain is that multiple Russian speakers are using throwaway phones from a particular seaside villa. NSA did go back over some old data, and they're pretty sure this burst of burner activity began two days ago. Before that, the place was quiet."

The duty officer suddenly excused himself to put out "an unrelated fire."

Slaton used the ensuing silence to weigh what he was being told. He appreciated the man's honesty—this new information *was* speculative. How often had he seen intelligence agencies push dubious data as being rock-solid? Still, the idea gelled with his own assumptions: that Ovechkin would go to ground in a nice place along the coast, something remote and secure. He tried to recall the specific villa, but it was hopeless given how many he and Omar had flown past.

With Ovechkin possibly located, the question became what to do about it. He considered hiring Omar for a follow-up flight to explore a "property of interest." Tempting as it was, repeated overflights by a helicopter would raise suspicion from Ovechkin and his security team. Even more likely—it could alert the man Slaton was truly after.

This final thought brought the end of any inward pretenses. He had come to Morocco to hunt down an assassin. A young man he'd missed by a day in the Davos outfitter's shop. A man who'd assumed the role of Slaton's own ghost. There was, of course, no guarantee the killer was even in Ovechkin's neighborhood. Might he stop his deadly run after having eliminated two of the three principals of MIR Enterprises? Perhaps he'd failed to locate Ovechkin as efficiently as the CIA had. Either case was possible, yet in Slaton's overdeveloped cautionary lobe he reckoned the opposite was true. The man was nearby. If so, Slaton hoped he wasn't too late. Hoped that, as he stood in a hangar talking to the CIA duty officer, there wasn't already a bullet in the air.

The duty officer came back on line. "Okay, where were we?"

"Do you have any overheads of this villa?" Slaton asked.

"Not yet. Our coverage in that area is less than optimal. We might have something tonight if we can get priority. Right now everyone is focused on what's happening on the Arabian Peninsula."

Slaton had already conceded that much—his priorities and Langley's were increasingly divergent. "Okay," he said, "but do you at least have something on file I could look at?"

"There's no terrain on the planet that isn't in one of our imagery databases. Recency might prove trickier, but I'll get somebody on it."

"And not just Ovechkin's place. He's only a reference point—the guy I'm really after could be nearby. I'd like a wide view, say everything within five miles. Close-ups of all residences and commercial buildings.

Vehicles too if you come up with anything in the last few days."

"You don't ask much. Whatever we find I'll have sent to the consulate in Casablanca."

"No, I can't go there."

"Why not?"

"Because it would be awkward for everyone when I walk out of a diplomatic post with the other things you're going to provide."

A long pause from Langley. "And what might that be?"

Slaton told the man, and for another long beat he didn't get a reply.

"If you have any questions," he added, "address them to the director. He'll approve it."

"Actually, I think he will ... in light of what he wants you to do for him."

It was Slaton's turn to go silent. He could almost feel the smugness from thousands of miles away as the duty officer said, "This is going to be a two-way street. Something has come up, and you're in a unique position to help us."

"Okay ... what do you have in mind?"

"A minor diversion, something you can do while we research your request. We need a bit of surveillance performed tonight ..."

FIFTY-FIVE

The hangar was hot, the big fans stirring the air to little effect on an unseasonably warm afternoon. Tikhonov used a shirtsleeve to wipe beads of sweat from his brow.

"What should the fuel load be?" asked Hamza, the young local who ran the fuel truck.

"Full tanks," Tikhonov responded, his elbows deep in the electronics bay of the MiG that would fly tomorrow.

He had been issuing orders nonstop since arriving back at the hangar, RosAvia's little band of employees rushing about the place to ready their only airworthy MiG for an unscheduled "live-fire test" tomorrow. *At least they don't have the burden of the truth,* he thought.

In the two hours since Colonel Zhukov had dropped his bolt of lightning, Tikhonov battled the obvious question. *How did I not see this coming?* The answer, of course, was obvious. He had become so distracted by the engineering, the technical hurdles, that he'd lost sight of the greater picture. The remote location and minimal staffing. All controlled by a lone military officer with no scientific background. Tikhonov's follow-up question—*How will this af-*

fect my career?—was answered even more easily. He would have no career. The funds transferred to the new account would have to carry him for the rest of his life. He would disperse the money elsewhere, of course, and disappear as quietly as possible. Yet professionally he would never be heard from again.

He watched the carefree Hamza turning valves on the fuel truck, and for the first time wondered how it would affect the others—thirteen men who had no such golden parachutes. Men as much in the dark about RosAvia's true goals as he'd been only hours ago.

Tikhonov pushed the thoughts away, Zhukov's parting words ringing above all else: *Your future is guaranteed to be restful, Boris. How long it might last . . . that depends very much on success.*

He stepped back from the MiG and tried to imagine what could go wrong tomorrow—the final flight of his crowning project. Today's mission had been perfection, but how often had he seen hard-won success followed by inexplicable failure? Advanced telemetry, cobbled-together flight-control software, an airplane that was older than he was. *What could go wrong?* he thought bleakly.

Tikhonov went to his laptop and began inputting the profile for the next day. The first change: plotting a course to a new operating area.

Sorensen got what she wanted after fifteen hours in Saudi Arabia—a meeting with the head of its National Guard.

She waited for the minister of the Guard, General Qasim bin Abdullah, in a grand conference room at the Riyadh regional headquarters. The room was a basketball-court-sized testament to gold and translucent fixtures, no expense spared in the glorification of the kingdom. The central hardwood table alone must have involved three great trees felled in some equatorial forest. The walls were lined with portraits of contemporary kings and princes. A few she recognized. None were smiling.

Sorensen knew a good bit about the Saudi Arabian National Guard, or as it was referred to in Langley, the SANG. She knew it was the country's lead organization when it came to dealing with internal threats, and that its regiments were dispersed across the country. Its leaders were drawn exclusively from tribes loyal to the ruling House of Saud, and its command and control structure was completely separate from that of the military. The reasons for these precautions were obvious enough. On paper the National Guard was tasked to protect Mecca and Medina, as well as select strategic targets—notably the country's oilfields. Yet the SANG's primary mission was far more elemental—it was sworn to keep the Saudi royal family safe and in power.

The great door at the head of the room surged open, and leading a small contingent was General Abdullah. He was a tall, long-faced man with a meticulously groomed beard. On seeing Sorensen, he spoke a few hushed words to the three men behind him—two wore robes, the other was in uniform—and all made a decorous exit.

The general came toward her, moving in a way that made her think of a great water bird, his long limbs graceful under the robe. His bearded face held a smile, the same one Sorensen imagined was in place for any American with official status. She'd been given a briefing on Abdullah: he was a fast-riser in the Saudi hierarchy, spoke flawless English thanks to a degree from Georgetown, and had a reputation as something of a womanizer despite having three wives.

"Miss Sorensen," he said, "it is good to meet you."

"And you, General."

The two shook hands and, penetrating gaze aside, Sorensen sensed Abdullah would rather be somewhere else at that moment. Coltrane had undoubtedly pulled strings to make the meeting happen.

He said, "Should I assume this is about the arms smuggling operation you've recently brought to our attention?"

"It is."

"I assure you we've taken your warnings most seriously. Units have been dispatched across the kingdom to track down these Shiite miscreants."

"Shiite?"

"Of course. It has been an ongoing problem for the last two months. The odd arms shipment here and there—small arms and explosives, barges across the Gulf and trucks from the Empty Quarter. These munitions are meant for the hands of those who would do the kingdom harm, but I can tell you we have intercepted every one."

"I hadn't heard about any earlier shipments," responded Sorensen.

"We have been keeping it rather to ourselves." The general shooed his hand in the air as one would for a bothersome insect. "As always, it is the work of Iran and their underlings. The mullahs across the Gulf live in an increasing state of fear."

"Actually," Sorensen said, "we saw convincing Russian fingerprints on this operation."

"Russian?" repeated the general. "Why on earth would Russia risk such a provocation?"

"That's a very good question. One we've been asking ourselves."

Abdullah looked at Sorensen with suddenly softened eyes. "You are very pretty," he said.

Sorensen was wearing conservative clothing, and her blond hair was pulled back beneath a tasteful scarf. Not sure how to respond—at least not without causing an international incident—she let the comment go.

"Tell your director not to worry," said Abdullah. "We will have these stray arms swept up in a few days, just as with the others." He leveled a finger at her. "And also tell him that next time he should share his intelligence with us before bringing in the likes of Mossad. I am sorry I cannot give you more time, but I am exceptionally busy this week with the family gathering." He turned toward the door in a flurry of white cotton.

"Family gathering?" Sorensen queried.

The general seemed to hesitate, then turned back to face her. Once more Abdullah looked at her appraisingly. Had he not been vaguely smitten, she was sure he would have kept going.

"Our king sets a careful course," he said. "Once each year he arranges a gathering of the royal family. It is an event like no other, a week in which the scattered hands of the kingdom become one. Policies are agreed upon for the coming year, alliances forged. This gathering is not comprehensive, mind you—the extended relations in the House of Saud number in the tens of thousands. Praise be to Allah, the most important in our kingdom number little more than a hundred."

"Where will this take place?" she asked.

"Most years the gathering convenes in one of the

main palaces, either Jeddah or Riyadh. As the head of the National Guard, it is my duty to secure things accordingly. This year, however, will be rather different."

"In what way?"

"Even to you, I cannot divulge specifics. Not for a few more hours. But rest assured that a few guns running around our countryside . . . they are inconsequential. Now, I really must go. If you are still in Riyadh next week perhaps we can schedule a more in-depth meeting." Flashing what had to be his most engaging smile, he spun away in a flourish of white cotton.

Sorensen stared incredulously as Abdullah disappeared through ten-foot gilded doors. The moment he was gone she reached for her phone. Her first two attempts to dial Langley failed, and she realized the building must be hardened against electronic eavesdropping—something akin to what would be called a SCIF at home.

She walked outside to get a signal, but before she could dial again Sorensen encountered a sight that left her standing in awe with her phone at her side. Across an expansive parking lot, shimmering under the lingering late afternoon sun, were more armored limousines than she'd ever seen in her life. All of them were empty, parked in wait of some great movement of VIPs. Sorensen realized there could be only one explanation. Without knowing where the royal gathering was taking place, she understood that the road to attend it began here.

She shook away her surprise, and seconds later her third call to Langley went through.

* * *

Slaton rounded a curve at speed, the big bike beneath him handling smoothly over the ribbon of high desert road. The motorcycle was a BMW, rented from a company that specialized in touring adventures of northern Africa. Slaton had considered a number of transportation options, but after receiving his surveillance assignment, he chose the bike for its blend of speed and maneuverability.

He was still traveling light: in the BMW's hardcase saddlebags were one change of clothes, a cheap backpack, a compact set of binoculars, and a high-end digital camera with a telescopic lens. All had been purchased in Casablanca, and all were perfectly in character for a lone Scandinavian on an adventurous Moroccan holiday.

His assigned objective was an airfield near a place called Ouarzazate, an hour's ride ahead. The CIA was convinced a small business jet would soon land at the airfield, and, for reasons he could not discern, the agency wanted him to photograph the lone passenger expected to disembark. It was a simple enough job, and as quid pro quos went, a small price to pay for the support he so desperately needed.

The latest word from Langley was that the target of his surveillance would arrive in the early evening—the timing was tight, but feasible. Slaton had also been asked to take pictures of the airfield and anything that looked "interesting." He recalled how many times Mossad had launched him into such missions. Speculative intelligence forays where operatives were put at risk to prove or disprove some analyst's hypothesis. Or, in other cases, the conjecture of a senior operations chief. Whatever the source, he would approach the whole affair with a due sense of caution.

He accelerated out of a series of curves, the BMW

commanding over roads that were in surprisingly good condition. If that held to Ouarzazate, he would arrive with time to spare. With any luck, he could get the desired pictures, return to the coast, and find a place to rest for a few hours before the real work began: in the early hours of tomorrow morning, he intended to be scouting the area where Ovechkin had gone into hiding. Looking for a man who was killing in his name.

The dry desert air swept past in a ninety-mile-an-hour rush, snapping at his clothing and keeping his head below the windscreen. As Slaton raced eastward, the sun touched the mountains behind him in faltering shocks of orange.

FIFTY-SIX

Slaton had no trouble locating the RosAvia complex—against the pitch black desert, twenty miles outside Ouarzazate, its cluster of floodlit buildings stood out like a neon-clad Vegas casino.

He dismounted half a mile short of the facility, and walked the bike carefully into the brush beside the main road—ease of concealment being another reason he'd not opted for a car. The air was thin and crisp, the warmth of the day already giving way to a still mountain coolness.

With the bike out of sight, he took his bearings carefully. He saw a traffic sign nearby, and a hundred yards to the east was a distinctive curve in the road sided by a high guardrail. Hiding transportation was a useful bit of tradecraft, but one that backfired readily if you couldn't find your ride on the way out. Particularly when one was on a dead run with gunfire blazing behind—something Slaton had had the displeasure of experiencing more than once.

He set out toward the floodlights under a dim moon. He moved with the land where he could, keeping to wadis and avoiding high ground. The terrain was scarred and dry, the earth's skin suffering the harshness of the elements. Slaton slowed as he neared the tiny airfield, and three times he paused to study the complex under its array of high-mounted amber floods. From a distance he saw a few small buildings nested beside the lone hangar. There was one long runway, and the standard mesh of taxiways connecting it all. It struck him that everything looked relatively new. The corrugated buildings appeared freshly painted, and the concrete was neither potholed nor weed-encrusted. The tall floodlights had not a single failed bulb in their luminous arrays.

When he was a hundred feet shy of the perimeter fence, Slaton turned right and moved parallel to the boundary. He'd so far seen no sign of security. No roving guards with dogs, no vehicles parked at the fenceline with headlights trained outward. He also saw no sign of intrusion-detection hardware—no wiring or hardware for motion sensors, no pole-mounted infrared cameras.

As his angle of view changed, he noticed that the hangar's big main door was partially open. Inside, under the hard fluorescent light, he saw the first signs of life—a pair of men wearing drab coveralls. Slaton lifted his binoculars and watched for a full minute as they disassembled what looked like an equipment stand. From the tight angle he couldn't see what else the hangar contained, but as he imagined it Slaton was struck by the airfield's one glaring deficiency— there was not a single airplane in sight. He kept moving, knowing there had to be something in the hangar, and was rewarded fifty feet later. First a nosecone, then a fuselage, and finally a tail. He did a double take before yielding to the unexpected—he was looking at a vintage MiG-21. Of all the aircraft he might have expected here, that hadn't made the list.

For Slaton, it was a throwback to his early days in

Mossad. He'd seen MiG-21s in Syria, and knew that the Egyptian Air Force had once flown them. Today, however, even those countries, which weren't known for fielding state-of-the-art fighters, had put their 21s to the dustbin. *So what's a relic like that doing here?* he wondered. *And at a brand-new airfield on the edge of the Sahara?*

He saw what looked like a second jet behind the first—same make and model, but missing an engine and some panels. Then, far inside, the tail of a third. All three jets shared one peculiar commonality— bright orange paint on the tail. This too Slaton recognized: He'd seen test aircraft at Israel's Palmachim Air Base with similar markings. Those jets, however, had been cutting-edge experimental aircraft, not fifty-year-old Russian cast-offs.

He looked out across the rest of the airfield. Aside from the lack of aircraft, he saw the same things one would see at any airport. A fuel truck and some support vehicles, two standard shipping containers. A pile of discarded sheet metal next to a stack of empty wooden crates. RosAvia seemed a compact setup, a tiny flight operation in the middle of nowhere. To Slaton, that remoteness, combined with the lack of security, suggested one of two things. Either what was going on inside was harmless and didn't need protecting, or someone was trying to make it appear that way. A variation of hiding in plain sight.

Ready to document his finds, he moved toward a rock outcropping that would give some elevation. He climbed from the backside, and on reaching the top he had what he needed—a line of sight to the hangar that cleared the perimeter fence. He set up shop quickly, choosing a flat stone shelf for his platform. He was removing his recently purchased camera and binoculars from the backpack when his phone vibrated with a message:

TARGET ARRIVING FOUR MINUTES

Slaton swept his eyes toward the ebony sky to the north. Sure enough, along the extended centerline of the runway, he saw an aircraft beacon. It twinkled red in a halfhearted warning, like the heartbeat of a weary traveler looking for respite. He checked his watch. Eighteen minutes ahead of the estimated arrival time the CIA had given him hours ago. Not bad. Perhaps an unexpected tailwind. Or a pilot with a hot date.

How Langley had tracked the jet across the wilderness of airspace that was northern Africa Slaton couldn't imagine. Was it some new kind of satellite capability? Had they hacked into the air traffic control systems of a half dozen countries? Whatever the case, they'd gotten it right.

The red beacon was soon lost to the glare of bright landing lights, all of it sinking with precision toward the end of the runway. The jet landed and taxied a short distance to the hangar. The engines spooled down, an entry door was lowered, and a lone figure descended to the ramp. A figure that, even as a shadowed silhouette, set Slaton immediately on edge.

He picked up the camera, adjusted the focus on the long lens. The man was momentarily caught in the spill of the ramp lights, his face clear in the viewfinder. In that moment, Slaton realized why the CIA had sent him here.

It was, he was quite sure, a face he'd seen before.

* * *

President Petrov sat fidgeting behind the desk in his Kremlin office. He looked at the secure phone as he had done a hundred times in the last day. Or so it seemed. After so many years in power, he was not a man used to waiting.

As far as he knew, his plan was going well. Yet things would move quickly now. He spun a half turn in his chair and gazed out the window. Red Square was lost to the gloom, winter ahead of its cruel schedule. He thought acidly of the infernal Paris Accord, the climate agreement he'd signed, but had no intention of honoring. *Try to convince a Russian the world is getting warmer.*

The square was quiet now, yet there had been a protest two days earlier. Kremlin security had stamped it out quickly, but such outbreaks had been materializing more often. More spontaneously. Something had to change, and very soon.

His musings were interrupted when his secretary announced a visitor.

"Send him in immediately!" Petrov said.

He spun to face the door, but remained in his seat to receive Sergei Durov—the man he'd anointed as director of the FSB.

"What news from Saudi Arabia?" the president asked, knowing Durov wouldn't be here for any other reason. Not today.

"Our source there tells us everything is operating on schedule."

"Is he sure?"

"He is only a mid-level man in the National Guard, but very conveniently placed. He's never been wrong before. Our staff from the Riyadh post have also been keeping their eyes open—everything they've seen correlates. The royals will be under way soon."

Petrov nodded, relieved. "Good. And what of our attribution plan?"

"That is why I came. We finally managed it—the phone intercept we were working on."

"You can influence our target as hoped?" asked Petrov.

Durov, who was relatively new to his position, said confidently, "Our man will be in place soon. Everything is lining up perfectly."

Petrov almost relaxed, but saw fit to add a bit of incentive for his latest FSB head. "For your sake . . . let's hope that it does."

FIFTY-SEVEN

The sergeant set out from his little house on the cliffs shortly after nightfall. He had spent the day under the pergola, sipping tea and using his shooter's optic to scout out a path along the high ledges by which he could reach the southern peninsula. There was nothing nearing a trail, but the terrain just below the crest appeared less sheer than that of lower levels. It was time to put his work to the test.

He brought with him one of the large shipping cases and a standard set of army-issue night-vision goggles. He started out slowly, glad to have the night optics and stepping carefully with the big case strapped to his back. He found the footing difficult, the scrub near the top of the cliffs more dense than he'd expected. He had seen worse, of course, most notably in the Caucasus with its swampy broadleaf forests. Fortunately, tonight the sergeant was in no hurry.

He bypassed the lone house at the foot of the peninsula, and was encouraged to see no signs of occupancy—as had been the case since his arrival. From that point, the promontory that was his objective extended roughly two hundred meters seaward and was perhaps half that in width. In the greater coastal scheme of things, it was a minor outcropping that he supposed was not even worth a name. That might change in thirty years, when developers worked their way south and gave it one. Today, however, it was merely a blunt finger of land jutting into the Atlantic, barren and isolated, no different from a thousand others on the left-hand shores of Africa.

He kept on through the dark, relying on the NVGs, and his pace slowed fifty meters short of the seaward tip of the point. There the sergeant turned left, toward the opposing southward-facing cliff, and made his way through thickening brambles. Burrs collected on his clothing, and dry branches snapped under every step. Then, all at once, the vegetation fell away and he saw the ocean again, a theater of black raked by moonlit whitecaps.

He saw Ovechkin's place right away, even without the optics. Far down the coastline, it lay under the dome of stars on its own stunted outcropping of rock, a lone villa reaching out to the sea like a wary handshake. It was a decent-sized place with multiple balconies, a complex roof, and a terrace that was lit like a carnival.

He spent ten minutes scouting the area before settling on a pad of firm ground in a depression between stands of trees. He shrugged off the equipment case and set it near a jagged stump where a seaward tree had long ago given way. The case was watertight, and he didn't bother with any kind of camouflage—he doubted that more than a handful of people visited this clearing in any given year. All he needed was a few hours.

He looked once more at the distant villa, more a matter of introspection than reconnaissance. The sergeant had already done his homework. He knew that the difference in elevation between the two points was thirty-one meters, and that the prevailing off-shore winds swirled up the cliffs with a vengeance that defied any measurement. All inconsequential. In another scenario, he might have used some kind of optic to see if anyone was on the expansive patio at that moment. Ovechkin himself, cocktail in hand? A security detail fighting to stay alert? Tonight such musings were irrelevant.

The most essential detail, of course, was that of range, and this the sergeant had predetermined. Four thousand one hundred eighty-four meters—plus or minus a few, depending on where he set up shop.

That was the distance between the patch of dead grass upon which he stood and Vladimir Ovechkin's terrace. The distance across which the next faultless bullet would fly.

If the sergeant's deliberations along the coast had the benefit of forethought, Slaton's were far more extemporaneous. He watched closely as the man who'd gotten off the jet strolled across the tarmac. While his facial features seemed familiar, the distance was too great for that to be the sole arbiter. In a long-honed practice, Slaton studied the man in his entirety: the way he carried himself, the set of his thick shoulders and squat legs, the military-inspired haircut.

As a sniper, he had learned, exercised, and even lectured on the art of identifying people from a distance. It was among the most essential tasks for a shooter in the field—in a sense, even more important than marksmanship itself, because a target that could not be identified wasn't a target at all.

The case before him had arrived with supporting evidence. The CIA, who'd recently dispatched Slaton beneath a ship in the Red Sea, had also sent him here. The nexus between those assignments was increasingly clear. Altogether, Slaton was convinced. He was looking at the same man he'd seen two days earlier, on the deck of a ship that had since gone to the bottom of the sea. Only hours ago Sorensen admitted that the CIA had lost track of the saboteurs who'd sent *Argos* and the other ships down. Apparently they'd recovered spectacularly, at least with regard to this suspect.

But of all places, why has he come here? Slaton wondered.

As he watched the man approach the hangar, there was a part of him—a very small and righteous part—that wished the lens he was using was attached to something more persuasive than a camera. His trigger finger depressed, but touched only the camera's shutter button. He held it down for a sequence of shots, the whirring click circulating in the early night air. It could never be heard half a mile away, but even so Slaton admonished himself for not wrapping the camera's body in a cloth. His aversion to sound was hardwired.

When the man disappeared inside the hangar, Slaton got a good shot of the business jet, one that included its registration number. He then snapped images of the MiGs inside, the hangar itself, and each of the surrounding buildings. Two vehicles also got his attention: a small van and a larger truck, both topped by gear and antennas. In the end he had nearly fifty digital shots. That done, he weighed whether to call the mission complete. If he stayed a few hours, he might get better pictures. More likely, sand flea bites and a deficit of sleep tomorrow.

It was an easy decision—until one new thought

occurred to him. Could the man he'd just seen be the sniper he was chasing? The fact that he'd arrived in Morocco, where Ovechkin was bunkered up, fit the scenario. Yet Slaton was nearly certain that this man had been on *Argos*. When he crosshatched the timing of the deaths of Ivanovic and Romanov, it seemed impossible that this could be his shooter. No one could have made all that happen, even with a private jet at his disposal.

Still, there was a proven connection between *Argos* and Ovechkin, and by extension the man who'd just arrived. That being the case, Slaton considered following him. Might the man lead him to Ovechkin? Or was Langley's technology the more reliable method?

Slaton decided the odds favored the CIA.

He backtracked through the desert and reached the bike. After one careful survey of the area, he went to work. He used the camera's Bluetooth function to upload the pictures to his CIA-issued phone. Seconds later they were uploading into the sky, and then back down to Langley. He was just pocketing the phone when it vibrated with a message. He looked, expecting a confirmation that the photos had gone through. What he saw was better. A message from a new number confirmed that the CIA had the information he wanted. A meeting was requested: ASAP in Marrakesh, a particular street address. A map was included, and Slaton committed the route to memory. It was roughly a one-hour ride from where he stood.

Things were happening quickly.

After that meeting, Slaton would find a place to rest. While he slept, the machine that was Langley would process the photos he'd sent, spin them through whatever digital gears were necessary. Perhaps by the time he woke, they would find something useful in them. Yet Slaton had already gotten the best possible news. Ovechkin had been located, and the assassin he was after might well be nearby.

The bad news? The very same things.

He stowed his gear, fired up the bike, and was soon accelerating in a spray of gravel and dirt into the empty westbound lane.

Slaton's photos arrived in Langley with little fanfare.

The operations center there was focused on certain remote quarters of the Saudi peninsula. A particularly heavy zoom lay over a village called Tubarjal, where a detachment of U.S. SEALs was helping the SANG wrap up two carloads of small arms. Three suspects had been killed in the raid, and the survivor, who was speculatively deemed a young Shiite insurgent, had not yet offered anything of intelligence value. That would likely change in coming days as he endured the persuasions of the Mahabith, the kingdom's secret police, yet it was doubtful one shocked teenager had any revelations to share.

The SEALs had been the only Special Operations detachment in country when things kicked off. With Langley's strong encouragement, however, the DOD was now on board: every available SOG unit in theater was currently en route to join the hunt. Because Director Coltrane himself was deeply immersed in the fray, he was not informed of the arrival of Slaton's photographs from the high deserts of Morocco. Thankfully, in an ode to raw manpower, a mid-level analyst on the third floor, whose name was Dobbs, did look at Slaton's pictures.

It was here, as fate would have it, that a ninety-six-year-old dementia patient in a suburban Fredericksburg nursing home made an indelible impression on the balance of power in the Middle East. It began when she launched a spoonful of peas at her regular dinner tablemate. The unprovoked barrage instigated a flat-out food fight, two other tables joining in with glee. Soon cornbread was flying and mashed potatoes plastered the walls. The exchange was soon tamped down, but the facility's staff were greatly displeased—it wasn't the woman's first transgression. That being the case, her daughter, the wife of a third-floor CIA analyst named Dobbs, was asked to come in for a word. This dominoed to the cancellation of dinner plans with her husband, who in turn was faced with two options. He could go home to a frozen dinner, or stay late and work the photographs, then sleep in tomorrow morning.

In what would weeks later be characterized as a commendable example of diligence, Dobbs chose the latter.

FIFTY-EIGHT

Marrakesh, like any city, puts on display its most prominent districts. Websites and brochures celebrate La Palmeraie with its sparkling villas and energetic Club Med. Gueliz stands apart for its distinctly European heritage, sporting wide boulevards, trendy shopping areas, and a span of verdant gardens. Mouassine is famously endowed with grand *riads* and resplendent mosques. The shadowed warren called Rue Essebtiyne finds no such promotions.

In a town renowned for tight streets and frenetic crowds, the web of shops and markets compressed within Rue Essebtiyne is nothing short of claustrophobic. The neighborhood seems to pulse in the way of a failed urban arterial system, alternately clogging and leaking, in a constant state of arrhythmia. Taking the place of any master plan are generations of winding streets, some allegedly paved and others left to dirt, that curve and loop and seize, all of it lined by patternless walls that give no suggestion as to where one shop ends and the next begins. The scents of competing street vendors whirl through the air, lamb on one gust, spices the next, all of it intermittently overcome by pungent black clouds of diesel exhaust.

It was here that Slaton arrived with great expectations.

He stood up the BMW five streets from the address he'd been given, concealed behind a wall amid a group of smaller motorcycles and scooters. The big German bike was an outlier among the lighter machines, but having seen much of the neighborhood, Slaton doubted he would find a less conspicuous place to leave it. As if to amplify the point, fifty feet to his right a disinterested mule stood lashed to a bicycle rack.

He removed the backpack from the bike's saddle case, slung it over his shoulder, and resisted an urge to relock the empty case—any petty thief, of which he supposed there were many in residence, wouldn't have to go to the trouble of breaking in to learn it was empty.

It took ten minutes and two polite questions to locate the correct door—which in fact was no door at all. A gap in the earthen wall beside a trellis-covered alley was covered by a tattered blue curtain. The curtain served little purpose, and he looked past it on either side to see a long-neglected dirt courtyard. Weeds predominated, and the ground was striped with slatted shadows that implied lights and some kind of structure overhead. A plastic chair lay on its side, and trash had accumulated in one corner, a mongrel nosing through hopefully. After briefly wondering if he had the right place, Slaton knocked on the wooden frame at the threshold.

The dog ignored him, but a man appeared almost instantly. He regarded Slaton with not a trace of uncertainty.

He could only be CIA.

* * *

His name was Smith, or so he said. He was ten years older than Slaton, three inches taller, with gaunt features and a dismal smile that gave him the countenance of a gravedigger on holiday.

He thanked Slaton for coming in a voice that was surprisingly rich and mellifluous, then pulled aside the curtain and invited him inside. This in itself had implications. It told Slaton the man had probably been issued his photograph as a means of identification. Which, in turn, meant his photograph was on file with the CIA. Not terribly surprising in this day and age, but a previously unknown fact. And yet another chink in his off-the-grid armor.

With the gait of an arthritic giraffe, Smith led Slaton through the courtyard and into a shambles of an apartment. If the courtyard had been rundown, the tiny efficiency was positively derelict. The walls seemed held together by peeling paint, and a filthy shag carpet was covered in crumpled food wrappers. The ceiling above had a massive yellow stain adjacent to the bathroom—presumably where the bathroom was situated in the apartment above. Slaton weighed taking a picture for Christine, just to convince her that spies didn't always reside in embassy suites.

He noticed right away that there were no windows in the room, and when Smith closed and bolted the door to the courtyard things fell improbably quiet. A safe house, perhaps, whose appearance belied its robustness.

"Nice place," he offered.

"It serves its purpose," replied Smith as if reading Shakespeare from a stage.

The light inside was dim, which Slaton reckoned was intentional. Hovels had their place in any intelligence agency's portfolio of properties. Chosen carefully, they could be both practical and discreet, and were often close to the action.

Smith diverted into what might have been the kitchen: in one corner was a tiny table, and next to it a mini-refrigerator with a microwave balanced on top. The glass door of the microwave had scorch marks.

"Can I offer you a drink?" Smith inquired. He pulled a pint-sized bottle of something amber from one jacket pocket, and from another produced two small plastic cups. "I'm afraid on-the-rocks is out of the question," he added, gesturing to the silent mini-fridge.

"No," Slaton said. "I'm good. But thanks."

Smith tilted the bottle to pour a decent bracer, then, as an apparent afterthought, tilted it a second time. Screwing the cap back on his bottle, he said. "We've located this Russian you been looking for."

"Ovechkin?" Slaton asked, wanting to be clear.

"That's right. I've been given a file to pass on." Smith produced a folder from the only drawer in the small counter. He cracked it open and removed a handful of photos. Each was numbered, one through five, and Smith spread them out on the table like a cardplayer laying down a winning straight. "We should start with these."

Slaton looked down to see a series of overhead images. They ranged from very high-resolution to a ten-mile-square panorama. The tight shots looked too good for satellite footage, implying that a drone had been tapped for the job. Slaton kept the thought to himself, not caring from what altitude or platform his help was taken.

"We've tracked Ovechkin here," Smith continued. He dragged a bony finger across the wide-angle shot and settled on a particular villa. Slaton tried to place it from his scenic tour with Omar, but having covered so many miles of coastline it was hopeless.

"Where exactly is that?"

"Southwest of here, between Essaouira and Tamri."

As Slaton studied the tighter shots he heard scraping noises somewhere in the walls. Tiny claws scratching out a living.

Smith pretended not to notice. "There's more," he said. He removed another photograph from the folder, this an image of a printed page. "I'm to tell you that you 'owe one' to a certain duty officer in Langley."

Slaton saw what looked like a legal document, then a series of signatures below. It was all quite incomprehensible because it was written in French. "What is it?"

"A short-term property rental agreement."

"For Ovechkin's villa?"

"No. Your supporter in Langley knew you were focusing on nearby residences. Since there are only a handful within the five-mile radius you mentioned, he had someone run a check. One address generated particular interest. It was rented for one week, beginning three nights ago, all arranged through a particularly shady vacation operator in Kazakhstan—as it turns out, one we've linked previously to the FSB."

"Russian intelligence rented this place?"

"Loosely put . . . yes. Reference image number five."

Slaton did, and saw an excellent shot of a small house perched on a cliffside. There was a patio with a pergola, and beneath that the outline of a chair and small table. Partially masked by vegetation on the pergola was the figure of a man. He appeared to be standing and staring out across the sea.

"How long ago was this taken?" Slaton asked, not seeing a time and date stamp.

"When did you ask for it?"

"Roughly eight hours ago."

Smith gave a *so there you are* look.

Slaton decided he did owe a favor to the duty man at Langley. He looked again at the shadowed form, then reverted to photo number one, the "big picture." He estimated the distance between the two villas as roughly four and a half miles.

He tried to shoot holes in his assumptive theory, and right away saw two that were glaring. To begin, there was no line of sight between the two residences—a high promontory split the coastline. Secondly, the range stretched the ballistic limits of any fifty-cal round—guided or not. Yet a short hike, most likely to the peninsula jutting toward the sea, solved both problems. From there, the issues of both range and line of sight to Ovechkin's temporary residence were solved. *Take him through a window or standing on a balcony. While he's floating in the pool.*

Was it all too straightforward? Or was truth staring him in the face in so many pixels?

He concentrated on the promontory, and saw level ground that tapered in the middle to an hourglass shape. He saw a half dozen good setups, and certainly there were hides that could not be seen from overhead. *Like a ledge on a mountainside.* Then something caught his eye in the narrow waist of the hourglass.

"What spectrum is this?" he asked.

"I beg your pardon?" replied Smith.

"Is it infrared?"

"I'm no expert, but our imagery these days is increasingly a hybrid product. Multiple wavelength inputs are synthesized using software. It helps pull out the slightest details. Why do you ask?"

Slaton tapped on the large-scale picture of the peninsula. Smith leaned in for a closer look. Near Slaton's fingertip was a light-colored rectangle.

"What do you think it is?" the CIA man asked.

"I don't know . . . but it doesn't belong. It's the only man-made object on that spit of land. Can you get me more detail?"

The gravedigger's smile. "Possibly. But I can't say how long it will take."

"Do what you can," Slaton said. "Now . . . what about the rest?"

Smith walked across the room, reached behind a threadbare daybed, and produced a heavy canvas bag. He set it carefully on the mattress and extracted what Slaton had requested: a Heckler & Koch UMP45, two twenty-five-round magazines, and enough .45 ACP rounds to fill them. He'd wanted the higher caliber version of the gun for its close-in stopping power, allowing that his adversary—if it was who and what he expected—would have every advantage at long range. For Slaton to win a gunfight, he had to get close. With its stock folded, he also knew the UMP would fit in the BMW's oversized side cases.

Smith reached into the bag again and produced a set of lightweight body armor. No vest in the world was going to stop a fifty-cal round, but he wanted some protection against smaller calibers while allowing for maneuverability—which, given the field of play, might be critical. The last thing Smith provided was a set of night-vision binoculars, a military-grade German brand with image enhancing. They would be far more capable than the over-the-counter set he'd bought earlier.

"Will there be anything else?" Smith asked.

"No, that should do the job. Can I keep these photos?"

"Of course. Any new information will be sent to your phone." Smith dropped a key on the small table. "Stay as long as you like."

Slaton looked up at the stain on the dimly lit ceiling—it now appeared wet. "Thanks."

Minutes later Slaton was alone in the tiny flat, Smith having wished him luck and departed to the cacophony outside.

He went to the mini-fridge and cautiously opened the door. The temperature inside was below that of the room, but only slightly. He saw something unidentifiable in a leftover box, and a fuzzy mass on a plate might once have been cheese. Two water bottles appeared sealed, and he took both, downed one immediately, then began nursing the second. The cupboards were nearly bare, his only useful discovery being a can of tuna. A subsequent search of the adjacent drawers produced no can opener, but one sturdy kitchen knife. He had the can half open before the blade broke.

Minutes later he was sitting on the bed, the second water bottle and one damaged but empty tuna can beside him. Light wafted in through joints in the ceiling, highlighting clouds of dust that drifted like a microscopic galaxy of stars. He closed his eyes.

Slaton tried not to think about the burner phone in his pocket. It was so far unused. It felt like a tiny thread linking him to Christine and Davy—a thread that, once stretched taut, would quickly have to be broken. He yearned for some tenor of normalcy, to hear a trace of their day-to-day trivialities. The squeals of a night-ending game of chase. Davy giggling as Mom brushed his teeth. How quickly it had been lost.

All at once, the tenuousness, the fragility of the life they'd built together seemed bleakly apparent. What had taken years to create was at risk, threatened by a few days of madness. The only way out: to not permit failure.

Someone in Russia was condemning him, trying to hold him responsible for killings he'd had no part in. Someone needed a fall guy. Slaton realized he was a ready-made target. In giving up his career with Mossad, he'd cast himself as a rogue. An assassin without a country. In recent days he'd associated with Mossad and the CIA, both giving and getting help. Had that been a mistake?

Exhausted, he tried to push the thoughts away. He could not afford the luxury of thinking forward—not past tomorrow. He needed a full night's sleep. Slaton allowed himself half that.

Four hours. Then his operation would commence. A private mission that he would undertake quickly and quietly, and to the furtherance of no one's objectives but his own. Most critical of all: he would do it alone.

FIFTY-NINE

The CIA analyst named Dobbs worked well into the night, his enthusiasm mounting with each new detail as he scoured the images sent by their man in Morocco. He hit a number of roadblocks. In particular, much of what he needed could only come from DOD counterparts, and most of that crew had gone home for the night. One critical expert he reached shortly after nine o'clock as he sat on the bench during a softball game. On the unsecure line the DOD specialist, who was retired Air Force and the department's resident expert on Russian unmanned aerial vehicles, provided just enough detail to support Dobbs' burgeoning theory.

By ten o'clock Dobbs had enough to take his findings to whoever would listen. He went through three levels in the organizational chart before ending with a shift manager at Current Operations, Middle East Arabia section. She insisted they take his results straight to the operations center where, it was rumored, a crisis was being managed—one so serious that the director himself was working overtime.

As a mid-level analyst, Dobbs had never been in the ops center, and he was taken aback when he saw the intensity of the place. After a minor sidebar conference, he was given five minutes to lay out his findings to no less than the director and his senior staff. In a conference hall just off the main room, Dobbs passed out hastily copied images of the photos Slaton had taken. He then began his evaluation of what they meant. When he was done—five minutes and ten seconds later—there was an extended silence.

Director Coltrane was the first to speak. "You're sure about this?"

"Yes, sir. This hangar contains at least three MiG-21s that have been modified into aerial drones of some kind."

"We have that kind of thing, don't we?" a deputy director asked.

"Yes, we've converted a number of outdated airframes into drones—F-106s, F-4s, and even older F-16s. Operators fly them over test ranges as targets—live missiles, minus the warheads, are launched at them for test and evaluation."

"But this RosAvia . . . it's a Russian company."

"Yes," said Dobbs.

"Does Russia test missiles in Morocco?" asked Coltrane.

"That's the disconnect I keep coming up against," said Dobbs. "I've gone over RosAvia's history and talked to analysts at DOD. Without exception, all Russian missile testing is run from remote airbases on home soil—it's a matter of security. You don't want the performance of your latest weapons to be compromised."

"So why would they put an operation like this on the edge of the Sahara?" the duty officer asked.

Dobbs added, "There is one other curiosity." He referenced a blown-up image. "There are two vehicles parked near the hangar—a van and a large truck.

I'm quite sure they're some kind of mobile control centers."

Coltrane wanted to be clear. "What does that mean?"

"Well, there are a number of possibilities. We think the smaller van might be a local control vehicle, meant to handle the drone on the runway. The larger one, based on antenna configuration, is likely data-linked and could be sent elsewhere to control missions. In essence, you could operate these drones virtually anywhere."

It was clear by the silence that no one knew what to make of it all.

Coltrane then mused aloud, adding a final bit of sand to gears that were fast grinding to a stop. "The thing that mystifies me is the Russian who led us to this hangar. Why would he rush straight from sinking a ship to a drone research facility in Morocco?"

Not even the most speculative answer was ventured.

Eight time zones east of Langley, Sorensen woke just before daybreak in Riyadh. She was still at the SANG's regional headquarters, having been allowed to use a small guest room in the servants' wing. She'd not changed clothes since leaving Italy, and when she sat up her long-sleeve blouse and pants looked like they'd come from the bottom of a damp hamper. She reflexively checked her phone, and was surprised to see a message from headquarters—apparently there was a useable mobile signal in this arm of the complex. The news was that a Delta Force unit had arrived an hour ago, and was mustering somewhere in the building. Sorensen's instructions were to update them on the latest developments.

"As if I know what they are," she mumbled through a yawn.

She tried to call General Abdullah, but he didn't pick up. Her next call was to Langley where she ended up talking to a supervisor in the operations center. He explained that two new shipments had been interdicted in recent hours, one on the Yemeni border and another near Jeddah. Between the two raids, the Saudis had killed three men and taken two others into custody.

"So far, neither are talking," the supervisor said.

"Chances are, they don't know anything. They were probably told to haul a load of guns from Point A to Point B. Further instructions to follow."

The supervisor admitted that headquarters had reached the same conclusion.

After ending the call, Sorensen spent two minutes gathering herself in a tiny bathroom. She then began a search of the headquarters wing and found the Delta team assembled, rather awkwardly, in an ornate dining room. Between walls braided in silk curtains and beneath golden statues of raptors, seventeen serious men were seated around a dining table the size of a bowling lane. To a man, none looked impressed. They wore battle gear—body armor and equipment vests—but were not yet weighed down by weapons and explosives. Sorensen was sure that could fast be remedied.

A man with a buzz cut introduced himself as the unit's commander. Sorensen greeted him warmly, and explained that she was the local "CIA liaison." It was a nonexistent post, but seemed to fit the situation.

For thirty minutes they exchanged their respective understandings of what was happening on the peninsula. The Delta Force intelligence officer introduced a new wrinkle. "JSOC tells us there have been a number of other arms shipments recently. They go back nearly a month—each one small in itself, but a definite trend. Message traffic among monitored terrorist cells has been accelerating in recent days."

"We've been seeing the same traffic," echoed Sorensen.

The Delta intel officer said, "Our Saudi National Guard contacts insist it's nothing out of the ordinary. They write it off as the usual Iranian meddling—say they have everything under control."

"I talked to General Abdullah yesterday," said Sorensen. "He said essentially the same thing. But then, he seemed pretty distracted."

"By what?"

"Apparently the royal family is convening its annual bash sometime in the next few days. Everybody who's anybody in the House of Saud will be there."

"Sort of like Thanksgiving and a session of Congress all in one?" the Delta commander injected with typical SpecOps sarcasm. "Sounds like a great time. Where is this blessed event supposed to take place?"

"He wouldn't say."

"For reasons of security."

"Right."

On that note, the meeting staggered to its end. The commander explained that he had three Pave Low helicopters standing by outside, and that his team would remain on alert, ready to respond to any new threats that warranted their involvement.

At the end of the meeting, Sorensen realized her phone was again useless in the heart of the main complex. Wanting to try General Abdullah once more, she decided to go outside for a signal, and perhaps even more for a bit of fresh air to clear her head. She navigated to the main entrance, and checked with the security station before stepping outside.

Standing on the fine marble of the building's main entrance, she took a deep breath and stretched her arms over her head under the fast-warming eastern sun. That intake of air was interrupted when she realized what lay before her—or more precisely, what *wasn't* there.

The parking lot, which yesterday had been clogged with more limousines than she'd seen in her entire life, was completely empty. With refreshed urgency, she quickly dialed General Abdullah. There was still no answer.

SIXTY

The general didn't pick up Sorensen's call because he was at that moment a thousand miles west, thirty thousand feet above the Mediterranean, and observing the strict dictates of his own comm-sec protocol: all connections of mobile phones and email were to be shut down until arrival at their destination.

They were three hours into an eight-hour flight, although it was hardly a chore given the manner of their conveyance. The Boeing 747 in which Abdullah was traveling was nothing short of a marvel. Under a virtually limitless financial spigot, the engineers at Boeing had gladly fitted the king's jet with a wide array of custom equipment. A first-rate communications suite was hardened against attacks, and multiple electronic countermeasures had been installed to protect against missiles and confuse radar.

Where security ended, the decorators had taken over. The interior of the jet was resplendent in fit and finish, with furnishings that rivaled any palace. Boeing's performance engineers were hardly surprised when their calculations revealed that coaxing everything into the air would require more than the usual thrust. The gold-plated throne amidships alone weighed nearly a ton, meaning the massive GE engines had to be programmed for their top-rated thrust. Mercifully, the custom-built golden boarding escalator—on which the king himself drifted to earth as if descending from the heavens—was too unwieldy to leave Saudi soil.

As was his custom, General Abdullah occupied himself during the flight by dabbling in tribal politics, working the airplane's various compartments like an alderman at a barbeque picnic. In spite of the early hour, he was not surprised to find that as the jet cruised smoothly westward toward the House of Saud's annual gathering, the party had gotten well under way. Groups of princes huddled with favorite uncles in the main salon, and silver breakfast trays were fast emptied. In the royal suite a handful of high-ranking ministers debated the prices of oil and thoroughbreds, and the suspicious correlation between the two. In a pillowed lounge aft, two dozen princesses in brightly colored robes, the presumptive bon vivants of the Wahhabi kingdom, sipped champagne from fluted crystal and compared notes on the latest styles from Paris.

Amid it all Abdullah saw the usual interactions. Family and tribal affiliations were the rule, but not without the occasional thrust and parry of allies made and backs stabbed. It occurred to him that, notwithstanding their immediate location and means of carriage, it was a scene not unlike what had been taking place under sweltering tents for a thousand years. And across those centuries, there had always been someone like him: a guardian to keep an eye on the servants and crew, to coordinate the logistics of what lay ahead.

In that moment, Abdullah was content. Two dozen of his best men were doing their best to stay in the

386 | WARD LARSEN

shadows. No more were required here, yet that would soon change. For the next five days, he would be responsible for the security of the royal family in its entirety as they gathered for the first time in a foreign land. Sixty-seven principals in all: the highest-ranking princes, government ministers, and corporate titans of the Kingdom of Saudi Arabia.

He returned to the quiet security center behind the cockpit, lamenting what he would face in the days ahead. Nine hundred more of his men were already in place, and nearly as many Moroccan police. There would be countless servants, contractors, and guests from outside the family to screen. The workload would be crushing.

As he pondered it all, it never occurred to Abdullah that for the next five hours the very core of what he was charged with protecting—the House of Saud in nearly its entirety—was assembled in one confined space.

A thin-skinned steel tube.

Traveling miles above the earth.

At five hundred miles an hour.

"Where are the stars, Mommy?" Davy asked.

Christine tilted her head to one side as she considered it. Sunrise was still two hours away. She looked up at Rome's light-washed night sky and considered how to put it. "They're still there, honey. You just can't see them right now."

"Why not?"

"There's too much light."

He stared up with her, pondering, and she realized how perplexing it must seem.

Davy had awakened twenty minutes earlier with

a bad dream. In his father's absence, Christine had already moved his daybed next to her own. She'd brought him close and held him for a time. After the tiny shudders subsided, she'd taken him outside onto the patio, where a surprised Nick and another man adjusted their perimeter without comment.

Together with her son she stared up at the milky black sky, and soon Davy's breathing turned rhythmic in the crook of her arm. With an appreciative smile to Nick, she lifted her son carefully and carried him inside. He was soon sleeping soundly, his terrors forgotten.

If only it were so easy for the rest of us, she thought.

As she turned to her bed, Christine realized she'd forgotten to take the burner phone David had given her outside: during the last twenty minutes, and for the first time since he'd left, it had been out of earshot. She checked the call log and saw nothing.

Settling on the bed, she wondered where he was at that moment. What country or time zone. She wished desperately she could do something to help him. She weighed hanging out at the embassy command post, much as she'd done when he was in the Red Sea, but decided that was no longer an option. Her admittance then had been Sorensen's doing, and she'd gone to Riyadh.

Out of ideas, Christine closed her eyes and hoped for sleep.

Knowing it wouldn't come.

SIXTY-ONE

Slaton eased off the power, and the big bike coasted downhill for the final half mile. He'd reached the coast quickly, no traffic whatsoever in the predawn hours. The sun remained no more than a dim prospect beyond the low eastern hills.

The main coast road lay a mile from the jutting promontory of rock that was his objective. This worked to Slaton's benefit, as his final approach had to be on foot. He idled past two driveways that led to villas, and then a long-abandoned service road that was probably a remnant of the main road's construction. He remembered all three sidings from the photographs.

Slaton's strategy for the morning was based on two sequential assumptions. First was that the light-colored box he'd seen in the surveillance image of the cliffs had been placed there by the killer—most likely the targeting system for the long-range gun. The second assumption was an extension of the first: if it *was* the targeting unit, then it had been pre-positioned for a reason. Action was imminent.

Slaton gave the entire scenario a fifty-fifty chance of playing out. Not the best odds he'd ever had, but in that moment he felt he was closing in on the assassin. He was also driven by the perishable nature of his assumptions: if Ovechkin *were* to be eliminated, there was no telling where, or even if, the shooter would ever surface again.

On waking two hours ago, Slaton had tried for updates using his Langley-issued phone. Unfortunately, he hadn't been able to make a connection. It might have been a problem with the handset, or perhaps satellite coverage was erratic in this far-flung corner of Africa. As much as he wanted fresh intel, he couldn't afford to wait until the orbital gods were smiling. He'd briefly weighed using his burner phone, but decided to keep it in reserve.

After correlating the terrain before him with the reconnaissance image he'd memorized—the two always held subtle differences—he doubled back and rode down the service road. Slaton descended a modestly steep grade for a hundred yards. He then steered off the road and across hardpan earth until the BMW was well out of sight. He stood up the bike, broke a leafy branch from a tree, and dusted away the most obvious tracks. Fortunately, there hadn't been any recent rain—the big bike would have left deep ruts on softer ground.

From the saddlebags he removed the canvas bag. Slaton took off his loose outer shirt, donned the body armor, then shrugged the shirt back on with a much tighter fit. The spare magazine for the UMP went into the thigh pocket of his cargo pants. He considered keeping the gun in the canvas bag for the sake of discretion, but decided against it. This stretch of coastline was exceedingly remote, and the chance of encountering hikers or beachcombers at this hour seemed nonexistent. Far more likely: a surprise encounter with someone like himself. With one last check of the gun, he fitted its three-point sling to put the weapon across his chest for a right-handed grip.

He set out downhill, paralleling the service road for a time. In his back pocket was the folded "big-picture" overhead photo Smith had provided. Slaton didn't expect to use it, having spent twenty minutes this morning memorizing every gulley, outcropping, and tree line along this narrow section of coast. He knew precisely how he would approach the cliffs. Where to conceal himself once he got there. Where his eyes would be trained.

The only question: Would the Russian come?

Tikhonov was driving the command truck, his massive frame suited perfectly to the wide trucker's seat. "Where is the turnoff?" he asked.

Zhukov was next to him in the passenger seat. He referenced a map on his phone and compared it to the scene outside. "We are almost there, less than a kilometer to go."

The phone was dead-on—a gravel side road soon appeared, and Tikhonov slowed and made the turn. Just ahead they both saw a thin chain strung between two poles, a halfhearted attempt to discourage access. Tikhonov brought the truck to a stop. He stared at the chain, then stole a glance at the colonel.

Zhukov waved his hand forward.

Tikhonov shifted into first gear and accelerated, the massive truck snapping the chain like a ribbon at a finish line.

"The grade is steep ahead," Zhukov said, "but I walked all the way to the top on my survey—it shouldn't be a problem."

The climb took ten minutes. The grade was indeed

steep, and a few hairpin turns demanded caution. On reaching the top both paused to take in the scene. It could hardly be called a mountain—not after a night spent negotiating the High Atlas Range—but it *was* without question the highest point within miles. Which, of course, was why they were here.

"You didn't mention those," said Tikhonov. He pointed to a nearby clearing where a pair of modest antennas stood like steel sentinels.

"Are they a problem?" Zhukov asked.

"It depends. If they use a common bandwidth we could have inference in our signals. Chances are, they're only mobile communications relays—those operate on a different frequency than our equipment."

"How can we know for certain?"

The engineer shrugged. "We turn everything on and see if it works."

He guided the truck onto a patch of asphalt between the two antennas, the place where maintenance teams probably parked once or twice a year. With the nearest of the aerials fifty feet away, he set the parking brake and turned off the engine.

For a moment the two men simply looked out over the water. To the north a belt of rocky cliffs arced out toward the sea, and long-winged birds rode effortlessly on the updrafts. To the left, half a mile distant and hundreds of feet lower, was the villa where Ovechkin had taken up residence. Zhukov had wanted to simply park there, thinking it more secure, but Tikhonov convinced him that elevation was necessary to ensure signal integrity.

"Yes," Tikhonov said, having only seen the place on a map. "This will do nicely."

"It had better. There's not much time. Do what you

need to do." Zhukov got out of the cab, and was soon pacing along a gravel siding with his phone to his ear.

Tikhonov cranked up both generators, then went in back and began powering up the vital systems. Computers whirred to life, circuits energizing and fans spinning up. The antenna array on the truck's roof went through an extensive self-test sequence. It took twenty minutes to get everything up to speed, and Tikhonov saw no faults in the system.

As screens came to life at the control station, he programmed the sat-comm handset Zhukov had provided with the correct log-on settings. That done, he sat back and waited.

Waited for the arrival of an order that would change his life forever.

One hundred miles distant, on the darkened ramp of the RosAvia complex, the Russian named Ivan glanced at his watch. It was almost time.

He watched the MiG get towed from the hangar, less interested in the aircraft than the two men pulling it—one drove the pushback tug, and the other sat in the MiG's cockpit, presumably to operate the brakes if an emergency stop was necessary. There were six other men in the hangar, three in the office, and two near the runway—the last pair seated on the roof of a ridiculous van with an umbrella on top. It was all precisely as he'd been told. Thirteen workers in all, six Russian technicians and seven locals. All were busy this morning, preparing for a mission that none of them realized would be the last for this Ros-Avia outpost.

The tug stopped near the end of the runway, and the two men went to work. One removed the tow bar that connected the tug to the fighter, and the other began pulling safety pins from the landing gear. That done, they mounted the tug together, drove to a nearby taxiway, and parked. As they settled in to wait, the soothing light of dawn began painting the horizon.

Ivan looked again at his watch. 0635 hours.

It was time.

The small backpack was in his left hand. He unzipped it, put his right hand inside, and walked purposefully toward the office.

SIXTY-TWO

Someone did come to the cliffs along the peninsula. Whether it was the Russian, Slaton couldn't tell.

He'd been waiting over an hour, and was repositioning into shadows as the sun topped the hills, when a flash of distant motion made him freeze. The first thing he noticed was a handful of terns scattering from the rock wall that rose above the rocky beach. Slaton shifted the binoculars on the area, and distinguished regular flickers of motion inside the tree line at the crest of the ridge. A figure wearing dark clothes was weaving toward the peninsula. Not slow, not fast. A carefree man in no hurry. Or a purposeful one being methodical.

Slaton watched for a full minute, at which point he was confident it was a man, based on build and gait. He was dressed in earth tone clothing and a black stocking cap, and moved in a way Slaton recognized: on a deliberate path that kept within the heaviest foliage and below the top of the ridgeline. He veered left and right, whatever it took to remain concealed, yet it was clear where the greater course was taking him: to the high rocky point.

What sealed it for Slaton was a single glimpse caught in a clearing between a pair of tall trees. On the man's far shoulder was a soft case hanging by a strap, long and thin, roughly two-thirds the length of his body. Having carried such packages before, Slaton knew precisely what it was. A gun case, sized for a long-range rifle. Like a Barrett fifty cal. Almost everything Slaton saw fit perfectly with the scenario he'd been building.

Almost.

There was, however, one disconnect, and it gnawed at him. He knew precisely where the assassin's villa was located, the tiny cottage that, according to the CIA, had been tied to an FSB front company. The man Slaton was watching had not come from that direction. He'd appeared from the east, materializing at the forested curve where the promontory joined the mainland. From where Slaton was set up, near the tip of the peninsula and concealed among sea-rounded rocks on a mid-level ledge, he had a commanding view of the northern coastline. The one drawback of his position was that he couldn't see any part of the tiny cottage where the killer was supposedly based. Because it was set back in a gulley, and virtually unapproachable— sheer vertical faces of rock on one side, a thin road over cleared land on the other—Slaton had decided to wait for the assassin on neutral ground.

So what course had the man taken? Had he come by way of the distant main road? Had he set up last night to the south, perhaps to surveil Ovechkin's villa? Either was possible, but also unverifiable. It was decision time. The man would soon be lost to sight, and within minutes he would arrive at the clearing on the ridge where the equipment case was waiting. Slaton summed everything he knew, and decided it was enough. The rifle case the man was carrying was simply insurmountable.

He backed away into cover, then began moving toward the rock face at the tip of the point. After one last look, he set off on the route to the top he'd scouted earlier. It was a modestly difficult climb, two or three areas where he'd have to navigate steep walls. Slaton rotated the UMP until it was slung across his back.

He began to climb.

CIA director Coltrane had not gone home that night, opting to sleep in one of the quiet rooms he'd ordered set up with precisely that in mind. The tiny spaces—little more than closets with plush recliners and "Do Not Disturb" signs on the doors—had been installed to support the rank and file. Analysts, cyber specialists, and comm techs who found themselves headquarters-bound for excessively long shifts could find a few hours' rest without battling the Beltway's notorious traffic. Coltrane had discovered early on that the rooms' loungers and dense soundproofing were far superior to the couch in his office. But comfortable as it all was, he dozed fitfully for no more than an hour before heading back to the operations center for an update.

The duty officer filled him in. "The situation in Saudi Arabia is deteriorating. Over the last two hours NSA is reporting a major spike in message traffic. The Saudi National Guard is responding to three 'terrorist-related' events as we speak."

Coltrane listened intently as each dustup was covered in detail. Like the others in recent days, they appeared to be isolated incidents involving the distribution of small arms. But as the frequency increased, it became difficult to deny that something larger was in play. "What about this business in Morocco?" he said.

"We've been concentrating on the RosAvia complex in Tazagurt. It was nothing but desert three years ago, then the place seemed to get built almost overnight, a joint venture between Russia and Morocco. It was designed with test work in mind, although nothing very cutting edge. The idea was to support high-altitude, high-temperature testing for the certification of civilian aircraft. At least that's what the website says."

"Website?"

"Honestly, we're playing catch-up on this—we know a lot about RosAvia's Russian operations, but the complex in Tazagurt is pretty much a mystery. We found a website, although it hasn't been updated in years. RosAvia advertises the facility as being available for contract work. So far we can't find a record of anyone who's actually used it. NRO has done a handful of passes over the place in the last couple of years, but none of the images showed anything suspicious. Bottom line—this airfield just wasn't on our radar."

"It is now," Coltrane said pointedly. "First we have a hangar full of old MiGs that have been modified into drones, and now some kind of arms smuggler arrives by private jet after murdering the crew of—"

"Sir!" an urgent female voice interrupted.

Coltrane's head swiveled turret-like, and he saw a woman behind a communications panel. She said, "I have a call from Miss Sorensen in Riyadh. She says she needs to talk to you directly—something very urgent."

Coltrane hesitated, then reached for the black handset in front of him. "All right, put her through."

"Anna," he said into the secure phone, "please make it quick. We've got multiple crises here."

"I'm going to add another one," she said. "I think the entire Saudi royal family is being targeted for assassination!"

SIXTY-THREE

"What?" Coltrane said loudly enough for everyone in the room to hear. "How?"

"I'm not sure. I'm at National Guard regional headquarters in Riyadh, and I've been trying to get answers for hours. I can't reach General Abdullah, and nobody will talk about what's going on. But I can tell you that last night I saw a hundred limos in the parking lot outside. Every one of them is gone this morning. I'm convinced the family is gathering as we speak—it's an annual event where virtually every minister and prince is in attendance."

"Where?"

"That's the problem—nobody will say. If you put together all these small arms coming in, and the fact that the House of Saud is gathering in one place . . ."

Coltrane thought about it. "That only makes sense to a point," he said. "You're saying the family is gathering in one spot, and that's a vulnerability. But these arms shipments are being spread all across the country."

After a long pause, it was Sorensen who found a solution. "Maybe these arms aren't meant to be used against the family."

"But what then?"

"Think about it. If you could somehow remove the ruling family from the picture, all at once . . . what would happen?"

Coltrane saw what she was getting at. "A complete power vacuum across the kingdom."

"Exactly. Cut off the head, and all their fighter jets and tanks might as well be stuck in sand. If the government were to go rudderless in an instant, a committed rebel force of a few thousand with a good supply of weapons could wreak havoc. They might not take over the peninsula, but they could easily turn it into the next Syria."

For Coltrane the revelation was like a light flicking on. He saw not the maps on the monitors in front of him, but one in his head. Saudi Arabia, a bastion of regional order, surrounded by some of the most unstable regimes on earth. Sudan and Somalia to the south. Yemen, Lebanon, and Syria on the shoulders. Archenemy Iran to the north. The House of Saud had its faults, but remove that iron hand, and the entire Middle East would fall to chaos. Kuwait, the Gulf States, an already divided Iraq—none could possibly fill such a void. "This is finally starting to make sense. The three ships that were sunk, multiple fingerprints of Russian involvement—this is Petrov making a play to destabilize the region. It could drive up energy prices for decades."

"Possibly," Sorensen said hesitantly, clearly not having taken things to a strategic level. "Whatever the objective, we have to figure out where the Saudis are meeting and warn them."

"Wouldn't it be at one of their palaces?" Coltrane asked.

"It has been in the past. But I've been getting stonewalled here. Security is extreme."

"As it should be. The problem is, that kind of bunker mentality can backfire. The only way we're going to get answers is from my end," Coltrane said. "I'll talk to the king himself if that's what it takes."

Slaton moved fast up the steep grade. Behind him, a hundred feet below, the Atlantic beat its endless greeting, swells rising up in the shallows and hurtling over the rock-strewn beach. Nearing the top of the cliff, at the seaside tip of the point, he paused for a cautious look up the promontory. There was no sign of the man. He had to be near, but stands of brush and rock outcroppings obscured Slaton's view. The clear area at the narrow waist of the point—where he guessed the man was heading based on the rectangular case he'd seen in the photo—was roughly eighty yards distant.

He began moving again, fast and quiet, lacing between trees and boulders. The UMP was in front again, ready in a two-handed grip. Amid the dense undergrowth sound became more important than sight. He paused at intervals, straining to capture anything. He heard only the battering sea below, the occasional cry of a gull. With an estimated forty yards to go, Slaton got his first glimpse of the clearing. He saw the rectangular box—it remained on the ground next to a jagged stump.

In a crouch he shifted to his right, behind a fallen tree, to get a better view. Finally he saw the dark figure. He was a few steps left of the box, facing away. The gun case was resting against a nearby sapling. Slaton evaluated the man for other weapons, but saw no obvious holster or strap. Even so, if he was what Slaton presumed—an elite operator—there *would* be something else. He also saw no bulkiness to suggest body armor, only a natural musculature under his thin brown shirt.

For Slaton there was never any question of fair play. No urge to shout a warning or make an offer of surrender. No more than this man had given Pyotr Ivanovic or Alexei Romanov, and probably many others. A bullet in the back . . . as Slaton knew better than most, it was all too often an assassin's destiny.

Yet he did take pause.

His hesitation had to do with his own weapon. Slaton had checked the UMP thoroughly, but had not yet fired it. The .45 had excellent stopping power, but every gun had its quirks. He could conceivably spray wide from where he stood. Ever the perfectionist, Slaton wanted to be sure. Wanted to give himself every advantage.

Which meant getting closer.

He began to move, with no choice but to close the gap across open ground. With the man still facing away, each step became a process. A glance down at each projected footfall. Avoid twigs and loose stones. Avoid any sound whatsoever.

Thirty yards.

The man suddenly moved. Slaton froze, the UMP poised with his finger tense on the trigger. He held steady as the man leaned down toward the box. Slaton watched him unlock two latches and lift the lid.

Slaton began moving again.

At twenty yards, success was all but guaranteed.

The man stood still. He was staring into the box thoughtfully . . . or . . . as if he were perplexed?

For the second time Slaton heard an old and trusted

voice. *Something isn't right.* He never had time to process that warning.

It might have been the smallest of sounds. Perhaps motion in his periphery. Possibly even a scent carrying on the wind. Whatever the source, the man sensed Slaton's presence like a good operator would.

He whipped to his right, his hand reaching for his beltline. Slaton didn't hesitate. Three rounds later his earlier doubts were erased. The Heckler & Koch in his hands was a faultless specimen of the weapon.

It shot perfectly straight and true.

The MiG rolled down the runway in full afterburner, shattering the desert morning. The sleek jet rotated upward and lifted into the air. As it gained speed, the takeoff controller on the roof of the van worked his joystick furiously. He was one of the Russian technicians, and on most flights ran the mission truck. Today, for reasons he didn't understand, the lead engineer had taken that seat.

He adjusted his microphone and spoke to Tikhonov over their dedicated comm link. "Prepare for transfer."

"Ready to accept control," came Tikhonov's distant response.

"On my mark. Three . . . two . . . one . . . execute."

The technician watched the MiG carefully. Already two miles distant, it flew on straight and true.

"I have the aircraft," Tikhonov confirmed from the mission truck.

The technician watched the airplane fade from view. Soon it was little more than a thin shadow with wings. Then he noticed something peculiar. Instead of turning east toward the test ranges, the jet banked very distinctly to the west.

"Mobile," he said into his microphone, "confirm you have control?"

No response.

"Mobile, this is runway local! I am watching the aircraft and it appears to be making an unexpected turn. Confirm you have control!"

Still no reply.

The technician was about to make a third call when his thoughts were interrupted. He heard a metallic creak behind him.

He turned and saw a man at the top of the van's ladder. He recognized him as the visitor who'd been milling about the hangar this morning. Everyone had been told his name was Ivan, and that he was an official from RosAvia. They'd been instructed to answer any questions he might have. He'd never asked a single one. Now, as Ivan reached the roof and stood clear of the umbrella a few steps away, the technician knew he wasn't going to ask any here either.

He knew because the man had a large silenced handgun pointed squarely at his head.

The 747 carrying the Saudi royal family began a gradual descent.

The king had loved airplanes since he was a child, and while he'd never bothered to learn how to fly, he always enjoyed visiting the cockpit to mingle with the pilots—one of the many perks of royalty.

"We will begin our flyby in thirty-one minutes," the captain said.

The king looked out the left window, just behind the captain's shoulder, and saw the Moroccan coastline gliding past. In the early light the tan landscape looked strikingly familiar, accentuated nicely by an azure sea.

"Will the weather be favorable?" he asked.

"A beautiful day," the smiling copilot said. "We will make a memorable entrance."

The king beamed. He'd decided it would be spectacular to watch the proceedings from here—the best seat in the house.

"Your Highness?"

The king turned and saw General Abdullah. "What is it?"

"We have received a message from the director of America's CIA. He wishes to arrange a call with you."

The king flapped his hand as if waving away a bad smell.

"Forgive me," said Abdullah, "but he claims it is very important."

A heavy sigh. "The Americans have worked themselves into a lather over these arms shipments. Make arrangements for the call—we will put it through once we've landed. Tell him I'm very busy at the moment."

Abdullah seemed about to protest.

The king gave him a glare that sent him on his way.

SIXTY-FOUR

Slaton walked slowly toward his target, the UMP still poised. Not that there was any doubt as to his fate. Two of the bullets had struck center of mass in his chest, the third in his neck. The big .45 rounds left no room for error.

Three steps away Slaton paused. The man had come to rest on his side, his left arm twisted beneath. On the blood-soaked ground near his right hand was a Sig Sauer 9mm. All as expected. All according to plan.

In the next few moments, however, everything went wrong.

The first problem was the man's face. Slaton recalled the words of the salesman in Davos. *There was a younger man with an accent—I thought he might be Russian, or perhaps Latvian.* This man wasn't young at all—he was easily mid-forties. More damningly, Slaton realized he'd seen the face before in a series of photographs. Standing on the balcony of a dacha with three oligarchs. Hunting with the president of Russia. The dead man on the ground before him was none other than Viktor Zhukov. Former Spetsnaz, 45th Guards.

His unease growing, Slaton looked at the metal

container. That was what had first drawn his focus to this clearing on the windswept point. In his final moments, Zhukov had lifted the lid. It remained open now, and Slaton saw why the Russian had seemed so perplexed—the box was completely empty. The gun case leaning against the sapling? Slaton knew there was no need to look inside. A wooden crutch, or perhaps a tree branch—it would contain anything but a Barrett fifty.

The voice in his head was now screaming.

In that critical moment, and for reasons he didn't understand, Slaton shifted his gaze upward. He looked down the southern coastline for the first time, searching for a villa he'd seen before only in photographs— the place where Vladimir Ovechkin had purportedly taken refuge. As he did, disjointed thoughts surged through his head. An empty case on a wind-whipped clearing. A gravedigger named Smith in Marrakesh. A sat-phone that had inexplicably stopped working. The thoughts swirled mercilessly, but there was no time for them. *Not here. Not now.*

Slaton picked out the villa easily, and in the next instant he saw a distinct flicker of light from a balcony.

He knew instantly what it was: through the morning's shadows, he'd just witnessed the most fateful sight a man could see. The last vision of a million soldiers in a hundred wars. It was the muzzle flash of a rifle. Which meant a bullet was flying toward him at greater than the speed of sound.

A guided bullet that could track any target.

Sent by an expert shooter.

Slaton stood absolutely still.

* * *

The sergeant took the brunt of the Barrett's recoil in his shoulder, his firm two-handed grip mitigating the jolt. He reacquired his target through the special optics.

He had spotted Slaton the instant he'd emerged from the tree line. Then he'd watched him stalk Zhukov silently. All as predicted. Colonel Zhukov had reacted, but of course not fast enough. The colonel had been good in his day, but he was getting old. Getting soft. Slaton had finished him effortlessly, then eased closer to survey his work.

It was in the next moments that the sergeant had taken the slightest of liberties. In that tiny window of opportunity he should have taken his shot, no quarter given while Slaton was distracted. Yet he'd waited just a beat, watching through the optics for a reaction—he wanted the *kidon*, in his last earthly thoughts, to realize he'd been outwitted. And the sergeant *had* seen it in his face, in the instant the Barrett's trigger had given way—the legendary assassin knew what was coming.

The sergeant saw the bullet hit—of that there was no doubt. Slaton was lifted completely off his feet and thrown backward. There was an awkward half roll before the only unforeseen outcome—he went tumbling over the side of the cliff.

He pulled away from the optic. That hadn't been in the plan—the loss of the body. He realized his miscalculation—Slaton had been wearing a vest. It was no defense against a fifty-cal round, but clearly had absorbed a great deal of energy. Instead of a straight-through shot to the chest, the projectile's momentum had translated widely across the victim's torso, throwing him ten feet back and over the precipice.

The sergeant decided it hardly mattered.

Dead was dead. The police would recover the body at some point.

Lesson learned.

SIXTY-FIVE

Slaton was hanging by his right hand. Hanging on for dear life.

His fingertips strained to keep the barest of grips on an exposed root. His left shoulder screamed in pain, and when he tried to raise that hand to grasp the root, a bolt of lightning shot through his arm. Feeling his fingers slipping, he explored blindly with his feet and found one slight toehold in the sheer rock wall. The sound of the ocean thundered from below. Slaton glanced down, ignoring the sea for the face of the cliff. He *had* to get better purchase.

The UMP was still with him, hanging in front and digging into his ribs—in that moment, no more than added weight. He looked down and saw a second root by his left shin. It looked old and rotted—from what he remembered, there wasn't a living tree within twenty yards of the spot where he'd gone over.

He bent his left knee, and managed to twist his foot onto the root. He tested it with a bit of weight, and there was a momentary slip. He heard clots of dirt tumble down the cliffside, but then, thankfully, things seemed to hold. It gave him three points of contact. Progress of sorts.

He wanted to look at his left shoulder, but couldn't turn his head in that direction. It had to be dislocated. Writing off any chance of using that arm, he surveyed his predicament. Climbing back up wasn't an option given his limited mobility. It also failed from a tactical viewpoint—staying below the crest of the cliff kept him out of the sniper's gunsight. He saw a few possible holds to his right, and ten yards in that direction, slightly below, was a narrow ledge. If he could reach that, he might get a reprieve.

What began as desperation evolved into a process. With two feet and one good hand, he began inching along the sheer rock wall. Another attempt to use his left arm brought blinding pain. Afraid he might pass out, he stopped trying altogether. Slaton tested every cleft that looked promising. He moved as slowly as he dared—even seasoned stonemasons had limits to the endurance of their grip. After clawing across the stone face for five painful minutes, and with his right hand beginning to tremble, he fell the last two feet to the ledge.

He came to rest in a heap, rolling carelessly on his injured shoulder. The lightning struck again. The ledge was less than a yard in width, and with his back against the cliff his folded right knee was out over the edge. He didn't move for a time, laying motionless as he took stock of things. His shoulder was the biggest problem. His vest was ripped from bottom to top, a longitudinal tear that ended in a graze of the soft flesh near his collarbone. Aside from that, he noticed nothing beyond a few scrapes and contusions.

It could have been far worse.

When he'd seen the muzzle flash, there had been an overwhelming urge to hit the dirt. That's what soldiers did for incoming fire. Yet something had held Slaton in place. Something based more on instinct than reason. And it had saved his life.

Only now did he have time to weigh all the variables. He remembered his first thought being that the flash had come from a fifty cal—a pessimist's view, he supposed, since any round from a smaller-caliber weapon would never have reached him. But it had turned out to be accurate. Notwithstanding the tremendous muzzle velocity, he knew it would take a ballistic eternity for the round to cover two and a half miles. Now, having time to calculate, he reckoned something near seven seconds. More or less. Yet in that critical moment, Slaton hadn't tried to crunch numbers or count Mississippis. He'd only understood that if he dropped immediately, any steerable bullet—assuming that's what was being used at such extreme range—would have time to alter its course. It would have struck him dead center as he lay on the ground.

So Slaton had stood waiting for a bullet with his name, knowing his only chance was to remain statue-like until the last instant. If played perfectly, the round might not have time to react if he moved in the final milliseconds. Slaton had done some nervy things in his day. Standing perfectly still, waiting for a bullet to arrive, was perhaps a new personal best. Yet that was what he'd done.

He'd stood motionless.

And waited.

Waited until he couldn't take it anymore.

Now, looking at his vest, he realized he couldn't have called it any closer. If he'd waited even a few more hundredths of a second, the bullet would have ripped him from belly to shoulder. Game over. He'd tried to throw himself down and to the right, but before he hit the ground, when he was practically horizontal, the bullet had ripped into his vest. The vest did its job in a sideways fashion—it absorbed much of the big round's kinetic energy, only from bottom to top. That energy translated directly to his body, propelling him back toward the cliff. Somewhere in that tumultuous fall he'd landed awkwardly on his shoulder, throwing it out of joint. Problematic as that was, Slaton saw only success.

He had, quite literally, dodged a bullet.

He tried again to look at his shoulder. This time he managed it and saw the unnatural set. It had happened once before in training, so the pain was not unfamiliar. Yet on that day he'd had the benefit of medical attention, a doctor who'd set the joint right within minutes. Today—on a windswept precipice in a foreign country, with a killer lurking nearby—that level of care was an unattainable luxury. He looked seaward along the cliff. His best chance at safety lay twenty yards distant—a gulley carved into the vertical wall. From there, he thought, he might be able to climb to the top. But how could he reach it with his shoulder in agony?

Slaton could think of only one answer.

He reached into his pocket, pulled out his burner phone. The coast road was a mile away, and the signal there, which he'd made a point of checking, had been strong. But here? On this desolate ledge with his back against a rock wall?

It all depended on where the towers were situated.

He powered up the phone and prayed.

By God's grace, he saw a tenuous signal.

* * *

The burner phone in Rome was on the veranda table next to a fresh baguette. Christine answered before the second ring.

"David?"

"Hey . . . it's good to hear your voice."

She didn't like the sound of his. It seemed strained and breathless. "Are you all right?"

"Honestly, I could use a little medical advice."

Christine felt something inside her turn cold. "What is it? What's wrong?"

"It's nothing dire," he said. "But my left shoulder . . . I'm pretty sure I dislocated it."

"Then you need a hospital."

"At the moment, that's not really an option."

She heard a dull roar in the background. "Where are you?"

A hesitation. "I'm in a place where I can't get help—not anytime soon. I'm on my own, and I was hoping you could help me work through this."

"We *are* talking about your shoulder here?"

"Uh, yeah."

"Mommy?" Davy said. "Is that Daddy?" He was sitting across the table fingering cereal into his mouth.

"Yes, honey, it is. But he can't talk to you right now—Daddy's very busy."

David had surely heard that little exchange, she thought. The fact that he didn't ask for a minute with Davy spoke volumes. He *really* needed her—not as a wife, but as a doctor. "Has this ever happened before?" she asked.

"Yeah, once in training, maybe ten years ago. A doctor fixed it on the scene."

"If you've dislocated it once, you're prone to recurrences."

"He might have mentioned that."

Through the line she heard his breathing, sharp and irregular. A seagull cried in the background. Christine put it all aside. She made him describe the injury, and when he did she decided it was the most common type—an anterior dislocation in which the upper arm was pushed forward out of the socket. "And it hurts like hell?" she asked.

"It really does. For what it's worth, I'm also wearing body armor."

Christine held steady, no inquisition about how he'd injured himself while wearing body armor. "Will that restrict your movement?" she asked.

"Not much. It's a lightweight vest, just canvas over the shoulder."

"Okay. You have to understand, it's not always possible to do this yourself. And you've really got to be careful. We don't want to damage any tendons or blood vessels."

"I know. But from where I'm sitting, trust me . . . it's very important that we try."

SIXTY-SIX

Slaton put the phone to speaker as Christine walked him through it.

"First of all," she said, "make sure you're in a safe place. There's a chance you could lose consciousness."

Slaton looked past his right hip. He saw a hundred-and-fifty-foot drop, waves crashing over boulders in a maelstrom of energy. "Next?"

"Do your best to relax the muscles in your arm and shoulder."

"Okay."

"Now, reach your bad arm out to the side, slow and easy."

Slaton did. The pain was excruciating, daggers through nerve bundles that radiated into his arm and neck.

"Now try to bend the elbow, like you're trying to reach the back of your neck. Imagine a baseball pitcher winding up to throw. I know it's hard, but the more you can relax the better chance you have of this working."

Slaton did his best, grunting from the pain. "Okay," he said. "Hand's on the back of my neck."

"Good! Now just a little more—push it farther to the opposite shoulder."

He seemed to hit a stop. "I don't think this is going to—"

"Do it, David! Fix it!"

He made a final push, and through a torrent of pain he felt a distinct *pop*. He felt light-headed and his eyes closed. When he opened them again he was looking down at nothing but sea. He clutched a cliff-side rock to steady himself.

"David?"

He looked at his shoulder and saw a more normal profile. "Yeah, I'm good. I think we did it."

He heard a long release of air over the phone. "Are you okay otherwise?" she asked.

"Never better. But now that I've got you, I need something else."

"Anything."

"I think the phone Sorensen gave me is compromised. Go to the comm room at the embassy and make sure Langley gets this number. I may not answer right away, but they can use it to reach me."

"Okay, I'll do it now."

"Thanks."

She was silent for a time, then asked, "Will you be back soon?"

"Yeah. I'll explain everything then. And Christine . . . I mean it, thanks. You really are a life saver."

At Langley, the threat level had risen to the agency equivalent of a five-alarm fire. In rapid succession it was learned that the royal family had hours earlier boarded the king's Boeing 747, and that the flight had initially taken up a westerly course. Since no palaces existed in that part of the kingdom, one question rose to the forefront: Where was the family gathering?

It wasn't long before the operations center had its collective palm-to-the-forehead moment. The monarchy had recently put the finishing touches on its first official palace abroad—in of all places, Morocco.

"Security at the new palace might be loose," one analyst surmised.

"Or someone could ambush the convoy on its way from the airport," another said.

Coltrane began issuing orders under the highest priority.

The duty officer began getting results within minutes. "We've located the jet carrying the royal family. Right now it's eighty miles north of Casablanca. We still have no comm link established—we're getting the runaround from SANG headquarters. I'm guessing General Abdullah and most of his senior staff are on that airplane."

"Can we put together some kind of response in Morocco?"

"According to JSOC, we have no Special Ops detachments anywhere near. Team Six, Delta . . . every available unit in theater was sent to Saudi Arabia to deal with the crisis there."

Coltrane sat in silence. He felt far behind in a fast-moving situation. Uncomfortable associations began brewing in his head. He thought about the RosAvia complex. About a Russian killer who'd flown in hours ago from Yemen. He considered the pictures Slaton had sent—a hangar full of MiGs that had been modified as drones.

He repeated one of his unfulfilled requests. "Do we know Slaton's whereabouts yet?"

"I'm just getting word on that now," said a voice in back. "It appears the phone we issued him has been compromised—sometime in the last twelve hours."

"*Compromised?* What does that mean?"

"Comm says it was some kind of hack and grab. Someone broke the encryption and altered the routing."

Coltrane didn't know exactly what that meant, but he was quite sure who was responsible. "So do we have *any* assets in Morocco?"

"Our standard CIA contingent at the embassy in Rabat. That's about two hundred miles from the palace."

"Sir, I'm getting something from NRO now," a technician said, breaking in.

Coltrane had put in an urgent request with the National Reconnaissance Office for coverage of a number of sites in Morocco.

"Something on the palace?" Coltrane asked hopefully.

"Actually, no. It's RosAvia's airfield near Tazagurt. Apparently . . . sixteen minutes ago . . . one of those MiGs took off."

Slaton negotiated his way to safety with limited use of his left arm. The bolts of pain were gone, but it remained sore from shoulder to hand, and he sensed nerve pain with certain movements. To the positive, everything seemed to function—at least well enough to grip a gunstock.

On reaching the gulley, he had little trouble climbing to the top of the bluff. There he melded into the brush and paused long enough to check the graze near his collarbone. The bleeding had nearly stopped. He maneuvered southward until he saw the villa where the shot had come from.

Slaton's vision had always been exceptionally sharp,

and even without binoculars he could discern two men standing on the distant terrace. He could not say who they were or what they were doing, but the fact that they were standing in the open spoke volumes. The assassin was confident he'd succeeded. And why wouldn't he be? He'd minutes ago watched his target take a hit from a fifty cal and go careening over a cliff.

With his immediate tactical crisis behind him, Slaton began to deconstruct what had happened. In essence, the assassin had set him up—and he wasn't the only victim. The killer had clearly put Zhukov in harm's way. He'd made sure the colonel was carrying what looked like a rifle, and sent him to a rendezvous that put him squarely in Slaton's sights. *I kill Zhukov,* Slaton thought, *then the sniper kills me.* The calculus of why it was done that way escaped him. But it *did* make sense.

As he thought about it, a great deal more fell into place.

At some point in the last twelve hours, his CIA-issued satellite phone had been hijacked. Taken over in support of an assassin. His conversations had been monitored, his messages tracked. Then, at the most critical moment, that electronic lifeline had been severed, leaving him to drift alone in the wind. A very cold and deliberate wind.

Slaton saw all the hallmarks of a state-sponsored hack, and there could be only one suspect: some shadowed cyber arm of Russia's FSB. Taking that idea further, he considered the surveillance photos he'd been given showing the obvious lure of the case in the clearing. The discovery of a rental agreement for the nearby villa. The UMP, body armor, and optic—all of it was promptly forwarded as per his request to the

CIA, yet now he realized it had been cobbled together not by that agency's Morocco station, but instead its Russian counterpart. The Rabat *rezidentura*. And handed over by a most convincing gravedigger—in retrospect, a curiously apt impression.

How could I not have seen it? he thought.

The response to that question came in the form of a second.

What am I going to do about it?

To that, Slaton had a resounding answer.

SIXTY-SEVEN

Ovechkin stood by the pool of his borrowed villa absorbing a view he would enjoy for a few more minutes—and then never see again. It truly was spectacular. *Perhaps I can find something like it,* he mused. *Chile or Ecuador.*

"It's done!" The voice, coming from behind, shattered his daydream.

Ovechkin turned to see the assassin emerge from the main house. He carried the massive gun effortlessly. The man had spent all morning on the northern balcony, the weapon and its guidance system poised and ready. Waiting. When the shot finally came fifteen minutes ago there had been no warning. Ovechkin had instinctively recoiled.

The man set the gun on a cushioned lounge chair, walked toward him, and handed over a compact set of binoculars. Ovechkin trained them on the distant cape. At this range the scene was not particularly detailed, but he could see enough. Poor Zhukov lay crumpled next to the empty equipment case. Ovechkin scanned the surrounding area for the second body.

"I don't see Slaton," he said.

"I finished him—doubly so. The bullet struck with such force it sent him over the cliff."

Ovechkin pulled away from the binoculars. He saw perhaps a trace of amusement in the man's expression. He felt nothing close to it. He had arranged his share of violence over the years, but rarely did he find himself in such close proximity to its execution. "He fell into the sea?"

"I can't imagine otherwise. It's a sheer drop of sixty meters."

Ovechkin set the binoculars on a table that was stocked with pastries and coffee. "That could be a complication."

"Not really. The body will be found. When I place the rifle there later, I'll create a bit of evidence to show the police the way. The scene was never going to be perfect from a forensic standpoint—which is in line with our objective. The more confusion the better. It will be enough to fix responsibility for the elimination of your corporate partners on an elusive Israeli assassin. Anyway, the police in Morocco are not the world's best."

"But the world's best will become involved . . . given what is still to come."

"It doesn't matter, I tell you. Combine the scene we will build here with the one being set in Tazagurt. There will be far more questions than answers. And don't forget—Petrov will insert his own investigators into the process to muddy things further. What's happening at the RosAvia complex assures Russia a stake in the inquiry."

Ovechkin eyed the killer pensively, trying to grasp his thinking, his motives. He always preferred that—to know, as the Americans were fond of saying, "what makes a man tick." In this case, the divergence between the two of them seemed unfathomable. He could only trust that their objectives were one. He shifted his gaze to the distant hill where the big truck was parked between two aerials. The engineer would be inside, guiding the MiG. Ovechkin wondered how far away the jet was at that moment. Thirty miles? Fifty? He nodded upward and said, "It's almost time. You'll need to deal with the engineer as soon as his part is complete."

The assassin casually selected a pastry from the table and took a bite, bits of sweet icing crumbling to the stonework below. He patted the partially visible holster beneath his unbuttoned outer shirt, the matte-black grip of a semiautomatic obvious. "I am ready. But I think I will delay my hike for a few more minutes. The airshow we are about to see is not to be missed."

Ovechkin nearly rebuked the sergeant, but something held him in check. Perhaps the fact that his own security staff had largely departed, only two men remaining at the villa. He checked his Rolex, a Christmas gift from Estrella. In thirty minutes they would all be gone—he and his detachment in one car, the assassin going his own way in another. Ovechkin wondered if he would ever see the man again. He found himself hoping against it.

The assassin poured a cup of coffee, having put his most recent murder behind him. The two locked eyes, and the sergeant lifted his cup in a mock toast. Ovechkin had to grin. Standing side by side, the two Russians turned their eyes skyward. They looked eager and expectant.

Like children waiting for a fireworks display.

Three miles south of the patio where Ovechkin and an assassin stood gazing skyward, a crescent-shaped tract of tan beach swept pleasingly out to sea. It was situated just beyond the next seaside cape, at the threshold of what had long been among the least developed and pristine shores of Morocco's Atlantic coast. Above the high-tide line, gently undulating dunes carried inland as far as the eye could see, a minor geologic curiosity in a country that abounded with them.

It was on an eighty-acre plot of this shore, cradled in the swale of a bluewater bay, that the Kingdom of Saudi Arabia had been granted special dispensation for the most unique of undertakings: the construction of its very first palace outside the Saudi peninsula.

The king himself had been the driving force behind the effort. For a ruler who spent considerable time abroad, the idea of another penthouse in London or New York had long lost its appeal. Everyone was doing that. Instead, the king envisioned a necklace of great palaces across the globe, residences whose scope and grandeur would reflect the monarchy's ambition. After considerable debate, he selected Morocco as the trial for his royal expansionism. The choice was as practical as it was esoteric: situated in a stable and friendly Muslim country, the site offered wondrous views of the Atlantic with its seemingly endless bounds. On any number of levels, it was a new frontier.

Four years under construction, the palace north of Agadir was without question among the most extravagant ever commissioned. The main residence was as majestic in scale and finish as any in the Saudi realm. There was a string of lavish guest villas, four separate kitchens to rival the five-star restaurants of Paris, and brilliant blue helipads dotting the compound like so many focal points on a grand mosaic. The parking lot of the main residence had spaces for over a hundred cars, those behind the service buildings three times that.

It had all been completed only weeks earlier, just in time to fulfill what had been the king's wish from the outset: that his new palace would make its debut as the venue for this year's family gathering.

If the construction of the palace had been impossible to conceal, the royal assemblage now taking place had been held far closer to the House of Saud's vest. As secrets went, it had been reasonably well kept, yet no event of such grandeur could be shaped without hints of what was to come. No fewer than a thousand members of the Moroccan Royal Guards were on loan to secure the grounds. Twice that many drivers, cooks, housekeepers, and gardeners were in well-compensated attendance, although most with minimal forewarning.

As vital as they would all be for the coming week, in that moment there was one group of hirelings who were of outsized importance. They were a small contingent who in the last hour had scattered to various points around the palace grounds. One was lying prone on a helipad, while another had saddled into the umpire's chair of a tennis court across the street from the main residence. There were twelve in all, a tiny battalion of photographers and videographers making final checks of batteries and foregrounds and sun angles. The product of their efforts during the coming week would be packaged in commemorative albums to be distributed to attendees. There would be posed group photos along balustrades, and candid shots of every pool party. Yet for all the photo ops, none would be more spectacular than the opening scene.

At that moment, the king's 747 was making its final descent along the coast. In fifteen minutes, the world's most expensive airliner would perform a low altitude flyby in front of the world's grandest vacation home. Shutters would fly and lenses zoom as each photographer composed their best shot, hoping it might become the signature image of the week.

In those breathless, anticipatory minutes, none of the photographers could imagine how it would play out in the end: that the pictures they would so meticulously capture would never see the light of day.

SIXTY-EIGHT

The sun was rising, edging above the hills. Slaton pushed through foliage wet with dew as briny air swept up the cliffs. He'd been moving on a steady run since leaving the point, but as he came close to the villa he was forced to slow.

Maneuvering carefully, he tried for an angle that would give a comprehensive view of the place. He paused in a small stand of trees eighty yards distant, slightly below the level of the main house. Slaton spotted two men near the front door and easily pegged them as security—manner, physique, not to mention the weapons they displayed openly in shoulder holsters. They were standing under the large portico, engaged in an animated discussion. He wondered how many like them were inside. One of the men was thin and rangy, and wore dark sunglasses in the dim morning. The other looked more like a mob enforcer than professional security, all crude thickness and muscle.

Two cars were parked nearby. Both were sedans, one tan, the other white. The trunk of the tan car was open, and on the ground next to it was a case similar to the one he'd seen on the promontory. He also saw four standard rollerbags—three were lined neatly on the driveway next to the white car's rear quarter-panel, one by the tan. The implication was clear—departure was imminent.

The rangy man was doing most of the talking, and he pointed off in the distance. Slaton followed his gesture and saw something he hadn't before—a big truck parked at the top of a nearby hill. Then he did a double take. There was no mistaking the vehicle's stout frame, nor the array of antennas on top. It was the truck he'd taken a picture of last night at the airfield—or at least its twin. Last night the truck had seemed lifeless, but now one of its rooftop antennas was rotating, and light shone distinctly in the front window. Taken with the fact that it was situated on the highest terrain, he could draw but one conclusion—some kind of operation was in progress.

Slaton had silenced the burner phone in his pocket for obvious reasons, yet he'd checked it minutes earlier and seen a missed call. It wasn't from Christine's number, which left but one possibility—she'd gotten word to the CIA about how to reach him. He'd ignored the call, thinking he had more pressing matters. Now Slaton revisited that conclusion.

What the hell is going on here?

An impulse to check the phone again was interrupted by movement on the villa's sprawling seaside terrace. Two men came outside and paused by a table stocked with food and a coffeepot. One Slaton recognized instantly: the thickset form of Vladimir Ovechkin stood with a coffee mug in hand, gazing out at the northern sky. The other man Slaton had never seen. But of course he knew who it was. In his late twenties, he was wearing drab olive pants, and an untucked cotton button-down over an undershirt. He was of medium height, lean and fit, and moved with an economy Slaton recognized all too well. Standing on the veranda sipping coffee, he could not have appeared more casual. A visitor to a pleasant seaside retreat. Or an operator basking in the afterglow of a successful mission.

That these two men—a shady oligarch and a confirmed assassin—were sharing coffee on a patio held any number of implications. Slaton had already considered the possibility that the two might be in cahoots, but something about that scenario seemed simplistic— even more so considering the cold-blooded setup that had put Zhukov under Slaton's own sight. Whatever their interactions, it was beyond what Slaton could compute in that moment. These two men had tried to kill him. By extension, they were a threat to his family.

That was all he needed to know.

Slaton made one last update of the picture before him. The truck on the hill was unchanged. The two men under the portico had begun loading suitcases into the white car. He studied the terrace, and for the first time noticed the unmistakable profile of a Barrett fifty cal resting on a lounge chair in a shadow. The assassin was ten steps away from the gun. Twelve steps after he sided up to the crumpet table. Slaton watched him stab a toothpick into a cube of cheese.

He began to move.

The CIA was efficient. It was also lucky.

By virtue of Morocco's position as a gateway to sub-Saharan Africa, the NSA had years earlier established a standing hack into that country's air traffic control network. It was a weakness that was rarely leveraged, but occasionally useful in monitoring arms smuggling, state-sponsored meddling, and the odd warlord taking flight. The Saudi royal 747 was easily extracted from the banks of traffic, and could be seen at that moment descending through thirty thousand feet, marginally south of El Jadida along the coast. There was still no contact with the aircraft, despite repeated attempts, and as far as anyone knew the Saudis were not yet aware that a threat to the royal family was brewing. Director Coltrane sensed a specific manifestation of that peril, but he needed proof.

It was here that luck came into play.

The technician manning the ops center's "internal comm" station was by chance a retired Navy air traffic controller. "Are we filtering this air traffic data to exclude primary returns?" he asked.

"What are those?" Coltrane responded.

"Raw reflections of radar pulses. Right now what we're looking at involves participating aircraft— airplanes that use transponders to verify airspeed, altitude, and call signs. Primary data is no more than a blip on a screen. If a jet was trying to stay off the scope, that's all you would see. What we're looking at seems to be a managed feed, with the primary returns screened out."

Since discovering that a MiG had taken off from the RosAvia complex, all focus had been on finding it. There hadn't been time to debate the implications, but the prevailing assumption in the room was clear—that the MiG might be targeting the king's 747.

Coltrane gave the go-ahead to look for primary radar data. Fortunately, it didn't take long. The source data was reconfigured, and the main screen flickered. A new air traffic map presented only raw reflective returns. Of these there were but a handful. A very low and slow target paralleling the beaches off Casablanca was, according to the Navy man, most likely some kind of single-engine propeller plane towing a banner. Two blips to the east were also low and slow, most likely training aircraft flown by student pilots. Then a fourth primary target blinked into view—quite literally. It was situated southeast, and on an azimuth that could well have sourced it from Tazagurt's airfield. The reflection displayed only intermittently, a tiny white dot ghosting in and out of view. The former controller said, "That one's sporadic because he's flying low."

Erratic coverage aside, two more facts soon became evident. First, the aircraft was traveling at a very high rate of speed. The second revelation was even more disconcerting. When the sporadic new track was overlaid with that of the Saudi 747, the two aircraft were clearly—for lack of a better term—on a collision course.

For the next five minutes the ops center shifted its focus, and three salient points were nailed down. First, unsure if the MiG might be armed, analysts renewed their study of the photos from the Tazagurt hangar. They saw no evidence whatsoever of air-to-air missiles—no rails on the MiG's hardpoints, no loading equipment in the hangar. Second, with a satellite brought to bear on the coastline, it was discovered with some surprise that the antenna-laden truck that had yesterday been at the RosAvia complex was now parked on a hill near Ovechkin's villa. The final revelation came from a different tack, and was perhaps the least surprising of the three—they'd learned that Slaton had a burner phone in his possession, and its location had been triangulated. He was presently near the villa. And moving closer.

"Still no luck with the Saudis?" Coltrane asked impatiently.

"We're trying constantly," said the comm leader. "They're not responding."

"What about Slaton?"

"No contact there either."

"Keep trying!"

SIXTY-NINE

Moderation in war is akin to surrender. That being the case, Slaton's only decision was in what order to kill the men he was watching.

Based on what he'd seen, the disposition of cars and suitcases, Slaton thought it likely that there were no others inside. "Likely" being the operative word. He was facing four men. The most capable, he was sure, was in back, a highly trained operator who at that moment seemed distracted. The two in front could not be underestimated, and showed evidence of training. It occurred to him that there might be others on the distant hill, but he discounted that for the time being since it was roughly a mile away. Into his calculus Slaton added angles and terrain and known weapons. Vladimir Ovechkin, standing next to the blue-aqua pool with a coffee cup in hand, was the least of his worries.

Slaton closed the gap expertly, keeping to cover and shadows at every chance, and moving in absolute silence. His immediate objective was a massive boulder on the villa's northern shoulder. From there, he estimated, he would have a good view of all three primary threats at an acceptable range—assuming no one moved. He was ten steps from the boulder, and thirty from the villa, when his tactical plan collapsed.

As a trained sniper, Slaton was practiced at observing targets. Consequently, he had a knack for recognizing when they'd alerted to his presence. It was like seeing a deer going still when it caught a predator's scent, or a guard dog getting its hackles up. He saw it then in the rangy security man. A subtle rigidity that fired into his limbs. An abrupt straightening of the spine.

Caught in the open, Slaton went to a crouch. He watched the guard pull his phone from his pocket and check it hurriedly. Then, damningly, he half turned and looked directly to the spot where Slaton had taken a knee.

Slaton held his breathing instinctively, knowing he'd missed something. A motion sensor in a tree. A pressure pad beneath the forest floor. He had rushed in, overconfident, and resultingly lost his greatest ally—the element of surprise. That would have allowed him the two kills before any resistance could organize. There was no getting it back now, which meant speed and accuracy were his new best friends.

He rose to height and settled the UMP on the rangy guard. Caught in the open, the man reached for his holstered gun. He got a hand to it, and managed to bark out a warning before Slaton's first round struck home. The second bullet caught him falling. Slaton shifted to the thickset guard, who was trying to dash behind the car with his weapon in hand. Slaton's first shot caught him obliquely, and he spun against a fender. The next caught him right between the collarbones, and he dropped once and for all.

Slaton didn't stand still long enough to even glance at the patio. He lunged toward the boulder, and in the next instant small-caliber fire began shredding the brush around him. The boulder was stout cover, but instead of stopping—the most natural move—he ran straight past it. After a brief hesitation, the operator on the terrace opened up again. In the longest two seconds of his life—the time it took Slaton to get out of sight behind the side of the house—three rounds came singing in. One found its mark, but thankfully on the back of his vest, jerking him off balance as he threw himself behind the wall.

With a moment to breathe, Slaton double-checked the two guards—both looked quite dead. He had shifted the odds in his favor, but the most dangerous adversary remained, along with the wild card that was Ovechkin. He reached behind with his good right arm and felt the tear in his vest where the round had hit. When he brought his hand back in front he was happy to see no blood—adrenaline had a way of masking injuries.

The man on the terrace had fired either nine or ten rounds—an uncertainty Slaton saw as a bit of rust creeping in from his year on the high seas. Either way, the man would be palming in a fresh mag. Slaton still had eighteen in the UMP, and a spare mag in his pocket. As things stood, he had superior firepower. The Barrett was impractical for a close-in fight— like trying to use a howitzer in a closet. He weighed whether the soldier might have anything else, and decided it was unlikely. He'd brought the Barrett with a specific purpose, and the semiautomatic handgun was his insurance. He would never expect to need anything more. What about Ovechkin? Would he be armed? Slaton thought it unlikely, but couldn't discount the idea.

He realized that the man on the patio held one

distinct advantage—he knew the layout inside the house. Slaton ventured a glance ahead, to the south-east corner of the villa. He saw no motion, heard no movement inside. On the far side of the front facade he saw a pine tree close to the house. Its branches laddered upward perfectly. *The shooter might know the inside,* he thought, *but I know the roof as well as he does. When in doubt, claim the high ground.*

Keeping below the front windows, he ran in a crouch toward the tree. He tested the lowest branch, and it held his weight easily. More importantly, it did so without a sound. Looking upward, he was sure he could reach the rooftop.

Slaton began to climb.

He planned each step carefully, avoiding one dead limb. When he reached eye level to the roofline, he paused to study things. The roof was complex and angular, ruddy barrel tiles joined at multiple peaks. He heard a noise from the house, like a chair being pushed across a tile floor. At least one of them was inside.

Slaton silently crawled onto the roof. The clay tiles were warm under his hands, the rising sun taking hold of the day. Keeping to his belly, he shifted the UMP behind him once more, not wanting it to clatter against the tiles. He bypassed a secondary peak for the main crest which, if he remembered correctly, would overlook the back terrace. As long as he remained silent, it would be a commanding position.

He neared the peak soundlessly, inching toward the row of semicircular cap tiles that joined the two sloping sections. Slaton edged up and peered over the ridge cautiously. What he saw was a surprise.

Not two feet away, a set of bright blue eyes stared back.

SEVENTY

There was no time to think. Only to react.

With the UMP behind his back, and seeing a hand-gun in the Russian's right hand, Slaton launched himself over the crown of the roof. His own weapon out of reach behind him, Slaton's only play was to lock up his adversary's arm. They grappled across the hard tile, struggling for control of the weapon. A wild shot rang out, the gun's barrel canted skyward in their combined grip. Slaton felt the man's finger on the trigger. He locked the finger down and twisted the gun viciously, heard the crack of bone and a grunt of pain.

Slaton had the advantage of size, and was confident he would win a close-in fight. The Russian sensed it too, because as Slaton tightened his arm bar, the man made the best possible move—he rolled and pushed with his legs, sending them both tumbling down the pitched roof. They fell intertwined, and the handgun caromed free. It clattered across the tile, and Slaton saw it slide toward the edge and disappear to the patio below.

He tried to arrest their entangled drop. The Russian did his best to promote it. Slaton knew what he was thinking. *The bigger they are, the harder they fall.*

Slaton dug his heels into tile grooves, but each time he gained purchase, the Russian countered with a push of his own. With gravity on his adversary's side, they both tumbled one last turn before careening over the roof's edge. In midair the two men let go of one another, survival instinct kicking in. In the next split second Slaton saw the second-floor balcony rail coming. It struck him square in the chest, but his vest spread the impact.

His body bounded out into space again, and he reached out with his right hand for the rail, trying to arrest his fall. As he did, the UMP's sling caught on something, twisting his body awkwardly. He grabbed the rail for an instant, braking his descent, but the force was overwhelming and his hand twisted free. It was a ten-foot drop to the stone terrace, and Slaton landed as best he could, legs bent and rolling onto a hip. New pains seared in, but he ignored every one and bounded to his feet.

The Russian had landed a few steps away, yet he too knew how to survive a fall. He was up before Slaton, his eyes sweeping the fine Italian tile, searching for his weapon.

Slaton did the same—somewhere in the fall he'd lost the UMP.

They spotted the handgun at the same time, a dull black L on the bottom of the kidney-shaped pool. It was much nearer the Russian. Slaton searched for the UMP. He didn't see it, but noticed his burner phone on the tile ten paces away. Then a sway of motion overhead caught his eye—the UMP was hanging by its sling from a wall-mounted light fixture. The gun was ten feet above him, and he guessed he could jump high enough to slap at it. He might knock it down on the first try. More likely, the second or the third.

He didn't have that much time.

The Russian dove into the pool head-first, his hands clawing for the bottom. He retrieved his gun six feet under, and started back up. Slaton was trapped in the open on the broad patio. There was no cover he could reach soon enough to dodge an expert marksman. And that's what this man would be. He saw one chance: on the nearby lounge chair the Barrett lay as if sunning itself.

Slaton leapt for the big gun and grabbed it by the barrel.

In retrospect, he would later realize that this was where the Russian faltered. Perhaps he wasn't experienced in the water. Not comfortable with shooting through refraction, or concerned about the ballistic degradation imparted by a few inches of over-chlorinated water. If he had only paused where he was and raised the gun toward the surface, fired at a stationary target a few feet above him, he would have won the battle. Won their whole private war. Instead, he tried to come up for air before taking his shot.

Slaton intervened decisively.

With both hands on the rifle's barrel, he ignored the pain in his shoulder and raised it over his head. In that same instant the Russian's head broke the surface. Slaton swung down like a lumberjack trying to part a log in a single blow.

He missed the man's head as it came out of the water, but no such precision was necessary. The gun weighed twenty-eight pounds, and was traveling on a moment arm of nearly five feet. The steel stock crashed into the Russian's neck with all the certainty of a sledgehammer, crushing bone and tearing sinew. The man crumpled instantly, stunned to stillness. Slaton's second blow was far more exacting, and probably fatal. The Barrett's stock caught him flush on the crown of his head.

The Russian went still in the water, facedown in a fast-diffusing cloud of red. Never one for half-measures, Slaton leapt into the pool and held the man's head under until he was sure. Absolutely sure. There was one flutter of movement, likely no more than an involuntary spasm. Then nothing at all. Slaton retrieved the handgun before scrambling out of the pool. With the gun poised, he scanned the villa for any sign of Ovechkin. He saw nothing.

Dripping wet, Slaton pocketed the gun, which he recognized as a Sig Sauer P320, and recovered his phone. He jumped up, knocked the UMP off the light fixture—it took two tries—and rushed into the villa. He was barely through the seaside French doors when a car engine fired to life out front. He heard the engine rev and the squeal of tires. Slaton burst through the front door with the UMP poised, but saw what he expected—a flicker of white disappearing up the driveway.

Ovechkin was gone.

The tan sedan remained, and Slaton checked the ignition. No keys. He took a deep breath, ratcheting down. He lowered the UMP, reconnecting the damaged sling and putting it across a shoulder.

As the adrenaline ebbed, he regarded the two vanquished guards. Then his eyes drifted to the equipment case near the car's trunk. It wasn't an exact twin to the one he'd seen on the promontory, but seemed similar in size and shape. He walked over, unlatched the lid, and after a brief pause threw it open.

There, cradled in solid foam, was the rest of the system. A thick optical lens that was connected by an umbilical to a processor of some kind. Two heavy batteries and a tripod stand, the rectangular feet of which matched the impressions he'd seen beneath a rock ledge on a Davos mountainside. And to one side, an ordinary ammo box. Slaton picked up the ammo box and opened it. What he saw inside was anything but ordinary. There were three shaped-foam cutouts, and one of the spaces was empty. The other two contained plastic cases the size and shape of a fifty-cal round. He opened one and saw a pristine example of the mangled projectile he'd recovered in Davos.

Slaton repackaged everything, then stood wondering what came next. He glanced up at the truck on the distant hill. It hadn't moved. He then considered whether the CIA might be able to track, or even intercept Ovechkin. He decided it was worth a try.

Slaton checked his phone.

He saw eighteen missed calls.

SEVENTY-ONE

Boris Tikhonov had spent most of his adult life indoors, yet as a child he'd summered often at his family's modest dacha deep in the game-rich Urals. That being the case, he knew gunfire when he heard it.

The shooting had begun a few minutes ago, a rapid-fire exchange of different-caliber weapons. Then it ended as abruptly as it had begun. The reports of the shots arrived muted inside the heavily insulated truck, but he suspected it was sourced from the villa Zhukov had pointed out earlier. Tikhonov drummed the fingers of one hand nervously. The colonel should have been back by now—he'd gone off over an hour ago, promising to return in time to view the intercept. The combination of those circumstances—unexpected gunfire and Zhukov's disappearance—did not bode well. It was even more disturbing in light of what was about to take place.

Tikhonov got up from his workstation and went to the driver's cab. Through the front windscreen he could just make out the villa's red tile roof, yet there was no sign of activity. He hurried back to his workstation, stopping on the way at a small equipment cabinet. There he removed a 9mm semiautomatic.

Tikhonov thought it a reasonable precaution given how unpredictable things had become. Zhukov. Ros-Avia. Great sums of money transferred. A mysterious Russian who'd shown up in Tazagurt last night on a private jet. The engineer had no hope of understanding it all. No more than he understood the reasons behind the crime he was about to commit. The atrocity he'd been coerced into performing.

Back in his seat, he set the gun on the console and concentrated once more on the MiG. The jet was forty miles east, and closing rapidly. Tikhonov had been told to fly a high-speed, low-altitude profile, which implied an intent to avoid radar coverage. He could only manage that to a point—if he went too low he might interrupt the integrity of his own signal and lose control of the drone.

He referenced the target on his monitor. The 747 would arrive in just over ten minutes—well within the window Zhukov had been promised. Whatever the colonel's source of information, it was proving accurate. He wondered who exactly was on the big jet. Zhukov had never entrusted him with that information. Tikhonov tried to tell himself it didn't matter, and as he did a surge of acid spewed in his belly.

He looked worriedly at the door behind him. *Where the devil did the colonel go?*

He checked the MiG. Thirty-eight miles.

Tikhonov again referenced the 747.

Performing a bit of mental math, he nudged the throttle forward ever so slightly.

When Slaton finally returned the CIA's call he got no greeting whatsoever—only Director Coltrane's voice bellowing across the Atlantic. "No time to explain!

We have a crisis and need you to intervene immediately!"

"*Intervene?*" Slaton repeated, feeling as though that was what he'd been doing since well before dawn. "Intervene in what?"

"One of the MiGs you saw last night is airborne and approaching your position. So is a Boeing 747 carrying the entire Saudi royal family. We think the MiG is going to take down the bigger jet."

"You mean *shoot* it down?"

"No. The MiG is configured as a drone—we believe whoever is operating it intends to crash it into the bigger jet. You're the only one in a position to stop it."

Sniper that he was, Slaton naturally thought of the Barrett. Newly bloodied, it was laying on the stone terrace. "If you think I can shoot down a jet fighter, you have a bit too much faith in my marksmanship. How could I—" His thoughts locked up midsentence. He looked at the nearby hill. "The truck," he said.

"We've been watching it and think it's our only chance! We're almost certain the MiG is being controlled through that vehicle. You need to move— these airplanes are getting *very* close!"

Without hesitation, Slaton did exactly that.

The tan sedan would have helped, but there was no time to search for the keys. He struck out on a sprint up the long paved driveway. "How much time do I have?" he asked, trying to hold the phone steady.

A pause, then, "Six and a half minutes."

The top of the hill was a mile away, a steep climb all the way. "What's the quickest way up?" he asked.

"There's a service road along the north side of the hill. It's slightly longer than a straight climb, but it'll be faster than fighting the terrain."

Slaton saw a section of the road on the hill above him. He cut across rock and scrub to reach it and began driving upward, his lungs straining for air.

"Four minutes," he heard Coltrane shout over the line.

At a bend in the road Slaton got a clear view up the coast. There was no mistaking what he saw—in the distance, a Boeing 747, identifiable by its distinctive upper deck. The jet was flying low and slow, as if making an approach to a runway. But there were no runways here.

Slaton pocketed the phone and sprinted flat out. He was gasping with every stride when he reached the top of the hill. His injured shoulder throbbed in pain. The truck was fifty yards in front of him, and he saw a door midway along one side. An integral set of exterior steps had been lowered like an invitation. There was no time for reconnaissance, no time to study alternate ingress points.

How many people are inside? he wondered. *Two? Ten?*

He paused long enough to palm a fresh mag into his weapon, hoping the UMP hadn't been damaged in the fall from the roof. The 747 was almost abeam the villa, the scripted words *Saudi Arabia* clear on its tan-and-white fuselage. A sudden roar from behind caused Slaton to spin around. He saw the MiG hurtling in like a thrown dagger.

Heading straight for the Saudi royal family.

With the UMP ready, he curled his finger over the trigger and ran toward the truck. He flew up the steps and battered his good shoulder into the door. It slammed back with almost no resistance. Slaton crouched with the UMP ready. The interior was dark, but he sensed movement to his right. He rotated his weapon and saw a huge man turning in a chair with what looked like a handgun. Slaton sent two rounds into his head from ten feet away. The massive man collapsed in his chair, then tumbled to the floor with a grunt.

Slaton spun left and cleared the rest of the place.

He saw no one else.

The MiG thundered overhead, the pitch of its engine altering as it passed.

Slaton rushed to the workstation, ignoring the dead man on the floor. He saw a control panel that reminded him of an airliner's cockpit. There were instruments and lights. Countless buttons and two joysticks. A monitor showed a view that could only be sourced from the MiG—the 747 centered in crosshairs.

For an instant Slaton was heartened to see that every switch was labeled. In the next he was stymied—the labels were all in Cyrillic. He considered using the UMP to annihilate the entire panel. Instead he began reaching for one of the joysticks, not sure how it worked or what effect it might have on the jet. Before he could touch it, a lone red-guarded switch caught his eye. It was labeled in Cyrillic like the rest—but with one of the few Russian words he'd ever had the occasion to learn.

Взрывчатка.

Explosives.

Slaton flicked up the guard and slapped the switch.

In the front window an instantaneous flash of light overwhelmed the rising morning. It was followed by the sound of a tremendous explosion.

SEVENTY-TWO

Slaton had no idea what had happened. The team watching from Langley could do nothing but sit helpless as, fifty miles above Morocco, a state-of-the-art infrared satellite lens blinked like a human eye trying to stare at the sun.

They would all learn the specifics in days to come. In cruel irony, the attempt on the king's life was captured in high resolution, and from a dozen different angles, by the photographers he himself had commissioned. Yet in that moment, as the cataclysm played out over Slaton's head, everyone feared the worst.

The 747 was directly above the cape to the south, just coming into view for the flock of waiting photographers, when the MiG reached its closest proximity. It would later be determined that the drone was 143 meters away, and on a perfect collision course with the widebody's central fuselage, when it exploded in midair—at the detonation of the self-destruct charge Tikhonov had installed as a precaution. From the Saudi point of view, it would have been far more useful had the self-immolation occurred ten seconds earlier. As it turned out, the MiG was traveling at such a high rate of speed that in spite of its obliteration as a functioning machine, a large number of fragments carried on to reach the Boeing.

Fortunately, the king's pilots were the king's pilots for a reason. Drawn from the most elite ranks of the Saudi Arabian Air Force, the two senior officers were among the most steady and highly trained aviators on earth. So it was that, when remnants of the MiG's third stage turbine punctured a wing spoiler actuator on the 747, the resulting loss of hydraulic pressure in system number two brought barely an intake of breath on the flight deck. No fewer than twelve pieces of the MiG penetrated the plane's hull at various points, but because the big jet was at very low altitude, the loss of cabin pressure was a complete nonevent. The most pressing concern arrived in the form of a slab of the MiG's vertical tail which sailed straight into the outboard port engine. The engine immediately caught fire and began disintegrating, throwing off shrapnel of its own that damaged an adjacent fuel line running to the inboard port engine.

It was at this point that the king, who'd remained on the flight deck for his sightseeing excursion, heard a most unprofessional word from the seat in front of him.

The pilots became a blur of motion, working levers and silencing warning bells. Checklists were run while the captain fought the controls to keep the jet airborne. In short order the crew secured the number one engine, little of which remained on the wing, and were able to coax the number two engine to keep running, albeit at a reduced power setting. With a bit of rudder thrown in to keep the behemoth flying in nearly a straight line, the hulking jet passed beachside of the king's new palace within seconds of the prescribed moment. Less according to plan was the picture it presented: the Boeing limped through the air in a decidedly uncoordinated dance, black smoke trailing one of its engines and fuel vapor streaming from another.

And that was exactly what Slaton saw when he stepped outside the control vehicle. From the highest hill on the coast, he watched the massive jet claw for altitude and begin a very gentle turn seaward. It rolled out on a northerly heading, certainly making for the nearest emergency airfield. When Slaton lost sight minutes later, the jet was marginally higher and still trailing smoke like a barnstormer at an airshow.

Slaton started back toward the villa, a host of new aches and pains governing his pace. After trotting downhill, he reestablished contact with Langley and explained what had happened.

When he finished, Coltrane said, "I'd like you to wait there at the scene."

"Why?"

"We've dispatched a team from our embassy in Rabat. With any luck they'll arrive before the Sûreté Nationale. We'd like to go over the place before the police get involved."

Slaton didn't respond for a time. "Did the royal family land safely?" he asked.

"A few minutes ago—a military airfield near Casablanca. You just saved the House of Saud from annihilation. I think the king will be surprised to find out that it was a former Mossad man who—"

"Actually," Slaton interrupted, "I'd like to keep my name out of this mess. *Completely* out."

"All right . . . I think I understand. We owe you that much."

"No—you owe me a *lot* more. And I'm going to start collecting right now."

Slaton explained what he wanted.

Before Coltrane could respond, the line went dead.

In fact, the CIA squad from Rabat beat the police to the scene by thirty minutes. They discovered three bodies at the villa, along with one in the truck on the nearby hill, and began taking pictures immediately. What they didn't find was one weary and severely bruised *kidon*. Slaton was gone, as was the tan sedan.

In fact, the operations center at Langley, still referencing their satellite feed, had noted his departure. When the duty officer inquired whether they should track the car, the director's answer had been unequivocal.

"No, let him go."

In time, detailed reconnaissance images of the villa would be compared to onsite photographs taken by the embassy team. After painstaking analysis it would be determined that, aside from Slaton and Ovechkin, two items had gone missing from the villa. One was a large rectangular shipping case. The other was a fifty-caliber Barrett sniper rifle.

SEVENTY-THREE

The back-slapping at Langley was still under way when a junior technician, who'd begun coordinating with Moroccan first responders, stumbled upon reports of a second calamity: the RosAvia complex in Tazagurt was falling victim to a raging fire. By the time Ouarzazate's distant fire brigade reached the facility, there was little left to salvage. More disturbing news soon followed: a number of bodies had been found amid the charred wreckage.

The improbable timing of the tragedy escaped no one at Langley, and their bleak outlook was confirmed when evidence of accelerants was found. Another body was discovered near the runway, on the roof of a curiously equipped van—a victim whose demise had nothing to do with fire and everything to do with two 9mm hollow-point bullets.

All too late, Director Coltrane ordered yet another retuning of the agency's priorities. In the frenzy to prevent the destruction of the House of Saud, all regional surveillance assets had been directed toward the Atlantic coast. The NRO quickly retrained its nearest bird eastward, and analysts scoured RosAvia's tarmac for the small business jet that had arrived twelve hours ago carrying a single Russian.

The jet was nowhere to be seen.

In the following days, Moroccan authorities issued a stream of disturbing press releases.

In his grave initial account, the minister of foreign affairs announced that an attempt had been made on the life of the king of Saudi Arabia. By grace of God, the plot targeting the monarch's jet along the southern Moroccan coast had been foiled. Great credit was given, and rightly so, to the king's pilots, who had skillfully brought the damaged plane to safety. The specific nature of the attack was characterized vaguely as a "drone incident," and requests from the press for amplification on the point were shot down for reasons of national security, no mention made as to whose secrets were in jeopardy.

The minister also linked the tragedy at Tazagurt to the attack. He noted that the facility, run under license by the Russian corporation RosAvia, had been integral to the plot. Yet the extent of that involvement would be difficult to measure: all thirteen employees had been killed execution style, and the hangar and outbuildings had burned to the ground. Little remained of the few aircraft inside. The minister also mentioned, perhaps through clenched teeth and with a degree of pith, that RosAvia representatives were responding dutifully to investigators' questions from their distant Moscow headquarters. At the end, he left no doubt that the inquiry would be a long and arduous one. Subsequent updates did nothing to dispel that notion.

Curiously, the most headline-worthy release of information came not from the Moroccans, but rather the Russian ambassador in Rabat. In a freewheeling news conference on the second day after the event, he spilled word of what had been discovered in the wreckage of RosAvia's hangar. Surviving the inferno were countless ISIS pamphlets, prayer rugs, and two laptop computers containing a virtual library of radical Islamic literature. Perhaps coincidentally—or perhaps not—within minutes of the Russian ambassador leaving his podium, a number of crude videos began circulating on the internet in which ISIS claimed credit for the attack.

With the bit between their teeth, reporters besieged Morocco's Sûreté Nationale, who reluctantly confirmed the ambassador's assertions. The police had hoped to deflect mention of ISIS involvement, not wanting to fan fundamentalist flames in their strongly Muslim nation. The dashing of the Sûreté's hopes was made complete the next day when headlines across the world labeled the attack as the latest radical jihadist assault.

An ocean away, the CIA followed every dispatch. The consensus opinion there was nearly universal, and distilled to two points: As attempts at false flag attribution went, it was perhaps the clumsiest job anyone had ever seen. And by all appearances, it seemed to be working.

EPILOGUE

TWO WEEKS LATER

Corruption is not born spontaneously. It festers in fine hotel rooms, hatches in five-star restaurants, and is birthed on yachts in faraway anchorages. It takes root in the dusty file cabinets of small-island law firms, and smiles in the reflection of washbasin mirrors in government ministry bathrooms. At that moment, it was coming together nicely on the paths of a palace garden along the shores of the Black Sea.

It was the richest of absurdities that if any palace in the world could rival those of the Saudi kingdom, it was one built for the man who had plotted to murder its sovereign. At a cost of a billion dollars—skimmed from state accounts intended for health care and infrastructure—the "Southern Project" held distinct differences from its Arab competition. There was a chapel in one wing, a casino in another. Multiple theaters showed first-run Hollywood movies, and ballrooms and swimming pools were so plentiful as to require numbers to distinguish between them. The palace by the sea was compulsive in scale, thieving in style, and, not by chance, reminiscent of the houses built for Russian Czars in the eighteenth century.

Situated high on a densely wooded plateau at the head of the Caucasus Mountains, the estate kept an authoritative watch over the eastern shores of the Black Sea. In whose name it did so was an ill-kept mystery. The property's provenance had proved maddeningly untraceable, this despite research campaigns by a dozen Western media outlets. For every official record reporters unearthed, two more seemed to appear. As shell games went, it was more transparent than most—the opulent manor north of Sochi had but one lord. And while he visited rarely, his sojourns were generally designed with one thing in mind: discretion.

As was the case today.

President Petrov roamed the eastern gardens with two men in tow. He looked out across the sea until a frigid breeze swept in and turned his gaze shoreward. Isolation aside, he'd hoped the southern palace would prove warmer than Moscow. As it turned out, any difference was marginal.

Vladimir Ovechkin, who was on his right, pursed his lips thoughtfully, and said, "I read this morning that oil prices have begun falling again."

"Unfortunately, yes."

"At least there was a brief spike. It took the Saudis a week to put down the insurgents we armed. And the rumors of an assassination plot against the entire House of Saud—it *did* rattle the markets. We were on the right track."

The president frowned. "I'm not so sure. The revolt was put down decisively, and now the Saudis will double down on security for the royal family."

"Perhaps. We can at least be happy the CIA hasn't gone public with what they know about our . . . involvement."

"Let them try," Petrov said dismissively. "There is

no real evidence. Nothing we can't deflect and obscure. If we have gained one upper hand in recent years, it is our ability to manipulate information. Our cyber teams are unmatched."

They reached a broad set of steps rising to a stone terrace that spanned over an acre. The president began climbing and Ovechkin followed suit. Three steps behind them the third man kept pace, a pit bull to Ovechkin's corpulent poodle. His name—as he had truthfully told the crew of a ship named *Argos*, and workers in a hangar in Morocco—was Ivan.

Ovechkin said, "We made the right choice in silencing Ivanovic and Romanov. They would not have been reliable under such pressure. But it's too bad about your young gun."

"The sergeant?" the president replied.

"Yes. Who was he?"

They reached the top of the stairs, and Petrov began walking toward the overlook of the southern glade. "A soldier—a very competent one, or so I was told. I believe his name was Nikolai."

"Nikolai. Another in the long line of men giving the ultimate sacrifice for the Rodina."

Petrov looked at Ovechkin and saw the sly grin. "Yes," said the president, "the Rodina. I'll make sure he gets a star on a wall somewhere. Perhaps a statue in a square."

"That's more than I'll ever get," said Ovechkin reflectively. "Not that I care. I'm happy to take my accolades in this life."

"You always do—in whatever denomination you can get."

Ovechkin's grin became forced, and he turned pensive. "What about Slaton? Apparently he is alive after all, and better than anyone thought. The fallout from our operation seems mostly contained, but he could be a problem."

Petrov's gaze hardened. "By all accounts, he was instrumental in our failure—he put a hatchet to three years of work. Last week I gave the SVR orders to hunt him down."

"Have they made any progress?"

"A few leads," the president said, "but he's proving elusive. We think he may be aware of our effort to eliminate him."

"How could that be?"

"He apparently keeps loose ties with the CIA, and perhaps Mossad. He's getting information from somewhere. But we'll find him. As long as I keep a target on his back, it is only a matter of time."

The two men stood along the high balustrade, looking out across the sea.

Ivan came closer and stood next to Ovechkin. He said, "If you locate Slaton, I would like to do the honors."

Petrov eyed him, then Ovechkin. "You have both proved yourselves in recent months. Our little effort went astray, yet I think that going forward we should—"

The president's words were interrupted by what seemed like a rush of air, and in the next instant came an explosion. An explosion of flesh and blood and fabric. Ovechkin dropped to the terrace like a stone. Ivan seemed to pirouette, then fell in a heap next to him.

A stunned Petrov reeled back a step. He looked at Ivan and saw a massive wound from rib to rib—he'd nearly been cut in half. Centered in Ovechkin's chest was a glistening crimson hole. The terrace all around was covered in blood and tissue. The president looked down to see his own fine suit misted in red.

Petrov stood inanimate, disbelieving.

The next thing he knew, he was tackled to the cold stone by his personal security detail.

As the shaken Russian president was locked down in the palace's inner sanctums, a spirited response was launched. For three hours Russian security forces searched the surrounding forest. Roadblocks were established for containment, nearby airports locked down. Service was suspended at the nearby Sochi train station as police and counter-terrorism forces beat down doors and scoured the countryside. A two-mile search radius around the palace was increased to three, and by seven that evening, with the president taking a cautious dinner under light sedation, there was still nothing to report. The best counter-terrorism forces in Russia could find no trace of the assassin who had shot two men dead with a single heavy-caliber bullet—a bullet that had passed within inches of the presidential lapel.

It went that way until just after sunrise the next morning. That was when Petrov himself ordered the search perimeter expanded. The shooter's hide was discovered soon after, and with surprisingly little trouble—the assassin had not bothered to conceal his temporary residence. There were energy bar wrappers and water bottles, fresh footprints on the wet earth. An expertly built blind made from vegetation had actually been set aside, in the way one might pull back the curtain on a stage.

By the account of one security man, who'd had some training as a sniper, it was as if the assailant was

460 | WARD LARSEN

making an effort to advertise his presence. Yet the same man gave pause in his assessment for one very simple reason: if this was indeed where the shooter had holed up, it would indicate a shot of six thousand yards. Nearly three and a half miles. Without question—and even against recent rumors from Capri and Davos—the longest sniper shot ever recorded.

Aside from the detritus of occupation, the hide provided one striking bit of evidence: a standard ammo box. Not sure what to make of it, and wanting to provide some sign of progress, the head of Kremlin security, a neckless man named Vasiliev, brought it straight to the president. Wearing gloves to ensure the evidence wasn't contaminated, he set it on a Louis Quinze desk in the president's private study for Petrov's inspection.

"It's an ammo box," Vasiliev said.

Petrov stared at the man with some irritation. He'd long cultivated his image as an outdoorsman, and he hunted regularly. He knew an ammo box when he saw one.

Vasiliev explained about the hide. "It's almost as if he's daring us to find him," he said at the end.

The president gestured toward the box with an upward flick of his finger. Vasiliev raised the lid. Petrov stared at what was inside for a very long time. He then ordered Vasiliev to stay put, and deferred to the far side of the room where he made a phone call that lasted five minutes. When it ended, Petrov returned to his desk and stood hovering over the box.

"This is precisely as you found it?" he asked.

"Yes," said Vasiliev.

"And you are certain that only one bullet was fired yesterday?"

"I can tell you a single spent casing was recovered

from the shooter's hide. We have also confirmed that both victims were struck by a single round. We analyzed their injuries, and know precisely where each man was standing in relation to the shooter's position. We actually have video from cameras on the terrace. There was no more than a ten-second window in which the two were standing perfectly in line. For one shot to strike them both—it was a terrible bit of bad luck. The bullet was found embedded in stone at the foot of the main residence. It is in poor condition, yet seems to be of a very curious design. Our forensic people are going to—"

"No!" Petrov barked. "I want the bullet brought to me!"

Vasiliev was dumbfounded, but knew better than to argue. "Very well."

Petrov stared at the box like it was a grenade with a pulled pin. After a period of silence, Vasiliev screwed up enough courage to ask, "Sir . . . it is my sworn duty to protect you. I will do as you ask, but if there is something I should know, something that has bearing on my duties . . ."

The president lifted his stony gaze from the box and settled it on the man whose job was to keep him alive. Petrov's rise to power was based largely on ruthlessness, yet as with most long-tenured tyrants, he recognized the occasional need for pragmatism.

"What I am about to tell you will never leave this room."

Vasiliev nodded cautiously.

"The phone call I just made was to a certain team of engineers. Some years ago they undertook a very special armaments project . . ." He told his security chief about the development of a steerable bullet and its capabilities. At the end he pointed to the ammo box. "A few weeks ago, three of these bullets existed. One, I've been told, was used in Morocco. It was employed by one of our best marksmen against a target who somehow survived. That man, as it turns out, is himself an accomplished sniper. He managed to overpower our man, and take possession of the remaining two rounds along with the weapon system. Yesterday he employed one of these bullets. You have seen the results."

Now it was Vasiliev who stood staring at the ammo box. There were three foam slots. In two of them were empty plastic cases shaped like large-caliber cartridges. The third slot was quite empty.

"You see the problem," Petrov said. "One bullet remains."

The head of Kremlin security, who had never conceived of bullets that could reach out miles, was quick to envision how such a technology could complicate his job. "The area we will have to clear everywhere you go—it has just more than tripled. Any public appearance will become a monumental undertaking. I dare say, there are certain venues that could never be made safe."

"Actually," the president said, confidence returning to his voice for the first time in nearly a day, "I think it may not be so difficult."

"We have to find this man, eliminate him," Vasiliev said.

"The SVR has been trying to track him down for weeks. They've gotten nowhere." Petrov actually smiled, at last seeing the theatrical double murder for precisely what it was.

A message.

"No," the president said, more to himself than Vasiliev. "I think we need to do quite the opposite."

* * *

President Petrov spent the next hour on the phone issuing orders. All were carried out to the letter.

In a soulless industrial park west of Moscow, a small and mysterious research project was ordered shuttered that day. All equipment was to be packed up and shipped away, and by the next morning every member of the support staff was lined up for exit briefings at two separate doors in the fast-emptying building. Behind the first door a pair of beefy FSB agents, straight from central casting, impressed upon everyone the continued level of secrecy expected regarding their work. One by one, the employees advanced with some trepidation toward the second door where a far more positive message was delivered. Two options were presented by an attractive young woman whose government affiliation was left unmentioned: each worker was offered either an early and remarkably generous pension, or a plum assignment in an unrelated engineering project. Among the support staff, none left the second room without a smile.

In an ode to compartmentalization, the only two people in the building with full knowledge of the project were the lead engineers. The man and woman took the news with predictable despondency: the research they'd committed four years of their lives to was having its plug pulled. Both had long tenures in the defense establishment, and so they'd seen such shutdowns before. Usually it involved a lack of progress or dismal test results. The two were convinced that their steerable bullet had shown great promise, yet any hope of resurrecting their work was shot down in a private briefing with the head of the FSB team. The choices they were presented, by a bespectacled pock-faced man, were considerably more narrow than those offered their underlings. Each of the engineers would be given a comfortable severance in exchange for never working again. More pointedly, they were warned against ever discussing any aspect of their recent work. The only alternative to this arrangement, alluded to obliquely and with a dead gaze, centered around something called Camp Number Six in Central Siberia. The man and woman signed agreements and left the room in silence.

Closer to the center of Moscow, the director of the SVR was taken by surprise when he was ordered by the president to shutter his agency's search for an elusive former Mossad assassin. Yet he was not unhappy. In the two weeks since the president had initiated the manhunt, there had been a notable dearth of leads. A paid informant in Lebanon swore the man could be found at a resort in Beirut. No trace of their target was ever seen, and not surprisingly, the informant himself fell untraceable when sought for a follow-up interview. There was a nibble in Madrid, but two SVR agents there were left backpedaling from the apartment of a retired Mossad officer who bore no resemblance whatsoever to their suspect, and who owned at least one large-caliber handgun.

The most promising tip, as it turned out, had come from an informant tied to the U.S. embassy in Rome. A plumber who performed occasional work there, and who much to the SVR's delight fancied himself a secret agent, claimed to have overheard rumblings that an "Israeli contractor" had taken up residence in the embassy with his family. The SVR set up watch outside the mission, and for three days saw nothing notable. They were in the process of pulling their surveillance when, less than twenty-four hours ago, the plumber had followed up with one more snippet: the Israeli in question was further rumored to have departed the embassy for a sailboat docked in Amalfi.

Weary of so many false leads, the SVR dispatched but a single man to the southern coast, although it wasn't quite the token effort it appeared. As far as anyone knew, the man they sent was the only person still living who had seen Slaton—just over two weeks ago in a derelict apartment amid the darkest dens of Marrakesh.

The tall and gaunt man, who when it suited him called himself Smith, cut no less somber a figure in Amalfi than he had on Rue Essebtiyne. He arrived on a sunny Saturday morning to a sparkling sea and the bluest of skies.

As an experienced field officer, he was well versed in all manner of surveillance. Resultingly, as he spent hours scouring the municipal docks, he did so with no small degree of discomfort. Because of his appearance—his unusual height and gait, and strikingly angular features—he was generally considered unsuitable for "street work." It was his strong language skills—honed by repeated postings to America—that had caused him to specialize in a far different role. He was, as he himself claimed in the parlance of Hollywood, something of a character actor. Someone who could play a bit part with the utmost of conviction.

The posting to Amalfi had not really surprised him. He was, after all, the only SVR officer who'd ever encountered Slaton. That meeting had taken place under mostly agreeable circumstances, yet there was something about the Israeli that unnerved him. Left to his druthers, he'd be happy to never see the man again. Unfortunately, orders *were* orders. So, in keeping with his calling, he presented himself that morning as best he could: as an American in search of a friend's boat.

"He told me the marina and slip number, but I've lost it, and he's not answering his phone. A bit over six feet tall, gray eyes. His family is with him."

A dockworker with an oar under his arm only shrugged and replied in broken English, "I don't know this man."

And so it went. He knew there were marinas up and down the coast—indeed it seemed there were more boats in the harbors than gulls on the beach. By eleven that morning, with aching feet, he was nearing dehydration. He attacked a steep path, and near the top found a tiny store that sold a bit of everything. Back outside, he nearly emptied a one-liter bottle of water before deciding to continue upward, thinking a good look up and down the shoreline might be useful.

The sidewalks fell to a maze, and a poor choice of turns led to a dead end. He reversed, and soon found himself hopelessly lost in a warren of alleys. He would have asked directions, but there was no one in sight. He paused momentarily to get his bearings, and as he did so his mobile phone vibrated with a message:

YOUR MISSION IN AMALFI ABORTED. RETURN MOSCOW IMMEDIATELY. ACKNOWLEDGE.

It was the best news he'd had all day.

He sent the reply, spun a half circle, and decided to go back the way he'd just come.

* * *

The man whose name wasn't really Smith never knew how close he'd come to dying. Six steps farther up the narrow alley, in a recessed doorway, a muscular gray-eyed man stood in wait. In his right hand was a classic Smith & Wesson revolver, recently stolen from a union boss in Vieste—although that probably wouldn't have been necessary.

What saved the Russian was in the assassin's left hand: a mobile phone.

Thanks to the CIA, and in a reversal of the advantage the Russian had held in Marrakesh, the phone displayed the very message from SVR headquarters that Smith was then reading. Word for word, translated into English:

YOUR MISSION IN AMALFI ABORTED. RETURN MOSCOW IMMEDIATELY. AC-KNOWLEDGE.

Luckily for Smith, he did precisely that.

One hour later the ersatz Smith was finishing an extended lunch in a café overlooking the harbor. Relieved that his mission had been curtailed, he'd booked an early evening flight to allow himself a few hours to celebrate. He mopped his plate with a crust of bread, and tipped back the last of a nice Sangiovese. He paid his bill, walked to the entrance, and paused just outside. With one last look at the sea, he turned away to begin eighteen hours of travel that would return him to the snow-encrusted streets of Moscow.

Had he looked seaward one last time, just beyond

the breakwater, he might have glimpsed a modest catamaran nosing gently into the waves. The boat, which was running a more or less westerly course, was too far away to discern any real detail. Without binoculars he never could have seen the name on her stern, which had recently been changed. Nor could he have made out the three people at the helm. They were grouped together tightly, almost as if trying to stay warm on what was a wondrously balmy day.

A man and a woman sat arm in arm. Directly in front of them, a tiny boy stood at the wheel like a seasoned captain of the sea.

ACKNOWLEDGMENTS

I would like to recognize my hardworking co-conspirators: without you there would be no stories. Thanks to my editor, Bob Gleason, for your boundless knowledge, experienced eye, and the occasional beer. There are none better than the wonderful team at Tor. Linda Quinton, Elayne Becker, Kevin Sweeney, Deborah Friedman—my sincere thanks for all that you do. To my agent, Susan Gleason, thanks for your longtime support and chasing what you chase.

I would also like to express my appreciation to independent booksellers. A few among you were the first to believe in my work, and I can attest that no one does a better job of bringing together readers and writers.

Finally, thanks as ever to my family. The next ten books will come much more easily.